DEATH AND TREASON

SEELEY JAMES

Published by
Machined Media
12402 N 68th St
Scottsdale, AZ 85254

DEATH AND TREASON released Sabel Security #4 version 3.14
Original Publication, v3.13 January 23rd, 2018
This version is v3.14 12-April, 2019
Print ISBN: 978-0-9972306-7-3
ePub ISBN: 978-0-9972306-5-9
Distribution Print ISBN: 978-1-9731911-9-3

Formatting: BB eBooks
Cover Design: Jeroen ten berge

FOR MY SISTERS
Margo and Susan

CHAPTER 1

I WAS WALKING MY PUPPY through Central Park on a beautiful summer day when I heard the President of the United States say, "Because rigging the election is illegal. Why? What's in it for me?"

The conversation was live-streaming to my earbud from a mic I'd hidden in a billionaire's library. Chuck Roche, the refinery king, had spent the last two minutes explaining how he could win the election if President Veronica Hunter would just do what he told her. The third person present, hastily retired FBI man David Watson, had advocated killing my boss to seal the win.

Bugging POTUS is illegal on a life-in-jail level so I wasn't sure what I could do about it or even who I could tell. But that quickly became the least of my problems.

Mercury, winged messenger of the Roman gods—my friend and personal deity—snapped his fingers in front of my nose. *Yo dude, you see what I see?*

Walking toward me were two mothers with baby strollers, side by side. Their mouths were wide open in horror; their eyes focused on something behind me.

I spun around.

Kasey Earl, an old nemesis from my Ranger days, charged me, brandishing an eight-inch knife.

Mercury grinned. *You got this, right?*

Yeah. Yeah. Yeah.

I know what you're thinking: *Mercury? You should go back on your meds, pal. It's all Jesus versus Allah these days with the smart money on the Prince of Peace because of His advantage in nuclear warheads.*

I get that a lot. My first Army-issued psychologist told me Mercury was a manifestation of my PTSD-induced schizophrenia. What did he know? The soldiers who lived and fought and died beside me knew Mercury's divine guidance made me the beast of the battlefield. Under his celestial direction, I rampaged through Afghanistan and Iraq and several other places that I'm not allowed to discuss until 2058. But the Army, in its infinite glory and wisdom, put me on meds. My life went downhill fast. Eventually, it became obvious that the godless life wasn't working for me. I quit the pills. Heck, he's the only god who talks to me. Just because he's been homeless for fifteen hundred years is no reason to make fun. He's not much, but he's mine. Does your savior appear before your very eyes, complete with period costume?

Yeah. What I thought.

Where was I? Oh yeah, Central Park. Guy with a knife.

The moms assumed Kasey was attacking them. They expected me to be their knight in shining jeans and t-shirt. Which was fine with me. I'm up for saving damsels in distress anytime, especially when the embodiment of evil is Kasey.

Years ago, on a secret base outside Karachi, he bragged that he'd raped an Afghan woman and got away with it. That pissed me off. I'd taught him a lesson by removing his left ear with a Fairbairn-Sykes knife. It's the classic dagger used by British commandos in WWII, featuring a double-edged blade for slashing back-and-forth and a needle-sharp point for stabbing.

I steeled myself for the fight. Anoshni, my puppy, chose the run-like-hell option and yanked the leash—and my arm—as he fled. My body twisted half-way around with my right arm fully extended by the lead, and my left arm flung opposite for balance. I looked as if I were going to welcome Kasey with open arms.

That would never happen, even if Orcus froze over. I live for danger. My adrenaline kicked up another notch at the prospect of putting down this man-animal once and for all.

Kasey launched himself into the air, holding his very own Fairbairn-Sykes knife over his head. I dropped on my back, raised my left foot, keeping my knee bent. As Kasey flew over, I kicked hard, hoping to use his forward motion to launch him over me. Didn't work. His body ended up a foot above mine, balancing on my foot and left hand.

I managed to grab his knife-wielding wrist before he drove it between my ribs and into my heart. He screamed four-letter words; his face was red with heat and anger. He strained and I strained and the knife slashed my shirt.

Anoshni realized someone was threatening his meal ticket and came back to join the fight, barking like a rabid animal. He sank his razor-sharp puppy teeth into Kasey's calf. Kasey howled.

Mercury said, *Dude! Nothing beats watching a death match. Ima get me some popcorn. Don't let him kill you before I get back.*

I said, *Could I get a little divine intervention here?*

Mercury, already several strides away in his cringe-short toga, replied over his shoulder. *You got this, my brutha. But you're not going to like how* you get this.

You might expect something more comprehensive from a god. Is the occasional lightning bolt too much to ask? He's kinda unpredictable about dispensing the divine assistance. Probably because he gets a kick out of watching the multitude of ways humans die. His favorite is when a man drinks heavily before cleaning his weapons.

Yeah. *That* kind of god. Hanging around on street corners gets boring after the first millennium. Apparently.

Still on my back, I wrenched Kasey's wrist, hoping to dislodge his nasty dagger. He fought hard. The blade nicked my shoulder before he freed himself from my grip and reared back for a death blow.

A gray mist shot between us.

I instantly recognized the small cloud for what it was: Oleoresin of capsicum—pepper spray.

Army Rangers are required to pass several OC training courses, all of them comprehensive and extremely painful. To this day, I can determine the strength and type of a spray the way a connoisseur of fine wines can identify grapes. This wasn't a simple self-defense pepper spray; it was a Level III formulation with 1.3% capsaicinoids—the highest level you can deploy before they call it a war crime.

Kasey and I choked and spluttered and cried like babies.

He dropped the knife and rolled off me.

I could see nothing. My skin burned. My eyes swelled up. The tears flowed. I writhed and rolled over, face down, trying not to let anything touch my skin. I let my tears wash out enough irritant to let in little slits of light. I fought to catch a breath. Every inhale drew pepper deeper into my lungs.

A woman's voice screamed in agony. "Julie, what the fuck?"

"Cover your mouth," Julie said. "I'm going to shoot 'em again."

I jumped to my feet, peering through the tears gushing from my damaged eyes, and grabbed the woman's arm, wrenched the can away and tossed it. "Cover the babies. The spray will drift."

Too late.

Julie and her pal started choking. Two seconds later, the babies started crying. A short distance away, the shrill rattle of a police whistle raised the tension level.

"Do you have milk?" I asked. "Douse the babies with it."

"You're crazy," Julie cried.

"Base neutralizes acid. Trust me."

The authorities arrived en masse, even a guy on a horse. Cops and paramedics swarmed us. First, they took care of the babies and moms. Then the paramedics helped me.

AFTER AN HOUR, THINGS CALMED down. At least I could breathe. The police took statements.

"We can charge him with assault." The cop nodded his chin toward Kasey.

"Nah." I glanced at my enemy, cuffed a few yards away. "He's just a brother-veteran with a grudge."

The cop looked skeptical. His buddy slapped him on the shoulder and leaned toward the boulevard. He wasn't interested in more paperwork. My cop shrugged. They uncuffed Kasey and left us to work out our tangled relationship on our own.

I checked my pockets. My phone had shattered in the melee. My earbud was lost in the grass. Roche, Hunter, and their goon Watson were plotting to throw the election without me.

I stared at Kasey. Kasey stared at me. Fifteen feet separated us. He flinched like a meerkat watching a circling lion.

I nodded at my adversary. "Heard you were some kind of big shot over at Roche Security."

"It's pronounced row-SHAY, not roach." He looked angry for a second. "How come you ain't gonna press charges?"

"You've tried to kill me plenty of times—and always failed. Why take another shot at me now when you know it's going to put your fancy job at risk?"

Kasey stared at the ground.

Mercury walked up licking an ice cream cone. *Whoa, I missed you flexin'? Did you cut off his dick?*

I said, *Where the hell were you?*

No popcorn. Believe that shit? Then I ran into Sedna over there. Mercury pointed behind him and slurped a drip off his cone. *She and Kadlu are in town to see* Hamilton.

I said, *Who?*

Dude. Sedna. Inuit goddess of the seas? Like Neptune, only she's got some cakes, ya feel me? Kadlu is heartbroken about the igloos melting, so they came here for a little downtime. When it comes to goddesses, they don't get much hotter than the Inuits. Oh. Say, uh. Doesn't look like you need any miracles right now, and they got an extra ticket ... so. Yeah.

Sometimes dealing with an immortal is more trouble than it's worth. I said, *Where's the ice cream?*

Kasey pointed at a cart across the grass. "Over there."

My eyes swiveled between Kasey and the ice cream cart while I tried to figure out how long I'd been using my outside voice. "Want a cone? I'm buying."

Kasey gave me the once-over. "What're you playing at, Stearne?"

"Time to put our differences behind us, brother. We're hardened veterans living in a world full of clueless civilians." I stuck my hand out. "Tell me what's going on in Earl-world."

He shook my hand while maintaining an awkward distance. He kept his cynical gaze fixed on me. "You ain't pissed about me almost killing your boss back in Germany?"

"Dude, you didn't even singe her mascara." I struck out for the ice cream vendor. "Last chance."

He paused a few seconds, then followed.

"Yeah." Kasey trotted alongside. "I was running Roche Security operations until that thing in California."

"We caught you helping terrorists, and they fired you?" His motivation for trying to kill me was coming into focus. Every job he'd lost—and there had been a few—he lost because of me.

"Nah. They didn't fire me. Nothing like that." Kasey looked around while he thought up a way to spin his demotion. "They brung in this dude from the FBI. Said he had more experience or some shit."

"Those idiots. They picked a desk jockey over a battle-scarred veteran?"

"Yeah, right?" Kasey grinned at me.

"They're making a big mistake." We got in line behind a boy and his dad. "You'd think corporate America would value a guy who's killed terrorists. You don't deserve to be treated like that, Kasey. Ever think about how you could get back at them?"

"Every fucking day."

"Who's the Feeb they put in charge? Some peckerhead from the reservations or something?"

Kasey looked over the menu as if it were a tough decision: vanilla, chocolate, or strawberry.

Agent Kayla from our NYC office slipped in line behind us. She shoved a replacement phone and a backup in my back pocket with a wireless earbud. Then she was gone. Kasey never saw her. He placed his order while I checked my phone. An updated version of the old phone was halfway downloaded to the new one. In a few minutes, I'd be up and running. Sabel Security is one smooth, professional operation.

I texted Bianca Dominguez, the chief sorceress of Sabel Technology, who helped me set up the bug in Chuck Roche's home. She texted back right away. The transmission had broken when Kasey tackled me. She patched the system during my wrestling match and recorded it straight to the cloud. I could catch up on it later. I asked her to set up my backup phone for undercover use. She didn't ask why just transferred the info so it looked like a burner with no trace to Sabel Security.

Kasey took his vanilla scoop on a sugar cone and waited for me. "The man was some kinda Mister Big from FBI Counterintelligence. That's the spies and shit. Says he turned down a job at Sabel."

I ordered. While the guy scooped chocolate into a waffle, I gave Kasey a sympathetic look. "Older guy, thinks he's all that, gray crew cut?"

"Yeah." He squinted a suspicious glance my way. "You know him?"

"Counterintelligence sounds cool, but he wasn't James Bond. He ran the economic espionage division. Copyright infringement, intellectual property theft."

"You shittin' me?" Kasey stomped a boot and almost threw his cone. "Paper-pusher? He never fired no gun?"

"At the range, maybe." I licked my cone.

Kasey looked off into the distance, his mouth drawn tight, his face pulsing red with his rising heart rate. He ignored a drip that rolled down his fingers. "I gotta go."

He chucked his cone in the trash and started to walk away.

"Kasey, hold on a second." I attempted to look conflicted, then reached for the undercover phone. "Here. Take this. It's secure, encrypted. In case you ever want to talk or something. Just dial 6-1-1 and ask for me. They'll connect you. No questions asked."

He looked at the phone in my outstretched hand. His gaze rose to mine with a degree of suspicion.

Anoshni cocked his head and gave Kasey a you-can-trust-us look. He instinctively knew what I was doing.

Good dogs are watchdogs. A great dog is an accomplice.

"It's my undercover phone." I kept my hand extended. "You call me. You know, if you ever want to talk to someone who thinks veterans matter more than pencil-pushers."

His face softened, and he took the phone. "Any chance I'd get hired on up at Sabel?"

I sighed and shrugged. "You tried to kill the boss a couple times. That might be—"

"Only that once. Them other times, I never got the chance." Kasey was never quick-witted, but even he knew how off-key that sounded. "Well. Y'know how it is. It's just business. Ain't it?"

"Ms. Sabel's all about forgiveness." I whistled and looked skyward. "I'll sound her out next time I see her. First thing she's going to ask is, why should we trust him?" I patted his shoulder. "How could you prove yourself? Think of something, give me a call."

"Yeah. I can think on that some." He gave me a weak smile, then shoved the phone in his pocket. "Maybe we can grab lunch, talk about it."

"Sure." My stomach turned at the thought of spending another second with him. "I'm open. Give me a call."

I walked away without looking back.

WITH THE NEW EARBUD SCREWED in and the puppy sniffing along the sidewalk, I resumed my tour of Central Park while listening to my illegal bug. The whole reason for eavesdropping was to uncover who killed Ms. Sabel's parents. This stuff about the election was a whole new headache. Especially since I could get myself, my boss, and her company in a world of trouble just for having it. Only Bianca, Ms. Sabel, and I would listen to this recording, but secrets always end up in the FBI's lap eventually.

I pictured the three of them in Roche's library. Chuck Roche looked like an old lunch sack taped together with willpower. He wasn't a guy to mess with, though; people who knew him claimed he'd blow up your life if you crossed him. President Hunter reminded me of a Roman statue, her broken and weathered marble held together with foundation and lipstick. Her yearbook probably had her tagged as, "most likely to start a war just to get reelected." David Watson was a short, angry man with a grey crew cut and a colossal Napoleon complex who blamed the failure of his FBI career on everyone around him.

I backed up the recordings of the co-conspirators and caught up with where I left off. The audio had a gap before Bianca switched everything to the cloud. In that break, something major had happened between the three schemers. Their voices strained just short of yelling.

Hunter was in the middle of a sentence. "…sell all your refineries, investments, everything."

Roche said, "I won't have to sell anything after I'm elected. What're they going to do, un-elect me? So what if I take investment capital from companies like Santalum? No one's ever heard of it, much less who owns it."

"You're dreaming if you think you can take over the Republican Party two weeks before the convention, Chuck." Hunter sounded confused. "Teddy VII has the nomination wrapped up."

She was talking about Teddy Roosevelt VII, a guy who believed in family dynasties.

"I've got that handled."

"You'll get your ass kicked by the press," Hunter said. "You'll look like a fool in the debates. Why endure the humiliation?"

"Someone has to clean up the country, and you're not getting the job done." Roche's volume nearly blew out the mic. He brought it down a notch. "I'll bring sound business principles to the table. I'll clean up all these damned treaties and sanctions and regulations. I could run this country with my eyes closed. But don't worry, I'll take care of you. My word is good."

Hunter sounded angry. "I don't want the Supreme Court."

"Yeah. I know what you want." Roche scoffed. "Forget it."

Watson chimed in quickly. "You're forgetting Sabel."

"The hell I am." Roche didn't tone it down for his lackey. "We need her. We'll get her onboard. I'll promise her funding for foster care—whatever stupid charity she's crying about this week."

"You want to bring her onboard?" Hunter was screeching now. "What does Pia Sabel have that you need?"

Roche blasted back. "She has a hundred million bucks to spend."

"Hey," Hunter said. "She's giving that to my campaign."

"Wrong," Roche shouted. "She was going to give it to Maddox, not you. Good thing those terrorists took him out. Saved the country from holding hands and singing campfire songs for four years—like a bunch of losers. You've got nothing to offer her. I can make her the Secretary of Education or something. Hell, why not? No one cares about that shit."

Hunter said, "The Senate will never confirm someone without a career—"

"That's why you're a failure," Roche barked. "You don't know how to make deals."

"Bad idea, boss." Watson sounded like he was cowering in a corner. "Sabel's a time bomb. She finds out what we did and she'll—"

"She won't do anything to a candidate or a president. She'd never do anything that would hurt her precious little country. As long as we win, we're safe." Roche dropped his voice to a whisper I could barely hear. "If she doesn't get onboard, you'll be inside her organization. You take care of it for us. You have more reason than the rest of us to kill her."

"Uh."

"How did the interview go?" Roche asked.

"She liked me." Watson backed off. "I think. She offered me the job anyway."

"Well," Hunter snapped. "Whatever happens, I insist you do nothing to harm Pia."

"I would never hurt her." Roche lied like the salesman who sold me my last car. "That's just our last resort. Don't get hung up on her. She's young and naïve. I'll convince her. Easy."

"OK, then." Hunter sounded satisfied.

There was some crosstalk I couldn't decipher. Then Watson broke out in a panic.

"You guys are underestimating her." Watson's voice rose. "She'll never stop coming after us. Our only option is to infiltrate Sabel Security and kill her—now."

Roche blew a gasket. The windows rattled with his bellowing. "How many times do I have to tell you two? I'm bringing her inside the campaign. She'll come around. But, just in case, you need to be close to her."

There was a long silence in the recording. I checked my phone twice to make sure it hadn't disconnected.

The voices picked up again with President Hunter, her voice low. "What if I win?"

Roche: "Have you seen your approval ratings? Not a chance."

Hunter started to object, but Roche and Watson laughed over her. The noises in the room indicated they were moving toward the exit. Pleasantries were extended in muffled voices. Social-laughter followed a few attempts at humor. *Ha ha heh.*

The last thing audible was Roche: "Work your way into her inner circle. Don't make me regret picking you, Watson."

Back in the real world, three teenage girls were oohing over Anoshni. He was eating it up with his nose in the air as they stroked his back. Not bad work if you can get it.

I texted Ms. Sabel. "Do not hire David Watson under any circumstances."

A second later, she texted back. "He starts Monday."

CHAPTER 2

MAJOR YURI BELENOV BOWED HIS head and averted his eyes in the general's office in Kaliningrad. He didn't need to look at the old man's vodka-reddened face to know what was coming.

"You're not happy with my orders?" The general, known by his codename, Strangelove, rose to his feet. "Your little banda is nothing but criminals. The others are full of soldiers. Real soldiers. Men who know how to follow orders and do what they're told without having therapy every five minutes."

Yuri interjected as Strangelove kept ranting. "I always respect and obey your orders, sir."

"I warned you that bunch would never do anything important, and now you come to me begging for bigger assignments."

Yuri longed to push his earbuds in and crank up the jazz on his phone, tune the old man out. "Respectfully, sir, my banda has proven itself. That is all I meant to say."

"There are words we say, and there are messages within our words." Strangelove shook a meaty finger at Yuri. "I know what you're trying to say."

Yuri bit the inside of his cheek to stop himself from speaking. Long past retirement, the general was shaped like a pear with a ring of white hair around a shiny bald spot. He gave the impression there was little fire left in him.

"You are nothing, Yuri." The old man waddled out from behind his desk. "There are many ambitious young men in the GRU. Men who work hard and ask nothing. You are not so special."

"I understand, sir." Yuri dipped his head.

"These message boards, they are a waste of time for time wasters."

"Social media is not the same as message boards, sir." When the general didn't object, Yuri took a deep breath and charged ahead. "We kept Sweden out of NATO. We played an important role in Brexit."

"So you say." Strangelove pushed past him and crossed to the window. "Where are the hard facts? How many died? Who suffered? Does anyone live in fear of you?"

The old man clasped his hands behind his back and looked out of his top floor window in the *Informatsionny Tsentr*. The general reminded Yuri of a garage mechanic who never learned fuel injection, a man out of synch with his era.

"Minds have been swayed." Yuri kept his cool. "Voters have gone to the polls. There are no numbers, but the results—"

"Your reports are empty, and you ask for more work?"

"I ask only how we can best serve our country." Leaning to the side, Yuri tried to glimpse the old man's face.

The boss kept staring out at Kaliningrad's skyline without a reply.

Finally, Strangelove said, "What is it you think you deserve, Yuri? My job?"

Yuri fought the urge to say yes.

"There are powerful people close to the Kremlin who like your little project." The general shrugged. "If it were up to me, I would shut it down, give your work to the other bandas. Why spend so much time and effort on these stupid little posts?"

"It is more powerful to control a mind than to kill it, sir."

"Hate controls people. Fear controls people. We made them hate and fear Muslims by blowing up apartment buildings." The old man turned and waved off Yuri's objection. "Can you do the hard things? When your country calls on you, can you do whatever is necessary for the Motherland?"

"Yes, sir."

"Even if it hurts your beloved America?"

"I only studied there," Yuri said. "On the orders of my commander at the time. I gathered intelligence and—"

"You eat their greasy hamburgers. You listen to their jungle music.

You've given up Tchaikovsky and Mussorgsky."

Yuri bowed. It was true; American jazz called to him when he first set foot on Columbia's campus. He never touched his oboe or listened to Russian composers again. When he returned to his military career, no one—except Strangelove—noticed the change. Isolated in Norway as he and his banda evaded detection from cybersecurity experts, he had become even more Westernized. Most of the men in his banda were the same, often leading him to forget the fierce pride and nationalism of his fellow Russians.

"I may have an assignment that will further your career." The old man stepped close. "Something that might suit your hackers."

Yuri could barely contain his swelling pride. Strangelove had always been a difficult commanding officer. There were no privileges, no favored officers, no easy assignments in his operation. Any failure could end a career. Being considered for a high-profile assignment was the closest Yuri had come to a nod of approval from the aging general.

"These will be difficult tasks." Strangelove glared. "Risky, dangerous missions for bold men, not cowards. Does that bother you? Are you afraid?"

"Not with your guidance, sir."

"Your English skills will help you." The general sighed. "You know the USA fairly well."

"Thank you, sir." Yuri nodded and kept his gaze on the floor.

"When you get them, you will memorize my orders—then destroy them. No traces." The old man looked over his shoulder and lowered his voice. "Some Americans might die. That is my problem, not yours." He turned and grabbed Yuri's shoulders like a father. "My mother had a proverb: you need a sharp ax for a tough bough. You are my ax, Yuri. Are you sharp enough?"

Yuri's mother also had a proverb: *a fly will not get into a closed mouth*. He nodded.

Strangelove stepped back to his chair. The spring creaked and the cushion whooshed and he turned to his computer screen. He glanced at Yuri once more before scanning his email. He leaned forward to read one and typed. "Something bothers you. What is it?"

"When angered, the Americans stop at nothing to destroy their enemies." Yuri shrugged. "My team understands Georgia. We understand Sweden and Scotland, Europe and the Middle East. But why antagonize America?"

"Why do you think my orders will antagonize America?"

"You said some people might—"

"Your banda makes up these little—" Strangelove waved his hand in the air "—conspiracy theories. People have noticed your proficiency at getting Americans to believe them. The orders to keep generating those ridiculous 'memes' remain in place." The old man paused for effect. "We have a new opportunity in American politics. We are going to help our friends there. Your new orders will come from Director Popov."

Yuri tried and failed to contain his surprise. Victor Popov, Strangelove's boss, was just the man Yuri wanted to impress. He noticed Strangelove's knowing smirk.

"I will endeavor to achieve the greatest results." Yuri saluted.

"I'm sure you will." Strangelove batted away his words with intentional cynicism. "Popov is my kind of leader. We prefer the old ways: blow up bridges, shoot down airplanes, make accidents in factories. These bullshit social media campaigns are the ideas of strutting young peacocks like Yeschenko, Gazinski, and Shishkin."

Yuri noted the name of the oligarch Yeschenko among the Kremlin's SVR generals. He said, "Americans perceive deaths of their citizens as an attack on their country."

"Americans." Strangelove tsked. "They are so stupid they have to write 'open here' on their milk cartons." Strangelove finished another email. He faced Yuri and scratched the nasty scar that ran from his ear to his collar.

"You're worried they will destroy us like Iraq?" He laughed. "They do descend like the Baba Yaga." He turned back to his screen. "Then you must work like the Viet Cong or the Mujahideen. Don't let them find you."

"You can count on me, sir."

"This will be a highly sensitive assignment." Strangelove did not look up. "You will be tested as the defenders of Stalingrad were tested in the

Great Patriotic War. You will be responsible for making sure your banda does not get cold feet. No one will speak about the mission. Not even to their girlfriends. It takes only one man to destroy an important mission. Eliminate the weak before they infect the others. Now get back to your office, wherever it is, and play with your virals."

CHAPTER 3

PIA SABEL WATCHED PLAYERS PRACTICING on a summer afternoon in Washington, DC. Her phone buzzed in her hand. She sent the call to voicemail without a glance.

She felt the longing she so often fought. She wanted to be back on the grass, chasing a ball, pushing past defenders to send in a cross to her forward. At twenty-six, she could easily play for another ten years. Life had been simpler when she played for her country in the Olympics and World Cup. The rules were clear; the skills were practiced, the players civil. At least, some players.

Pia smiled and let her mind wander back to the first foul language that ever assaulted her young ears. Playing for her future high school while still in sixth grade, she'd tried to weave around the other team's sweeper, who was a slower but massive senior. A hip check from the girl sent Pia sliding across the grass on her butt. "Don't come back," the defender yelled. "Ya fuckin' punk."

Pia came right back—only to be knocked on her ass again. Then a third time. And a fourth. On the fifth, she nutmegged the senior, leapt the girl's outstretched leg and launched the ball over the keeper's reaching glove and into the upper corner.

That was the language she preferred: actions over words.

The executive office she'd left an hour earlier was a foreign land to her. It was all words: analyses, reports, synergies, metrics, excuses, results—words, words, words. Business is a game of lies and secrets and half-truths and circumstances. Soccer is a game of actions: attempts, successes, and failures.

Her adopted father, Alan Sabel, had built an international

conglomerate that ranged from technology and satellites to security and finance. Money poured out of the company coffers and into her hands like an overflowing fountain. She had no idea what to do with it. All it meant to her was the chance to improve a few lives. Today was one of those chances. She intended to block out the business world and relive her passion for just a few minutes. On the field before her, the inner-city team she sponsored played a practice game. Her heart ran with them.

Charnay, center mid, struggled to get ahead of the competition. Tired and angry, she committed foul after foul.

Pia kicked off her business flats and ran onto the grass in her pantsuit. She pulled up to Charnay's shoulder. "Stop trying to score. They know you're the power on the field. They're double-teaming you. Keep the ball, draw the defenders, and pass when your teammates are open. Play only for name on the front of your jersey, not the back."

The ball came to Charnay. Pia grabbed her shoulder as the high school senior began to run.

"Don't look at the goal—look at your options." Pia pointed left and right where the opposing team's players ran. "Who's open?" Then in a whisper. "Fake, and when she lunges, fake a second time, so her backup also lunges. Look left, then pass to the right."

Charnay did precisely what the retired star of the national team told her. She turned upfield, dribbling into a row of defenders who crowded around her. Just before they closed her down, she passed to her wide-open midfielder.

Pia admired her work for a moment as the action moved to the other end of the pitch. It made her wonder if her boyfriend's children—since he'd suddenly acquired a family—would play soccer. But then, what did she know about toddlers? Or, more to the point, was Stefan still her boyfriend?

Pia sighed at the question and jogged back to the sidelines.

Agent Miguel waited for her with a stern look. The tall Navajo handed her a phone.

Halfway into the first syllable of Pia's greeting, Bianca Dominguez interrupted her. "A man named Pozdeeva has been frantic to get hold of you, *flaca*. Something just came up, and I think you should meet him.

Our people who monitor passport control for the NSA picked up Pozdeeva's arrival in DC. He's a Russian national. Several FSB officers on that same flight turned around and immediately flew back to Moscow."

Pia watched as Charnay repeated her lesson. Again, she drew three defenders and crossed to her forward. "Sounds like spy stuff. Why would I be involved?"

"I don't know." Bianca lowered her voice to scolding-mode. "But your assistant says you've been ignoring calls from Director Shikowitz all afternoon."

Ignoring the FBI director was not a good thing. Especially since he had been a lifetime friend of her father.

"Do you know what he wants?" Pia asked.

"Something about Pozdeeva." Bianca hesitated. "By the way, I told Mr. Pozdeeva where to find you. I figured you and Miguel could handle him if he turns out to be a nutcase."

Pia thanked her and clicked off. As she started to dial Shikowitz, a voice shouted from the street. Miguel planted his feet and faced the man running across the grass.

The figure staggered more than ran. He called out Pia's name and dropped an overcoat and trudged a few more steps. Miguel and Pia exchanged a glance. The man was now thirty yards away, his arms stretching to reach them. He shouted something unintelligible, then fell.

Pia ran to offer aid. Miguel tracked slightly behind. As she approached, the man rose to his hands and knees. He pulled something from his pocket, tossed it on the grass, then threw up pink-and-yellow bile.

Instinctively cautious about his condition, Pia slowed and stopped two feet away. "What's wrong?"

"They kill me." The man's Russian accent was thick. He barfed more. "In the … *tashnit*."

The man rolled on his back and thumbed at his pool of lunch slowly sinking into the grass.

"What is *tashnit*?" Pia looked at Miguel, who was busy dialing 911. "What happened? How can I help you?"

"No help. Too late." He coughed uncontrollably. "They kill me. Kaliningrad."

"An ambulance is on the way. Hang in there. Who killed you?"

The man spluttered, "Job fifteen…verses fifteen and sixteen."

Screeching tires on the street drew her attention. Eight men jumped from two plain sedans and ran toward them, shouting over each other.

"Are you Pozdeeva?" She knelt next to the man.

He ran his fingers through his thin, black hair and pulled out a shocking handful. "Poisoned. Like … like Litvinenko."

His eyes rolled back in his head.

A mass of men in dark suits crowded around them. "FBI. Stand back."

"Wait a second!" Pia pushed her shoulder into one of the agents. "He was trying to talk to me."

"We've got this under control, ma'am. This is an international incident. Step away. Now."

He and another man politely pushed her back.

Pia finished dialing her call and spoke in a loud voice. "Director Shikowitz, this is Pia Sabel. I'm sorry I couldn't take your call earlier. Several of your men are here along with the man I think is Pozdeeva."

The FBI agents stopped what they were doing and faced her.

"Pozdeeva is a Russian officer trying to defect," Shikowtiz said. "It sounds like they got to him. Let me speak to an agent."

Pia handed the phone to the nearest Feeb. After the director spoke to him, the tight circle opened wide enough to let her in. One agent held Pozdeeva's head up and gently poured water into his mouth.

"Can you hear me, Mr. Pozdeeva?" Pia knelt again, her phone on speaker for the director. She examined his cold, clammy skin. His lips looked frozen despite the summer heat. More clumps of hair fell as the agent holding him up adjusted his grip.

"Radiation." Pozdeeva opened his eyes. "In my drink. I was … not careful." His head lolled. He tried to raise his hand to Pia's face. It fell into his lap. "You remember me?"

She wanted to help him, remember him, cure him, but the threat of radioactivity froze her in place. Pia tried to remember his face—round and pleasant, the far end of middle-age—but came up with nothing. She shook her head sadly.

"Job." He coughed again, deep and horrible, ending with a spit of blood. "FSB. FBI. CIA. Don't …"

He puked again, this time on the knees of an agent. Everyone but Pia stepped back.

"You remember …" He gasped for air and reached for Pia's hand. "You will love your neighbor as yourself."

He spasmed and shook. The life blinked out of his eyes. Black bile oozed from his mouth.

A siren preceded the ambulance. No one moved from the dead man. They stood and stared at his form while the paramedics grabbed their gear and ran to join them.

The huddled group backed up to give the first responders access.

An agent turned to Pia. "Did he give you anything?"

"No. He was puking his guts out. I didn't get too close."

"Did he tell you anything?"

"All he got out was that they killed him."

"What did he mean?" The agent leaned into her personal space.

"I have no idea." Pia planted a hand on the agent's chest and pushed him back a foot.

"Why did he tell you to love your neighbor?"

"Your guess is as good as mine."

"What's your guess?"

"He's religious, maybe? Jesus said to love your neighbor was the second most important of the Ten Commandments."

The agent squinted and took a moment to think. "You sure he didn't give you anything?"

"One hundred percent." Pia held her hands out as if to invite a pat-down.

She could see the gears working in his head: did he want to search a friend of the director, or take her word for it? He said goodbye and turned away.

The agents went through Pozdeeva's pockets and bagged everything. Then they returned to their car and drove off. The ambulance crew packed the body on a gurney and wheeled him back to their ambulance and roared away.

Pia pulled up a translator app on her phone and thumbed in a few phonetic spellings of *tashnit* until one of them made sense.

A respectful distance behind them, the practice squad had lined up to watch the commotion. They stared at the empty place where Pozdeeva died.

"Charnay," Pia called over her shoulder, "would you bring me your water, please?"

A moment later, the midfielder handed her a one-gallon Bubba Keg. Pia opened the spout and poured water over a specific place in the puke. A shiny piece of silver and black emerged.

A large USB drive.

CHAPTER 4

A MONTH AFTER HAVING ICE cream with Kasey Earl, I strode down the halls of the Sabel Industries corporate office in Bethesda, Maryland. I was on the someteenth floor pretending I wasn't lost while I searched for a clue about where they moved the big meeting room. Huge office buildings give me the creeps. They're full of zombies wearing suits and shiny shoes, the most dangerous of our species.

Mercury matched my stride in his party-toga. *You're going to include me in the conversation again, right, my brutha?*

In case you're wondering, Mercury looks like Will Smith on steroids and claims the Roman artists were white-gazing their work.

I said, *We had a deal: you saved my ass—and I introduced you to Ms. Sabel as promised. She didn't see you—because you're a FIGMENT OF MY IMAGINATION! I'm not going to risk my job by voicing my delusions again. End of story.*

Mercury rose on his tiny bronze wings and floated around me. *Dawg. She spoke to me. We made a connection. Pia-Caesar-Sabel is down with the program. C'mon, man. A new day is dawning. The Dii Consentes is going to make a comeback thanks to—*

I said, *She didn't even look in your direction.*

Mercury said, *Aw homie, you know she was averting her eyes. Conditioned by all that Judeo-Christian crack about God being the almighty lord who you're not worthy to look at. The burning bush and all that. She's not used to us chill gods. You gotta tell her—the whole Roman pantheon is street. You can hold a ceremony in my honor and escort her to—*

I said, *I'm not escorting anyone anywhere. I gotta go back on my meds.*

I stuck my head in the nearest office door and got directions. The big meeting room had not moved in twenty years—the guy claimed.

I was two floors off and headed for the elevator. I checked my watch while the elevator music tried to extract my soul. Three minutes late. Not bad for most corporate meetings, but the young lady holding this one was not like most executives.

When I opened the door, all eyes turned to me. Including the president of Sabel Technology, Bianca Dominguez.

Bianca—who could have easily won the Miss Latin America contest every year for the last decade but instead chose to attend MIT and work for the NSA before joining Sabel Technology—stood in front of a wall-sized screen, pointing at a chart with a hundred circles and arrows. She loathed late-comers and stopped talking mid-sentence. She waited in silence and watched me search for an open chair. Everyone followed my painful progress.

I tried to become invisible as I took the last few steps.

From the head of the table, Ms. Sabel fixed her gaze on me. "Jacob, thank you for running that errand for me. You can begin now, Bianca."

Saved by the boss.

In the world of brown-nosing, nothing pays off like dragging the company owner's unconscious body out of a burning wreck before it erupts in a scorching fireball. Yeah, I did that. She's been covering for me ever since.

Everyone turned back to Bianca.

"The USA is at war—and most people don't even know it. Russia is waging a psychological war against us. The battleground is unfamiliar territory for the US: traditional print and television media, online advertising, social media, even our political leaders." Bianca changed slides to a diagram of a brain. "The war is being fought in the human mind. What we believe, who we trust, and where we find information to form decisions is being controlled by actors we believe to be working for the Russian Federation."

She brought up a photo of Ilya Pozdeeva, the man who died at Ms. Sabel's feet.

"Thanks to Mr. Pozdeeva, we have an inkling of their capability, but we still don't have enough information to fight back. He left us hundreds of clues that my team has been trying to untangle for weeks. Since Kryptos, the coded sculpture in the CIA courtyard, took years to crack, we don't feel bad. However, in consultation with Ms. Sabel, we've decided to put more great minds to work on this project. That's why you're here today."

Out of the twenty people in the room, Bianca focused a skeptical gaze on me. I didn't blame her. Her team had some of the smartest people on the planet. Even I wondered what I was doing in the meeting.

Bianca gave us background on Ilya Pozdeeva. His career started in Russia's *Glavnoye Razvedyvatel'noye Upravleniye* or Main Intelligence Directorate, GRU. The GRU functions like the Defense Intelligence Agency, DIA, only with twenty-five thousand spetznatz troops to help them. Later he transferred to the *Sluzhba Vneshney Razvedki* or SVR. They are Russia's foreign intel service—spies and clandestine operations like the CIA, except that they report directly to the President of Russia. Pozdeeva was a liaison who carried top-secret orders from SVR officials in the Kremlin to various GRU units scattered around Europe.

"As an example of what the GRU can do," Bianca said, "a man named Yevgeny Bogachev runs one of their projects. According to Treasury, he authored Cryptolocker, a ransomware program that shuts down a company's servers until they pay a hefty fee. Bogachev's believed to have earned over $100 million from his exploits."

She changed to the next slide.

"Top-secret groups called *bandas*, Russian for team, run the GRU's scariest operations. We aren't sure how many are operating. Estimates run as high as twenty. Some bandas are special ops groups; others are purely technical, hackers. Some are in-between. One of them wrote an app that reduced artillery calculations from twenty minutes to fifteen seconds. They posed as Belgian software developers and sold their app to the Ukrainian Army. Once the Ukrainians started using the app, the Russians hacked in, retargeted the trajectories and caused terrible friendly-fire incidents."

Having been fired on by US Army artillery, I felt the pain of the

Ukrainian gunners and victims alike. Fratricide is among the most horrific and rarely discussed aspects of war.

"Democracy itself is under attack," Bianca said. "Our country is built on trust. We trust our government, even if our favorite politicians are not in power. We trust our free press, even if our favorite sources are slanted left or right. We trust our two-party system to work out compromises. We have trusted our democratic system for over two hundred years. The information Mr. Pozdeeva gave us proves Russia is trying to break that trust to influence our elections. What we don't yet understand is why or to what end."

Bianca turned off the screen and nodded to Ms. Sabel, whose gray-green eyes swept the room like a colonel looking over the battalion before battle. She strode to the front of the room, looking like a tiger trapped in a business suit.

"Ilya Pozdeeva died of polonium-210 radiation poisoning." Ms. Sabel started to speak, then stopped, winced, and took a moment. "I'm sorry. Until we did the research, I'd forgotten that I'd met him. His daughter played for Russia. We met after a game in Leipzig a couple years ago."

She took a deep breath. "While Mr. Pozdeeva had ample opportunity to give this data to the FBI, he chose to leave an encrypted USB to me. The CIA won't tell us anything about him. It took our people several days to crack the encryption. We're now in possession of a significant cache of data.

"The only items that stood on their own was a group of reports about a network of tens of thousands of users on Facebook, Twitter, Instagram, and other social media. There's also a list of Russian-sponsored news sites. They're all small and appear to be coordinated. Here is a meme posted by one of these groups." She clicked to a picture of a woman wearing a headscarf shaking hands with President Hunter. Beneath them in Arabic-looking script it read, "American Muslims support Veronica Hunter." Bianca clicked again, and another meme came up. This time a woman cried on a casket draped in an American flag. The caption read, "Veronica Hunter calls them acceptable losses." Her third slide showed Jesus arm wrestling Satan. This one quoted Satan, "If I win, Hunter wins," while Jesus replied, "Not if I can help it."

Bianca waited while we processed the memes. She said, "Each of these came with a 'Learn More' button that took you to a dubious site. We traced those sites back to Kremlin-run media companies. These news sites will post a related, but dubious news story. Another site will quote the first site, and others will quote the second site, covering up the trail to the original. After the posts are shared all over the place, yet another Russian news site will post an article about their own fake news being ignored by traditional media outlets. Then their coordinated social media users pile on and create a fake news storm."

"Excuse me," Tania raised her hand. "H-h-how do we know the news is f-f-fake?"

Tania is Ms. Sabel's best friend and my partner in leading the Sabels' personal security operations. She wore a black beret over her wild hair to conceal a white bandage that covered a good portion of her head. A terrorist's bullet had cracked her skull and left her recovering from a serious head injury. She was on the mend, but an annoying stammer remained. The doctors thought her speech would eventually heal.

"Whether you like mainstream media or not," Ms. Sabel said, "professional news organizations do two things that give their work credibility. They name the publisher and reporter on each story, and they verify every detail from independent sources. They may not always get it right, and their sources may request anonymity, but they take responsibility for their stories as professionals. We can tell fake news because there is no confirmation, no verifiable facts, and no way to find the reporter who first posted the story."

"Then we've found the source of all the fake news?" Miguel asked.

"Before you think we can stamp them out," she replied, "all of the news sites in this database have been closed. The user accounts have been deleted as well. They put these up and take them down in a matter of days. But the conspiracy theories remain in circulation and take on a life of their own."

"Why is-is-isn't the FBI working-ing..." Tania flushed when her words refused to come out.

Ms. Sabel pointed to Miguel.

An Indian who grew up in LA, he spent his summers learning the ancient ways from his grandfather back on the Rez in Arizona. The stoic Navajo philosophy didn't leave him with an affinity for public speaking.

He stood and cleared his throat. "Just before Pozdeeva died, he said, 'Job fifteen, verses fifteen and sixteen.' Not my religion, so I looked it up on Biblegateway. It reads, *God puts no trust even in his holy ones, and the heavens are not clean in his sight; how much less one who is abominable and corrupt, one who drinks iniquity like water!*" Miguel shrugged. "My take: if your God doesn't trust anyone, who can you trust? We think Pozdeeva meant, trust no one. Because of that, we decided not to share this with anyone outside this room."

Miguel sat back down. It was more words in one stretch than I'd ever heard out of him.

Ms. Sabel said, "Social media companies and government agencies are constantly trying to shut these people down. But there's only so much you can do when a government shields the perpetrators. Being a nuclear superpower means any small escalation can become a world-ending escalation all too quickly. I think that's why Pozdeeva gave this to me. He might not trust the FBI or CIA. Or he might have given this to them already. We'll never know."

The group around the table murmured and nodded. The job seemed simple enough to me: find some hackers and pull the plug on them. But then I thought about it—how do you pull the plug on hackers? Posting fake news isn't exactly a capital crime. It's more like a bad-boy crime. A couple of months in jail, if we can crowbar them out of Moscow and pin a serious charge on them. Maybe we should punish the Americans who repost the stuff without verifying the news source.

Wow. That could wipe out a lot of innocent grandmothers—including mine.

I asked, "You want us to track down the people who set up the fake sites and eliminate them?"

The desk jockeys in the room turned to me like a school of fish that had just spotted a shark. I need to watch my language around the suits; they just don't appreciate how many of the world's problems can be solved with a well-placed bullet.

Ms. Sabel said, "If it were that simple, I'd have sent you after them weeks ago."

Bianca retook center stage. "Each of you has been given access to a secure cloud folder with the contents of Pozdeeva's drive. We'd like you to look them over. Give them some thought. See if you spot any patterns."

She brought up another slide with some photos on it. "These are some items we find interesting. We think there's something here, but we can't figure out what it's telling us. There are photographs taken over several years. Most of them do not have Mr. Pozdeeva in them. Four stand out because they do have Mr. Pozdeeva in them. The oldest—taken almost thirty years ago—shows him standing in the inner courtyard of CIA, Langley. We have no clue who cleared him to enter the building, much less why he was there. The next oldest shows him in the lobby of Sabel Industries, but our visitor logs don't go back that far. Third, is this picture of him with an unknown woman in an office setting. The final image is Pozdeeva at the Hirshhorn Museum about a year ago. We believe he meant for these pictures to tell us something."

Tania asked, "What a-a-about the rest of these f-f-files?"

"We have no idea. They include everyday items like bills of lading for coal, orders for office supplies, employee transfers for people like janitors. Some are from the Soviet era; others are dated a couple of months ago. There's a bank statement from Rossiya Bank for a company we've never heard of. There are canceled checks, parking tickets, all kinds of junk." Bianca turned off the presentation. "Look at them, see if you find any common threads."

People began asking the obvious questions: Are there translations? Yes. Have they tried sequences like dates, places, alphabetical? Yes. And so on.

Mercury leaned over my shoulder, scaring me enough to make me jump. *Listen up, brutha.*

I whispered, *Don't sneak up on me like that.*

Mercury said, *Hey, I'm here to help, homie. Read the news on your phone.*

He slipped to the back of the room.

The last thing I needed in my career was a used god showing up in the middle of an important, executive-filled briefing. I pulled a bottle of meds out of my pocket and rolled it around in my fingers while Bianca took more questions.

It was time to find my sanity.

Mercury squeezed my fingers, which shot the bottle from my hand. It spun across the table at the speed of light and rolled near Miguel. He scooped it up and shoved it in his pocket. My best friend from the 75th Rangers didn't look at me—he always has my six.

Mercury said, *What the fuck, dude? I tell you to read the news and all a sudden you go thinking you gotta pop some pills? Need I remind you of the good people who died the last time you were taking mind-numbing drugs? Tony was a good guy.*

The ancient deity knew how to pull my guilt-chain better than a Catholic nun. Agent Tony fell to his death on my watch. I was on my meds at the time. If I'd been clean and sober—and psychotic—maybe I could've saved him.

I pulled my phone out of my pocket and glanced at the news screen. All the major outlets had headlines: Only three days before the convention, Republican front-runner Teddy Roosevelt VII abruptly quit the race and pledged his delegates to billionaire Chuck Roche.

I looked up and discovered Ms. Sabel, phone in hand, looking at me with her piercing gray-green eyes. She could communicate an encyclopedia with those eyes. *We need to talk.*

The meeting broke up the way meetings do, with the self-important guy looking at his phone, announcing to the air that he had to run. Two ladies compared calendars and made a follow-up appointment. Three brown-nosers tried to get an extra minute with the boss. Ms. Sabel shook them off and headed straight for me.

"Roche told Hunter he'd do this." She looked pale. "I didn't believe him."

It took me a minute to realize why she seemed unsteady. She'd never committed a crime against her country before. Not that I had. Intentionally. Bugging the President of the United States isn't something you brag about since it could get you tossed in jail until the next ice age rolls around.

"How the hell did he pull it off?" I asked. "And, how does he think he can win after saying, 'They're bringing drugs, they're bringing crime, they're rapists?'"

"You're too idealistic about where we are as a country." She looked disappointed in me. "Did you notice the Major isn't here? She was pulled over two hours ago for failing to signal a lane change. They're searching her car."

Ms. Sabel referred to the company's Chief Operating Officer, a.k.a. "the Major". A successful African-American who dared to drive a shiny Mercedes in Bethesda, Maryland.

"You should always send the limo for her."

Mercury leaned over Ms. Sabel's shoulder and scowled at me. *Hey, dawg, here's a thought: maybe the cops should pull over all the white people who leave their blinkers on forever and search* their *cars.*

I said, *They'd get a million lawsuits ... Oh.*

Mercury crossed his arms and gave me a look.

"Only the three of us know about the recordings," Ms. Sabel said, referring to Bianca, herself, and me.

I looked back and forth to make sure no one was listening. "We should take it public."

"President Hunter would toss us in jail in a heartbeat."

"The recording would be like a get-out-of-jail-free card."

"Who runs the jails?" She waited until I got it. "We can't just blunder onto the national stage with this. Hunter is cunning and ruthless. So is Roche. To take them down, we need a plan. A strategy."

That was reassuring since she usually went to war on a whim. I thought for a minute. "You need to talk to your dad."

"Why?" Her voice strained high.

"He knows more about politics than all three of us."

"You're right." She bit her thumbnail and looked away.

Mercury said, *Aw bro, why'd you go and tell her that? Sycophants are supposed to tell rich people how great they are, not, 'hey, talk to Dad.'*

I said, *He'll have a solution. Besides, I'm not a sycophant.*

Mercury said, *Which is why you didn't get as big a bonus as Tania this year.*

I said, *Tania got shot in the head. She deserved ... I'm not having this discussion again.*

Mercury said, *Whatever, homeboy. She's not going to tell the Alan-Caesar-Sabel that she has a recording that'll save the election but wreck the reputation of the multi-billion-dollar empire he built for her. It would crush him. And get her tossed in jail.*

"Dad's in Europe on an extended business trip." She looked like she was convincing herself a delay was justified. "I'll talk to him face-to-face when he gets back. In the meantime, we should come up with a plan to box in Roche."

"Roche said Watson has more reason to—" An irrational fear of jinxing her by saying it out loud made me shut up.

Her eyes flashed. "They were going to ask me for a hundred million first, remember? That's our strategy."

"What about Watson?" I asked.

"He's finishing up Sabel Security boot camp in a couple weeks." She squeezed my arm. "He'll be on your team."

CHAPTER 5

Yuri Belenov shoved his Aeron chair back from his workstation in Stavanger, Norway. He glanced out the window to find the rainy September afternoon had grown cold and dark. He stood and stared at his order from Strangelove. Unbelievable. The general said it would be a big task. Yuri never expected anything this big, this provocative. Did Viktor Popov really give this order to Strangelove? What were either of them thinking?

The idea infuriated him. The Americans had no idea about Yuri's annoying intrusions into their cyberspace. If they did, they would hold hearings, discuss privacy and freedoms, and drag it out for years. But they would destroy him at the snap of a president's fingers over an operation like the one Strangelove had outlined. The Americans would call it an act of terrorism. An act of war.

He was a soldier. These were orders. He had to change his attitude. He took a deep breath and scratched his beard.

Strangelove's instructions came over the self-erasing chat system. There would be no paper trail. Yuri sent a message to Strangelove requesting confirmation of the order. He explained his concerns about getting caught. Strangelove's reply was instant. "Don't get caught. If you do, do not worry. I'll handle everything. Delete this thread immediately."

He deleted it and thought for a moment. If Major Belenov wanted to become Colonel Belenov, executing his orders—especially the stomach-churning orders—was a matter of mental attitude. He had to get himself under control, come to terms with the mission, and then get the men on board. That is the heart of leadership.

He glanced around the room to see if anyone had noticed his concerns. The men were all hard at work creating social media accounts. This week's goal was to create twelve thousand grandmothers in the American Midwest, each connected to the friend or family member of a reporter. They were on track to hit the goal by afternoon. No sense distracting them until he had it worked out.

He rubbed his neck and announced he was going for a walk.

Down the stairs, he left the office building and walked out into the lane. He distanced himself from the business district to walk on the docks. After briskly taking the corner, he realized he was going too fast. He looked guilty. Which was understandable because he felt guilty. He slowed to stroll, like a tourist out to admire the eighteenth-century homes and offices along the wharf. Stavanger meticulously preserved its small-town feel and twelfth-century heritage by retaining ancient architecture on the outside. Inside, everything had been remodeled and modernized.

He pushed his earbuds in and selected *Jumpin' Jack* by Big Bad Voodoo Daddy. It put a smile on his face.

He turned up Kirkegaten—Church Street—wandering aimlessly. How should he explain the assignment? Strangelove had sent it to him in plain, unambiguous language to test him. *Do this or you're out.* He could see the old man stroking his scar.

The men in his banda were modernized and westernized—and that was a problem. Working on the internet of the West every day, they had adopted values foreign to Russian military commanders. The men would not like the assignment.

Gray clouds hovered over gray cobblestones. Yuri looked at his gray reflection in a coffee shop window. He went inside, ordered a cup of American coffee and sat at a small table with a street view. Stavanger, home to Statoil and NATO's Joint Warfare Center, had the best internet service in northern Europe. Choosing it for his special operations team was a simple decision. Its international population covered their Russian origins well. It rarely snowed, which made it ten times better than that tiny sliver of Russia stranded between Poland and Lithuania that Strangelove called home, Kaliningrad. The electricity was always on.

The internet was always fast. They were in the perfect location for his career trajectory to reach its potential.

This crazy assignment could push his career into an even higher trajectory.

But if the Americans caught him, it would be a death sentence.

Don't get caught.

None of his other assignments had been set aside. The massive database sent by Strangelove's strutting young peacocks was the kind of assignment the banda relished. It contained more data on Americans than anyone thought possible. From their favorite foods to their political views, the information contained every fascinating detail imaginable except one: credit data. That last bit disappointed the banda. They had been successful hackers before being forced to serve the Motherland and they were always on the lookout for credit data.

"May I join you?" A sandy-haired American spoke in broken Russian and sat next to him. "My name is Brad. I'm—"

Yuri shoved his pistol into the man's ribs discreetly behind their thick coats and spoke in perfect English. "Are you a spy handler or a queer—Brad?"

The American didn't bat an eyelash. He stared for a calm moment, then picked up his coffee and pushed off his chair. "I've caught you at a bad time. My mistake. Perhaps another day."

Yuri didn't take his eyes off the man until he'd disappeared down Kirkegaten. The last thing he needed was a CIA agent trying to turn him.

He sipped his coffee and gazed across the street. He watched a beautiful young woman walk into the pub next door. Then it came to him: Cirkus, the pub, had a private room. He crossed the lane and made arrangements with the manager. He texted his group to join him for a celebration, an early dinner, and vodka. A few drinks would open their ears and minds to his carefully chosen words.

The banda arrived a few hours later after the workday ended.

The chilled vodka was poured. Each man raised his glass and faced Yuri.

"Tvoe zdorovie!" To your health.

Every glass turned up then slammed back to the table. Eyes filling with the first flush of the evening swept the room. Grins spread. The Cirkus manager arrived with a round of zakuski: pickled cucumber, tomato, mushroom, and pumpkin.

Lieutenant Vasili, Yuri's second in command and the only other career soldier in the banda, poured the second round. *"Vashee zdaróvye!"* Your health.

The pickled vegetables disappeared moments before the Cirkus staff brought more food: smoked salmon, halibut, and salted mackerel. He hadn't given them much time, but they had managed to find real Russian hor d'ourves.

More vodka was poured and another toast given. This time, they sipped.

"My friends," Yuri said, "we are about to transform the balance of power in the world. Russia's GDP has tripled—300%—since the turn of the century. How has the USA faired in those same years? They grew only 25%. Under President Vladimir Medevtin, the average Russian income has doubled. In America, only the rich get richer. Change is coming, my friends. Russia will be the twenty-first century superpower, and you will be the engineers who make it happen."

His men looked quite proud, their faces glowing with vodka's sheen.

"Nuclear bombs defined power in the last century." Yuri smiled. "But no longer. To use one, even a small one, would bring the immediate dissolution of the country that deployed it. No, today's superpower controls minds. The future belongs to those who control the truth. And we know how to shape alternative truths better than anyone."

One of the newest men, young and fair-haired Alexi, raised his glass to offer a toast. Yuri waved him off.

"The Americans think they are in charge of the world. They have missiles and drones and armies and navies. They use their power to oppress Russia. We tried to liberate Georgia and Libya. And what do they do? Sanctions. Our diplomats are shunned. Our business leaders banned from travel. Our overseas bank accounts frozen. Our jobs are threatened by their actions. The Motherland strains under the American yoke. And who are they to impose such things? Who made the Americans masters of the galaxy?"

"The devil is not as frightening as he is painted," Alexi said.

Yuri and Vasili shared a quick glance. Was the young man's use of the old Russian adage aimed at Yuri or the Americans? Vasili shrugged.

A waitress darted in carrying a tray of piroshki: buns with cabbage, raisins, and meats stuffed inside. She was the same woman who drew him to the establishment earlier in the afternoon. He lost his men's attention as the beautiful young lady put her tray on the table and then, unnerved by fifteen men staring at her like wolves, fled.

Yuri smiled and quoted the meme his men passed around soon after they covertly moved their operation to Stavanger. "The Vikings didn't bring back the ugly ones."

Everyone laughed and grabbed a piroshki. Yuri tasted one and found it almost as good as his mother's.

"The American sanction is a weapon of oppression." Yuri spoke loud enough to draw their eyes as they enjoyed their food. "Why do the Americans oppress us? Because democracy is outdated."

"Nations are outdated," Roman, the anarchist, called out. He, Igor, and Petr clinked their glasses.

Yuri ignored his comment. "Americans are bloated with conceit and entitlements." Yuri caught their attention by bellowing. "From the poor who feel entitled to free food, to the billionaires who feel entitled to free stadiums, to the elderly who feel entitled to free retirement, they only worry about themselves. They don't care about each other. And how do they get their entitlements? By devaluing Russia's natural resources. They've flooded the market with cheap nickel, aluminum, oil, and diamonds. Those are Russia's primary economies." He pounded his fist on the table. "Their decadence must end."

A round of cheers went up. A couple fists pumped in the air.

"Have you seen them?" dew-faced Alexi asked. "Even their poor people are fat."

Yuri topped off everyone's glass and toasted. They sipped.

"Our banda is more powerful than their nuclear missiles. We control information and disinformation inside their country. Distrust and suspicion are the most powerful weapons—the very weapons we wield. They gave it to us like a gift. Factions within the USA have been denigrating the American government for decades. The American people no longer trust their political leaders. They vote out corrupt politicians and replace them with the very billionaires who corrupted the politicians in the first place."

A burly waiter came in with a tray of food.

"We are on the verge of ending sanctions against the Motherland." Yuri raised his glass. "Within a few years, maybe months, we will be tugging the American leash, and it is they who will come to heel when we whistle."

"To the Motherland!" Igor said with a distinct note of satire in his voice. Everyone sipped.

Alexi looked around the table, a little confused. "What do we have to do?"

"We have to stand together." Yuri clenched his teeth, lowered his voice, and scowled. "We must be brave and do the things that no coward could do."

Most of his men had served only their required time in the Russian military. They were young men who made ends meet by hacking into publicly traded American companies, reading their quarterly reports before they were officially published, and trading on the information. In the US, they would call it insider trading. To Yuri, it was simply smart business. Several members of his banda had made plenty of money.

That was also a problem. Some of his men made a lot of money before he caught them. When bringing them in, Yuri offered each man a choice: be extradited to the US and go to jail, or give up his illegal profits and work quietly in Yuri's banda under the protection of the Russian Federation.

Alexi had been one of the best. Smart and quick, he had moved his money offshore. Yuri had frozen the man's accounts. Alexi came to terms with Yuri's rule quickly. But the boy kept an attitude of moral superiority. They both knew he could slip away one night and rebuild his small fortune from Panama or Singapore or anywhere he chose.

"*Payékhalee*!" Alexi said. *Let's get started.* He raised his shot glass and sipped half.

Yuri had no choice but to follow suit.

As Yuri drank, Alexi asked another question. "Exactly how will our courage be tested?"

"We will follow orders." Yuri stared hard over the top of his glass. "We will change some coordinates in a few systems. A few people might be harmed. Americans only."

"Innocent Americans?"

And there it was—Alexi's moral superiority unleashed before the group. For Yuri's career to go higher, he would heed Strangelove's warning: *it takes only one man to destroy an important mission.* Insurrections were best put down quietly, without fuss.

"When is an American innocent?" Roman asked with a smirk.

"The day before he is born!" the others answered the old joke in unison.

Yuri said, "*Davayte vyp'yem za uspekh nashego biznesa.*" Let's drink to the success of our business.

Alexi raised his glass and gulped. The others raised their glasses and sipped. Yuri raised his glass slowly, watching Alexi carefully, and sipped.

Someone told another joke. They settled in and drank and told stories and ate and drank and told more stories. The evening went on in the ancient Russian tradition: a lot of vodka and a lot of talking and laughing. Roman and his group discussed the global hacker community and the growing sentiment that governments were unnecessary. Yuri laughed and left them to it.

When the manager announced it was closing time, Yuri offered one last toast. "*Na pososhok*!" One for the road, but literally meaning, *for your walking stick.*

They put on their coats and staggered to the door, laughing and pushing each other. On the street, they said goodnight and went separately into the dark.

Yuri stayed behind. He paid the bill and inquired about the pretty waitress, who turned out to be the manager's daughter. Yuri complimented the man on his fine genes and left.

On the street, he pulled his phone and turned on the tracker. Alexi had staggered near the fish market by the dock. He pulled on his gloves and hurried there.

The docks were desolate except for a pair of drugged-up folk singers who hadn't noticed the tourists were gone. Thirty yards away, Alexi stood by the water's edge, weaving in place. Perhaps he was trying to regain his bearings. The young man drank as young men will: too much and too fast.

Yuri strolled to the singers, at the corner of a nearby building. He watched their drug-glazed eyes and listened to their off-key strains. They couldn't see Alexi from where they stood, but Yuri could. Taking a hundred krone note from his wallet, he bent down, put it in the guitar case, and snatched a spare guitar string. He looked both ways as he crossed the cobblestone wharf and approached Alexi from behind.

They were alone on a moonless night, in those few fleeting hours of darkness so close to the Arctic Circle. Alexi heard his footsteps and swung around to face him.

"Contemplating the whale in the harbor?" Yuri asked.

Alexi's brow creased in alcohol-fueled confusion. He turned to face the water. "What whale—"

Yuri slipped the guitar string around the boy's neck and pulled tight. Too drunk to fight, Alexi vainly reached for the garrote in strangled silence.

It had to be done, Yuri reasoned as the brilliant young man flailed ineffectively. Yuri's promotion was too close to let an idealistic young man poison his banda with moral questions. *Eliminate the weak before they infect the others.*

Yuri held the man for several minutes to let life slip away. While he waited, he pulled Alexi's wallet from his pocket. When it was time, Yuri kicked the body over the edge where it slipped quietly into the sea. Alexi's heavy boots and coat would take him to the bottom.

Yuri pushed his earbuds in and listened to John Scofield playing *Past Present*. As he strode past the addicts, he dropped the guitar string and Alexi's wallet in the open case.

CHAPTER 6

PIA STEPPED OFF THE ELEVATOR and into Terrat, the rooftop restaurant on the Mandarin Oriental, Barcelona. Handing her bundle of roses to the maître' d along with a hundred-euro note, she pulled a ragged, second-hand skirt and blouse out of her shoulder bag and slipped them over her running shorts and racerback top. She added a dirty-hair wig and pulled a scarf around it to obscure the side of her face. After giving the shocked man a wink and trading her bag for the roses, she hunched over and stepped outside. She did her best to diminish her tall stature by shuffling in her scruffy shoes on the terrace.

The stunning afternoon view across Barcelona's rooftops almost threw her out of character. She managed to sell a rose to a table of confused Kuwaitis. Gypsy peddlers were never allowed in the nice hotels.

She shuffled closer to her target, the table of four near the pool where her dad sipped a beer. Big, loud, and brash, Alan Sabel exuded confidence that infected everyone around him. Entering a room with him felt like being the guest of honor at a surprise party. Usually.

Alan leaned forward, listening intently to the two smartly dressed men across from him. Jonelle "the Major" Jackson, his Chief Operating Officer, sat next to him.

Pia scuffled to the table behind them and listened with one ear while an indignant local couple shooed her away in Catalan. Their rejection sent her beyond eavesdropping distance.

She didn't know the men. They had Slavic accents. Possibly Russian. Their tone was conceited. They made demands. From appearances, her father found them disturbing. Alan countered in some way. The men scoffed, batting away his words with their hands.

Two more tables waved her off while a handsome young man called her over. He held a twenty euro note out and rattled something in Spanish. With her head down, she approached him. As soon as she was within reach, he grabbed her bundle of roses and replaced it with a five euro note. He gave her a shove and laughed.

Pia's blood rose quickly. Rudeness to gypsies was commonplace throughout Europe, but it pissed her off. She grabbed his wrist. His gaze rose. He saw her rage and shrank back. He called for the waiter in a cracked voice. She stuffed his money in his mouth and snatched back the flowers.

For the first time, she glanced at his companion, a lovely young woman. Still gripping the man's wrist in her vice-like fist, Pia bowed and offered the bouquet to the lady. "May you find a better man."

The incident reminded her of her own boyfriend, Stefan. He was off traveling the world to find himself. In his case, for good reason. But, would he abuse a gypsy to impress Pia? The old Stefan would have. But, the new, improved Stefan? Had he really changed? She wanted to think so.

In the corner of her peripheral vision, the two men left her father's table with their chins tipped high.

She rose to her natural height, and let go of the man's wrist. The woman gasped. Pia glanced down at her and realized her height didn't fit her disguise. She pulled off her wig, tossed it on an empty chair, and shook her ponytail free. The blouse and skirt came next, revealing her toned, lanky form in athletic wear. Across the terrace, the Kuwaiti couple applauded. She took a bow.

Her father looked over at the Kuwaitis, then followed their gaze to his daughter. He swallowed hard.

She crossed to him and took one of the recently vacated chairs. "Hi, Dad."

"How nice to run into you so far from home." He picked up his beer and sipped.

"Hello, Major." Pia smiled.

"You've been working with our DAO?" the Major asked Pia.

"Our what?" Alan asked.

"Denied Area Operations," Pia said. "Disguises and gadgets that get us in without knocking."

"When did we open that?" he asked.

Pia said, "My idea."

No one spoke for a moment.

"You've been avoiding me." Pia leaned in. "What brings you to Barcelona?"

"We're looking to expand Sabel Satellite in Catalonia. Spain feels left out of the *Thales Alenia* deal. They help finance it, but all the jobs and production go to France and Italy."

The Major snapped a glance his way.

"You left town the day Pozdeeva showed up and haven't answered my calls since," Pia said. "Why?"

He shrugged. "I didn't build a twenty-billion-dollar company sitting on my couch."

"Dad." She leaned toward him, her elbows on her knees. "You're hiding something."

He clenched his jaw and stared into her gray-green eyes.

"Who is Pozdeeva?" she asked. "Why did he die bringing me encrypted data that's old news in the intelligence community?"

Alan looked across the skyline at red tile roofs. "Has Bianca decoded them yet?"

"Yes."

"What's in them?" he asked.

"What are you afraid might be in them?"

"Are you accusing me of something?" Alan met her gaze and huffed. "I thought we put your parent's murder behind us. I did the best I could raising you. I went to nearly all your games. I built a global conglomerate for you. You should be grateful. Not condemning me for being 'afraid' of what's in some random USB drive. Show some respect."

The Major leaned closer to him, her eyes watching him carefully, and laid her fingertips on his forearm. A calming touch.

"I forgave you for your role," Pia said, "innocent as it was. But why would you keep any secrets going forward?"

He shifted his weight in his seat.

"Who were those men?" Pia asked.

Alan took another sip of beer. He set the glass down and brushed a drop of condensation off his trousers. He glanced at Pia and squinted into the distance.

"Why aren't they mentioned on your calendar?" she asked.

"They represent an old business partner." He crossed one leg over his knee and kept his gaze on the horizon. "They want to renegotiate an outdated agreement."

Pia leaned back in her seat. A waiter approached. She smiled at him and shook her head before he asked. He took the hint and left.

"In the data, there's one picture of Pozdeeva in the lobby of Sabel Industries. Who was he?"

Her dad looked skyward and took a moment to compose his answer.

"Polonium-210 is the signature poison of a Russian assassination." He sighed and sipped. "The most famous case was Alexander Litvinenko, the FSB agent who accused Vladimir Medevtin of terrorism and corruption. Litvinenko claimed Medevtin ordered him to kill oligarchs who disagreed with Medevtin's tactics. He also accused Medevtin of bombing two Moscow apartment buildings and killing 293 innocent civilians just to start a war. Medevtin expected that war with Chechnya to launch him into the Russian Presidency, according to Litvinenko. It worked. Medevtin became president.

"Litvinenko came forward to accuse Medevtin in public. Several Russian military officers and dissidents confirmed his accusations. It didn't go well. Litvinenko fled to London and worked with MI6. He wrote two books making credible accusations linking the FSB and Medevtin to the bombings. He named people, places, and events that were verified. Someone in Russia didn't like his dissent. In 2006, Russian FSB agents slipped a dose of polonium no bigger than a grain of sand into his tea. It killed him."

Alan faced her. "Pozdeeva was one of the men who confirmed Litvinenko's accusations. He disappeared for several years." He made air quotes with his fingers around the word disappeared. "When he resurfaced, he recanted the indictments.”

“Pozdeeva went against Medevtin?” she asked.

“Yes and no. When he backed Litvinenko, he was high up in Russia’s military intelligence. When he came back from the gulags, he was reassigned closer to Moscow where they could keep an eye on him.”

“How did you know Pozdeeva? Did you meet him when we used to go to St. Petersburg?”

“You were so young.” Alan gave her a tight smile and softened his tone. “You still remember those trips?”

Pia nodded cautiously. “Pozdeeva’s drive has thousands of documents. Most of them are random. Three of them are twenty-year-old visas for you, me—and Chuck Roche—to visit a bank in St. Petersburg. It dredged up memories.”

“Chuck Roche.” The Major rolled her eyes. “What a nutcase. Did you hear his campaign speech? Hunter’s administration is wrecking the FAA. Airliners will fall from the sky. Ridiculous.”

“If you believe the polls,” Pia said, “he’s already pulled ahead of the Democrat, William Charles.”

“Don’t worry.” Alan glanced her way. “I’m going to ruin that guy before the election. It’s my number one goal.”

“Let me help you,” Pia said. “We could work together.”

Alan thought about it. Then looked to the sky.

“After Roche was caught bragging about sexual assault, I thought he’d drop out,” the Major said. “So why’s he ahead?”

“What makes him worse than Veronica Hunter?” Pia asked.

“Did you hear his campaign platform?” Alan shot a stern look her way. “He promised everything: jobs, health insurance, ending terrorism, lower taxes, no more deficits. He has no idea how to accomplish any of that.”

“True.” Pia shook her head. “But America always falls for hucksters like P.T. Barnum, Charles Ponzi, and Bernie Madoff.”

“Enron, Lehman Brothers.” Alan nodded. “But it’s worse than that. He’s not qualified for the office. He has no morals. He’s nothing more than a narcissist surrounded by sycophants.”

“That doesn’t make him dangerous,” Pia said, “it makes him foolish.”

"How dangerous is a narcissistic fool with nuclear weapons?" Alan raised his voice. "He refused to rule out using nuclear weapons in Europe. He boasted he'd launch Trident missiles at ISIS-held cities, ignoring the millions of enslaved civilians. He thinks we have a trade deficit with Germany. That's like saying Canada has a deficit with Tennessee. He doesn't understand they're part of the European Union. He has no idea what he's talking about."

Pia looked away after his tirade. She came to Barcelona hoping to connect with him in a new way, to work with him on the Pozdeeva project. Instead, they sat in silence for a minute. She considered telling him about the recording of Roche and Hunter. How they casually discussed her murder if she didn't join the campaign. But Dad was in the wrong mood to hear that news.

"What do you know about Pozdeeva?" Pia leaned forward and held out her phone with pictures loaded. "Why is he in these?"

She swiped through the four shots of Pozdeeva from the files: at the Hirshhorn, at the CIA, at Sabel Industries, and in an office with an older woman.

"Twenty years ago, he worked for a man codenamed Strangelove. I can't prove it, but I believe Strangelove was responsible for Litvinenko's death and Pozdeeva's time in prison. Strangelove also bailed out Roche Refineries many years ago. Maybe Pozdeeva was trying to tell you something about Roche."

"We didn't find anything like that in Pozdeeva's data." Pia pursed her lips in thought. "We have hundreds of random documents that don't make sense. So why was he willing to die to give them to me?"

Alan rocked back and forth as if he were indecisive about saying something. He sank back, looked around, and found the waiter. He rubbed his fingers together for the check. "Pozdeeva didn't die just to drop old vacation photos in your lap. There's something more in there. If it's about Roche, we need to know it. Roche is the Siberian Candidate."

"I have a meeting with bankers from Rossiya Bank." Pia watched his quick reaction. "What aren't you telling me?"

"How did that come about?" His voice sounded rushed and agitated.

"I inquired about this bank statement." She showed him a photo on her phone. "They wanted to talk in person. They sent me an offer for a billion dollars of expansion capital with no interest."

"Dollars, US? That's twenty percent of their capital." He picked up the napkin under his beer glass and wiped his brow. "I'll take the meeting. Where is it?"

"St. Petersburg."

He pounded the arm of his chair with his clenched fist and looked skyward.

After a moment, he brought his hot glare back to Pia. "A year ago, the leader of the Russian opposition party, Boris Nemtsov, was gunned down in the streets of Moscow. It was the day before he was to lead a protest rally. All the surveillance cameras on the street were turned off just before the shooting. Nearly two hundred Russian journalists have been murdered since Medevtin first came to power. There's even a Wikipedia page called 'List of journalists killed in Russia'. In Russian-friendly countries, a GRU operator simply shoots Russian critics in the street. They reserve polonium-210 for high-profile murders in western countries. The GRU is the only organization with access to polonium. They're the people who murdered Pozdeeva—and they're the people who invited you to St. Petersburg."

CHAPTER 7

THE WIPERS SQUEAKED AN IRRITATING rhythm that matched my exhausted mood. I was driving home from Sabel Gardens on a dark night in late September after a long shift. It started when I tried to keep up with Ms. Sabel's exercise routine at four in the morning. She's a world-class athlete. I'm a former bullet-chewer. I'm also the only employee capable of running close to her speed and distance.

My phone rang. Kasey Earl. We exchanged pleasantries for a moment before he came to the point.

"You got anything for me at Sabel?" he asked.

"We're about to dispatch a clearing team to Darfur." Clearing being shorthand for bomb-squad, or more specifically, digging up land mines so children can play without losing a leg.

"Funny."

"I'm serious," I said. "We need thirty guys and only have twenty-five qualified right now. Pay's good. Accommodations suck. But the danger's fair to high. If you want Ms. Sabel to forgive-and-forget, it would be a—"

"I got something better." He waited for me to ask. I didn't. After a few awkward seconds, he continued. "How would you like insider information about Roche's contract bids you're competing on?"

"That would be dishonest. We don't do that."

His despondent sigh traveled over the air all the way from NYC to my ear.

I broke the silence. "How is David Watson working out?"

"Ain't you heard?" he asked. "He's done gone to your side."

"Get out. When did that happen?" I heard him snicker in the background as he moved away from the mic. "Who took his job?"

"Sure as hell weren't me." He scoffed.

"They should put you in. There's something wrong there."

He grunted his agreement.

"What did Watson do that got him fired?" I asked.

"I dunno."

"Well, if we just hired him and he's a terrorist or a child molester, that would be important to Ms. Sabel. So, here's your chance to get on her good side."

"Oh, hey, yeah. I should look into that shit."

I clicked off and sighed. Spy handling was not my thing. I preferred shooting people to making them betray their employers. Especially when they're as despicable as Kasey.

But I couldn't care very much. All I could think about was crashing face-first into my big soft bed, clothes and all.

I rounded the corner off the main road into my quiet, tree-lined neighborhood, going fast. I splashed through a puddle. Water sprayed out higher than the roof of my car. I love that. The guy walking his dog was less enthusiastic. It's shocking what kind of language people use sometimes.

When my eyes returned to the street, a pale figure stood in the middle of the road. I slammed on my brakes and skidded to a stop, expecting to hear the thud of a body hitting the hood of my car. Instead, it disappeared.

Mercury reappeared in the seat next to me, his mini-toga soaking wet. *Aw, dawg, do you have any idea how much I love blowing your mind?*

I peeled myself off the ceiling. *Please, don't ever do that again.*

Mercury said, *Bro, you got one heavy schedule ahead of you tonight. Let's get moving.*

He was wrong: the only thing left on my calendar was an appointment with the pillow.

My headlights swept the driveway. Their reflection lit up my yard when they hit the rising garage door. In that single second of illumination, I could see a dark figure huddled on my doorstep. I parked, drew my pistol, and snuck out as the garage door rattled back down.

A quick peek around the corner revealed a woman in a black hooded cape curled up on my stoop. An overhang slightly larger than a doormat kept the rain off but left her little room. Her posture was non-threatening, so I holstered my weapon and approached.

Emily Lunger, the *Post's* embedded reporter at Sabel Security, and a former lover, looked up with a pale, frightened face. The hood framed her like a movie star from the black-and-white days.

I'd fallen in love with her once. Then I left her at a coffee shop waiting for a romantic weekend that never happened because … I was an easily distracted jerk.

I've matured since then. I left my prowling days behind and was actively seeking a life-partner. Ever since I bought my house, I've become serious about the matter. Whenever I look at my backyard, I can picture children frolicking in the weeds.

Maybe I should mow that.

Anyway. I'm ready to meet the right woman. I want someone worth cooking a five-course meal for. I want someone worth asking how her day went. I want someone worth listening to when she answers me with every excruciatingly microscopic detail of exactly how her day went. I'm ready to share my future with one woman—and only one woman. Probably.

So far, none of the women I'd been serious about were serious about me. For them, it's all fun and games until her husband comes back from his business trip. Then she ghosts on me and my calls are blocked.

I had my chance with Emily. That ship sailed a long time ago. She was in love with someone else now. Someone who treated her right. Someone who invited her on romantic weekends—and went with her.

Emily had tears in her eyes.

She rose and stood before me with a despondent mixture of longing and pain. She held something in her hand. It was hard to see in the dark, but it looked like a small velvet box from Tiffany's. She pushed it to me like an offering. I looked at the box. I looked at her.

She twitched a pained smile and opened it.

A giant diamond ring sparkled in what little light spilled from my living room window.

I gawked at the size of the thing. Shafts of light radiated in all directions like the big scene in a romantic movie that blew its budget on special effects. I didn't know they could do that in real life. I was frozen with curiosity and fear at the same time.

"What should I do?" She broke down in sobs.

Mercury said, *Dang, dude! Do you always have women hanging around waiting for a chance to propose?*

I said, *In my dreams.*

When I slipped my hand around her to unlock the door, she snapped the box shut and curled under my arm. I opened the door. Anoshni ran out, jumping and barking with excitement. I pushed them both inside.

I took Emily's coat and hung it while she stood in the foyer, staring at the ring. She wore a sleek black dress, tight and short, with heels and pearls. Her matching black pumps showed off her legs. She was dressed to impress. I moved to the kitchen, gave Anoshni a treat, and pulled a shrimp ceviche out of the fridge.

She followed slowly, stopping between every step to break down in soft tears.

When she reached the archway to the kitchen, she leaned against the wall. "You don't like it?"

I pulled a shrimp from the lime sauce, held it over a cocktail napkin, and offered it to her. She crossed to the kitchen island. Her gaze locked on mine while she leaned forward and took the offered bite.

As soon as her mouth was full, I said, "It's not my size."

She was in the middle of an eyes-closed culinary orgasm—because I'm that good a chef—when her eyes blew open. She almost spat her shrimp. She chewed and gulp-swallowed keeping one hand up to stop me from talking. "It's not for you, idiot. Bianca proposed."

Mercury said, *Idiot. That's a lot nicer thing than she called you the last time you two were alone. You're coming up in the world, homie.*

I said, *Can you give me a minute? She's upset.*

Mercury said, *Whoa, Sherlock, the power of your deductive reasoning is awesome. Just don't forget, she shot a guy in the face with a shotgun once. So. Like. Be chill here.*

I said, *Forget? She saved my life with that shotgun—no thanks to you.*

I handed her a tissue. She looked up at me and sniffled.

I didn't know what to say. "Uh. Congratulations, then?"

Wrong. Apparently.

She broke down again.

Anoshni had enough with the tears. He darted out the doggie door.

There are things a veteran with eight tours of duty under his belt can do well: call in airstrikes, shoot bad guys, make playgrounds safe for Afghan kids. Consoling someone after a marriage proposal isn't on the list. I tried handing her another shrimp. She waved it off. I pushed the dish to the center of the counter and grabbed some red leaf lettuce and arugula. I tore the lettuce into bite-sized pieces and added tomatoes that I cut into thin wedges. Slivered olives and figs with torn basil topped the growing bowl. Then, goat cheese crumbled with care. I drizzled olive oil and balsamic vinegar over the top, and coarse-ground salt and spicy pepper. I twirled it and dumped the mixture onto a salad plate, added two forks and handed her a napkin.

Emily's eyes watched my preparations with growing interest. She placed the ring, open, on the counter where she could see it and climbed the bar stool.

I leaned over and took the first bite. I waited until we were three bites in. "Bianca is the smartest person I've ever met."

"Yeah, she is."

"I've only known you for a couple years, but these last six months, I've never seen anyone as happy as you."

"I know."

I ate my salad and waited.

Mercury, standing behind her, pointed at the backyard. *Hey homeslice, you need to keep your ears open. You hear that?*

I said, *I'm busy. Warn me if I need to chase the neighbor's dog again.*

Emily focused on eating. After she whittled it down to the last couple bites, she looked up. Then her gaze fell to the ring and tears streamed down her cheeks.

Mercury said, *Homie, this is all nice and sweet, but have you checked out your back window lately?*

I took a quick glance out the kitchen window and saw lots of dark. *Leave me alone, she's in pain.*

"I can't do it." She caught a rolling tear with the back of her wrist. "I'm not gay. I mean. Well. Sure, you might call the last six months … whatever. And there was Carmen. And before her, there was Julia and … But I'm not gay. I wear makeup. I've never owned a Subaru."

"You? Kicking out the stereotypes?"

"I know." She looked embarrassed and sniffled into a tissue. "I don't know if I could be gay the rest of my life. I mean. I'm still attracted to men. Maybe. I don't know what I prefer."

Mercury's grin grew like the Cheshire cat's. *Oh dawg, you're in for some hot sex tonight. Hot hot hot.*

I said, *No way. She's not hitting on me.*

Dude, help-me-find-my-gender-preference is the best kind.

I said, *And you wonder why nobody worships you anymore.*

I heard a strange noise at the back of the house and cocked my ear.

"Maybe." Emily reached across the island to put her hand on mine. "You and I had some great times, Jacob."

"You had better times with Bianca."

"But. What if I cheat on her?"

Mercury said, *Not hitting on you? Brutha, you're in! She's going to jump your bones. You should get Bianca over here and squeeze in the middle. Everybody loves a sandwich.*

I said, *I will not take advantage of the situation.*

CRASH.

The window in my back door exploded. A hand reached in and turned the knob. The door swung open, and a slim man in a sleek Brioni suit stepped in. His Prada shoes crunched on the broken glass.

I reached for my pistol on the far end of the counter.

Mercury said, *Oh yeah, tried to tell you. Russian gangsters are crawling around your property. You're surrounded.*

I said, *You tried?*

You were one zipper away from having Emily's dress on the floor, homie. Tell me the truth. What's more important: your heartbeat or your sex life?

We looked at each other and whispered in unison as if reading from the Sacred Book of Men, *Sex life.*

I added, *But, for the record, I wasn't going to take advantage of the situation.*

Mercury shrugged. *Shuuurre.*

My senses picked up two more figures entering from different directions. One stepped behind me and grabbed my wrist, the other behind Emily.

"Do I interrupt special occasion?" Brioni-suit said. His mostly-gray hair was styled by a pro. His watch glittered behind the PSM Baikal-441 in his hand. If I remembered my Ranger training correctly, the initials stood for *Pistolet Samozaryadny Malogabaritny,* meaning compact self-loading pistol. A small gun that was all the rage among high-ranking Communist Party members and top KGB officers back in the Soviet era. In today's Russian Federation, it's passé.

In his other hand, he held Anoshni. My puppy had been fitted with a duct tape muzzle. The dog's failure to subdue three large men weighed on him. His puppy-eyes looked to me for forgiveness.

Emily and I stared at Brioni with blank expressions. He nodded at the sparkling diamond on the counter. Her eyes followed his. She burst into tears again.

Brioni gave me a sympathetic shrug. "Not so good night for you?"

"What can I do for you?"

"I want Pozdeeva drive."

"Poz-what?" I tried to free my wrist from a man built like a refrigerator.

"Don't be dumb with me. Ilya Pozdeeva die at your boss feet six weeks ago." He gave me an ice-cold stare.

Refrigerator-guy pressed a barrel to my temple, let go of my wrist, and slipped a leg-sized arm around my neck. I put my hands on the counter. Emily sat up straight. The goon behind her put her in an equally hope-crushing headlock and pulled her off the chair.

"We came for Pozdeeva drive." Brioni put his gun away.

"You came to the wrong place." I turned my hands up.

"You are Sabel's lover, no?"

Emily gurgled her words. "She has more class than that."

I did a long slow turn to look at Emily.

She gasped. "Just saying."

"Lover, boy-toy, whatever—" Brioni snapped his fingers "—does not matter. What matters is she want her Jacob to have all finger and toe— and everything else—attached."

Mercury leaned over Brioni's shoulder. *Boy-toy? You been holding out on me, bro?*

I said, *If you're omniscient, why don't you know he's lying?*

"Want me to make a call?" I choked out.

"You know where it is?"

I shook my head. "I know someone who knows. Probably."

He tilted his head to the side and waited for me to tell him.

"If you let Emily go." I nodded at her.

He shook his head slowly.

"Your guys killed Pozdeeva two months ago." I struggled for breath. "Why wait so long to find it?"

"Concern yourself with keeping your lady alive."

"I can get you a copy," I said. "They said there was nothing on it, just some old emails from a couple decades ago. A few fake-news pools that are closed. Nothing that means anything today."

"Pozdeeva was old-school," Brioni said as if thinking out loud. He shifted Anoshni's weight in his arm. "I want original drive. You find it, give it to me, tomorrow. I give you woman back."

Brioni turned and opened the back door. The guy holding Emily leaned back, pulling her off the ground, and started to follow him.

"You're not very smart then." I waited for Brioni to look over his shoulder. "Taking a reporter from the *Post* will bring down the wrath of every journalist in the city. It's the only thing worse than cop-killing in terms of getting unwanted attention."

Brioni faced Emily. "This is true? You are reporter?"

"Journalist." She squeaked over the musclehead's arm.

Brioni nodded at his man. The guy dropped her. She staggered and put a hand to her throat. He squeezed Anoshni. "I keep dog."

He stepped outside.

"Hey!" I called into the darkness. "How am I supposed to find you?"

"Not worry. I find you. Tomorrow."

"I'm scheduled to be in Istanbul tomorrow."

"Too bad for dog." His voice trailed into the distance.

The guy holding me took my Glock and let go. He covered for his buddy as the two of them followed their boss into the dark.

"Tell me you have security cameras." Emily had eyes the size of Frisbees. "Holy shit, Jacob—Viktor Popov just stole your dog."

"You're welcome. I'm not sure Anoshni thinks trading his life for yours was worthwhile though."

Mercury said, *Sometimes you should listen to your girlfriend, homie.*

I said, *She's not my girlfriend. She's Bianca's—when she comes to her senses.*

Emily scrambled to her phone and started dialing with shaking hands.

Mercury's advice made its way through my thick skull.

"Wait." I grabbed her wrist. "You know that guy?"

"Director of the SVR. Kremlin spies." She pulled her hand away and resumed dialing. "But he comes to the USA pretending to be the cultural attaché at the Russian Embassy. That guy is a legend."

I texted Bianca from my secure Sabel phone. "Get yourself and the original Pozdeeva drive to Sabel Security HQ or Sabel Gardens, whichever is closer. Don't reply or ask questions. Do it NOW!"

My expertise with Arabic-speaking jihadis didn't help in this situation. What little I knew about Russians came from a few incidents in strange corners of the world. Corners where there weren't supposed to be any Russians. Whenever I ran into them, they made Mafia goons look like altar boys. "So who is Viktor … whatever-his-name-is?"

Emily had reached voicemail and disconnected. She dialed another number. "In 1985, Hezbollah kidnapped three Russian diplomats in front of the Beirut embassy. Popov was a young, green lieutenant back then. He picked up the brother of Hezbollah's leader, stuffed the man's severed genitals in his mouth, and dropped his carcass on the front steps of Hezbollah headquarters. An hour later, the Russians were released."

"And you let him walk away with my dog?" I asked.

She failed to see the humor in my question and pressed the phone to her ear. "What the hell is on that drive, Jacob?"

I shrugged and called Montgomery County Detective Czajkowski to report a kidnapped dog, extortion, home invasion, etc.

"You've come up in the world, Stearne." CJ sighed. "Last time it was felons on parole. Now you're going global. If the body count is under a dozen, I'll send a squad car over in the morning for the details."

"Morning? CJ! Did you hear the part where the top Russian spy kidnapped my dog?"

"We're not your personal police. If he's who you said, he has diplomatic immunity—nothing we can do. Besides, you're the great big fancy security guys. Why not invade the Russian Embassy with your super-secret special-ops team?" He clicked off.

I looked at Emily. She looked at me.

"My editor doesn't think it'll sell." She snapped her ring box shut and popped it open again. "He wants me to put a paragraph on the website, see if it gets any hits."

Chasing a Cold War legend back to his sanctuary would be an international incident. My only hope for getting my dog back was to hand over the Pozdeeva drive. I was too tired to think straight. Viktor would come out of his safe space eventually. Tackling the problem after a good night's sleep sounded like the best plan.

I left Emily in the kitchen madly thumbing a blog post on her phone and staggered back to my bedroom. I hit the sack dejected.

Mercury leaned over the lamp as I switched it off. *Bro, you gonna sleep after Viktor gave you that big fat clue? Cannot believe you.*

I said, *I can't believe you. What kind of a god lets his chosen one get robbed by the Russians?*

Chosen one? You? Aw, homie, I got better worshippers than you, believe me. Big time people. Important people. Powerful people.

Powerful, huh? I said, *If you care about those 'important' people, tell them they can get a free meal and a warm bed at the Salvation Army. Goodnight.*

Three seconds later, I was dead to the world. I dreamed about a lady on a bicycle riding away with Anoshni in a basket. The scene morphed into the face of Pia Sabel asking me why I slept with Emily. I pleaded my case, over and over, to a shifting sea of faces that turned into a crowd who picked up fist-sized rocks. Before they stoned me, I was late for someone's wedding. Running somewhere. Running in knee-deep mud until a bomb went off.

"Old school!" Covered in sweat, I sat bolt upright and shouted into the dark. "Microdots."

I grabbed my phone off the bedside table and texted Bianca my instructions. Then I looked at Anoshni's empty doggy bed. "No way that's gonna stand."

Throwing back the covers, I jumped out and grabbed my gear.

Twenty-seven minutes later, alarms were ringing, and soldiers were shouting on the far side of the compound as I secured Viktor Popov's mouth with duct tape. I waved Anoshni in front of his plasticuffed hands. I propped the pillows under his head so he could see better and aimed my pistol.

He grimaced in anticipation.

I fired a silenced 9mm into his right tibia. "You ever touch my dog again—you're a dead man."

CHAPTER 8

YURI LEANED OVER HIS HACKER'S shoulder in the darkened room and watched the center of three screens. The Russian heavy metal pouring from the man's headphones almost drowned out Yuri's jazz. Yuri was streaming the Mambo Kings' Latin-influenced version of the 1950s classic *Blue Rondo a la Turk*. There was the one thing he missed about living in America: live jazz. They invented the music and evolved its many forms from ragtime to big bands to modern. Going to a trendy club with a live quartet gave him tremendous joy. Moscow's jazz clubs were nothing by comparison.

One day he would return to the clubs in Chicago, New York, New Orleans. He would arrive in style with the Cirkus manager's daughter on his arm. He savored a few more notes of the pounding piano melody, then paused his music and tapped the programmer's shoulder. "Status?"

"The first was underbooked." He dropped his headphones to his neck and faced his boss. "They changed equipment. Nothing I could do."

"Monitor that one and keep looking."

"There will be one that is perfect. Give it time."

"We don't have time. We have an hour. Maybe." Yuri glared at the man. "Keep looking."

The programmer shrugged and returned to his screens.

Yuri stood in the center of the room and surveyed the round wall of computer screens. There had to be a perfect pair somewhere.

Roman looked up and pointed to his screen. Yuri crossed to him.

"There is a message in the database they sent us yesterday." Roman tapped a screen full of social media data about Americans. "Someone named Brad wants you to call him about hackers without borders."

"What is wrong with you?" Yuri's blood rose with his voice. "Everyone is working on the assignment. The social media projects are on hold."

"It's worth checking out because the guy seems to know—"

"Most likely, this 'Brad' guy is FSB. He's testing for spies. Answer him, and you're a dead man. Now get to work."

Yuri pushed his hand into his pocket to stop himself from decking the young man. With all the western influence in the room, an officer couldn't hit a man anymore. He calmed himself and returned to the center of the room. He checked off each of the monitors to see if anyone else had strayed from his assignment.

One of Lieutenant Vasili's displays looked promising. He resumed the Mambo Kings and watched the numbers scrolling by. Vasili sensed his stare and glanced over his shoulder. Yuri raised his brows. Vasili shook his head and turned back to his monitors.

Strangelove sent Yuri a text via the GRU's homegrown version of Snapchat that deleted everything after being read. "Are you working on my project? Expected results by now."

Yuri bit the inside of his cheek to prevent writing back something snarky about the banda's growing workload. He texted back "soon".

There was something impersonal in Strangelove's orders lately. As if he no longer cared about Yuri's banda. Strangelove's previous direction was chilling. *Don't get caught. If you do, do not worry. I'll handle everything.*

Strangelove knew nothing about Americans. They were fierce individualists until someone attacked their country. Strangelove might think he could handle things, but he was no match for them. More troubling was the fact that Strangelove was a seasoned veteran who came up during the Cold War. He would know that. So. Why no written orders? Did Popov really approve this assignment? Was Strangelove playing some game in which Yuri and his banda were pawns? Yuri scratched his beard.

Whatever the cagey old general was up to, Yuri would have to untangle it after the fact. For now, he would rely on Russian *Avos'*. His nation's reliance on fate. Hope. Destiny. For a people ruled by autocrats for a thousand years, Avos' was a reasonable way to deal with impossible situations. Great writers from Cantemir to Solzhenitsyn had championed the mindset as the heart of Russian character. They soldiered on in the face of overwhelming odds. It was their Avos'. He sighed.

He straightened up and took a deep breath. Failures do not get promoted to colonel or general.

Minutes ticked by as his playlist cranked up the next song, *Hurricane Season* by Trombone Shorty. He snapped his fingers to the beat.

He turned his attention to Igor, who drummed his fingers on the desk. "You have something?"

Igor looked over his shoulder. "No. It's just that … I'd rather be at the trial."

"Do your job!" Yuri clenched his fists. "Whether or not those damned addicts are convicted, Alexi will still be dead."

"I want to look them in the eye."

"Watch the displays." Yuri ripped his earbuds out and leaned into Igor's face. "Filthy street musicians are not your problem."

Igor turned red and clenched his teeth. His lips formed words that he bit back after glancing in Vasili's direction. He inhaled and held his breath for a second. "Yes, sir."

With an impudent flourish, he turned back.

Yuri leaned over him. "What about that one?"

"It's the right path," Igor squinted and looked up the tables on his right-hand monitor. "Schedule looks good."

"Keep watching it. If it stays on time, shout."

Igor nodded. Yuri resumed his watch and put his earbuds back in. The trial for Alexi's murderers couldn't have come at a worse time. His plan could unravel at any minute, and Igor wasn't the only one losing focus. Everyone had a news feed open on their desktops. He had cut their bereavement short to get on with the mission. Maybe he should've given them more time to grieve.

Then he stopped thinking. Major Yuri Belenov never second-guessed his decisions.

The mission was in motion. Nothing could stop him now. The

window of opportunity was short. Their man had inserted the code in the Cleveland ARTCC system an hour earlier. It had gone undetected. Sixteen possible scenarios had been studied and modeled. So far, eight had been eliminated. The timing would have to be perfect. Sending the revised code would have to be timed to the second. If the Americans discovered their connection, it would take months to get back inside.

Les McCann's pounding piano on *Compared to What* danced in his ears.

"I've got it." Roman snapped his fingers and pointed at his monitor. "These two."

Yuri ran to him and followed his finger on the first screen, then looked at the second. "Definitely. They will work." He shouted over his shoulder, "Vasili! We have them. They've already received instructions from TRACON."

"What are the numbers?" Vasili shouted.

Roman called them out, and Vasili repeated them.

Yuri listened intently and confirmed. "Go! Go!"

Igor ran the math through the simulator. "It will work. They'll hand off to ARTCC in five minutes."

"Quickly, quickly." Yuri felt his voice rising with his excitement. "Get it loaded now."

Vasili pounded his keyboard, sending the revised math to their Trojan subroutine. His fingers clicked like an orchestra of crickets, then stopped. Everything in the room went quiet.

"Check your work. Confirm everything." Yuri shouted. "We only get one chance at this."

Vasili called out the numbers. Roman repeated them, pressing a finger to his screen as he read them off. After he confirmed each set, he called out, "Correct."

When his men finished, all eyes in the room turned to Yuri. "Proceed."

The lieutenant dramatically pressed the enter key with the index finger on his outstretched arm. Then he stared at his monitor for a long, agonizing moment. He jumped up and shoved his fists in the air. "Upload confirmed!"

The entire group shouted for joy.

"Not yet!" Yuri held up a hand, stop.

They ran to Roman's display and watched as two dots blinked and moved and blinked again. They crowded in for a closer look. The dots moved ever closer to each other on a triangular path. Five minutes inched along like as many hours. No one spoke, no one moved. The whir of the computer fans the only sound in the room.

Everyone's eyes remained glued to Flight 1028, New York to Chicago, and Flight 31 from Boston. The first carried 212 people, the other 153.

For what seemed like an eternity, the two dots remained side-by-side. Blinking. Blinking. Blinking. Then they disappeared.

Everyone in the banda shouted and gave high-fives. Even Yuri smiled. Mission accomplished. He pulled his phone and sent a text to Strangelove: "It is done."

Strangelove texted back: "Reported in the news?"

Yuri's fist tightened around his phone. Of course, the media hadn't picked it up yet. The mid-air collision had just occurred. It would take an hour for a major news organization to confirm the story and post it online. He watched his team celebrating. They had worked hard for weeks to reach this point. They had lost a brother. They had executed an impossible string of math in seconds. They were careful and diligent in their work. They deserved a moment to revel in their accomplishment.

Vasili noticed him staring and tapped one of the others. Roman looked up next. The voices died down. They faced Yuri. "Well done. Now the next step."

The men nodded and returned to their workstations. They brought up the social media accounts they'd created in the general vicinity of the crash. They posted online about a loud noise. They posted about seeing airplanes falling from the sky. They posted about President Hunter's failure to upgrade the FAA. They posted about how obviously avoidable this horrific accident was. They posted about how no one in the media was publishing the true story. They posted that there were no news reports because lamestream media were covering up for their favorite establishment candidate, Veronica Hunter. They posted that President

Hunter should be called "the Murderer of Flight 1028." They posted that Chuck Roche had blasted President Hunter for failing to fix the outdated FAA. They posted that Chuck Roche would never have let this happen.

Roman started a meme: #HuntersFail.

Yuri liked it and had everyone copy it.

All the social media accounts had been set up in advance. All the fake-accounts had friended or followed someone connected to a major media outlet—but not reporters. The reporters would hear the Russians' spin from friends and thereby find it trustworthy.

Everyone in the banda waited with twenty news browsers open.

The first mention was a banner on a major website: *Mid-Air Collision, 365 Lives Feared Lost*. Then another and another. A specialty news site took the bait: *Hunter's Failure Costs Hundreds of Lives*. Then another and another. CNN was the first to pick up Roman's meme, #HuntersFail. Then Fox, and moments later, the rest followed.

Yuri walked behind his men and watched over their shoulders. He sent the confirmation text to Strangelove.

An odd quiet fell over the room. Only the computers hummed.

Igor groaned loudly. He turned his chair around, his back to his screens, and held his head in his hands. "What have we done?"

CHAPTER 9

Pia and Tania sipped coffees while waiting for an overdue limo. They sat in a booth at the otherwise empty Finnegan's Pub a block north of Rossiya Bank in Saint Petersburg, Russia. The proprietor wiped tables and swept floors in preparation for the evening crowd.

"What a-a-are you reading?" Tania asked.

Pia looked up. "Roche called the press the 'enemy of the people'. A term used by Stalin and Hitler."

"His s-s-supporters called th-th-them the *lügenpresse*." Tania stirred her cup and savored the aroma. "Lügen means l-l-lying in German. If I remember m-m-my West Point studies correctly, th-th-the Nazis used the phrase it b-b-before they closed the newspapers."

Pia checked her watch. "I have a feeling the limo isn't coming."

"That guy f-f-from the bank is still w-w-watching us."

"Does he know how obvious he is?"

"He was rushed i-i-into this." Tania took a casual look out the window, her gaze rolling by the man in the gray coat. "He's a local guy. Someone called him and told him to w-w-watch the meeting, s-s-see what we do afterward. Or else he's with the mob—but, s-s-same result in the end."

Pia texted the limo driver one last time.

"D-d-did that piss you off when the banker asked if y-y-your dad was coming?" Tania asked.

"He built Sabel Industries. It's natural for everyone to think he owns the company."

"So, why did he p-p-put nearly all the stock in your n-n-name?"

Pia took a long, slow sip of coffee. "Guilt."

"N-n-nah, that's OK." Tania raised her brows and flopped her hands out. "Don't tell m-m-me anything. Just because I'm your best f-f-friend doesn't mean you owe me any explanations."

"All right, but this is not a story I want talked about—ever." Pia caught Tania's gaze and drilled into it. "Dad lived next door to my bio-parents and me. A couple guys came to him, told him they were CIA investigating my parents. Asked him to track their comings and goings."

"And they were a-a-actually the guys who m-m-murdered your parents? He b-b-became their lookout before the killings? Holy shit." She held her cup to her lips. "Wait. He's not really c-c-complicit if they fooled him. Oh. Yeah. I get it. Even then, that's g-gotta weigh on a person's mind." Tania rolled her eyes to the ceiling. "That's why he a-a-adopted you?"

"He couldn't let me fall into the foster care system."

Tania dropped back in her seat. "That's h-heavy."

They sat in silence, contemplating Alan Sabel's act of atonement twenty-two years earlier.

Tania put her cup down and leaned forward. "Is that why w-w-we came here? You're trying to help y-y-your dad pin something on Roche?"

Pia tilted her head. "No. Pozdeeva gave us those files. I wanted to know more about the bank statement." She looked out the window. "They sure tightened up when I put that out there. I think there's something to it."

"Don't g-g-give me that." Tania touched her friend's wrist. "You could've c-c-called or sent s-s-someone. You came here because your d-d-dad brought you here when y-y-you were little. You're trying t-t-to connect with him."

Pia pursed her lips and sipped her coffee and looked out the window at the man across the street.

"Are you going to t-t-take the Russian's deal?" Tania asked.

Grateful for a new topic, Pia turned back. "Expand Sabel Security into Moscow with a zero-interest loan? Hard to resist, isn't it?"

"What about the p-p-part where they pay ten times the going rate for services, and you give them a r-rebate in Euros?"

"What's the matter, Tania? You don't think we should get involved in money laundering?" Pia smiled.

"N-n-n… N-n-n." Tania looked out the window at the blue sky and frowned. "S-s-so frustrating. Words in my head. Not in m-mouth."

"All wounds heal." Pia reached across the table and squeezed her hand. "Afterwards, you should keep the beret. It looks … jaunty. Perfect for you."

Tania turned her watery gaze outside.

Pia's phone buzzed with a text from Bianca telling her to check the news feed: *Hundreds Feared Dead in Disaster over Ohio.* She showed the headline on her phone to Tania, #HuntersFail.

Bianca called a second later. Pia put her on speaker.

"We have something related to this morning's crash, flaca." Bianca took a deep breath. "Jacob was right—the inside of the USB drive was sprinkled with both new and old microdots. Old microdots are tiny photographs. New microdots have a hundred megabytes on a disk the size of the dot in the letter i. We've found ten images so far. Some we think are Latin but in a code or something. They make no sense at all. There are hundreds more. The one we just translated is scary. Check your email."

Pia opened her tablet and found a snapshot of handwritten notes in what appeared to be Cyrillic on a yellow pad. A translation came with it:

> *Meeting with Badger, Barcelona:*
> *Talking point – FAA falling apart because Hunter*
> *Midair collision 3-4 weeks later*
> *More coordinated talking points to come*
> *Bring Sabel in by Oct or terminate*
> *Next comm 3 weeks*

In her email, Bianca pointed out that the notes were unattributed, but it was dated the day before Pozdeeva came to the US.

Pia returned her attention to the phone call. "The fact that Pozdeeva had access to this person's notes the day before he came to see me tells me this was the catalyst for him to act. He knew what they were planning."

"That's a plausible theory," Bianca said. "But it's too early to know that for sure. He might have been stuffing everything in this drive right up until he left. We don't know that he read this. But what about the 'terminate' order?"

"Nice to know someone's going to let me breathe for another month." Pia sighed. "Do we know who or what the code name Badger means?"

"Someone who w-w-went to the University of Wisconsin?" Tania offered.

"The Badgers," Bianca said. "Could be. But most codenames are pulled out of a hat."

Pia felt sick. "Roche has been complaining about the FAA ever since these notes were taken. And the midair collision happened exactly as these notes predicted. To the voters, he looks clairvoyant."

"Yo-yo-your dad's right, we g-g-gotta take down Roche before anyone votes for him."

"Is this what Medevtin did?" Pia looked at Tania. "The apartment bombing? An American wouldn't do something like that. Right?"

"Let's s-s-shoot him." Tania's eyes narrowed to slits. "Just to be sure."

"Whoa," Bianca said. "These notes have no origin and no reference point. We can't jump to conclusions. It doesn't look good, but let's not look to murder as a solution."

Tania scowled and crossed her arms.

"Did they do this on purpose?" Pia asked. "Is there a way to cause two passenger jets to crash?"

"The investigation might tell us. But these notes indicate someone thought so."

"How would it work?"

"I'll have to ask our experts for theories." Bianca thought for a moment. "Flight navigation is a simple, aging technology, point-A-to-point-B math. It's connected to the internet because they rely on input from a variety of sources for local weather, microbursts, temporary conditions, that kind of thing. They feed the flight path into a simulator and subroutines figure out the mile-by-mile route. They automatically upload any changes needed to the airplane's autopilot."

"They would keep something that critical hack-proof." Pia kept staring at the note.

"There's no such thing as hack-proof. But, tampering with that system would leave a trail of some kind. You could do it, but you could only do it once."

"Ilya Pozdeeva wanted us to know about this." Pia pushed her mug away. "If only he'd lived long enough to explain it. We might've saved those people."

"Y-yo-you can't think like that," Tania said. "It'll d-d-drive you nuts."

"That brings up a different question," Bianca said. "Why did Popov wait so long to get the drive back?"

"He didn't know about the microdots." Pia thought through the implications. "They knew which emails Pozdeeva took in electronic form on the USB drive and didn't worry because they were ambiguous. That's why we never figured them out—they were there to obscure the real secrets. But later someone told them about the microdots. Which means Pozdeeva had an accomplice. And the Russians figured out who it is and caught him. If we can find him and free him, maybe he can help us—if he's still alive."

Tania pointed out the window. The man in the gray coat shook hands with a new man in a gray coat. "Changing of the g-g-guard."

They ended the call.

The first man walked away. The second man, short and wiry, looked at their window, pulled out a newspaper, and occupied the park bench.

"We have to go," Pia said. "The limo's not coming."

"Which i-i-is a very bad sign for your s-s-safety." Tania shrugged. "But I'm n-n-never going to talk you o-ou-out of walking, am I?"

They shouldered their bags with a flourish meant to be seen from outside despite the late afternoon glare. Exiting the front door, they took a left and marched down the side street. Halfway down the block, they found an open gate leading to a parking area.

Tania backed to one side of the gate where she would be obscured when it opened. Pia waited until she heard their shadow's clicking footsteps on the cobblestone sidewalk. When he slowed to peer into the gate, she walked away, her back to him, and slipped around a corner at the far end.

He followed her at a quicker pace, closing fast.

Pia turned into a dead-end walkway and waited for him. When he came around the corner, she threw her forearm under his chin, slamming him against the wall. Surprised, he wrenched himself free, only to find Tania scowling over her pistol sights. He raised his hands.

Pia relieved him of a GSh-18 handgun, hunting knife, passport, keys, and wallet. The wallet had a few rubles and a license in Cyrillic. She dropped the items on the ground and rifled through more of his pockets. She patted him down and found a pocket pistol, brass knuckles, and a phone in hidden pockets. Using it to dial a Sabel Technology phone number, she uploaded a copy of the man's phone to their central system. While it sent data upstream, she picked up the passport.

She stepped into his personal space, towering over him. "Mr. Ivanov, what do you want?"

She handed over his passport.

He gave her an ice-cold stare and said nothing.

"If you don't answer," Pia said, "I have to assume your assignment is to kill me. Since I'm not in the mood to lose my life, I'll kill you first. So, last chance: what do you want?"

Ivanov said nothing.

Pia aimed his own gun at his groin. "Who sent you? What did they ask you to do?"

He covered his genitals. "I am to report if you call a taxi."

"From the pub?"

He nodded.

She held his keys up and jingled them. "You give us a lift to the airport, and I'll let you report."

He reached for the keys.

Pia snatched them back. "Tania drives. You ride in back with me and answer some questions."

A quick walk took them to his parked car.

Inside and underway, Pia held the muzzle to his kneecap. "What happened to the limo driver we hired?"

"Arrested."

"Who ordered you to follow me?"

Ivanov chewed the inside of his cheek and stared at the passenger-side headrest.

She moved the barrel an inch, just under his knee, and fired. Exhaust gasses burned his pants and probably his skin. He gritted his teeth and breathed deeply.

"You're a tough guy." She ejected a round for effect. "I get that. But talk now, and you can explain the broken nose as the result of a sudden stop. But how will you explain shooting yourself in the knee with your own gun—twice?"

Ivanov gritted his teeth and pursed his lips, anticipating the pain.

"One last chance." She raised the weapon to his kneecap. "Who ordered you to follow me?"

He exhaled. "FSB. You will be detained."

Tania cranked the wheel and drifted into a side street. She downshifted, floored the little car, and made the next right, tires squealing.

Pia yanked Ivanov to the floor and bent over him, keeping both of them below the seatbacks. Tania kept up her aggressive turns, racing forward.

"You're a local cop?" she asked.

He grunted, too compressed for regular speech.

"This d-d-dork was supposed to detain us until the FSB arrives?" Tania asked. The car slid sideways again, on a longer trajectory this time. "You c-c-can dump him now."

Pia opened the door as Tania slowed to school-zone speed. She shoved Ivanov onto the airport tarmac and let him roll. Tania sped up again and skidded to a stop in front of the Sabel jet. They bounded up the airstair and closed the door behind them.

The jet began taxiing.

Pia and Tania panted their adrenaline and high-fived each other in the galley.

"Good evening, Pia." Dad's voice brought her head up.

Alan Sabel sat in a chair at the forward table. A glass pitcher of lemonade and bottle of vodka sat on the table in front of him. Three glasses filled with ice waited.

Pia slid into the chair opposite him, Tania next to her.

As the wheels lifted off, he raised the bottle. Two fingers of Stolichnaya Elit Himalayan Edition tumbled into each glass. "Made with Himalayan water and Russian winter wheat. No one comes close to the Russian's expertise in alcohol. Combined with Meyer lemons for the lemonade, you have the finest refreshing end-of-summer cocktail."

She took her glass and held it up for a toast. Tania raised hers.

Alan lifted his and said, "Here's to making Finnish airspace before the Russians shoot us down."

CHAPTER 10

OUTSIDE MY FRONT DOOR, A voice shouted something about police. I staggered forward in my robe, still exhausted from my nocturnal wanderings. Anoshni barked like a demon. I told him to sit. He obeyed.

Mercury stood in front of the door with his hands up. *For the record, bro, I did not advise you to invade the diplomatic enclave of a nuclear power. I told you Viktor gave you a clue on the microdots. The rest was you tripping.*

I pushed him aside and pulled the door open. A flash of midday sunshine hit me like a brick in the face. A round-faced man in a suit held an ID in my face. After a squint, I made out that he was a DC detective named Eddie Harris. Behind him stood my old frenemy, Montgomery County Detective Czajkowski.

"Any relation to Eddie Harris, the king of soul-jazz saxophone?" I asked.

He frowned. Not only no relation, the man had no idea what his namesake had done for improvisational jazz in the sixties. He reorganized himself and opened his mouth to speak.

CJ jumped him. "Harris is investigating an embassy invasion."

Harris glared over his shoulder at his local counterpart.

"Just letting him know," CJ said. "In case he's wondering who's going to be arresting him."

"Do you have any evidence to warrant an arrest?" Harris asked. When CJ looked away, he continued, "Let's not be escalating things here."

CJ nodded.

Harris turned to me. "May we come in? I'd like to ask your professional opinion on something."

He held up a laptop and handed over my newspaper.

I checked the *Post's* headlines. "Holy shit, #HuntersFail? 365 dead? Worst air disaster since Tenerife and—"

"Been all over the news, Stearne," CJ snarled. "Where you been?"

Harris tossed another hairy eyeball at him, then gestured inside.

I ushered them into the kitchen and seated them at my breakfast table. "Coffee?"

"Kind of late for that, isn't it?" CJ asked.

"I'd love me some." Harris smiled a little gratitude.

I put the kettle on and joined them at the table.

Harris set up his laptop and started a video. A black-clad figure flitted between buildings, an assault rifle slung over body armor, a pistol in his hand.

"Do you recognize this man?" Harris asked.

"Do you have any close-ups of this person's face?" I asked.

"He's about your height."

"So that's a 'no' on the face?"

"He's wearing what looks like body armor."

"You don't say."

"I do say. And to me, it looks like Sabel body armor."

I reached over his wrist and paused it on a full-frame view of the intruder and pointed at the screen. "Sabel armor doesn't have a Nike swoosh on it."

Both detectives looked at the swoosh as if seeing it for the first time.

Mercury stood between them pumping a fist in the air. *Hey homie, who's an awesome god now, huh? Who told you to slip a Nike shirt over your armor? C'mon, bro—props!*

The kettle whistle started building up. I got up, folded a cone filter into my Chemex coffee maker, ground some beans, and put them in. I called over the growing whistle, "Do you have a head shot?"

"He wore a balaclava," Harris said.

I poured in steaming water. "Let's see."

Coffee pot in hand, I filled the filter and let it drip. I rejoined them at the table. Harris teed up a clip, paused it, zoomed in, and pointed.

"Quite a chin on that guy," I said.

Both detectives snapped their eyes to the screen as if seeing the significant chin for the first time.

CJ looked up at me, then at the picture, then at me. He reached over and clicked fast forward to a different camera angle. My eyes were shielded by night vision glasses styled by Oakley. Standard-issue for Sabel agents, but indistinguishable from common Oakley safety glasses. CJ compared the still frame to my face. After three takes, he pushed the laptop away and let out a sigh.

I pulled the Chemex filter and put it in the trash, returning with two coffee mugs. "Want to tell me what this is all about?"

"This guy—" Harris pointed at the screen while nodding thanks and taking his cup "—broke into the Russian Embassy last night and shot Viktor Popov in the leg. Popov claims you're the man. Are you?"

I looked surprised. "Someone shot the guy who broke into my house last night and stole my dog?"

Both detectives nodded then glanced at Anoshni. My puppy did his accomplice-look: *you can trust us*.

"You mean someone did exactly what you told me to do?" I looked at CJ.

Harris gave CJ the once over. "Say what?"

"Oh. Hey, look, that was a joke. It was late, he called my cell." CJ's eyes bounced back and forth between us. "Wait a second. He's avoiding the question."

Harris turned his questioning gaze back to me.

"So, karma is a real thing then, eh?" I poured myself a cup, took a sip, and leaned back. "That must be terribly embarrassing for a country calling itself a superpower to have a break-in and assault like that." I shook my head in dismay. "Think they're grasping at straws?"

"The reason for our visit," Harris said, "is to get your professional opinion as former special ops, Commando, Delta Force, whatever you were. Who could pull this off and how do we find him?"

I gave them my full soldier-stare. It's the stare that comes from facing certain death for days on end and leaving behind nothing but vanquished enemies and all remorse.

After they flinched, I said, "It looks to me like your perpetrator stuffed his balaclava with toilet paper to throw off facial mapping software. You know the difference between toilet paper and regular tissues? Toilet paper dissolves in water. When you flush it, it's gone. After that, I imagine, he would've ditched his outer layer, one piece at a time, in various public trash cans that are on the morning pickup route. And—again, just guessing—he would've re-bored his pistol to change the ballistics profile."

Harris looked at CJ and CJ looked at him. Harris leaned forward and spoke quietly. "Jacob, do you own the tools needed to alter the bore of a pistol?"

"I do. Lots of gun enthusiasts and many veterans have them. A lot of guys make a little extra cash doing it for others. They're available on the open market. I can refer you to some of the better tool makers if you're looking to open a side business."

Harris nodded slowly, thoughtfully. "You saying there would be no way to trace the perpetrator?"

"I don't know much about police work, detective. I'm just saying the evidence trail might be thin. You make judgment calls every day about which crimes need to be solved and which don't. Thin evidence trails or thick trails—which one looks better on your record? If I were you, I'd punt this case. Besides, isn't a diplomatic mission some kind of sovereign territory? Was any crime committed in your jurisdiction?"

"Embassy grounds are outside my territory. But we try to help when assistance is requested." Harris looked at Anoshni again. The puppy cocked his head and gave him the look. Harris closed the laptop and stood up. "Glad to see your dog found his way home. Thanks for the coffee."

CJ pursed his lips and gave me the meanest glare he'd given me to date. He rose and stuck his index finger in my face.

Harris grabbed CJ's finger before he could say anything.

"International incidents are a sticky business." Harris handed me a business card. "Strange things happen between foreign diplomats and US citizens. Maybe they're lashing out like you said. But it's not a case I'm going to drop. I'll find the evidence I need, and I'll put this guy in jail."

He gave me his professional detective stare. It was pretty good. He's stared down more than a few criminals in his day. Maybe even a killer or two. But it's not the same as facing down hundreds of men who believe—from deep in their marrow—that they're doing God's work.

Harris blinked first.

He yanked CJ and they let themselves out. I waved goodbye and shut the door.

Mercury said, *You might have fooled Harris and CJ, but reality check: you declared war on a great humanitarian who has plenty of covert operators at his command. You ready for this?*

I said, *Bring it.*

"You shot Viktor Popov?" Emily's voice came from behind me.

Spitting my coffee, I spun around. "That does *not* get into print."

One of my dress shirts covered what I suspected was a naked body. I spun away. "Whoa. You spent the night?"

"The way you bolted out of here at three in the morning, I figured you'd need an alibi." She stuffed a wad of clothes in a grocery bag. "Bianca's picking me up in five. Can I get a cup to go?"

"You're wearing my shirt." I grabbed a paper cup from the stash I keep for scrambling out on missions.

She winked. "Jealousy sex is the best kind."

"No way," I pleaded. "You are not putting me in the middle of your … indecision."

"Don't worry, I'll tell her you were a perfect gentleman—but not until after." She took the coffee and gave me a peck on my stunned cheek. "Ciao."

She swished her way to the front door and out into the warm sun. I slammed and locked the door behind her.

Mercury blocked my return trip to the kitchen. *Vulcan and Mars are laying ten to one odds the Russians come in and slit your throat tonight. My money's on Bianca killing you first. Let me see now.* He tapped his chin and looked at the ceiling. *How would a math genius, tech-geek go about it? Reprogram your car and drive you off a bridge? That'd be fun to watch.*

I moved left. He swayed to block me.

I said, *Anyone ever tell you, you look just like Will Smith?*

Don't be talking smack. Will Smith looks like me because I fashioned him from clay. I taught him how to rap. I gave him his big break. And what did that ingrate do? Turned to Scientology. Scientology! They don't even have a god. Holy Vesta, Earthlings are going to drive me to drink.

Kasey Earl, my favorite rapist, called. I slid around Mercury and answered.

"I got something solid, Jacob." He giggled. "I got something you don't even know you need to know."

"What did you find?"

"No way, dude. I meet Pia Sabel face to face. I tell her. Not you."

"Not happening. She's a busy woman. If you want a meeting, you give me a reason why."

I could hear the squirrel that powers Kasey's brain running on his squeaky little wheel. "It's about Roche Security payroll from way back. I'm not looking for a job no more. With this information, she's going to pay me loads of cash."

He clicked off the call. The weasel had grown a pair in the last few weeks. Maybe he really did have something.

I packed a duffel, grabbed a dog dish and a bag of dog food and tossed everything in the car. On the drive, I couldn't get Emily out of my head. I'd been searching for a life-partner and soul-mate for years and, so far, had come up empty. She has the perfect soulmate descend from heaven, ask for her hand in marriage—and she freaks out. Do we ever recognize happiness when we see it?

Mercury appeared in the front seat. *See? Now that's what I'm talking about, right there, homie. All y'all humans don't appreciate shit. We give you this, and we give you that—and when do we hear from you? When your kid gets cancer. Not a minute sooner. It's always 'Why do the gods do bad things to good people?' Well y'know what? Y'all ain't no kind of 'good people'. We keep them on a different planet.*

I said, *You mean, we're living in hell?*

Mercury said, *For every dollar you spend on the military—to kill each other—you spend fourteen cents on making your children smarter. If that isn't hell, what is?*

I said, *I quit my second year of college to go kill people.*

Mercury said, *I rest my case. But as long as they're the people who need killing, I'm down with you, bro.*

A few minutes later, Miguel stood in his doorway and looked us over like we had Ebola. "You declare war on Russia and want to make your last stand at my place?"

"What are friends for?" I ducked under the big guy's arm and put Anoshni's dish on the kitchen floor. "Hey, if I asked you to marry me, would you get all weird about it?"

Wow. Sometimes thoughts sound different when you say them out loud.

"Maybe you should stay over at Dhanpal's." Miguel's nose curled. "Wait, is this about Bianca and Emily?"

"How did you know about them?"

"She slid over here last night." He leaned against the kitchen island.

Mercury mimicked his posture. *Ouch, homes. She took her questioning-my-sexuality to the big Indian first? That's gotta hurt.*

I said, *Doesn't matter. He didn't take advantage of her.*

Mercury said, *How do you know?*

I did a double-take at Miguel.

"What?" He gave me a skeptical glance. "No. Of course not. Bianca would kill me."

My phone rang. When I answered, Viktor Popov's accent assaulted my ear. "Maybe little policemans believe you. But my men find you."

CHAPTER 11

Yuri looked up and down the concrete hallway of the crusty, sparse building in Kaliningrad to make sure they were alone. He tried Strangelove's office door. Locked. Pulling a set of picks from his jacket, he steadied his hands and took a knee. After a brief look, he began feeling his way inside the old-fashioned tumblers.

"Are you crazy?" Vasili whispered, his head swiveling left and right. "Strangelove will kill you."

"We need to know. That outweighs the risks." Yuri stopped and looked over his shoulder. "Think about it. We killed 365 Americans. They will stop at nothing to find us. Worse, what evidence do we have that he gave the order? Our lives are at stake here, Vasili. Knowledge is the best protection."

"We are soldiers. They owe us no explanation."

In Vasili's reticence, Yuri could see the downside to Russian Avos': a superstitious resignation in the face of enormous problems. "Igor raised a perfectly good question: what have we done? We will have to answer for it sooner or later."

"This is a bad idea."

Yuri ignored him. He felt the third tumbler click. One more. Why did it always look so easy in the movies? The last one clicked over. He opened the door. "Take watch. Go to the toilet and back. Text me if he shows up. Remember, he'll kill you too."

Yuri slipped around the door and closed it quietly behind him. He waited, knowing Vasili could agonize about things for hours. When he finally heard the lieutenant march away, he relaxed and began his search. On the desk were a few papers and a photograph of an old woman who could be the poster lady for babushkas from the Baltic to the Bering Strait.

He flipped the keyboard over and removed the backing. The small proximity keystroke logger came out easily. He plugged it into his laptop and retrieved Strangelove's password: 0503Stalin53. The day, month, and year Stalin died and, coincidentally, Strangelove's birthday. Classic. Yuri could've guessed it if he thought about it long enough.

He logged on.

Strangelove's email was empty. Nothing in the inbox. Nothing in the sent file. Nothing in the trash. Nothing in junk or spam or anywhere else. That wasn't right. Was the old man that concerned about security that he wiped everything when he went to lunch? Yuri logged off quickly and wiped his fingerprints from the board. There had to be some explanation. He had received almost daily emails and texts from Strangelove.

He rose and stepped to the window. For all the ugliness of Soviet architecture, they knew where to place a window. Across the muddy river flowing below him, the fourteenth-century Königsberg Cathedral rose in red-brick glory. The Prussian masterpiece stood for six hundred years until one night in World War II—when a hundred children sought refuge in it—British bombers demolished their church and their souls. Strangelove had made a point of that story on their first meeting.

The old general was always telling stories. The old man reminded Yuri of his uncle—closing in on retirement, passing on the wisdom of his years. The endless prattle of the washed-up and soon-to-be-forgotten. Strangelove's time was over. He should step aside.

Vasili texted, "Strangelove coming."

Yuri scurried from the office and closed the door behind him. He took the bench opposite and opened an ereader on his phone. The pounding of the old man's weight echoed down the hall. Yuri rose to attention and saluted.

Strangelove gave him his typical stern glance, waved off the formality, and unlocked his door. He stopped, one hand on the knob. "Where is that lieutenant of yours?"

"Toilet."

The general glanced down the hall and shrugged. He went in,

gesturing for Yuri to follow. He sat at his desk and scratched the scar that ran down his neck. He gestured for Yuri to sit in front of him.

"You are to be congratulated." Strangelove leaned back. "Your banda did quite well with #HuntersFail. Have your men gotten over their concerns?"

Yuri looked over his shoulder at the door, then back to Strangelove, then leaned forward. "For the most part. But I'm concerned there are lingering doubts they are not voicing in front of me. What is your advice?"

Strangelove nodded slowly while thinking. He crossed his arms and stroked his chin. "I suppose Alexi was a self-appointed saint and that his fate was not as random as it would seem."

Yuri shrugged.

"And yet others are concerned?" Strangelove asked.

"There was a great loss of life. The Americans were outraged and have been searching for our tools. We covered our tracks well, nonetheless ..."

"What are the signs?"

"My men read American news sites. Follow the investigations with alerts and popups."

"Remorse is a serious problem." Strangelove rose and paced to the windows. "Soldiers cannot allow it. You will talk to them. Get it out in the open—American style. Listen to them, agree with them, argue with them, then turn them toward the future."

"Very good, General. 'American style.' I like it. They will like it." Yuri paused and stroked his beard in thought. "'American style' to them means understanding the bigger picture. What should I tell them? What is the value of this mission to the Motherland?"

Strangelove shrugged. "Someone wants to play a part in the American election."

"Why? How would that affect us?"

Vasili opened the door a crack, poked his head in, and knocked.

Strangelove waved him in and returned his gaze to the cathedral. "Your major wants to know why the Kremlin wants to mess with the Americans. You tell him, Vasili."

Vasili looked to Yuri, who shrugged.

Vasili cleared his throat. "I would not be so bold as to guess the motives of my superiors."

The general turned slowly with a wry smile and shook his finger at Vasili. "You are Trotsky's New Soviet Man. You know that? Selfless, learned, healthy, and enthusiastic. Not like Nietzsche's romantic fatalists who lay down to die. You will go far." He turned back to the window. "Ah, we would still be Soviets united in the collective struggle if more men thought like you."

Gray clouds rolled across the sky. Yuri and Vasili shared a glance. No one spoke for an awkwardly long time.

Strangelove inhaled a long, tired breath. "An old problem from the past has arisen. I need trustworthy men to rid me of this problem. New Soviet men like you and Vasili."

Yuri glanced at Vasili before answering. "You can count on us, sir."

"I count on my '89 Lada. I drive it every day even though I must rebuild every moving part each year." Strangelove faced them, his face warm with romantic nostalgia. "It gets me to work, and sometimes it gets me home."

They chuckled respectfully.

"My car was still new when I first met Alan Sabel. I thought we were through with him many years ago. This month, calls have come in from contacts in Cyprus, Barcelona, and Luxembourg. He is digging into things. Old things he should leave alone. He is meddling in our efforts to aid the American election. These things are none of his concern." He leaned against the window casing and faced them. "Twenty years ago, I could read Alan Sabel's emails. He discovered our hacks and changed his system. Since then, nothing. Every day we try to get in, nothing. He left us alone. We left him alone. Years went by.

"Now he's attacking us. One of his men shot our cultural attaché in Washington. Sabel has become aggressive and dangerous. He could testify against our favorite candidate in court, which would be his word against the word of others. But if he finds any proof, we would be in great jeopardy. We believe one of our people gave him that proof. He could sink years of work. We need to eliminate him."

"We will take care of him, sir," Yuri said.

Strangelove laughed in his face. "You know the old proverb: do not praise yourself going into battle; only coming out."

Vasili said, "He meant we will do our best, sir."

"Come here, Yuri. I want to show you something." The old man raised an encircling arm.

Yuri stepped under it and felt a patriarchal embrace as the arm tightened around his shoulder.

"You see that cathedral? You know what happened there. But those children were far from Berlin or Moscow. They had nothing to do with the war. Ah, so sad. The children put their faith in those ancient bricks only to be sacrificed at the whim of political powers far away. Be careful where you put your faith, Yuri."

Yuri heard the distinct snick of a switchblade opening. He felt the oddly-painless incision between his ribs followed by the sound of air escaping his lung. An instant later the pain arrived at his brain. He faced the old man but couldn't summon a breath to question, *why?*

Strangelove's cold, remorseless eyes watched him as he gasped for air.

The general held up a proximity keystroke logger identical to Yuri's. He turned to Vasili. "Unless you want to be sacrificed at the whim of political powers far away, get him to a doctor. If you want to live another month, make sure Sabel does not. Three weeks. Plenty of time."

CHAPTER 12

"YOU G-G-GUYS KNOW HOW TO flee in style." Tania slurped her vodka lemonade as the Sabel jet roared west, high above Helsinki.

Alan sipped his drink and smiled.

"I had the meeting under control, Dad." Pia tilted her glass toward her father for a refill. "You didn't need to show up and 'save' me."

"Bianca called me." He poured vodka into her glass and topped it with lemonade. "She had a team monitor mobile phone traffic in St. Petersburg. Her team believes the FSB was in the process of detaining your driver, filling the limo with remotely detonated explosives, and putting an ISIL captive at the wheel."

"She warned me, too." Pia looked at her glass. "That's why we kidnapped the cop and rode with him instead."

"Clever. But the trip was ill-advised." He sipped his drink. "What did you hope to accomplish?"

"Expanding into Moscow with a zero-interest loan for operations." Pia waved off the objection before Dad could get the words out. "I wanted to follow some of the clues Pozdeeva gave us. It surprised me how shamelessly they talked about money laundering."

He shrugged as if it was normal.

Pia looked him over. "You knew I could handle this trip. Why did you come?"

"I had the Major drop me off because we need to disappear for a while."

Pia's eyes opened wide. Dad wasn't given to dramatic statements. "What happened?"

"We have a Russian issue."

"I thought Chuck Roche was your issue."

"Chuck Roche is either a well-intentioned amateur or a saboteur working for a foreign power, depending on your views. Either way, he's a threat to the country. But, at the moment, the key to stopping him is in Russia."

Pia sipped her drink. "What's wrong with an amateur? Professional politicians have done a pretty terrible job."

"Have they?" Alan's voice boomed. "Those politicians produced the largest, most productive economy in the history of civilization. Why would anyone vote for a guy who wants to disrupt it? Roche's campaigning to destroy NAFTA despite fourteen million American jobs depending on it. He claims he's going to bring back manufacturing when even China's moving to robotics. We went to robotics years ago."

Tania raised her finger to inject a point. "Where is he g-g-going to build that wall he's talking a-a-about? Half the border i-i-is the Rio Grande. The M-Mexican's aren't going to build it o-o-on their side. You can't build it in the m-m-middle. What's he going t-to do, build it on our s-s-side and give Mexico the whole r-river? The best he can do is b-b-build half a wall."

Alan nodded and pointed to at her in agreement.

"What does that have to do with me in Russia?" Pia asked.

"Viktor Popov showed up at Jacob's house." Alan gave her a serious stare.

"Jacob figured it out. We found a boatload of microdots hidden in the USB drive."

"He opened up Pandora's box." Alan sat back and finished his drink. "But that's a long story. What was in the microdots?"

"More questions. We think there's some key to piecing it all together. Bianca's team has found a few obvious items." She pulled out her phone and showed him the note about Badger and #HuntersFail.

Dad stared at it for a long time, horror coloring his face. His finger dabbed at the image as tried to find words. "That's Strangelove's handwriting."

He reminded her that Strangelove had bailed out Roche's failing refineries and that Pozdeeva had once worked for the general.

"Where does Popov fit in?" Pia asked.

"He holds Strangelove's leash."

Pia thought about it for a minute. "Meaning, Strangelove might still hold something over Roche's head. If Roche wins the election, there's a good chance Popov can pull Roche's strings."

"Bingo. And if you've seen the polls, he's pulling ahead of President Hunter. We can't let that happen."

"How did Pozdeeva get this?" She asked.

"He had access because he was the liaison between Strangelove's GRU bandas and Popov at the SVR. The CIA and NSA have been trying to find Strangelove since the Cold War." He poured himself another drink. "We have to find him and take him out."

Alan Sabel rarely spoke in absolutes. His ice-cold stare and his tight face caught by surprise.

"How do you know all this?" she asked.

"Remember the old visas Pozdeeva gave you?" Dad poured a refill for Tania as he spoke. "You and I traveled to St. Petersburg with Roche."

He took a deep breath and composed himself. "When I was trying to build Sabel, I couldn't get capital. Banks don't loan money to startups operated by single dads fresh out of grad school. And I had no idea how to find investors. At the time, Chuck Roche was a high-flying playboy who inherited billions in refineries. Out of nowhere, an old professor called and said Roche wanted to meet me. I was ecstatic and went to see him right away. Roche didn't want to invest, but he introduced me to venture capital people in St. Petersburg. They were enthusiastic about my company.

"They gave me hundreds of millions of dollars. The company took off. Then, when the company could've made them billions going public, the VCs sold their stake to a company in Zurich. That company turned around and sold it to a company in Cyprus called Santalum. Santalum was owned by a cellist in the Moscow Symphony." Dad sipped his drink, set it down, and looked at Pia. "The cellist paid a dollar for a three hundred million investment."

"I could l-l-learn the cello," Tania said. "What I gotta do?"

"The Luxembourg guys wrote off all that money?" Pia asked. "Was the company sinking?"

"It's called offshoring." Dad stirred his lemonade. "In a kleptocracy, where government insiders are taking public assets, like oil, nickel, aluminum, or diamonds, they need to get the money out of the country."

"Why?"

"In case of a revolution. And when you're robbing the public trust, the likelihood of a revolution rises as fast as your eventual falling out of favor with the dictator."

Pia felt her gut tighten. Nausea crept over her. Sabel Industries, in which she was the majority shareholder, had been built on laundered money.

"How do they make money, then?" Pia asked.

"At that point, the cellist owned virtually all of Sabel Industries. The next step for them was to sell my company to the highest bidder, take the laundered cash and bank it in Panama. With a few mirrored trades, they could have it back in Cyprus for the next opportunity." He paused. "Businesses are bought and sold all the time, so I didn't worry about it until the auditors came. We had several government contracts. The auditors were supposed to be looking over the books to make sure the cellist was getting his money's worth. But I found them digging through our intellectual property. They were auditing our science and engineering. I kicked them out."

The jet banked hard to the right. The pilot announced they were in a holding pattern.

"The next day," Dad continued, "Strangelove came to see me. He had photos of you on the soccer field and at school. He'd been watching you for a week."

Pia had been unnerved by overzealous soccer fans during her career. Creepy stalkers who hung around the team hotel at three in the morning. But a Russian general taking pictures of her? Invisible spiders crawled over her skin. She shivered.

"Is that when you started Sabel Security?" Pia asked.

"No, first I turned to Roche Security. They made a great show of keeping the Russian auditors out. But a few months later, I discovered the Russians had been there the whole time."

"Roche Security was h-h-helping them steal your trade secrets?" Tania asked.

Alan nodded.

"Chuck Roche was working for them all along," Pia said. "That's why you hate him."

"Was he working for them? Did he have any idea what low-level guards ten rungs down the corporate ladder were doing?" Dad sighed. "I can't prove what he was doing then or now. When I kicked his people out of our company, he was less than magnanimous about it."

"Yet you remained on friendly terms."

"There's no point in making enemies," Dad said. "It only makes a bad relationship worse. However, you'll notice that I never did business with him again. And I warned you not to do deals with him."

"Was he helping Strangelove or not?"

"I've never found proof. Back then, I had an investigator looking into the death of your parents. The man was murdered after rifling through Roche's records. I took his murder as a message from Strangelove that I was getting too close."

"Wait a minute." Pia felt like her chair was a bottomless canyon and she was falling backwards into it. "When we lived in the old house, we were on the back porch having lemonade, and someone lobbed a rock with a message tied to it."

"That's why I bought Sabel Gardens. You can't see the house unless you're inside the Garden walls." Alan nodded. "Roche Security was working with Strangelove. So, I did some digging. Chuck Roche had blown through his inheritance in the '80s and went bankrupt. No one in North America would loan him a dime."

"He took money from Russian oligarchs, laundered it, and rebuilt his empire."

"Maybe." Dad tossed up his hands. "But not exactly Russian money. Santalum bought up a series of loans through ventures in Cyprus, Luxembourg, and Panama."

"We can't let him become president. We have to take your story to the press."

"I did." Dad took a long sip. "Way back then. I wanted to bury him for letting spies into my operations. National security depended on it. Despite people crying and whining about the biased press, the press double-checks stories to make sure they're true. They wouldn't print anything unless I could prove it. I went looking for confirmation, sources, emails, documents, anything. It took a lot of work, but I found some."

"And Strangelove s-s-showed up?" Tania asked.

"Any self-made man will tell you," Alan said, "at one critical juncture in his career, his great leap forward was the result of a single stroke of luck. I collected the documents I needed and went to your soccer game. Kindergarten or first grade, I forget. Anyway, Strangelove showed up. He followed us home, looking for an opportunity to kill us both. Bobby Jenkins of Jenkins Pharmaceuticals ran a red light and plowed into our car. We lived through the crash. Strangelove had been following us. Luckily, the cops were only a block away. If they had arrived a couple minutes later, Strangelove would've killed us and made it look like part of the accident. As it was, Bobby Jenkins was riddled with guilt. He became my mentor. He helped arrange bank loans, got us clear of Santalum, helped me get Sabel Security started, and just like that, we were clean."

Pia felt herself breathing again.

The jet's nose tilted down, the engines throttled back.

"But you have proof." Pia took a big sip of lemonade.

"Had." Dad sighed. "Strangelove managed to steal everything while pretending to pull us from the wreckage. While the paramedics were treating us by the side of the road, Strangelove waved the briefcase and told me, 'I'll keep this safe. If you forget about it, you and I are good. If you go digging again…' and then he looked at you. He was offering a stalemate, and I accepted."

All three sank back into their seats, each thinking through the story.

"Pozdeeva showed up, and you ran away. Why?" Pia tilted her head.

"He didn't show up—he was murdered at your feet. By coming to us, Pozdeeva unintentionally gave Strangelove reason to think I was digging into things again. And then Jacob invaded the Russian Embassy. I had no choice but to pick up where I left off decades ago. I hoped to draw his attention away from you.”

“Who were the men in Barcelona?”

“As I told you then, they were looking to renegotiate an old deal. They represented Strangelove. They delivered his declaration of war.”

“And Strangelove owns Chuck Roche?” Pia asked.

Alan shrugged. “It’s no small secret that he’s been doing business with Santalum for decades, but that doesn’t seem to bother anyone.”

“That’s why you said Roche is no longer our biggest threat.”

“Roche is either a genius, a fool, or a traitor. But that’s a long-term problem. We have to prioritize the threats against us.” Alan finished his drink. “Pozdeeva gave us ammunition to use against all three of them, but we can’t wait around to decode it. We must crank up our operations.”

The jet touched down, tires squealed, the engines reversed thrust. The jet taxied to the executive terminal. Another Sabel jet sat on the tarmac. Waiting next to it stood a tall woman, a broad-shouldered man, a mixed-race woman, and the Major.

“Body doubles,” Pia said. She felt a little pride growing inside her along with a combination of angst and excitement. She’d always wanted to work on an important project with Dad.

“Why?” Tania asked. “Where we g-g-going?”

“We’re taking the first step.” A smile crossed Pia’s face. “We’re going to track down Strangelove.”

CHAPTER 13

I FACED THE METRO'S TRANSIT Authority officer with my hands up. She trained her shaky pistol on me. Miguel stepped sideways to get clear of her field of fire. Even though they're trained for this kind of encounter, few law enforcement officers are ready for them. Life-threatening danger leaves them scared as hell and flooded with adrenaline. She wasn't mentally prepared to confront heavily armed men duking it out on the nice clean platforms of the Capitol's mass transit system a minute before closing time.

The Russian with the bloody nose, slumped against the shiny Metro car beside me, would regain his senses shortly. If he resumed the fight where he left off, there was a good chance that he'd pull the trigger on his PSS, a silent assassination pistol developed by the Spetsnaz during the Cold War. Which would probably make the brave cop pull her trigger. With her arm shaking like that, it was anyone's guess as to who would catch the bullet.

Mercury leaned his elbow on the cop's shoulder. *Dude, this is so not-awesome. You survive the professional assassin only to get wasted by the subway guard? That just not be worthy of my believers, brutha. Jumping on a nuclear bomb and riding it to glory, now that would be cool.*

I said, *Help me get out of this or shut up.*

Why you gotta be so salty? Mercury asked. *Scary Spice here is looking to get off work, not fill out three hours of paperwork and spend the next six weeks talking about it with a therapist.*

"My brother's a drug addict," I told the subway cop. "Mom sent me to find him. I'll take him home."

She relaxed her shooting stance.

The Russian bear-man stirred. Like any good soldier, the first thing he thought about was his weapon. He tightened his grip. His eyes remained closed.

Not good.

"Is it all right if I take his gun away from him, ma'am?" I asked.

She looked at me down the sight of her pistol, then aimed at him. The PSS is a funny-looking pistol. It's stubby, with mechanicals above the barrel instead of below. A piston in front of the standard gunpowder charge transfers energy from the blast to the bullet. But the piston stops at the end of the barrel, trapping the explosion—and the noise—inside the gun. It can kill at a distance of up to fifty feet without a sound. Which is why the Commies used it for assassinations. Which is, presumably, what the bear had in mind for me.

"You can have the weapon." I began to lean toward him while still looking at her.

She nodded. I put my foot on his wrist and twisted the hunk of metal away. Holding it with two fingers, I handed it to the cop. She took it.

The Russian said something unintelligible and rocked back and forth.

"Does he need an ambulance?" she asked.

"Only if they carry an antidote."

She holstered her sidearm and nodded over her shoulder at the exit. "Get him out of here. If I ever see you guys again…"

She walked away, shaking her head.

Miguel and I each grabbed an arm and pulled the guy to his feet. He staggered a couple steps with us. I put a shoulder under his armpit, and Miguel grabbed him by the neck. We pushed our man down the ramp toward the Grosvenor Metro parking lot.

Outside the station, we sat him down on a bench and popped a Sabel Dart in his leg. It's a projectile the size of a bullet filled with a nonlethal dose of Inland Taipan snake venom backed by a heavy sedative. The venom produces instant flaccid paralysis long enough for the sedative to put our victim to sleep. Once we had him propped up, we called Dhanpal for a ride.

Twenty minutes later, the three of us shoved the Russian's dead weight into the back of Dhanpal's Porsche Cayenne. After we closed the hatch, I admired the car for a noticeably long moment.

"Pia didn't like it," Dhanpal said. "So, she gave it to me."

Ms. Sabel gave me a Volkswagen after I saved her life. A few months later, a not-very-nice guy blew it up with a homemade bomb. No word yet from my favorite billionaire about a replacement. Some things are below her radar, I guess. I glanced at Miguel, who drove a Mercedes SUV—also given to him by our generous boss.

"You keep drooling over her McLarens and Lambos, man." He shrugged. "She keeps those for herself. If you want a cast-off, mention an SUV. She hates them."

I sorted through the Russian's personal items. According to his passport, his name was Ivan something-unpronounceable. His phone had what I was looking for: Viktor Popov's mobile number.

Viktor answered his phone with a question in Russian.

"I hate to disappoint you," I gloated, "but Ivan the Terrible isn't coming home tonight. If you want him to live, have your people drop you off—alone—at the Grosvenor Metro station."

He ranted a threat laced with Russian obscenities.

I hate sore losers. I never listen to them. I clicked off and tossed the phone across the parking lot.

Dhanpal stayed behind to work the trap while Miguel and I took Dhanpal's car. We laid Ivan the Terrible on the grass outside the Cabin John Indoor Tennis Courts, several miles from the Metro.

From there, we drove to Sabel Security's Ops Center.

We marched into Meeting Room Zero, our NSA/CIA/FBI-proof room: a few indoor acres encased in concrete. No one could eavesdrop, electronically or otherwise, without walking a hundred yards to the middle where a glass table with four Aeron chairs waited under halogen lights. Miguel and I took seats and waited for our guest of honor.

After a long wait, my mission team reported from the Metro station. The Russians tried to swarm the area with only eight men. Our hastily arranged crew of thirty Sabel agents easily overwhelmed them.

They brought Viktor to us ten minutes later. Three agents wheeled him in, pushed him to the table, and removed his hood. He and I maintained a lengthy soldier-stare. I didn't speak. He didn't speak. His gray hair was still immaculately coiffed. His expensive watch glistened. Instead of the Brioni suit, he wore a bathrobe that barely covered his most inglorious parts. His leg was elevated. Titanium pins protruded from his skin to a two-foot-long shiny metal rig holding his damaged bone fragments in place.

It was enough to make a normal person feel bad.

"Your man tried to kill me." I drummed my fingers on the table. "That pisses me off. Not as much as stealing my dog, but still."

Viktor kept up his tough-guy look. He wasn't half-bad at it, either. There was a good chance he did a couple tours in Afghanistan back when the Russians spent a decade learning why the English fought and lost three wars in those poppy fields. God only knows why the USA went there after everyone else failed.

After a long silence, Viktor shrugged.

"You know I can hurt you." I glanced at the oil derrick holding his leg together. "Yet you send men after me. What's up with that?"

He gave another tired shrug. "Preemptive."

"Something happens to me, my friends will come for you." I nodded at Miguel.

"So many try." He gave my friend a taste of his glare.

"Let's de-escalate things," I said. "Tell me why you want the Pozdeeva drive. I told you there's nothing on it."

"The lies Pozdeeva brought you are of no concern to us. We know they are lies." He shifted his weight and winced. "What is true does not matter to American press. Only what is sensational. What sells papers."

"Free press sucks, right?" I tossed the original USB drive on the table. "Here you go. Now we can walk away from each other."

"You discover microdots, *da*?" He leaned forward and flicked the drive back at me. "Too late for detente."

"They mean nothing to us."

"What else would you say?" He leaned closer to me, shifting his titanium armature and causing himself pain that showed on his face. "Do not challenge me."

"The only reason we had a translator take another look at them was due to your interest."

"Forget about Pozdeeva." Viktor sat motionless except for his lips. He controlled his breathing, but he blinked several times. "Tell your Sabels to forget about him."

Something about the dog-napper pissed me off. Maybe it was the look in his eyes: the arrogant murderer who killed whoever he pleased to achieve his goals. Maybe it was his disrespect. Or his cold threats. Whatever it was, I wanted to shoot him right then and there. No doubt I would save the world from a good deal of pain and anguish. But I'd end up in a world of hurt as well. Killing a diplomat, even if everyone knows he's a spy, is frowned upon in certain circles.

"See this?" I held up my stained sleeve. "This is where Ivan bled all over me. Your threats are nothing more than laundry bills to me. Tell me what's so special about those memos, and we'll think about letting you go."

"You let me go anyway. It is not in your power." He snorted. "Peasant."

Miguel grabbed my shoulder before I leapt across the table to strangle the bastard.

My phone buzzed with a text from the front desk: "Got a small army of county, state, and Federal agents swarming the building looking for a diplomat named Popov. They have search warrants. Seen him?"

"Never heard of him," I texted back. "Show them around. We booked Meeting Room Twelve. Probably."

And that pissed me off even more. He had the law on his side. He was a malicious killer who was getting away with it, and it showed in his eyes.

"Is that it then?" I asked Viktor. "You're going to try to kill twenty thousand Sabel Security employees?"

"The Sabel Industries building, well-guarded." He gave me a long sneer. "Three men in underground garage. Two in lobby. Two more on floors. Sabel Technologies headquarters in Columbia, eight armed guards wandering location. Ah, but Sabel Gardens, so many acres and so many trees."

CHAPTER 14

ON THE FLIGHT BACK TO Stavanger, all Yuri could think about was the general's expertise with a switchblade. Slicing between ribs without the steel glancing off bone was a practiced skill. The placement had been perfect. Higher and it could've severed a vital artery or vein. Lower and it could've slashed the diaphragm or intestines. But Strangelove cut him deeply where it would do no permanent damage. It would leave him in pain, carrying a memory of who was in charge for weeks afterward. Every breath was unbearable, every movement excruciating. And every second filled with hate.

He held himself together with drugstore painkillers because he refused to seek help in Kaliningrad. But the agony finally overwhelmed him. He collapsed on arrival in Norway. Airport security sped him to the local hospital, where they worked to inflate a collapsed lung. After a couple of hours, they moved Yuri to a room to recuperate.

Yuri told the nurse to let Vasili in. Through the painkiller-soup of his mind, he grabbed his lieutenant's wrist. The movement sent shockwaves of pain rattling through his body. "How did he find the keylogger? Did you tell him?"

Vasili turned away.

"I'm sorry." Yuri let his lieutenant go. He took a deep breath.

"I told you it was a bad idea." Vasili stared out the window.

"My country has betrayed me. My commanding officer has betrayed me."

"Talk like that leads nowhere." Vasili faced him. "Maybe one of the banda is a traitor? You picked only half of them. He sent the others."

Yuri vetted them all, regardless of how they came to him. He tried to visualize each man, but the drugs swirled his focus and kept bringing him back to the ultimate betrayer. Strangelove.

What the hell was wrong with the old man? The general waited until Vasili was back in the room just to humiliate him. From the beginning, Strangelove talked only of sacrifice. Good soldiers are fully prepared to make the ultimate sacrifice. Over time, the general had extended the concept: anything—friends, family, even morality—could be sacrificed for the greater good.

Through his soggy mind, Yuri came to the slow realization of why he was stabbed. Why there were no written orders. No confirmation of Popov's approval. Extra security sweeps of Strangelove's office. That's how the old man found his keylogger. Yuri and his banda were sacrificial lambs. They were to be sacrificed at the whim of political powers far away. Men in Washington and Moscow would one day come to an agreement that #HuntersFail must be avenged. The people must be given blood. *Don't get caught. If you do, do not worry. I'll handle everything.*

Indeed, the fat old general would do just that.

Yuri was done. Never again would he make sacrifices for Strangelove's Motherland. He'd talked his men into murdering 365 Americans. Why? What outcome could possibly be worth it? Yuri and his banda took all the risks. And what did he get? Stabbed. He didn't need Strangelove. He didn't need Russia.

Yuri looked up quickly to see if Vasili was reading his mind.

His lieutenant stared at a TV screen in the corner. The American Presidential Debate was in progress. The three candidates stood at podiums. William Charles, the Democratic candidate, shook his head in disbelief as Roche expounded on unfounded conspiracy theories to explain why Hunter should be in jail. President Hunter cast a longing gaze at Chuck Roche. It occurred to Yuri that Hunter was in love with the billionaire—although he couldn't be sure his assessment wasn't due to the drugs they'd given him.

Yuri retreated back to his thoughts. There was only one way to get out from under the general's command. Strangelove must die.

But to reach that goal, he had to earn the general's trust. He had to crawl back into Strangelove's good graces to be close enough. Or was this all a revenge fantasy that would go away when the drugs wore off? Maybe he should accept his Avos' and let Strangelove stab him at will. He pushed his earbuds in and brought up the music app on his phone.

With thick fingers, he accidentally played a song that brought back memories from his childhood—Verdi's *Requiem, Dies Irae*. He was innocent back then. Trying so hard to impress his mother. He played the oboe in the Moscow Youth Orchestra. It was quite an achievement just to be accepted. He pictured his smiling face looking up to his mother, desperate for her approval. She told him to keep practicing.

He switched songs. Annie Lennox poured her soul into *Strange Fruit*, the classic 1937 song protesting the lynching of African Americans. An appropriate lament for his mood.

Roman and his anarchist friends were right about going rogue. It was possible. After all, he'd kept several million dollars of Alexi's ill-gotten gains in an offshore account. He alone knew it existed. He could use it to start something. Then one day he could be an oligarch like Yeschenko. He could tug the general's leash. But first, the old man would have to give up his secrets. Why kill Sabel? Who is he? Could an enemy of Strangelove prove useful?

"He thinks he owns me." Yuri clenched his fist.

"He knows he owns us." Vasili turned from the TV. "We are soldiers. He is our commander."

Yuri scowled at his lieutenant. Neither man spoke. Yuri calmed himself. Vasili was indeed the New Soviet Man. He would run to Strangelove at the first hint of mutiny. He could be turned in time, but only with great care and patience.

Yuri took a deep breath and let the jazz flowing through his head calm him.

They looked out the window and watched the city lights until a thought struck him.

"Why did he give us so much time to take care of Sabel?" Yuri frowned. "It doesn't make sense. They've doubled our social media assignments. His superiors order new conspiracies by the hour."

"Sabel owns a security company." Vasili kept his gaze fixed on the debates. "He's giving us time to come up with a plan."

They thought for a moment to process their schedule.

"Go get our laptops. Bring them here. We should get started."

Looking relieved to get out of the place, Vasili left. In his haste, he nearly knocked over the pretty waitress from Cirkus.

She carried a tray covered with a kitchen towel and stood at the door, shy and unsure what to say.

"Come in." Yuri waved. "We've not met formally. What's your name?"

"Andrine." She blushed. "My father sent food."

He relished her pronunciation: ahn-DREE-neh.

She lifted the tray an inch. He waved her in closer and pointed to a rolling stand. She set it down with a glance his way. He watched her every move. She wheeled the dinner tray to the bed and looked up again. She smiled quickly, then turned aside.

"I apologize." Yuri knew he would never win her without taking a risk. He lowered his gaze. "The medication makes me forget my manners. You are quite beautiful, and so I stare shamelessly."

Her face brightened, revealing a conflict between anger and pride. After thinking it over, she softened and removed the towel.

Yuri couldn't believe it—homemade *piroshki* with salad. "There is a Russian in your family?"

"My mother." She smiled. "She escaped in the '80s."

He felt like a child in her presence. Or was that the painkillers? He laughed at his thoughts and looked up to see Andrine watching him.

"I like your beard." She blushed again and lowered her eyes. "I must go. I will come back for the tray."

"Wait." He felt his voice too harsh and softened it. "Tell me about you, Andrine. You are at university?"

"I graduated last year." She lifted her face with pride. "University of Oslo. I have a Masters in Human Rights."

He ate his food and rolled his hand for her to keep talking.

"Someday I hope to champion the people oppressed by dictatorships." She looked up at him quickly. "I don't mean to insult your country."

"You don't like Vladimir Medevtin?" When she shook her head, he laughed. "Politics is your area of expertise, I will trust your opinion."

"You approve of him?"

Yuri shrugged. "I did not choose Russia, I was born there."

"Is that why you moved to Stavanger?" she asked. "Was it too hard?"

"What about you? Are you going to change the world from this fjord?" He took a big bite and waved her on.

"Stavanger is not in a fjord."

He felt himself flush with embarrassment over his limited geographical knowledge. She was kind enough to look away.

"I had a job lined up with Amnesty International in London, but ..." She stopped and looked out the window.

He waited and ate, but she didn't continue. "Oh, is there a boy keeping you here?"

"No." She smiled and then drooped. "I was too shy. Homesick before I left."

"Surely you are ready to see the world, Andrine."

"Have you seen the world?"

"Not Australia or Antarctica, but the rest of it." He shrugged. "It's nice."

"Have you been to America?" She stepped to the bed and gripped the rail. "San Francisco?"

"Yes." He laughed. "They're crazy. The bridge is not golden—it's red."

"Did you like it? America?"

"The only problem with America—it's full of Americans."

She laughed and covered her mouth. Andrine paced back to the window and threw open her arms. "I want to see it all. Especially New York City and the Grand Canyon."

He finished his food. "It would be a lucky man who would escort you—"

"I couldn't find your other battery pack—" Vasili stopped three feet in the door, his eyes bouncing from Andrine to Yuri.

She grabbed the dishtowel, threw it on the empty tray, scooped it up, and fled.

For a minute, the two men stared at the empty doorway, hoping the young beauty would return. Then Vasili, several laptops slowly slipping out of his grip, staggered to the rolling table.

Yuri paid no attention to his lieutenant. He could still smell her perfume. Andrine. Andrine. The name evoked the scent of flowers in a child's hand. An open meadow in the Urals.

"You're going to abuse the barkeeper's daughter?" Vasili opened one of the computers and booted it. "I liked the place, and now we can never go back."

Yuri grabbed Vasili's arm and squeezed hard. "Never speak of her like that again."

CHUCK ROCHE LEANED AROUND THE jamb of the office door in Air Force One. "What the hell were you doing?"

Hunter looked up. "What are you doing here? Who let you in?"

"Wrong question." He stepped around the corner and pointed at her assembled aides. "Everybody out."

Hunter glared at him, then looked at her people. She snapped her fingers and pointed to the door. They filed out silently and closed the door. When they were alone, she stepped out from behind the desk and crossed her arms. "The press watches everyone who gets on and off my jet."

"Don't worry about it." Chuck grabbed a decanter on the sideboard and dropped a couple ice cubes into a glass and poured himself a bourbon. "I told them I'm here to negotiate your surrender. They bought it."

Hunter rolled her eyes before bringing them back to focus on the drink. She needed a drink.

"What the fuck were you doing in that debate?" Roche swirled the bourbon and ice. "You made me look like an idiot. We had a deal."

"You were utterly unprepared." She stepped in front of him. "What happened at your practice sessions?"

"You had a part to play." His voice shook with rage. "You were supposed to go easy."

"Keep it down." She put her hands up and glanced over her shoulder at the door. "My staff knows nothing. They'd all quit." She looked him over. "Tonight was about as easy as it gets, Chuck. If I went any easier, people would be asking questions. You have to prepare. Study. Read. Practice. Take this seriously."

"Screw the debates. I'm not going to do them anymore. Nobody cares about that crap. I'm a genius at this presidential stuff. I could renegotiate all our treaties in a couple months. I'll be the greatest president ever."

"Of course you will."

"Alan Sabel's poking around the Russian business. They found Pozdeeva's microdots. It's only a matter of time before they decode it."

Hunter gasped. "How do you know that?"

"I have sources." He took a sip of bourbon and winced. "This is terrible stuff."

"You're not still connected to Popov, are you? Chuck, tell me you're not talking to them."

"Hell, no. I'm not stupid." He set his glass down. "You should be worried about Sabel too, you know."

"Don't go near the Russians. You have to keep ten layers of separation from them."

"I'll do what I want." He glared at her. "Quit fucking me on stuff like the debate."

Hunter moved in closer and touched his arm. "Let's not argue."

"I'll never marry you." Roche pushed her away. "That was never part of the deal."

Hunter away. "Don't say never."

CHAPTER 15

AT THE END OF THE long flight from St. Petersburg, Pia waited in the Gulfstream's cargo hold for the pilot's signal. More than an hour after midnight, he sent a short beep before he drove off the tarmac at Ercan Airport. Seven miles west lay Nicosia, the capital of Cyprus. They were on a mission to retrieve caches of evidence Dad had left behind twenty years earlier. Time and the pace of his rapidly expanding business empire had obscured locations and content, but he was convinced they would bury Roche. Pia just liked working with him.

Her father and Tania remained silent beside her in the dark. Pia wore the coveralls of an aircraft mechanic, her hair under a male wig and a t-shirt. Due to her height and build, it was easier to disguise her as a man—a fact she didn't like but agreed to because the gypsy act had been too difficult. Tania wore a waitress's dress. Alan dressed like a bum with five-day stubble.

The Major and the body doubles had long since left for the hotel as a decoy convoy to throw off any potential covert surveillance. Later they would provide backup for the operation.

Pia opened the hatch and hopped down. Tania and Alan followed right behind her. The facility looked almost abandoned at two in the morning. They found car keys behind the tire of the only car left in the lot, a Suzuki Ignis.

Pia and Alan squeezed themselves in. Without an inch to spare, their shoulders rubbed against the windows on one side and each other in the middle. After the Sabels raked their seats back, eliminating the backseat footwells, Tania climbed in crosswise in back.

They drove away on the dark, rural airport road. Two miles north across a dry, barren plain, they passed a small shopping mall. A car pulled onto the road behind them.

"Am I being paranoid, or did they not take the bait?" Pia asked.

"If they didn't f-f-follow the Major, they're smarter than w-w-we thought." Tania sank below the rear window and loaded an assault rifle.

"You were right," Dad said. "They anticipated my visit. That's not good for Eleni. We must hurry."

He raised his phone to take a selfie and used the camera to zoom in on the car behind them. "Four men, considerably larger than the average Cypriot male."

Pia watched the mirror for a moment before taking the cloverleaf onto the main highway to Nicosia. The Mercedes sedan followed them. She downshifted, revved up the tiny engine, and accelerated halfway through the arc. As she expected, they matched her speed. She took it up another notch, and they stayed with her. Her car banged over a pothole. Pia and Alan smacked their heads. The much faster Mercedes closed in, tailgating.

"Now?" Tania asked, her finger stroking her trigger.

"If we start shooting now, do they have backup?"

"Let's shoot them and find out."

"Let's try bluffing first." Pia swerved through a tiny opening in the tree-lined median and drove into a dark petrol station. Their pursuers were unable to make the turn but went to the next break in the median and came back.

Pia's tires squealed around the large pumping islands built for tractor-trailers. She rounded the back of the empty building and slowed. Tania opened her door, rolled out, and disappeared into the dark.

Pia sped up. She rounded the next corner and slammed the brakes, bringing them headlamp-to-headlamp with their adversaries.

Two men, silhouetted by their brighter lights, held Kalashnikovs aimed at them. They were lightly dressed in clothing similar to the local farmers' garb. No room for hidden weapons or body armor. Two more men remained in the car.

"Are they going to kill us?" Dad asked.

"Not yet." Pia raised her hands. "You do the talking. My voice doesn't match the disguise."

The men with rifles motioned for them to get out. They complied. Alan stooped, keeping his head down, and pulled a few mangled and dirty euro notes from his pocket. Shuffling in his best approximation of a Cypriot bum, he moved toward them and held out the bills.

One of the men shouted something in Turkish. Alan shrugged and tried a pathetic look.

"Your ID," the man said in heavily accented English.

They pulled out their wallets. Pia had to think about where it was before remembering the back pocket. She handed it to her dad to keep her polished nails from becoming too obvious.

The man looked them over, comparing pictures and people. He nodded at his companion. The pair jumped back in their car and sped off.

"Dad, are you OK?"

"How do you do it?" Dad's knees were shaking. "I thought they were going to kill us."

"Consider yourself already dead at the start, and you won't worry about dying. Besides, we had Tania backing us up."

"N-n-not really." Tania stepped from behind the building with scraped knees and a dirty dress. "I forgot I was w-w-wearing a dress."

"They headed into town," Alan said. "We have to meet Eleni."

"For the record, I absolutely hate dressing like a man." Pia restarted the car. "They sit on their wallets. Their clothes fit like cardboard boxes."

They raced as fast as the little engine could manage. The Russians were long gone.

"There weren't any other planes at the airport." Pia willed the little car to go faster.

"They were KSO," Tania said. "The R-R-Russian version of SEALs. Matted, wet hair. I'm guessing they l-l-landed a Zodiac on the c-coast, stole a car, and tried to meet our jet."

Pia glanced at the map on her phone and kept her foot pressed hard to the floor. "Is Eleni Christoforou an obvious destination for us?"

"It was a long time ago," Dad said. "She was close to retiring back then. I'd hoped they forgot about her." He sighed. "But Strangelove sent these guys."

"What does she have?"

"What she told me then—and I took her advice to heart—was to stash a copy of the paperwork along the way. Hardcopies, she told me. You don't want geeks erasing or rewriting your data. Cyprus deals with companies and governments of all kinds. They aren't corrupt, but they don't mind banking for the corrupt. They know the importance of records to protect themselves."

"You kept copies then?"

"A few documents on Santalum and Roche in safety deposit boxes here and in Barcelona, Zurich, Singapore, other places."

"Let me guess," Pia said. "That's what you were doing when I found you in Barcelona. Your boxes were emptied?"

"Polished, clean and shiny. The bank had my signature on the form an hour before I landed." He clenched his fist and stopped himself from pounding the dash. "He's been one step ahead of me."

"Let's send agents out for the rest of them."

"One problem," Dad looked out the window. "At the time I left each box, I thought I would write them all down. I cross-referenced a few, but I was working hundred-hour work weeks and never had enough time to document their locations. Jonelle and I have been reconstructing the trail as best we can."

"You had time." Pia glanced at him. "You came to all my games."

"I, uh—" Dad took a deep breath "—made choices."

Pia gripped the steering wheel, wishing she could be more appreciative of what he had accomplished.

She twisted the car through wide and narrow lanes. They arrived in a suburb that looked as American as any in the USA. They parked at an unlit curb two blocks from the banker's house, got out and closed their doors quietly.

Pia opened the trunk and grabbed their gear. Tania ditched her dress for her more familiar ninja gear with liquid body armor and took the far side of the street. Pia donned her body armor. Both took a pistol with darts and a sound-suppressed MP5 with real bullets. She handed her father a pistol. All three of them slipped on the new dark-vision glasses from Sabel Tech. A combined night vision and thermal imaging display produced better-than-daylight sight in the dark.

They walked past Eleni's street. The Mercedes was nowhere to be seen, but Pia remained vigilant. Tania circled into the backyard. Pia and her dad slipped quietly back to the front door.

Tania's voice whispered in their earbuds. "Two Russians are inside, back of the house. Looks like a home office. They're tearing up the place in the dark. That means night vision goggles. There's a woman, slumped in a chair."

Pia tried the doorknob. Locked. She pulled a slide hammer out of her coveralls, screwed the end into the lock and slid the weight back quickly. The lock came out with a small bang.

"Wait here, Dad." She pulled her rifle around and tugged on the door.

"I'm coming with you." He raised his pistol. "I'm not letting you go in there alone."

Telling Dad what to do was hard enough; telling a self-made billionaire what to do was nearly impossible. If she left him behind, he would ignore her orders and rush inside to save the day. A well-intentioned idea that would lead to disaster. She knew because she'd done just that several times before she started listening to Jacob and Tania. Her best bet was to give Dad a role and make it significant.

"Cover the front." She placed a hand on his chest. "You're not trained for inside."

"But I couldn't let anything happen to—"

"I need you to cover our backs. Keep an eye open for the other two Russians." She squeezed his shoulder. "Covering our six is very important."

Alan stepped back and took up a position around the corner. He was content making a valuable contribution. Besides, the Major and her squad would be providing backup when they arrived in a few minutes.

Pia pushed the door and stepped inside. She could hear the Russians in the back. She crept through a family room into the kitchen. She slid the door open to let Tania in. Together, they stole down the hall.

The noises grew louder as they approached a narrow passageway with two open doors at the end, one straight ahead and the other on the left.

Pia recognized the danger. A noisy distraction could be a trap.

Tania tapped her, motioning for her to step aside. She wound up an underhand lob. A pan from the kitchen flew past Pia into the darkened room and landed with a bang. The noise stopped. A figure leaned out of the door on the left. The hidden sentry.

Pia pulled her pistol and put him down with a dart. Tania ran past her and rolled out on the office floor. Pia holstered her handgun and pulled up her MP5. She ran in behind Tania and fired twice. Her target didn't drop.

Which alarmed her.

The Russians were wearing body armor as advanced as hers. Which meant the dart probably didn't work on the first guy.

The target in front of her aimed at her.

Tania opened up on him with her muzzle aimed at his face.

Pia dove to the left and covered Tania's six. A bullet buzzed her ear. She emptied her MP5 in an upward arc at the man she thought she'd already dropped. The rounds hit the man in the groin, then stitched their way up to his head. This time he went down hard. At least one bullet had slipped between armor coverage to take him out.

Pia spun to aim at the last soldier. Tania rolled away as he fired into her empty space. Pia's magazine was empty. She swapped as Tania, and her adversary exchanged shots. Pia rose, located her target, but held her fire. The man had dropped to his knees.

Tania scrambled to her feet, pulled her pistol and darted the man.

Pia surveyed the room and found an older woman in an executive chair. Blood oozed between Eleni's fingers and dripped to the floor. Her face contorted with pain. Her body twisted in agony.

Tania flipped on the lights and went to clear the house.

"You're little Pia?" Eleni Christoforou reached out with shaking fingers. "You've grown."

Pia knelt next to the chair. There was a familiar feel about the woman. A memory of an ocean breeze came to her: an airy, white stucco house on a sandy beach where she'd played in the surf. "Did you used to live on the coast?"

"I had a cottage there." A smile tried to cross her face. "We used it for discreet meetings. I liked your father. He was a good man. He read poems to you from that funny book. He deserved better than …"

Pia stroked the woman's arm. She remembered the funny poems well. Shel Silverstein's books were her favorite bedtime reading.

Alan touched Pia's shoulder.

Eleni looked up and saw him. "Alan. Can I get you some tea?"

"Don't get up." Pia touched the woman as if she were keeping her down. "I'll get it."

"I'm sorry, I seem to be stuck in this chair." Her eyes wandered about the room. "Those men took your papers. Two of them left earlier. I'm sorry I could…"

Her voice drifted to a barely audible mumble.

"Is she going to be OK?" Dad asked.

Pia looked at the large pool of blood on the floor, then at the woman's clammy skin. She listened to the shallow, labored breathing. She looked at her father and shook her head.

CHAPTER 16

A COUPLE WEEKS AFTER MS. Sabel's trip to Cyprus, the cat-and-mouse game I'd been playing with Viktor Popov boiled over. The cops couldn't prove I was the guy who left three Russian operators naked and tied to the CIA's front gate. Nor could they prove I was behind the rash of Russian diplomats passing out in bars throughout the city, their blood testing positive for Inland Taipan snake venom and sleep medication on top of the alcohol. But Ms. Sabel knew.

She gave me an assignment out of the country and told me to cool off. Since Eleni's tragic murder, Ms. Sabel and her dad were hell-bent on taking down Strangelove and expose his involvement before Roche got elected. I wasn't too sure they would make it in time. It was late October, and Roche was leading the polls.

My assignment sounded easy enough. Work my way into Strangelove's circle by making friends with the guys who met Alan Sabel at the Mandarin Oriental, Barcelona a few weeks back.

And that's why I was standing on the tarmac looking at Sabel Three, the oldest company jet. It was a foggy morning. My gaze wandered over the misty outline of the Dulles executive terminal a hundred yards away. The scent of autumn drifted in on the chilly breeze. The ground crew took my car and parked it in the Sabel hangar.

The pilot called out from the top of the airstair that Miguel and Emily were already onboard. I glanced around the airport. In the distance, commercial aircraft taxied across several expansive runways to the public terminal. I searched behind me, scanning the road leading to the private entrance.

Instead of finding what I was looking for, I found Mercury in his formal toga, full-length with red trim.

Mercury grinned like a fool. *This is it, my brutha. Success is in the air. You pull this off and Pia-Caesar-Sabel's going to build me a temple. Can you see it? A hundred feet high, all marble—better than anything those lowlife Greeks ever slapped together.* He spread his arms across empty space. *Home of Mercury, winged messenger of the Dii Concentes, the dawg of commerce, the dude of eloquence, the demon of travelers—*

I said, *She's not building you a temple.*

He faced me. *Whoa now. Y'see that? Right there, bro. That's stinking thinking. It's because of that bad attitude of yours that we don't even have a shrine. She almost spoke to me. Get me a little more time with her, and I'll win her over.*

I rolled my eyes. *She's never going to believe the 'dude of eloquence' talks like ... you.*

Say what? Face it, rap is the language of the future. Rappers are the Shakespeares of tomorrow.

I said, *Maybe, maybe not, but you sound like my grandfather trying to be chill with the kids.*

It was a harsh thing to say to a god abandoned in the fifth century. But if you think dad-jokes are awful, try listening to a four-thousand-year-old.

The car I was expecting cleared security and drove through the gate. I pointed to the ground at my feet, and a confused David Watson stopped where I indicated. He was a lean, short older guy, who acted like a man eight feet tall strutting through a village of pygmies. Before they fired him, he'd been an FBI Special Agent in Charge, which is about the same as a colonel who thinks he's a five-star general. Watson argued with the ground crew until they convinced him they'd take good care of his aging Toyota. He glanced my way and looked around, his gray hair glistening in the early morning mist.

"Hoping for someone else?" I asked.

"I heard the Russians had you arrested."

"Why would they do that?" I gave him my innocent look.

The ground crew made Watson hand over his personal phone and double-checked that he had no other electronics; part of my idea to isolate his communications. Ms. Sabel wanted him to feel close but not be close. I didn't want him at all. I promised to return his stuff after the mission. I pointed him up the airstair.

He scowled and climbed. "Where're we going?"

"To look for some bad guys." I followed him.

"What's the mission plan?"

"When you work for Ms. Sabel, you wing it." We climbed aboard and moved down the aisle. "Working directly for the boss, you'll find yourself on a lot of hastily arranged assignments."

"Tactically, that's a dangerous methodology."

"Tell her. She'll fire you."

"Hey, what's with the reporter?" He pointed at Emily.

She sat at a table with Miguel, looked offended, and tugged Watson's wrist as he passed by. "Journalist."

"She's our embedded reporter. Uh. Journalist." I pushed past him. "She passed the Sabel Security advanced training program. She's fully qualified to kick your ass and write up a story about it."

Watson took the first open chair. "Where you going?"

"To get some sleep." I strolled down the aisle and stretched out on the couch. "Emily, if he keeps asking questions, toss him out the window."

THEY WOKE ME WHEN WE landed in Barcelona. Emily and Miguel rented a car and took off. I was stuck with Watson. We headed downtown to the *Plaça de Catalunya* and stopped at a sidewalk café. I sent him inside to fetch me a paper and coffee.

"What are we doing here?" He set a steaming cup and paper in front of me and slipped into the chair opposite.

"Waiting for a couple guys who have lunch here every day."

"You going to tell me why, or is this some kind of stupid game?"

I picked up the paper and started reading. It was in Catalan, which is like a cross between French and Italian but structured like Spanish. Considering Spain, including Catalonia, is barely larger than California in size and population, you might think they'd get their language act together.

I tossed the paper at Watson. "Get me an English paper, and don't tell me they don't have them. This nineteenth-century plaza is tourist central."

He sneered. "Get your own."

Mercury stretched in the chair next to me. *I expect more strategic thinking from you, dawg. You treat the man like he's your bitch when you got no leverage. Have yourself a nice I'm-in-charge-no-really walk back to the news rack.*

Mercury stood up.

I said, *Where are you going? Why are you all dressed up, anyway?*

Mercury frowned. *Time for my semi-annual report to the Capitoline Triad, my brutha. In case you forgot, that's Juno, Minerva, and the big man, Jupiter. They're not easy to please, yo. Every few months I gotta make another excuse about why we aren't on the comeback trail so they don't smite you. But this time, I think we're getting there. I mean, you did introduce me to Pia-Caesar-Sabel. And because of that, we be getting close to building that temple. I can feel it.*

With that, he lifted off on his tiny wings and disappeared into the sky.

Watson looked into the clear blue above us. "What're you looking at?"

"God, of course." I shoved my chair back and went inside. I grabbed a *Financial Times* and stopped short of the cash register. I could swear Mercury was taunting me from the sidewalk, but that didn't make sense—he was gone. I turned around.

Outside, my mission targets approached our table. I compared the picture Ms. Sabel took of her dad's meeting. Same guys. They were clean-cut guys in expensive suits who were surprised to see my new buddy. Watson looked up, saw them, and turned white. Which was not the reaction I expected from him. He glanced inside, but the strong sunshine produced too much glare on the window for him to see me. But I could see him just fine. The targets stopped in front of him and spoke. He shielded his face with his hand and waved them away. They looked around and scuttled off to a table at the far end.

The barista coughed, "*Señor.*"

I paid for the paper and rejoined Watson.

"So we understand each other—" Watson leaned across the table with a glare "—I'm not your water boy."

I opened the paper in his face and spoke through it. "Ms. Sabel told me to run you through the wringer to test your devotion to teamwork. Former soccer stars like Ms. Sabel are big on teamwork. You know what teamwork is? Doing what the team needs without question. So far… not so good."

The pride he swallowed could be heard down the block. At least he wasn't low enough to grovel.

I considered asking him when, where, and how he planned to kill Ms. Sabel, but she told me not to. This whole watch-him-closely plan of hers wasn't working for me.

After reading a few pages, and observing one of the Russians return with sandwiches, I folded up.

"Hey, let's go to Camp Nou and see if we can get tickets." I rose and started walking past my marks.

One of them glanced at me, then at Watson, then back to the sandwich in his hands. He faced a tough decision: do his job or eat his lunch? He dropped the sandwich and licked his fingers. I kept walking at a brisk pace. Their chairs scraped back across the stone sidewalk behind me. Watson's footsteps struggled to keep up with me.

I kept my pace down the block and around the corner. The entourage followed me at various distances. From three paces back, Watson asked me questions about where we were going and why. I crossed the tree-lined avenue and skirted the traffic circle, pretending not to hear him above the noisy motorcycles that filled the streets. I strode past the *Passeig de Gràcia* subway entrance and up the block to the Mandarin Oriental Barcelona. I stopped and used the reflections in Tiffany's window to observe my two targets ten yards behind me on the broad sidewalk.

They didn't appear armed, but I made no assumptions.

Watson looked in the window and elbowed me. "We're being followed."

"Really?" I turned around, looking past the men in dark suits as if they were signposts. "Who?"

"Idiot." He hissed under his breath.

Our tails examined their phones and mimicked a conversation. One of them pointed up the street. They started walking away. I turned in the opposite direction at a brisk pace. Once again, my short companion doubled his stride to keep up.

We took the glass elevator down to the subway station and hopped on a train. We settled into open seats, and the doors thwacked closed.

Watson rolled his Sabel phone in his hand, turning it over and over. "Where we going?"

"I told you, Camp Nou. Barca plays Valencia tonight. Maybe we can get tickets and see Messi play."

"Who?"

"Lionel Messi." I did a double-take. "You work for the best women's soccer player of all time, and you haven't brushed up on the sport? Bad form, little man. Bad form."

"There's a lot to digest. Coming to Sabel is like diving overboard a thousand miles from Honolulu."

"Have you been to Barcelona before?"

He looked away.

We got off at the Maria Cristina station.

"Map says Camp Nou is the next stop." Watson made sure he was even with me as we stepped off the ground-level train and crossed the wide boulevard.

"I wanted to see the *Facultat de Dret* while we're here." I glanced at his scrunched-up face. "Law school."

He did a big *oh* as he took a nervous glance behind us.

The law school was disappointing. A giant box with some mildly interesting windows, it hardly reflected the unique architecture one might expect from the city that gave us Gaudi's *Sagrada Familia*.

I ducked into a multistory parking structure and wound my way down a level in the stairwell. Watson followed, asking what we were doing in a loud voice.

"Why so noisy, Watson?" I asked. "Trying to give our location away to those guys who're following us?"

Beads of sweat broke out on his forehead.

It was nice and dark at the bottom. A weak lamp flickered nearby. Footsteps scuffed their way down the concrete steps a few seconds later. I pulled my Glock and nodded for Watson to follow suit. I gave him standard hand signals to tell him I'll shoot the first guy, you shoot the second.

I pressed my back to the wall next to the stairwell. Watson froze in place like a buck private fresh out of boot camp in his first firefight. The first target walked past me, moving straight ahead. The second followed two strides back.

I darted Watson in the forehead. Then darted both targets.

Miguel and Emily stepped out of the shadows and stared at the bodies.

CHAPTER 17

YURI BOPPED IN TIME TO Erik Friedlander's plucked cello streaming through his earbuds as he rode the tram up the mountains overlooking Zurich. He was headed for the popular overlook called Felsenegg. It was a beautiful, sunny view of golden leaves a day from going brown. Not quite the explosion of color he'd found in the American New England states, but a close second. He shared his tramcar with a small family and an entwined couple. He smiled and bopped and drank in the natural beauty.

It was too much to keep to himself. His burning need to share it with someone overcame his logical desire to keep his location secret. He pulled up Andrine on Skype and turned his phone's camera to the window.

When she came online, he heard the clatter of dishes, the shouts from the kitchen, the sound of an early-evening crowd. It was a bad time. She was working.

"It's beautiful," she said. "Where are you?"

"You have to guess." He took a seat, wincing at the pain in his ribs, and flipped the screen to his face. She was lovely. Too beautiful for him. He positioned the camera to catch some of the view. "I'll give you a hint, it's in Switzerland."

"Geneva? Lucerne?" She looked over her shoulder and held a finger, making someone wait.

"You're busy, you have to go."

"Father can wait, Yuri." She smiled. "I wish I was there with you. But not Switzerland."

"You don't like the Swiss?"

"They helped the Nazis, refused to help Holocaust survivors, and now they are the bankers to the kleptocracy in your homeland. Did you read the Panama Papers? Their work allows the subjugation of millions of people. They have no scruples. You're not banking there, are you?"

"Sightseeing, I swear." He laughed. "Next time I travel, I'll ask your father to give you a few days off. You can pick the place."

"New York would be nice." She hid her smile and batted her eyes. Someone called to her in the background. "Now I have to go. We can talk later."

The tram car slowed and bumped to a stop. The family got off first. Yuri followed. The young couple lagged behind, their arms wrapped tightly around each other, oblivious to the world around them.

For a moment, he imagined wrapping his arms around Andrine, picking her up off her feet, twirling her in a circle, and putting her down in front of the panoramic view. One day, perhaps. One day when he had become important and could hire servants for her. She may not approve of servants. But even a socialist would eventually warm to having household staff. Everyone does.

The family had gone the opposite direction. He was alone on the path. With a bounce in his step, he waltzed through the colorful trees. Despite the sunshine, the weather had a bite to it. Yuri shoved his hands in his pea coat and picked up his pace.

Restaurant Felsenegg's outdoor patio, with its famous view of Zurich, was closed. He strolled by and continued down the path. A hundred yards later, he found his contact. A bald man in a business suit sat in the shadows on an overlook bench. A stack of manila envelopes waited next to him.

"Herr Mandrake?" the man asked.

Yuri nodded and replied with the codename. "Herr Freimann?"

"The light's not good for pictures." Freimann spoke in German. He rose and held out the envelopes. "I hope you have a good flash. Just be quick about it. Alan Sabel is a powerful man. If I get caught, I'm as good as dead. I must get back to the bank in an hour."

Yuri pulled his PSS, the silent pistol, from his coat and put a bullet in the man's temple. The envelopes fell to the ground. Kneeling for only a second, he picked them up and tucked them under his arm. With a glance, he satisfied himself that Freimann was dead. He strode down the footpath another two hundred yards, then turned into the trees.

He walked down the mountain's north side through a few villages to the Reppischtallstrasse. Independence from Strangelove occupied every waking moment of his life. But extricating himself from Strangelove would require a master plan. Carefully staged and executed. He could take some of the men with him, but only the strong. There would be no second chances. Any failure, no matter how small, would mean death. It would have to be perfect. No mistakes. No loose talk. No weak links.

He met Roman at the café as planned. They drank coffee and ordered lunch. They admired the quaint farmhouse across the street.

"How did you like group therapy?" Yuri asked.

"It was good for Igor to talk about his concerns." Roman waved his empty cup at the waitress. "And talk and talk and talk."

Yuri laughed. "He had quite a few issues, didn't he? But I think he spoke for many others." Yuri shrugged and held his cup up to the waitress when she filled Roman's. "I was surprised to see Petr break down in tears."

"So many children lost … bothered everyone." Roman sipped and burned his tongue. "It bothers me, but not enough to cry in front of the others."

Yuri looked at Roman, whose eyes avoided his. He always saw Roman as a tough guy from the streets of Moscow. Late twenties and already a worldly cynic. He wore his hair buzzed to stubble like a black cap. His darting eyes took in everything around him as if evaluating its resale value on the black market. He was the first to laugh at the tribulations of others, never one to offer sympathy, yet he now admitted to feelings.

"Alexandr sat with his arms crossed and never spoke," Yuri said. "You know him well. Should I be worried about him?"

"You mean his mental health? No. He doesn't speak when there are more than two people in the room. It's his way."

The waitress brought potato rösti—what Americans call hash browns—for Yuri, and bratwurst with fries for Roman. Their eyes grew, and they dug in.

"You know, we still get messages in the data from America." Roman took a big bite.

"I met Brad once." Yuri watched his man carefully for a reaction. His man tried not to look surprised. "A brief encounter, just a few words exchanged. Who he represented was not clear, so I reported the contact to Strangelove."

Roman finished chewing, aware that Yuri watched his every facial twitch. "What did the old man say?"

"Nothing."

"That's not good." Roman offered his fries. "Does that mean Brad works for the general?"

"I don't know." Yuri waved off the offered fries. "It means my banda should be careful not to engage with people when they don't know anything about them. There are many spies in this world. Our value to the Motherland would diminish instantly if our methods and techniques were replicated by other bandas or unmasked by other countries."

Roman stopped eating and met his gaze. "I understand."

Yuri kept staring long enough to make his point, then picked up his fork. "Talking about #HuntersFail was good for me. Everyone said it made them feel better as well. Tell me, Roman, what do they say when I'm not there?"

Roman finished his bratwurst to buy time for an answer. Yuri waited patiently.

"Some of the men," he waved his fork, "are unhappy."

"Unhappiness is the Russian way of life. It is our fate." Yuri signaled for the check. "How unhappy are they?"

"We were happy to be unhappy when you dragged us into the banda. We lost a lot of money. But, we serve our country, we earn our freedom, we go back to hacking Americans. That is a level 5 unhappy."

"But?" Yuri gave their waitress his credit card.

Roman waited until the transaction was complete and the waitress walked away. He leaned across the small table and stared directly into Yuri's eyes. "There is a big difference between stealing a man's watch and murdering his child. Right now, we are at maximum unhappiness."

Yuri nodded and rose. They went outside. Yuri said, "Some in the banda are not willing to accept their fate, their Avos'?"

"That is an outdated superstition." Roman scoffed as they opened their respective doors, Roman driving and Yuri the passenger. They got in and buckled up.

Yuri said, "Nietzsche wrote about a Russian soldier who lay down in the snow to accept his fate. Either he would die, or the enemy would pass by and think he was dead. His willingness to leave it to Avos' put him at ease, lowered his metabolism. He entered a state near hibernation. It conserved his energy. The enemy passed over him. He lived."

Roman put it in drive and glanced at his officer. "Bullshit."

"Yes." Yuri pulled a thin, short knife out of its hidden slot in his belt buckle. "One might rely on his Avos', but keep something handy to help the odds."

Roman laughed and drove out to the main road. He turned left and headed for the unmanned crossing into Germany. Yuri took out his stack of manila envelopes and opened one. He found twenty-year-old bank statements.

"Why did you tell me that story about Nietzsche?" Roman asked.

"The trouble with being an officer is reading your men. Normally, I would rely on my lieutenant, but this time there is too much at stake. It is critical to understand what is not said in group."

"Your quote was from Nietzsche's autobiography, *Ecce Homo*, which is Latin for 'behold the man.'" Roman checked his commanding officer from the corner of his eye. "This is why you brought me instead of Vasili? You expect me to behold the hearts of my brothers?"

Yuri laughed and waved a finger at Roman. "The trouble with commanding a platoon of hackers is that you're all smart. Too smart sometimes."

"OK, fine." Roman put out his fist. Yuri bumped it. "I answer your questions as best I can. But I don't speak for everyone. I can say only what I believe to be."

Yuri opened another envelope and looked through it as he spoke. "Talking about our feelings in the group makes everyone feel better. But it is a step. Only a step. From there, one can step left or right or forward.

A feeling arose from the session that not everyone was willing to accept his Avos'. And that's OK. It was a difficult assignment. We did a terrible thing. What I need to know is, what do the men propose to do about it?"

They drove in silence for a kilometer or more. Yuri looked through the papers in the next envelope. They were also twenty-years-old. Documents of no value that he could see. Requisitions for toner cartridges, personnel transfers of bank employees, water bills.

"The answer is difficult to reveal." Roman stammered a little before he spoke again. "Before I do, I need to know something."

"We are having a conversation about theories, Roman. Nothing you say will be repeated outside of this car. This is American-style AMA: ask me anything."

Roman nodded. "There is a rumor that there were no orders for #HuntersFail."

"Interesting rumor." Yuri opened another envelope. "We are being honest here, so I will tell you the truth: there were orders. They were destroyed after I read them. But the result is the same. The record will show we were acting on our own."

Roman exhaled. "Shit."

"An eloquent analysis, Roman. 'Shit' is right. Look on the bright side—if the Americans trace our hacks, we will never hear the drone that will vaporize us."

Roman laughed. "Your concept of Avos' is a dark one, my friend."

"I know." Yuri twisted in his seat to look squarely at his driver. "Theoretically, if you could wave a magic wand, what does your life look like in six months?"

"Are you recording this?" Roman snapped. "Am I going to jail?" His harsh tone banged against the glass. His eyes flashed. Then he softened. "Perhaps we talk about where Alexi would've been in six months—had he lived."

"Fine."

"Alexi has an apartment overlooking a sandy beach in Brazil. The beach is populated by women in bikinis. Behind him are banks of computers, hacking away at firewalls around the world. He is not a citizen of any country. He does not need a nation. But he keeps several passports to suit his whims for travel. Bitcoins flow to his Coinbase account and on to banks in the Caymans. He has undergone facial reconstruction to avoid recognition software. His Lotus is parked underground. Life is good."

Yuri thought about the multi-million-dollar account filled with Alexi's money that he controlled. He never told Strangelove about it. Never turned the money into the Russian auditors. He'd promised Alexi he would give it back one day if Alexi behaved himself. Now, it was his, and he owed it to no one.

"Alexi would be happier in the Caribbean," Yuri said. "Each island belongs to a different country. If he had to flee in the middle of the night, all he would need is a fast boat. Cyprus is nicer about confidentiality than the Brits in the Caymans. And, a McLaren is much sexier than a Lotus."

"You've been thinking about this?" Roman asked.

Yuri shrugged.

He opened another envelope. Again, the contents were reams of useless information. He resealed them and tossed the lot in the backseat.

"There is another rumor," Roman said a kilometer later, "that Strangelove has ordered you to kill the industrialist Alan Sabel."

"How many other interesting rumors have you heard?" Yuri knew the source for that rumor. There were only two people there when Strangelove gave that verbal order. "We still have our full workload."

"Aren't you done killing Americans? Will you put us at risk again? Strangelove is setting you up. It's time to make a break. Get away from Strangelove and Russia."

"Talk like that will get you court-martialed," Yuri snapped.

He looked at the sharp teeth of the Alps on all sides of them. His men deserved better leadership. Better than Strangelove. Officers who would never stab their men. Officers who would find a way out of the Avos' Strangelove created for them.

"You don't just walk away." He took a deep breath. "You make plans. You find exits. You test your friends to determine the allies and the enemies. Who you can trust. You leave survival packages along the route. Until your plans are ready, you follow orders. No one should know what you're doing. That is how a wise man would do it."

Roman remained quiet for a long time. Then he twisted to look at Yuri. "Are you a wise man?"

"Extremely." Yuri faced his man. "Are you?"

Roman nodded slowly and returned his gaze to the road. "I'm going to be wiser as soon as we get back."

Something ticked in the back of Yuri's brain. Something that he'd seen but not recognized when he saw it. What was it? Paper that wasn't paper.

Roman glanced his way.

Yuri craned into the backseat and grabbed the envelopes. He rifled through them, checking each paper one at a time, then discarded them in the backseat. His hands and eyes worked like a madman's.

Roman watched him from the corner of his eye until his curiosity overwhelmed him. "What is it?"

Yuri froze when he found it. It felt like his heart stopped as well. He pulled something no larger than a postage stamp from where it was stuck to the back of a paper.

A tracking transmitter.

CHAPTER 18

PIA GOT OUT OF THE car a couple miles outside of Moûtiers near the French border with Italy. She stretched and pulled her jacket close. She gave her father a smile across the hood. Despite Eleni's tragic death, Pia had enjoyed working with Dad over the last few weeks. While their search for Strangelove had been fruitless, the time spent together was precious.

She nodded at the old stone farmhouse. "We've been here before?"

"You've b-b-been everywhere before." Tania pulled out her beret and capped her wild hair.

Alan returned Pia's smile. "Once, after a match in Marseille. I think you were in high school."

Pia examined the valley snuggled into the Alps. Most of the steep hillside was pasture. To one side, corn and wheat fields lay in post-harvest ruin, their lateral furrows covered with straw. Melons and squash ripened in another field near the house. A cow and chickens stayed close to the ancient barn. One wall leaned hard to the outside, propped up by angled oak beams.

All four levels of the house were built into the hill; only the top floor was free of the mountain. Everything had that classic European look: hand-hewn, pragmatic, and aged. The only thing that stood out was the living room's floor-to-ceiling picture window. It looked as if a Phillip Johnson glass house had been grafted into the middle of a classic French farmhouse. Yet somehow it worked.

A grandmotherly woman came to greet them, wiping her hands on her apron. Camille, the housekeeper, introduced herself in an accent so thick they could barely understand her. They went inside to wait for the owner,

Olivier Jallet. Camille begged off and left them in a living room with a magnificent view.

"Remember, let me do the talking," Dad said.

Pia flinched at his unnecessary words and swallowed her rising resentment. The downside to their time together: reopening the ten-thousand paper cuts of family relationships. At what point is the child an independent adult capable of accomplishing anything in her father's eyes? She bit the inside of her cheek.

"He was my counterpart in the EU," Dad said. "We worked together on several—"

"You've mentioned that—many times," she said through clenched teeth.

Pia watched her father turn to the window. She worried about him. Something more than Eleni's death and Chuck Roche's candidacy was bothering him. He was keeping a secret. Worse, she kept a secret of her own. She still hadn't worked up the courage to tell him how she'd broken several laws by bugging President Hunter. She wanted to tell him they were plotting against her, but the bug would put him in legal jeopardy. She couldn't risk his future. The issue left her with a better understanding of why he obscured his role in her parents' murders for twenty years.

Alan faced her. "Anyway, Olivier can be direct. Don't let him unnerve—"

"Thanks, Dad."

A few feet away, Tania looked over the valley and threw her hands up. "Where's the w-w-wine? I don't see any vineyards or a-anything. Isn't this supposed to be France?"

On cue, Camille entered with a bottle and glasses. She poured and served them. They sipped. She looked around nervously, shrugged and left.

"Olivier went through a lot of guilt about his involvement in the arms business."

"Dad. Stop."

"Believe it or not, Pia, I've learned a thing or two. Have you ever considered listening—"

"Alan!" Olivier, a trim, handsome man in his fifties strode in with his arms outstretched. "Mon ami."

They embraced. Alan introduced Pia and Tania.

"Mademoiselle." He never took his eyes off Pia's as he took her hand. "You have become so much the beauty. The gods bless you beyond measure. Surely you are turning down the bachelors of Washington by the dozens."

Pia appreciated his attempt to flatter her. Most men were intimidated by her stature and fitness. The few men who took an interest in her were more excited about her exotic car collection or riding on her jet than engaging with her. Oh. Pity the rich girl. She laughed at herself. Olivier was right, she was blessed and should remain grateful forever. She smiled.

The men began talking about old times, how Olivier launched his satellites from questionable Russian rockets while Alan had the luxury of American launches.

Pia's attention turned to the meadow below the windows. Olivier's two teenage boys played soccer on a sloped field while their younger sister played referee. The angled pitch produced a crazy game that made them laugh and run and push each other.

Pia wondered about Stefan Devoor, her maybe-boyfriend who had adopted two children. She'd followed their travels on Instagram from time to time. The little family looked good, but a short video and occasional picture didn't tell much about their mental health. Stefan had been forced to kill his own father to save Pia. She couldn't imagine the psychological damage from that decision. Stefan had handled his grief by giving all his wealth to charity, becoming a single dad, and taking off to see the world. It was a questionable therapy, but she had no reference point from which to judge.

Olivier's teens frolicked on the grass, far removed from the violence of life. They were lucky. Pia had not been so lucky. Violence and death followed her every step.

She took a deep breath and derailed her thoughts before they dove into that dark well where the ugly memories lay. The memories of her natural parents and their brutal murders. They were negative thoughts too stressful to consider when visiting Dad's old friends.

She heard her father behind her, bringing Olivier up to date. "So, we placed fake documents with a tracking chip in the remaining safe deposit boxes."

"How did they find the locations?"

"It took a while," Alan said, "but we realized Strangelove was following the company's credit card payments for each box. Because we would arrive in Cyprus at night, I had asked Eleni to bring the contents home. That was my mistake."

"Eleni was the wise woman." Olivier squeezed Alan's shoulder as he fell silent. "But Strangelove is her killer—not you." He gestured to chairs, and they sat.

Alan said, "We can't find a common thread in all the documents Pozdeeva left us. There are quite a few signed by someone named Olesya something. Does that ring a bell?"

Olivier shook his head. "You said the Russians were behind the airline disaster. You have found the proof?"

"Nothing concrete."

A recurring memory of impending doom surfaced. Pia could never tell if it was a dream. She stood on a cliff, the ocean pounding against the rock below her. Thousands of gallons of water shot high into the air, then fell back to earth. The ebb carried the kinetic energy out to sea leaving a harmless and placid pool below her. She felt it calling to her. She could jump in and momentarily become one with Earth's infinite seas. Peace. Serenity. She allowed herself to imagine the dive. The waves rushed back in, assaulting the precipice with such violence that it shocked her awake.

Pia shook her head and inhaled.

Olivier and Dad were looking at her.

"You have a wonderful farm." Pia sipped her wine. "You don't miss the satellite business?"

Olivier observed Pia for a moment before answering. "One day I listened to a man boast that his new suit cost more than the average car. During the time he spoke, the only thought in my mind was, the finest fashions in the world—and he is still the asshole. I didn't want to be the asshole in nice clothes. I don't want my children to grow up thinking human value comes from cloth woven in Bangladesh."

He sipped his wine and looked at the view. "Business partners, subcontractors, employees come bearing gifts. They are piling them at your feet as if the offerings were for the Emperor of Rome. Day after day, everyone wants to get the few minutes of your time to propose the next big business venture. They pin their hopes and dreams for the future on your thumb turning up or down. What good did it do me?"

Pia stayed silent.

"What good is it to you, Pia?" Olivier faced her with a piercing stare. "Does it bring the parents back from the dead?"

His words stunned her. She shook her head and buried her face in her wine glass. No one spoke to her like that. Olivier had hit the raw nerve she had kept carefully bandaged every day for the last twenty-two years. The toys, the dolls, the cars, the horses, the autographed soccer balls, the art objects, the fashions piled high—all meant nothing to her. Yet people, Dad especially, brought them every day. As if one more gift could erase the tragedy. They did just the opposite; they reminded her and amplified her painful loss.

She felt Olivier staring at her, sensing her reaction. For some reason, he was forcing her down that dark well of memories. As much as she didn't want to go there, she had to.

In her heart, she knew that people offer gifts to signal their desire to start a relationship. A small child will take a common object from a coffee table and offer it to a visiting adult as an overture to a relationship. When you take the offered object, you are obliged to speak to them, to recognize and interact with them. Gifts are offered with hope. But to Pia, they were offered as dressings for a wound. By their presentation, they became unintentional reminders of her agony. Cues that dredged up the image of her mother's body dangling by the neck from Leroy Johnson's outstretched hands. Reminders of her four-year-old hands stabbing Johnson over and over again with the vegetable knife from the kitchen counter. Reminders of the enraged voice in her young head telling her to strike harder and higher. Reminders of the fountain of blood her knife produced when it struck his femoral artery.

She put the wine glass on the coffee table, its deep red liquid suddenly repulsive.

"It was my wife, Bridgette." Olivier's voice drifted into her thoughts. His stare still lashed to her. "He tied us to chairs and—in front of the children and me—slit her throat."

She gasped as she met his gaze. He was cold and gray. A color she could feel in her soul.

He said, "Viktor Popov."

CHAPTER 19

MIGUEL GRABBED THE RUSSIAN'S ARMS, and I picked up his feet. We dragged his dead weight to the back of the SUV in the subterranean parking garage in Barcelona. Watson and the other Russian were sleeping off the effects of the Sabel Darts while crammed in the back of what would be a micro-SUV in America. Emily kept watch from the driver's seat.

A limo squealed up from the depths below us, rounding the corner in too big a hurry. Our truck partially blocked the ramp. The limo slammed on the brakes and stopped.

Miguel dropped his end, and I dropped mine. We kicked the Russian under the rear bumper, drew our weapons, and took a glance around the side.

The back door of the limo opened, and a stream of Spanish curse words flew out in a man's voice. A woman in a tight red cocktail dress, matching stiletto heels and clutch backed out of it, screaming a few choice words of her own in Spanish and slammed the door. The limo backed up, cutting a steep angle to get around our car, and body-slammed the woman. She landed on her butt. The stretch burned rubber up the ramp and out of sight.

I holstered my gun and pushed around Miguel.

The lady in red was sprawled like an upside-down turtle in a dress too tight to get her feet under her. She took my outstretched hand, and I pulled her up. She dusted off her designer rear end and rubbed at a spot of grease on her knee.

An angel face looked up at me: a button nose and rosy cheeks framed with auburn hair lit by pale blue eyes. A quick, engaging smile swept across her face. For a split-second, my heart stopped beating. She said, "Thank you."

Perfect, unaccented English was not what I expected.

Her smile vanished. She brushed a stray hair from her face and turned toward the exit without a second glance.

I said, "Uh, could I … you wanna … do you need a lift?"

"Fuck you." Also in perfect English. Without so much as a glance over her shoulder, she disappeared into the stairwell.

The driver's window buzzed down. Emily stuck her head out. "You need a lift? Are you kidding me? That's your best line? She's so far above you, you can't see the soles of her shoes."

The window buzzed back up.

Miguel shrugged and tugged the Russian's arms. I ran around, grabbed the feet. We tossed him on top of the other two. Miguel pulled the hatch down.

"What are you guys doing?" Again, perfect English.

I spun to face the beauty in red and noticed her lipstick also matched her ensemble. "Aaahhh. Well, um, drunk … friends."

"And you were going to offer me a ride in that? With them?"

Tongue tied, I pointed at the back of the car, realized we couldn't squeeze a kindergartner in there, then twisted to the front door, where Miguel was reaching for the handle, then flopped my arms by my side. "Can I call you a cab?"

"Yeah." She opened her purse and took out a packet of gum. "They don't have Uber in this New-York-Wannabe town."

I looked back at Miguel. He rolled his eyes and got in the truck.

To call a cab in a foreign country, you need a clue where to start, not to mention a rudimentary grasp of the local language. Since I didn't have either of those, I called the Sabel Security help desk. A cab was ordered in three seconds.

"I didn't mean to be so rude earlier." She pointed to where the limo decked her. "Not a good week. I'm volunteering at a fundraiser tomorrow in Monaco. I have to get there … somehow."

She shrugged.

"No offense taken." I grinned. "Cab should be outside in five."

She smiled as if she were mildly impressed and unwrapped her gum. She held it in her fingers and placed it on her tongue and slid it back into her mouth where her lips closed around it and sucked it the rest of the way in with a definitive *thup*.

My heart rate rose, and my lungs expelled all their air.

"What's your name?" she asked softly.

"Jacob." I prayed I wasn't drooling. "And yours?"

"Sylvia." All three syllables rolled from her lips like liquid, long *e*'s ending with a drawn-out *ah*. SEAL-vee-yahh.

She chewed her gum with deliberate slowness. Grace and sensuality in food consumption is such a rarity that its discovery can bring the meaning of life into focus on a whole new plane of existence.

Sylvia gave me a tease of her electrifying smile and finger-waved. "See ya."

She turned back up the stairwell and flexed every fiber of muscle in her amazing legs while disappearing up and away.

Emily blasted the horn. "We're committing a crime here, Romeo—GET IN THE CAR."

I squeezed in the backseat sideways since the two in front had raked their seats all the way back. Miguel because he was six-four, two-twenty, and Emily because she thought she was Lewis Hamilton in a Formula One car. She stomped on the gas, expecting the mini-SUV to burn rubber. The car's acceleration, uphill and fully loaded, lacked enthusiasm. The little engine revved up as best it could with six people. Eventually, we made it up the ramp, found our way to the W Barcelona, and snuck our drugged friends through the service elevator to our suite.

Watson and the Russians would sleep for several hours. We propped them in chairs, duct-taped and cuffed them, and went to sit on the balcony. We sipped wine and watched the evening shadows stretch across the Balearic Sea.

Emily talked about her favorite subject: Emily. She'd left Bianca hanging. Miguel and I shook our heads in dismay. I always wonder how people as smart as Emily could make such dumb decisions about love.

I've never done that.

I got up while they talked and leaned my forearms on the railing. The view was spectacular. Far below, beachgoers called it a day, packed their bags, and came inside. Sailboats bobbed on low waves and seagulls swooped in for seafood. Inside, I had two Russians and a traitor waiting to be interrogated. Life was good.

Mercury floated down from above. *Things were tough at the Dii Consentes review, homie. I had your life spared, but then you went and saved Sylvia. You guys were supposed to get nervous and shoot her by accident. So, it's on you. You messed up, and it's over. It's been nice, bro. But. Now they're down to arguing over whether you should die at sea, on land, or from the air. I guess technically that would be by land as well, seeing as how you don't die while you're falling.* He did a double-take when he looked in the suite. *What's with the bondage thing? Are you going kinky? Cause we might reconsider your death scenario.*

I said, *What? That's it? You guys are going to off me? I just fell in love. Again.*

Mercury patted my shoulder. *Don't worry, dawg, I'll make it slow and painful.*

But I wanted to get married, have a family, watch the kids grow up and go to jail.

That's what they all say. Hey, brutha, relax. I'm the one who guides you across the river into the afterlife. He looked over the railing. *Say, that's a long way down. And you'd land on the rocks. This might be just what Juno ordered.*

I said, *Wait! I'll build a shrine. I'll show it to the Caesar-Sabels.*

Too late for that. The wings on his helmet started flapping. He once told me that was how his intra-deity messages arrived. *Hang on a second. I gotta take this.*

Mercury rose thirty feet.

As I watched him, I leaned back against the balcony railing.

I heard a *ka-thunk.* Something halfway between metal and concrete. Or both.

In the next instant, the railing gave way.

The metal and glass partition on which my butt rested broke loose from one side and swung out over open space as if on a hinge. My weight had been counting on it and no longer had any support. I went backward over the chasm of nothingness below. All the wine in my glass flew out—but I maintained a firm, three-finger grip on the stemware because, in case of survival, a refill would be warranted. I flailed for purchase with my left hand. I flailed for purchase with my right pinkie. Nothing there. I continued to fall backward.

From deep in my brain, the ancient ape who once swung through trees took control. If my earliest ancestors could grip branches with their feet, so could I. My life depended on it. My toes curled to grip through the soles of my boots in a last-ditch effort to stay on the twentieth floor.

Apparently, a lot of water has passed under the bridge since we swung on trees. A lot of handy instincts were abandoned along the evolutionary river. My toes gripped nothing but sock.

I was falling to my death.

I hoped the gods were happy. One day they save you from an onslaught of a thousand Mujahedeen. The next day they save you from an angry husband with a loaded .44. And for what? So they can have a belly laugh watching you thrash two hundred feet.

Bastards.

Out of the clear blue sky above, Miguel's big paw grabbed my wrist. He yanked me back to the land of the living. Emily screamed. Miguel and I ended up toe-to-toe, staring at each other for an awkward second.

"Refill?" Miguel asked.

"Sure." I swung my glass into position.

He was nice enough to pretend my hand wasn't shaking and went to grab the wine bottle.

Mercury stood in the empty space Miguel left behind. *Navajos can fuck up a wet dream, you know that? Estsanatlehi can kiss my ass.*

I said, *Who?*

Estsanatlehi. Changing Woman. She walks to the east and meets her younger self and changes into a young person. Your main man Miguel there is in tight with her. She calls him Monster Slayer. The two of them can take a flying—

"Hey, they're waking up." Miguel stood in the sliding glass door. "Ready?"

Watson was still out cold. He was smaller than the other two; the sedative would last longer. The bigger Russian was coming around first. I had Miguel carry the others into separate bedrooms off the living room. While he moved the bodies, I observed how large the suite was. Everything in leather and glass and silver. Nice. Extremely nice. I wondered how he was planning to explain it on his expense report.

I splashed cold water on my prisoner. "Why did Viktor steal my dog?"

His eyes focused on me. I repeated my question. He squinted. I repeated it a third time.

When he finally heard me, his face blanched. He knew who I was: the man who had crept into the Russian Embassy's private living quarters and shot his boss's boss in the leg. In an organization the size of the SVR, a story like Viktor's could not stay secret long. Which worked well for me. My prisoner tried to look unfazed, but the beads of sweat on his brow gave him away.

"I was going to ask you a series of questions." I checked my pistol's magazine and gave him a smile. "I expect you'll refuse to answer—because you're a professional. So, I'll skip the formalities and go straight to the part where I blow a hole in your leg just like Viktor's. I mean, why not? You've earned it. Probably."

I pressed the pistol to his shin and watched his eyes blow up like balloons.

"Wait." The sweat on his brow formed rivulets that dripped down his temple. "I answer what I know."

I lifted the muzzle and nonchalantly waved the gun around, always keeping the inside of the barrel in his direct line of sight. "How do you know Watson?"

"Who?"

"I knew it would be a waste of time." I pressed the muzzle back to his shin.

"*Zhdat'!* Wait." He took a deep breath. "I need … how do you say, escape sheep?"

I rolled his phrase around in my head for a minute. "Scapegoat? You need someone to blame as the source? Yeah, I got you covered there, buddy."

Most professional killers punch a clock for the secret police in some country or another. They're not living the Mafia dream or a consumed by religious fervor. All they want is plausible deniability and a reasonable expectation of going home at quitting time. My guarantee of giving him a fall guy was almost what he needed to hear. But he still gave me a skeptical glance.

I pulled out the oldest insurance package available to men of our kind. "I give you my word, soldier-to-soldier, no one will ever learn my source."

He nodded. "He work for the Chuck Roche."

A genuine smile grew on me. The Russians purposely mispronounced the weasel's name the same way we did: roach. None of that fancy row-SHAY nonsense. They might not be such bad guys after all. Then I remembered who stole my dog. I kept the Glock in place and gave him another serial-killer smile. "Duh."

"He … he is important man."

I looked at his leg, then at him. "Watson comes to Barcelona?"

The guy nodded furiously. "Last summer. He come with Roche first time. He comes now, weekends, big meetings."

I gave him my soldier stare. He gave me the same right back.

Voices were coming from the other room. Miguel's hostage wasn't as chatty as mine. But then, the big guy didn't have my street cred working for him.

"What does Watson do?" I asked.

"He work on project with big general. Maybe kompromat on Alan Sabel." He referred to the Russian's love of getting or creating compromising pictures or documents on their targets for continuing extortion.

That didn't make sense. They wouldn't waste time looking for kompromat on Pia and Alan Sabel, who led exemplary lives. Given what we knew of Watson's mission, there was no way in hell that scumbag would get dirt on the Sabels.

Yet Roche had planted him in our midst, and Viktor Popov had gone to extraordinary lengths to retrieve Pozdeeva's drive. Roche and Watson held secret meetings with Russians in Barcelona. Watson carried the message about #HuntersFail back to Roche. They were smart enough to make it easily deniable. But why take the risk?

With the election a handful of weeks away, we needed concrete proof soon. I'd already mailed in my ballot. Most Sabel employees had. The voters deserved to know about these connections. But where could we find verifiable evidence?

"Who's the big general?" I asked.

The Russian shrugged. "Important man, very secret. Above my payment class."

I squinted. "Pay grade?"

"Da." He shrugged. "Only thing I know sure: from Kaliningrad."

Mercury tapped me on the shoulder. *Dude, can I have a word with you?*

I said, *I'm in the middle of something.*

Mercury said, *I might have found a reprieve for you. Getcha second chance, ya feel me?*

You worried I might start working with the Navajo gods?

Ah homie, don't be throwing them in my face. You don't want to hang with them. Ask Miguel. Scary as hell. Dancing around the bonfire, big ol' masks, and all that. He shivered. *Minerva and Ceres were interested in your shrine offer.*

"You are drinking?" My Russian's face scrunched up as if he'd seen something he shouldn't have.

I looked at him and tilted my head while I wondered if I'd been using my outside voice again. There was no reason not to be honest with him. I tapped the pistol to my forehead. "My bad. When I talk to the gods, I forget no one else can see them."

A look crossed his face as if his borscht had gone bad.

Someone knocked at the door. The knock repeated, and a man announced himself as the hotel manager coming to check on the balcony. Apparently, my high-wire act was visible from the street.

I pulled my other gun and fired a Sabel Dart in the Russian's leg. I heard the same pop coming from Miguel's room. I stripped the remaining duct tape off the guy and let the manager in.

"You are all right, señor?" the manager asked. "No one is hurt?"

"Nah, fine." I kept him in the vestibule. "Your railing wasn't built very well."

"I have workmen on their way up to secure it. I would offer you another room, but you are in the Extreme Wow Suite now. Anything else would be a downgrade. Would you like to look at options?"

Once again, my mind wandered to how and why Miguel picked this room and how much it cost. But his expense report wasn't my problem. Besides, it came with a free bottle of wine.

"May I come in?" he asked. "To inspect the damage?"

Without a good excuse handy, I waved him in through the rooms, hoping to lead him out to the wrap-around balcony before he noticed the Russian. It didn't work. He froze.

"Is your friend OK?"

"He's not a friend, and he's not well. We were going to party with these guys, but they got into drugs. We need to dispose of them. Drop them off at some addict-infested dump. Can you recommend a really bad neighborhood?"

"We will take care of them for you, *señor*. Right away." He pulled a walkie-talkie from his jacket and barked instructions in Spanish.

His willingness to dispose of overdosed guests without asking questions brought my attention back to the cost of the room. Dumping bodies didn't come cheap in any hotel. And this guy didn't bat an eye.

"How many?" he asked.

"Three."

CHAPTER 20

Yuri read the requirements for a new mission spelled out in an email on his computer in the banda's office. He pursed his lips as he thought how he would go about it.

What still bothered him was who benefitted. None of the American presidents liked the Russians. What difference would it make if a Russian-hating Republican or a Russian-hating Democrat became president? Even if the new NEXT USA party succeeded in their long-shot attempt to keep Veronica Hunter in the White House, what would change?

The American intelligence agencies loved Russia because to them, the SVR was the rival professional team. They respected each other. The SVR and CIA could go at each other the old-fashioned way: honey traps, booze, and money. No one in the Kremlin would want that to change. Middle Eastern jihadis considered torture at the hands of Americans or Russians a badge of honor that brought them closer to God. Russia should stick with the Americans as archenemies; it was easier.

The two countries were locked in an eternal love-to-hate relationship. No two countries could be more alike: relatively well-educated, predominantly white and Christian with large and diverse minority populations, and rapidly expanding economies. They were the first two countries to develop nuclear weapons. The first two countries to reach the moon. The first two countries to aim nuclear missiles at each other. They both rallied their populations to hate each other for nearly a century. They needed each other. One without the other would shrivel and die.

So why meddle in their election?

Maybe it was the Exxon deal to help Russia develop $4 trillion worth of oil reserves in the Arctic. Enough to double Russia's Gross Domestic Product. That agreement went on hold when Russia invaded the Ukraine and occupied the Crimea. US sanctions stopped the deal, and neither Exxon nor Russia were making money. Is that what the Kremlin wanted, the end of sanctions? Hunter put them in place so they wouldn't be excited about her campaign. The Democrat never got a word in during the debates. Which left Roche. A man who obviously knew nothing about foreign trade, sanctions, or America's role in world politics. What good would he do them?

He shook the thoughts from his head. It didn't matter. What mattered was Strangelove's mission. Like it or not, understand it or not, he had to form a plan and execute his orders.

And then he needed to rid himself of Russia. Carefully. Just as he had explained to Roman in Switzerland. He'd begun by moving a few of Alexi's accounts to new holding companies and banks. He'd researched locations and made a priority list. After manipulating a few more things, he would execute his plan right under Strangelove's nose. A month, two at most. And then he would be free. Free of generals who stab their men. Free of nations who murder innocent Americans. Free to make money hacking those Americans.

He leaned back in his chair, his foot on the edge of his desk. When he needed to think, he needed music. He pushed his earbuds in and clicked on Thelonious Monk playing the energetic and optimistic *Straight, No Chaser*. What he liked about his job was the creativity allowed in executing Strangelove's plan. It was just like jazz: improvise and riff off each other. That's how he would do this one. He snapped his fingers.

Vasili rolled over to Yuri's multi-screen workstation. Yuri pointed. Vasili read the mission objectives, then leaned back and joined him in thinking.

Yuri pulled his earbuds out. "The first stage is hardly a challenge, really. I say we let each man come up with a different plan and implement them all. We'll reward the first man to get his story on front-page sites. A contest with a prize."

"They would like that." Vasili squinted as he thought. "But why do this? What is the point to all these fake news stories?"

"The biggest killer of Americans is other Americans. Over thirty thousand of them will be shot to death this year, as they are every year. The USA is the world-record holder for mass shootings. There have been 132 mass shootings in the US since 1966, five times more than any other country in the world. But it's OK because all but three of those killers were born in America."

Yuri stroked his beard and Vasili scratched his head as they thought for a moment.

"So," Yuri said, "our people are bringing this angle because nothing binds supporters to a candidate like a common enemy. Medevtin made the Chechens the enemy. Everyone rallied around him. He was their hero because he saved them from those nasty Chechen terrorists. To Americans, these Mexicans must be like our Chechens."

"Did they kill hundreds of children like the Chechen rebels?"

"I don't think so." Yuri frowned at him. "It doesn't matter."

"I will get the banda working on it right away." Vasili started to roll back to his desk, then stopped. "But the second stage? We need to find a Latino and talk him into a rampage killing on a specific date? This is not possible."

"You find me a mentally unstable immigrant, I'll handle the rest."

"You're going to America?"

"I know the streets." And he could take Andrine with him, but he didn't need to tell Vasili that part.

"But we have a man there."

"Concentrate on mentally-ill Latinos in New York City." Yuri faced his lieutenant with a long, cold stare.

Vasili lowered his eyes and rolled his chair back an inch. After a moment of sulking, he said, "Why did you go to Zurich?"

Yuri watched the young man. "Why did I take Roman—is that what you really want to know? Because someone needed to watch the banda."

Vasili's looked unconvinced. Yuri patted his shoulder. "I showed you the paperwork. I sent it to Strangelove months ago. He's said nothing."

"I've done everything. I should be captain by now. I should be the one going to Zurich when he needs something. He thinks of me as your accomplice for the keylogger."

There was nothing Yuri could say to that. So he said nothing. He waited for an appropriate amount of silence to pass before changing the subject.

Yuri caught his man's gaze. "What do you think of the group therapy?"

Vasili nodded thoughtfully. "It is good. I feel better after each session. I sleep at night now."

"Yes, but you and I are soldiers." He lowered his voice to a whisper and nodded over his shoulder at the other men. "They are not used to spilling blood. Could we have trouble?"

"What kind of trouble?" Vasili leaned in, concern creasing his brow.

"I don't know. Maybe someone sneaks off in the night and reports us to the Americans or the Norwegians in exchange for immunity. Or maybe someone is overcome by guilt and commits suicide."

"Alexandr never speaks about his feelings." Vasili nodded as he thought. "But no. This is impossible. No Russian would do such a thing."

"What about you, Vasili? You are not worried about the risk we took?"

"If we are caught, then we are caught. On a battlefield or in an office makes no difference, we accept our fate. We die like soldiers."

Yuri took a long look over his shoulder at the others. "Will they?"

"If I hear talk of betrayal, mutiny, or treason, I will tell you right away."

Yuri laughed. "And what if it is me?"

Vasili frowned. "I would tell Strangelove immediately."

Yuri patted the lieutenant's arm. "Just a joke, Vasili. I would never abandon my men."

Wheeling his chair back to his workstation, Vasili gave him a noncommittal nod over his shoulder.

Yuri pursed his lips, regretting saying anything to the humorless lieutenant. He rolled his chair over and slapped Vasili's shoulder. "Focus on the new orders. I want ten stories about Mexicans killing Americans all over Facebook by nightfall and on page one of major newspapers by morning. Extrapolate, sensationalize, make them up if you have to."

"Did you see where they want them planted?"

"What do you mean?"

"They want specific areas targeted for these stories. Specific voting precincts."

Yuri pulled up the targeting database and scrolled through the data. He began to understand Vasili's concern. "This is American voter data."

"The kind their political parties keep. This could only have come from an American—inside a campaign."

"Or we hacked it." Yuri smiled.

"We are the banda that would've hacked a campaign database." Vasili lowered his voice. "This came from an American."

"The Americans listen to phone conversations all over the world. It's against Turkish law for the Americans to record phone conversations in Turkey—yet they do it every day. It's illegal in Germany, Qatar, Japan, in fact, it's illegal in all countries, and still, the Americans do what they please because they're in America." Yuri leaned back. "And now someone gave us their voter rolls. It would be illegal in America—" Yuri laughed "—but we're in Norway."

"You're going to New York." Vasili grabbed his arm and glanced left and right. "If they track you down and interrogate you for this, they might discover #HuntersFail."

"Are you serious?" Yuri clenched his teeth as he pulled out of Vasili's grip. "You're accusing me of cracking under questioning? Never insult me again. You know me. I would eliminate any threat to my men."

He grabbed his jacket and strode out the door. Despite Vasili's insult, Yuri was in a great mood. He would finally have something worthy to offer the beautiful Andrine: a trip to New York, New York. The city so nice they named it twice. She told him she wanted to go there. Now he could take her.

On the street, he strolled up the wharf with his earbuds in, listening to Ned Goold playing *Car Alarm*. Would she even go with him? So far, they'd only flirted. A trip abroad was a big step. He would get separate hotel rooms. She would like that. Her father would like that. Why was he so nervous? He'd had plenty of women. He'd cleaned up with American girls because he knew how to dance. Those foolish, awkward American boys were too stiff. He turned up Kirkegaten and felt like whistling.

Instead, he pulled his earbuds out and heard the footsteps around him on the sidewalk. A glance in a store window, a twisting look at a passing car, and his instincts raised the alarm. He stepped quickly into a narrow alley and waited with his back to the wall.

A sandy-haired man turned the corner, trying to look casual. Yuri slammed him against the opposite wall with his forearm under the man's chin.

"Who are you?" Yuri noticed a vague familiarity about the man. He was smaller, more compact than the average American, yet had that distinctly American confidence.

"Name is Brad." There was no fear in the man's voice. "We met a while back at the coffee shop up the street."

Yuri nodded. Spy handler or gay? he'd asked at the time. "Why follow me?"

"You're an impressive man, Mr. Belenov."

"Major Belenov."

Brad shrugged and gave him an arrogant grin. Yuri resisted the urge to knee the man in the balls.

"Some people see the future—and some live in the past." Brad grabbed Yuri's wrist and elbow and pushed his arm down. "People who grew up with the internet are different from the older generation."

Yuri stepped back and folded his arms. He stayed silent.

"Some people see the future and notice your work, Yuri. People in high places with vast resources."

"I would be honored by their praises—if they spoke in person."

Brad's arrogant grin disappeared. He lowered his voice. "Strangelove is stuck in the past."

"Who?"

Brad half-grinned to let Yuri know he appreciated the denial of the super-secret alias.

"Is there something you want?" Yuri asked.

"Ask yourself if you trust Strangelove." Brad pulled a phone out of his back pocket and slapped it against Yuri's chest. "When you're ready, call 6-1-1 and ask for me.”

Brad turned without another word and walked out of the alley and down the street.

Yuri took the SIM card out of the phone and stuck both in his pocket. It was a classic spy contact. An ambiguous offer with nothing concrete exchanged. Brad might be a cut-out, someone acting as an intermediary for a foreign power. Or he could be a false-flag, sent by Strangelove to test his loyalty. Covert operations like Yuri’s banda were always tested for weak links.

Yuri touched his wound. Just thinking about Strangelove’s stabbing stopped his heart and his breathing. He filled with hate like a propane burner lighting up. Escape plans danced through his mind. There were many options, but one constant remained: no matter how he separated the banda from Russia, Strangelove must die in the end. It would take time, and it wouldn’t be easy, but it would happen.

Yuri dialed Strangelove. It was his duty to report as long as he was still under the old man’s command.

The general answered.

Yuri explained Brad’s contact.

“You were right to call me.” Strangelove was the master of voice control. Nothing in the old man’s voice indicated whether he’d been the one who sent Brad. “Send me the phone.”

“At once, sir.” Yuri would make an electronic copy of the SIM card first.

“No doubt you’re wondering what is going on.” Strangelove sighed as if explaining to a child. “There are factions within the Kremlin. Not unlike your Americans with their right wing and left wing. I will take care of it. Nothing should keep you from your duties.”

“Of course, sir. We are already working on the Mexican—”

“Have you heard of a man named Jacob Stearne?” Strangelove asked.

“Not that I recall, sir.”

“He’s the one who shot Viktor Popov. He thinks this is some kind of game. Use your hackers to track him down. Interrogate him. Kill him. Do this now. Not an hour from now. Right now. He works for Sabel

Security. Last seen in Barcelona. Traveling with a woman and another man. Don't take him lightly. He's a highly-decorated veteran of the US Army Rangers."

Strangelove killed the call.

CHAPTER 21

"WE HAVE A COMMON ENEMY." Olivier leaned back and stretched an arm across the couch.

For the first time in her life, Pia was talking to someone who lived her experience. She had been wrong about his children. They had survived the same horror as she, possibly at the same age. His firm gaze gave way to a small nod. They understood each other in the unspoken language of survivors.

"Why did Popov kill her?"

"When the Soviet Union collapsed, the incompetent Yeltsin took over. His grand plans could not defeat the worst of human nature. Russia teetered on the brink of becoming the failed state run by the gangs of oligarchs. Medevtin used the legal system to strip them of their wealth. Now there is a balance in the Russian economy. Because they are the nuclear power, we can all sleep more soundly."

"Only the living can sleep soundly." Pia looked at her father. He shrugged.

Tania stood by the picture window. "Hey, where'd y-y-your kids go?"

"The farm is big." Olivier motioned to a chair.

Tania shook her head. Tania purposely caught Pia's gaze and gave her a nod, a silent message of concern.

"The oligarchs realized Medevtin could turn on them without notice." Olivier tilted the wine bottle toward Pia. She nodded. He refreshed her glass. "They became avid investors in offshore businesses—money laundering on an industrial scale. They arranged financing for my company in Luxembourg, Cyprus, and Panama. The debt was consolidated to a company called Santalum. They audit all the day and night. They send the questionable people. Their oversight was too much. So, I took Alan's advice to refinance. I thought I was free of them. They sent Strangelove."

"I warned him about Strangelove and sent our agents to help." Alan reached for the bottle and refilled his glass. "Our people kidnapped the Russian, explained our position that the Jallet family was off limits, and gave him a nasty scar in case he forgot. Our mistake was thinking that was the end of it."

"Your people went home," Olivier said. "Strangelove waited the year. I hired the small security team. Strangelove came back. They kidnapped us and took us places. A cold beach far away. He forced me into compromising situations. They took pictures. Kompromat." Olivier shivered. "When Strangelove finished, Viktor Popov appeared."

He left the name in the air while they each retreated into their thoughts about facing the horror that Viktor Popov unleashed on him.

"Do you have the documents?" Alan asked.

"In a moment." Olivier held up a hand and smiled. "Let's finish Pia's questions first."

"What the hell kind of n-n-name is Strangelove?" Tania asked as she crossed the room and looked into the kitchen. "Is he a m-molester or something?"

"It's from an old movie," Dad said. "A Cold War satire about nuclear war. If we dropped a nuke on Russia, they had a doomsday device that would light their entire arsenal and destroy the world. Mutually assured destruction. Ironically, within a year of the movie, that premise became the de facto strategy of the Cold War."

"He keeps kompromat on people as a doomsday device?" Pia asked. "If you come after me, I'll destroy you."

Olivier nodded.

She had no desire to know what Strangelove did to Olivier. He wasn't offering any clues, and if the punctuation was the murder of his wife Bridgette, it must have been horrific.

"Where does Strangelove fit in?" Pia asked. "I thought you said Popov did it."

"They are two arms of the same body. Strangelove's GRU is the left arm. Popov's SVR is the right. The GRU is military. The SVR sends the spy who kills in the night. These two have worked together for decades. This is how they survive the transition from the Union of the Soviets to the *Federation Russe*."

"Strangelove abducted you; Popov slit her throat."

Olivier nodded.

Pia said, "Your children survived the ordeal."

"Unlike Alan, I did not have the resources to start my own security firm. In such situations, our top priority is to protect our children." Olivier nodded at Alan. "I sold the company."

Pots banged in the kitchen as if a stack had been dropped. The three of them flinched.

"What do they have on Roche?" Pia asked. She craned over the seat but couldn't see through the doorway. She reached for her purse to keep her pistol close.

Olivier tossed up his hands. "No idea."

"I'm going to take them down." Pia stood. "They'll never be a threat to you again."

Another strange noise came from the kitchen. Pia drew her weapon and turned.

"It took long years for the wounds to heal for my children and me." Olivier's voice was strangely calm. "But I've just made the deal that should keep Popov away forever."

"Like Dad?" Pia rose and, aiming her weapon toward the kitchen, tiptoed around the couch.

Two men in balaclavas pushed Camille into the living room. One held a gun to her head, the other aimed at Pia.

Pia's muzzle flicked from one to the other.

"You son of a bitch," Alan hissed.

"Hand me the pistols." Olivier reached out a hand.

A shadow flitted behind the gunmen.

"OK," Pia said, "everyone stay calm."

Pia raised her pistol and turned slowly toward Olivier. "I'm handing it over in three, two."

After announcing the countdown, the assassins relaxed an

infinitesimal but crucial amount. Before she said *one*, Tania darted the first gunman from behind. Pia darted Olivier. A split-second later, Tania nailed the second man. Pia darted Camille as a precaution.

"I'm taking h-h-high ground, cover me." Tania grabbed a rifle off one of the thugs and was out the door in a dead run.

Pia took a pair of binoculars from Olivier's bookshelf and stuffed them into her shocked father's hands. "Be Tania's spotter. GO. NOW."

When the reality struck him, he ran outside, following Tania up the slope toward a shed above the farm buildings. Bullets raked their footsteps and splintered bark off the trees nearby.

Pia dropped her magazine of darts and loaded regular bullets. Outside, she rounded the corner, squatting low, and found a man in body armor aiming at Tania. She fired. He dove, rolled, and returned fire. He aimed high, expecting her to be standing. She fired three more rounds. He dropped.

There was silence.

Another gunman, also wearing body armor, stepped around the edge of the barn and aimed. Pia could see his eyes at the end of his barrel. She dove left. He fired. A chip of grass and dirt flew up near her toes.

Pia rolled behind a retaining wall and scrambled five yards to the left. Jumping to her feet, she saw the barn-man running toward her. He swung his rifle up to shoot her before she had her pistol leveled. For a second, she saw the inside of the barrel. She expected to see the bullet emerge from the dark depths of its interior. Instead, the rifle and the man holding it fell sideways with a shout of pain.

"Only got his armor," Tania said over their comm link. "The first guy is crabbing around behind Jallet's Land Rover. Can't tell if you wounded him. He's going for the side entrance. There's another guy—"

A burst of automatic gunfire crackled across the pastoral valley. The bricks in front of Pia sent up shards and dust. Looking around, she could find no solid cover. She scrambled back to the house and ran into the foyer.

She stood in a dark space. Everything in front of her was silhouetted against the living room's picture window. To her right were the dining room and kitchen, a parlor to her left and a hallway connecting the living and dining areas. Like many ancient homes, this one had been remodeled many times by many generations and was now a rabbit warren of rooms and halls.

A man's silhouette stepped into view in the living room. Pia fired and rolled and popped up to fire again. Her adversary fired three times. Splinters of wood exploded from a cabinet near her face. She ran right, jumped over chairs, slid across the dining room table, and fired into the foyer. Blood oozed from his unarmored shoulder. He drew back and shouted a curse in Russian.

Pia followed the sound of the wounded man's footsteps creaking down the farmhouse hallway. She kicked off her shoes and tiptoed to the pantry. She reached around the door frame and fired blindly into the hall. She heard a groan, and a body hit the floor.

In her last training session at the operations center, the instructor spent three hours on how things sound when they drop to the ground. The sound of an unconscious body falling was very different from someone going to ground intentionally. Without a brain to control it, a body would collapse in a heap, making single percussive note. A conscious body would fall with two or more notes as the person braced his fall with a knee or a butt or an elbow.

Pia had just heard a triple percussive thud: butt, elbow, back. Her prey was faking it.

She spun in place and fired through the plaster walls.

She heard her enemy scramble out of the hall into a different room.

Pia's biggest concern was the children's safety. If Strangelove showed up, Olivier and his children would pay a heavy price for failing. As pissed as she was at the traitorous Frenchman, she understood his last statement: he was protecting his family. Which left her no choice. She had to subdue these thugs and get the Jallets to safety.

Outside, Tania's rifle cracked the silence. On the comm link, she said, "I nailed a guy outside, but there's another coming in the back door."

Pia moved toward the kitchen but stopped in the middle of the large pantry.

An eerie silence made Pia keenly aware of the wooden floors squeaking beneath her step. The guy could find her the same way she had found him. She stopped and listened. Silence strained her ears. Her heartbeat became the loudest noise in the room.

Then she heard it. A floorboard creaked on the other side of the archway leading to the kitchen. She looked around the room. Flour, canned soups, boxes of staples lined the shelves. Fresh spices and vegetables hung in baskets from the ceiling. A wine cooler at the end of the room gave her the advantage she needed. Its glass front reflected the soldier. He was looking the other way.

Tania's voice whispered in her earbud. "You h-h-have two guys in the building. I'm coming in the f-f-front door. Don't sh-sh-shoot me."

Before she could talk herself out of it, Pia bolted four steps, slamming her body into the pantry wall, and fired three shots into the kitchen.

The soldier had stepped out of range. Luck or instinct, it didn't matter; her shots missed. They were now an arm's length from each other, separated by plaster.

Pia remembered a trick Jacob taught her: when ammo's cheap, take cheap shots. She pushed her pistol around the corner and fired three shots blind. Nothing. No exclamation of pain. No thud of collapse. Only the tinkling of broken glass.

Pia was up against a professional who anticipated her moves.

"I'm i-in," Tania whispered. "Where are y-y-you?"

Pia could hear the man breathing on the other side of the wall.

He jumped forward, into the space directly in front of her, his rifle inches from her face. Instinctively, she dropped to a crouch, leaving his muzzle over her head. She exploded upward, her shoulder shoving his rifle toward the ceiling as it unleashed a three-round burst. The heel of her hand extended her momentum into his lower jaw. His head bounced off an oak cabinet.

Any other man would've had a mild concussion. This man pushed her to the floor with his rifle stock and raised it to pound down on her head.

Pia rolled and kicked. All those years working out for soccer paid off. Her powerful leg hammered his knee, bending it backward. His rifle butt slammed into the floor next to her shoulder. He raised it back up to his shoulder. She kicked again but missed, her foot slamming the wall.

She rolled away and brought her pistol up a split-second ahead of him. She fired her last round. It bounced off his body armor. The stun effect gave her a second to jump up. She drove off her back foot, twisting her core, and unleashed a powerful elbow to the side of his head. He crumpled behind the kitchen's work island.

She felt her pack for ammo and found only the dart magazine. She slammed it in and aimed.

Two rounds splintered the wood next to her, fired by the last man. She dropped, crawled around the island, grabbed the Russian's rifle as he twitched in concussed agony, and aimed.

Her last adversary had ducked out of sight.

She rose slowly to look over the work island. Bullets buzzed her ear. She dropped back.

"Stay d-d-down," Tania's voice on the comm link. "Make a n-n-noise, keep his focus."

The last man's footsteps creaked the floorboards on her right side as he approached. Pia darted the concussed Russian next to her and readied her pistol for her approaching enemy.

Instead of appearing where she expected, his rifle reached over the top and brushed her head. With her back to it, there was nothing she could do. She jumped forward to get out of the way. A three-round burst blistered her ears.

She stood, aiming at the figure stretched across the granite counter and wondered why she hadn't felt any bullets hit her back.

Tania stepped in from the hall, her muzzle still smoking. "You g-g-good, sister?"

Pia wrapped her friend in a big hug. "Good. You?"

Tania didn't answer. She pulled an earpiece out of the dead Russian's ear and listened to voices for a second. Her face drained. She pushed Pia out of the room. "Russians a-a-are like ants: you f-f-find one, you're gonna find a whole b-b-bunch more real quick."

"What do you mean?"

"They have b-b-backup coming. We gotta get o-o-out of here now. N-N-NOW."

"We have to take the Jalllets with us."

"What?" Tania screeched. "Are y-y-you insane?"

CHAPTER 22

I WAS ABOUT TO OPEN a celebratory bottle of Marqués de Murrieta '93 from the suite's glass-enclosed wine wall when the text from Ms. Sabel came in. We were to meet her in Lyon as soon as we could get there. I glanced at the giant feather bed with down pillows and weighed sleeping on them against flying an hour away to meet the boss.

It would be a terrible loss, but she would have to get along without me.

Mercury said, *Dude, I am two votes away from sparing your life, and you're thinking of ghosting on a Caesar? She's the only reason you still breathe.*

I said, *You mean you don't keep me alive because you care?*

Mercury tossed up his hands. *Dawg, we care about you as much as we care about the cockroach that just fell off your balcony. I'm the god of commerce. The Sabels are commerce. You're ... well. Not. Looky here now. You promised to build a shrine and show it to Pia-Caesar-Sabel and Alan-Caesar-Sabel. So none of this slacker bullshit's gonna fly. Feel me?*

I said, *Wait—the twelve of you vote on my life? Do I get a chance to speak on my own behalf?*

You? Speak to the Dii Concentes? Wreck your chances for sure, bro. I got this. I'm on your side. Trust me.

I closed my eyes in disbelief.

When I opened them again, Emily and Miguel stood in front of me with duffels slung over their shoulders. One of Miguel's bags clanked as the barrels of assault rifles banged into each other. He unzipped the bag and stuffed a pillow off my bed between the weapons. With a frustrated sigh, I grabbed my duffel, shoved a couple bottles of wine into it, and headed for the front desk.

Miguel went to the valet, leaving me to check out, which should've been my first clue. The second clue was the look on the manager's face when he thanked me profusely—too profusely—and quadruple-checked that we were happy with our stay.

Then I looked at the bill.

Miguel had checked in under my name and my company credit card. The one-night stay exceeded fifteen thousand euros.

"Are you OK, señor?" the manager asked when my ragged gasps subsided.

"Did this suite come with a selection of sex partners I was supposed to choose from?"

"Señor, my apologies. We thought you brought your own." He nodded at Miguel and Emily, who were climbing into our car out front.

I glanced over the line items. They included the wine I thought I was stealing, Miguel's pillow, and *disposal services* of four grand.

Couldn't argue with that last one. The W's staff were the consummate Russian-disposers.

I felt a presence and looked into the shiny marble wall behind the manager. The vague reflection of a woman doing the supermodel-catwalk approached from behind. Each foot went down directly in front of the other as if she were on a tightrope. Her hips swiveled with each step in a rhythm that had me hypnotized in three steps.

Mercury tapped my shoulder. *You ain't falling for Sylvia again, homie. We're not going there.*

I heard my voice sounding distant and drugged. *Again?*

She killed you in the last life. And you killed her in the life before that. And before that she killed you. I think. I lose track. Anyway, that's why I had it set up for you and Miguel to shoot her when she got out of the limo. Just cut to the chase and spare us both the agonizing drama.

Again, distant and slow: *I met her in a past life?*

Sylvia, still dressed in red, walked right to me and hooked a finger through a hole in my t-shirt. She read it in a glance: *RELAX—A Ranger has arrived.* She looked up at me and slowly licked her lips. "You're leaving town without me?"

"Gotta meet … um."

"You asked me if I needed a ride." Her pale blue eyes softened. "Well … I do."

"I'm going to Lyon." I crossed my arms and leaned back against the lobby desk, trying to act casual. "Ever been to France?"

"I was born in Bordeaux."

"That sounds French." Behind me, I sensed the manager stepping away to give us some privacy.

"I need to be in Monaco, but it seems my ride had … expectations." A worried look crossed her face. "Could you drop me in Avignon on your way?"

French geography was never my strong suit. But the prospect of spending a couple hours with her had me dreaming up ways I could get Sylvia to her destination and still meet Ms. Sabel on time without losing my job. A smart man would just say no.

"I have a jet waiting." I paused for dramatic effect. Call me what you will, but I don't have a problem appropriating company resources to impress a lady. "Dropping you would require a parachute."

She looked more disappointed than impressed. Not the desired effect.

I asked, "What's such a big deal in Monaco?"

"A fund-raiser." She dropped the sex-kitten act and glanced away. "They're counting on me."

There was a hint of despair in her voice.

I tried to lighten the mood. "Good cause or criminal defense fund?"

She touched my arm as if to push me away, her eyes widened with worry and bounced from my right to left eye and back, searching for the serious side of Jacob. "Charity. We work with *Aide Sociale à l'Enfance*."

French rolled off her tongue like butter off a hot pancake. "The what?"

"Sorry." She reverted to English without a hint of accent. "ASE, the French social service that helps children in crisis. The forgotten, abandoned, and abused."

Something caught in the back of her throat. She looked away with a sniffle.

Working with Ms. Sabel made me aware that many people get involved in charities close to their world experience. In the back of Ms. Sabel's mind, she never forgot how close she'd come to being a homeless waif bouncing from one foster family to another. I'd served with plenty of soldiers who spent every spare hour helping veterans reintegrate into the utterly foreign landscape back home. Others had come so close to losing a limb they dedicated themselves to those who had. There was a personal connection to her charity she didn't want to explain.

"Follow me." I picked up my bag and marched for the car without looking back.

She took a couple seconds to think. Then her heels clicked across the marble behind me. "But, can you help me? It's really important to me. I have to be in Monaco—"

"We're going to Lyon." I held the car door open. "Trust me; you want to come with me."

She looked at me. She looked at the cramped space behind Emily's driver's seat. She looked back at me with no-thanks forming on her lips.

"Get in." I pointed.

"Wait a second." Her eyes flashed. "This isn't some kind of—"

"Don't worry," Emily called out from the driver's seat. "I'll keep him from being a pig."

With friends like Emily, what do I need with the Taliban? I shot her a nasty glance. Emily shrugged.

Sylvia reluctantly crawled in. I snuggled in beside her and kept deflecting her questions about how going to a city farther from Monaco than Barcelona was going to help. She stopped talking when Emily pulled through the executive terminal gate. Our headlights lit up the white jet with blue lettering across the fuselage. Sylvia's eyes popped. The ground crew swept the car away.

Four hundred miles later, while Emily and Miguel napped, Sylvia and I wrapped up a lengthy and comprehensive discussion about music. We disagreed about Billie Holliday's legacy. We agreed Rachael Price is the sexiest voice alive. And that a Trombone Shorty concert was not to be missed. We landed in Lyon. The pilots parked next to Sabel One. Ms.

Sabel's bigger, fancier jet.

The boss texted me to meet her between the jets, alone.

As I descended the airstair into a dark abyss. My heart raced with the certainty that I was about to lose my job for having breached a thousand protocols.

"You're fired." Her first words as we stood face-to-face. "Causing an international incident in Barcelona is against company policy. Feel better?"

Mercury said, *The vote is swinging against you right now, mo-fo. Watch for falling meteors.*

I looked into the night sky. "Not really."

"Well, at least you've been punished. You're rehired. Now explain why the accounting department wants you gone."

"Ah, that." I took a deep breath and cursed my best friend, who thought Ms. Sabel would let me spend anything without question just because I saved her life a few times. "They disposed of the Russians for us. There were fees involved."

"Seems reasonable." She nodded. "What did Watson say about the Russians?"

"Uh, he was one of the guys I had disposed."

"You're fired."

Holy mother of Ceres, homie. Mercury paced behind her. *You're toast right now. The vote's six to five against. They're thinking the meteor will take too long. You have five minutes to say your prayers while we arrange for a thunderstorm with a lightning bolt.*

I said, *Wait. That's only eleven votes.*

They're making me abstain. But I was going for the lightning bolt anyway, so ... whatever.

I pleaded my case to Ms. Sabel. "I had to sacrifice Watson to get information out of the Russian. He wasn't going to talk unless he had someone to blame it on."

She rolled her eyes and made a call. Three minutes later the American ambassador to Spain promised to extricate Watson from the Russian consulate in Barcelona—if he was still alive—and send him home. She clicked off. "Since we know he's the one charged with killing me, I'd like to know where he is. All the time.”

“Right. Sorry.”

“I should re-fire you for the incident with Popov. The company is taking all kinds of heat for your kidnapping idea. The FBI sent my lawyers a subpoena. There’s a Congressional investigation starting up.”

“He took my dog.”

“Yeah.” She looked at me, tilted her head, and let a long silence pass. “Understandable.”

“Thanks.” I couldn’t tell if it was sarcasm. “I guess.”

We looked at each other. Those gray-green eyes looked through me as if she was reading the serial number the Creator left on the inside of my skull.

I looked away. “Watson’s worse than an assassin. He’s a courier.”

She reeled back like she’d seen a discarded god. “That’s why we can’t find a paper trail. We have evidence, but it never points to Chuck Roche. He never put anything in writing or email or even a text. Everything is verbal.”

“Watson is his sacrificial messenger.” I faced her again. Her laser-gaze waited for me. “The man would die before he’d give up Roche. But we still don’t know if there’s any connection. Is Roche doing what the Russians tell him, or is he that naïve?”

She relaxed just a bit. “Dad thinks he’s in league with them. I’m not so sure.”

“Why not trust Alan’s opinion?”

“Roche promised to raise import tariffs twenty-five percent. That won’t benefit the Russians or anyone else.”

“Wouldn’t that cause instant, sky-rocketing inflation?” As I spoke, her point about his lack of basic economic knowledge became clear. “It would—but he’s not planning to do it, it just sounds great in a campaign.”

She nodded.

“Bianca’s tracking the chip from Zurich,” she said. “It went to a Danish island. Bring it back and discover what you can about the facility. Dad thinks it might be Strangelove’s compound. The *Asteria* is in the Baltic, but it’s too far away to get there tonight.” She referred to her massive yacht that we'd pressed into service on a few occasions. "You'll have to rent a boat."

"Why are we doing this?" I asked.

Mercury leaned over her shoulder. *Don't be asking about her motivations, bro. She's a complex creature, not just some single-minded automaton. You know she has a hundred reasons. She's doing it to save her country. She's doing it because someone needs to step up. She's doing it to save the millions of people who—*

"Dad." She looked happy for a second. "He's on this mission to stop Roche. I'm helping him. It's the first time we've worked together."

Mercury said, *And because she's Daddy's girl. But let's get out of here before she goes all philosophical on us. I had enough of that shit from Cicero. Man, that guy could talk in circles.*

She scowled. "But I'm more worried about your friend Popov than Roche. Anyway, the next step is tracking down Strangelove. Follow that tracker."

Normally, I would accept my orders, salute, and get moving. Instead, I stood there and checked out the pavement.

She brought up those piercing gray-green eyes again.

I fidgeted.

Nothing in life is as painful as coming clean about abusing company resources to impress a woman.

"What is it?" She tilted her head. "Oh, you have Emily with you. Right, she can ride with us. She can post Olivier's story."

"Uh, yeah. OK."

She kept staring. "What else?"

"I met a lady who asked for a ride and … um."

"You met someone? Is she nice?"

"There are differing opinions." I shot a glance at Mercury, who always wore his formal toga when he was in the presence of Ms. Sabel.

"A ride." She tilted her head, her eyebrows rose quickly. "She's on the jet?"

I nodded.

"Have her join me. Bring her luggage."

"She doesn't have any."

Ms. Sabel stared at me for far too long. "I can't wait to hear her side of the story."

"She volunteers with foster kids. She wanted a ride to Monaco to work a fund-raiser."

"And you thought I might donate to her cause?" She smiled and squeezed my arm. "You like her?"

I felt like a little boy trying hard to hide the truth while knowing my face had betrayed my feelings. I looked up.

"Send her over, I'll figure out how we can help her." Ms. Sabel walked back to her jet.

She called over her shoulder. "By the way, the Lyon office is fully deployed, so there's no one to spare. You and Miguel have to go it alone."

She climbed the airstair and stopped at the top. "How are things with Mercury?"

"Strained." I shrugged. "I might have to go back on my meds."

"I'm not a believer in chemical solutions." She nodded with an understanding look. "They always make me feel like a mud-brain. But do whatever you think best. Tell him I said hey."

With that, she disappeared into the fuselage.

I turned around to find Mercury jumping up and down, dancing with irrational exuberance, and generally acting like a circus clown. *Dude! Who's the MAN? Did I tell you she loves me? Oh, boy! We are IN, baby! That temple is on the HO-rize-ON. Can you see it?*

She was humoring me. I started for Sabel Three's airstair. *There isn't going to be any temple.*

Mercury said, *Oh really? Is that how you're going to be? That lightning bolt is five miles out, bro. Is that the answer you want me to give the other gods?*

I climbed up and faced three expectant faces. "Ladies, Ms. Sabel has requested your presence."

Emily beamed and grabbed her things. "Thank god. I hate riding in the little jet."

"Who?" Sylvia looked perplexed.

"My boss. She has deep pockets, and she's a big fan of foster care programs."

Sylvia brightened and gave me a big hug.

"C'mon, I'll introduce you." Emily tugged Sylvia's hand. They flowed down the steps and into the night.

When it was too late, I realized I'd never gotten her phone number. Maybe I would find her again someday. Maybe not. Maybe she would remember the guy who set her up with a billionaire philanthropist. Maybe not. I took a deep breath.

The pilot stepped out of the cabin. "Sir, there's an unexpected thunderstorm moving in. We should wait an hour before taking off."

"Let's go now and get in front of it." I gave Mercury a nasty glare. He shrugged.

"As you wish, but it could be bumpy." The pilot hurried back to the cockpit and roared onto the runway.

MIGUEL MAPPED OUT THE MISSION while I took a nap on the two-hour flight to Malmö, Sweden.

From there, we drove an hour to Ystad and rented a forty-foot cruiser with a Zodiac we could use as a landing craft. We set off across the Baltic a few hours before dawn. My interrupted nap resumed while Miguel piloted our ship across the rough, open seas and around the island of Bornholm.

It was dark, cold, and rainy when he woke me up. We slipped our augmented-reality visors on, giving us night vision with thermal highlights. We slipped ashore half a mile from the target, a lighthouse south of Svaneke on Bornholm, Denmark. Clouds kept the full moon muted. We made our way along a track between autumn trees whose foliage was clinging on to the bitter end.

We separated near the lighthouse. It was a red-brick place with a stone tower. The house had been modernized with a glass wall on one side. From our angle, it appeared unoccupied.

"Don't like it," Miguel said over our comm link. "Too quiet."

"They aren't expecting us." I backed up to cover our six from a wider angle.

"I mean too quiet a town." He moved back to a tree line. "Whoever cleaned out Alan Sabel's safe deposit box brought the stuff to a vacation rental?"

"You're right. It smells like a trap," I said.

"Exactly." Miguel ran to the walled yard around the house. "I'm going in."

CHAPTER 23

Yuri cursed Strangelove for ruining his plan to surprise Andrine. Unfortunately, his options were limited. Something he would soon remedy. The opportunity to take the young beauty to the Big Apple would be delayed. He could wait a little longer.

When he got back in the office, he caught Roman's eye and nodded toward the break room. Roman understood his idea and went straight there.

Yuri felt Vasili's cold eyes watching him as he made his way through the sprawling main room.

"Make some tea," he told Roman.

The younger man gave him a quizzical glance, then poured water into a kettle.

Yuri leaned his butt against the counter and folded his arms. He spoke in a low, conspiratorial voice. "What do you know about Brad?"

Roman stared at the wall in front of him. "Nothing. Only that whoever sends us the databases has coded messages from him in it."

"What do they say?"

"To keep an open mind and wait for contact."

Yuri took a deep breath and thought. "What do you think, FSB? CIA maybe? Strangelove?"

"At first, I thought, freedom. But after we talked, I see what you mean. Now, I'm worried. The data has been handled by ten people before it reaches us."

Yuri put a tea bag in a cup and passed it to Roman. "Have you made progress on your list?"

Roman looked up quickly and pursed his lips. "List?"

"Enemies, allies." Yuri dropped to a whisper. "To whom do you trust your life?"

Roman relaxed and almost laughed. "Then you are with us. You are thinking we need to break—"

"Thinking can get you killed." Yuri's anger hissed through his words. "You have tested your list, yes or no?"

Roman frowned and glanced behind him. "Yes. Everyone in the banda except one is ready. We all kept passports from our old days. We all have a small fund stashed away."

"You've been hacking Americans for cash on the side?"

Roman shrugged. "It is our nature."

Yuri weighed the likelihood that Strangelove knew about their extracurricular activities. There was a chance the old man let them think they were accumulating money but monitored their accounts as a method of leverage. And that made him consider his personal stash, Alexi's account with several million in it. He'd moved it three times. Opened and closed companies in Luxemburg that bought each other. The trail was long and complex. He'd relied on all the techniques used by the oligarchs. He was safe. Maybe.

"Who is not with us?" Yuri asked.

"Vasili."

Which confirmed what he'd learned from his conversation with the lieutenant.

He reached in his pocket for Brad's phone. "Make a copy of this SIM card, then send it and the phone to Strangelove. I want all the call logs, activation information, everything and anything."

"I heard my name." Vasili stood an arm's length from them.

Yuri's heart nearly stopped. "I asked him if you could hack a SIM card, but he offered to do it for you."

Vasili's gaze darted back and forth between them. All three of them knew Vasili couldn't hack a SIM card.

Roman poured the tea, then scooped up the phone. "I'll get right on it."

For several seconds after he left, Yuri and Vasili stared at each other. Yuri sipped his tea without breaking eye contact.

He set the cup on the counter. "What is it, Vasili? You are troubled. Speak."

The lieutenant looked left and right and over his shoulder. "The men are talking about abandoning their posts. I've heard them. They talk about becoming stateless citizens. Desertion. Insubordination."

"They are always talking about fantasies and conspiracies." Yuri waved his arms, keeping his voice light. "The oligarchs do this, and the Kremlin does that. Nationless hackers. International banks. I can't keep up."

"We must report this development to Strangelove."

Yuri leaned back and scowled. "You have emails? Recordings? Evidence?" When Vasili shook his head, he continued. "You want to ruin your career over their hallway fantasies? We're getting noticed, my friend. Strangelove said people in Moscow are paying attention to our methods. Don't derail our success just because the workload has grown."

"You're right." He bit his knuckle as he thought. "I'll monitor their calls, their emails, the sites they visit. They could be moving cash—"

Yuri grabbed the man's shoulders. "Vasili, you know what Strangelove will do to them? He'll kill their youngest child, their sister, mother. He will stop at nothing to make us fear him."

Vasili glanced at the thick bandage beneath Yuri's shirt. His face drained.

"Leave them alone for now. I'll do some checking." He let go of the lieutenant. "Say, have you finished your assignments? Have you tracked Sabel or the other guy, Stearne? Have you found an insane Mexican in New York City?"

Vasili straightened up, saluted smartly, and went back to work.

Yuri had his own research to do. He returned to his desk and checked the records his team had hacked from the US Government years earlier. They were old, but they held the one he needed.

Jacob Stearne was a decorated veteran who'd switched battalions several times to get more tours in war zones. He loved danger. The Americans placed no limit on battle deployments. The record number of tours was fourteen by a Ranger, a contemporary of Stearne's, who died in Afghanistan.

Yuri searched his files for a Pentagon study conducted in 2010 called *Red Book*. It concluded that soldiers who had three or more tours were "a growing high-risk population of soldiers engaging in criminal and high-risk behavior with increasingly more severe outcomes, including violent crime." Stearne had eight tours and had seen action on multiple missions each tour.

Yuri smiled. Strangelove was right: this was not a man to be taken lightly. A highly skilled killer who was going off the rails. This assignment was so much better than some billionaire hiding behind a wall of bodyguards. This challenge was the bodyguard himself. It would keep him occupied while he made arrangements to get free of Strangelove.

Roman texted Yuri with the information from the SIM card. He found the billing information and nothing else. There were no calls made on the phone. It was made in China but sold in Italy.

Yuri's desk phone rang. The caller ID was his own phone number. An easy trick for a hacker. He clicked on without saying anything and listened.

"You never called me." Brad's voice. "Don't tell me you trust Strangelove. You're not a stupid man."

"You're not high on my priority list. Our research shows your phone is paid for by a company in Cyprus called Santalum, but they don't have any employees."

"They told me you were smart. They must not know you're slow." Brad clicked off.

Yuri stared at his phone for a long time before getting online and researching Santalum's public records. Brad's insult stung. Yuri was not slow. He had more important things to do than tracking spy handlers.

With a minimal search, he found lists of Santalum's board members going back ten years in the Panama Papers. The Panama Papers was a trove of eleven million documents leaked by a disgruntled employee from a Panamanian law firm. It detailed shell corporations used by billionaires the world over for fraud, tax evasion, and dodging international sanctions.

Santalum's current board read like a who's who of Russian

billionaires, the lead director being Mikhail Yeschenko, the slippery youngish billionaire and deal maker. But the board was all new, having served for a little over a year. The previous board had been unchanged for over a decade. Then Yuri saw the previous lead director and nearly choked.

Viktor Popov.

That sealed it for him. Brad was connected to Popov, which meant he was connected to Strangelove, which meant he could not be trusted.

Yuri and Vasili worked through dinner and into the night. The men went home, leaving them alone.

Yuri dove back into Stearne's heavily redacted records. On his first tour, he had been just another *Matrosov*, an expendable infantryman, until he wiped out a company of Iraqi Republican Guards—singlehanded. Instantly a legend, his heroics exploded to the point of disbelief. One report cited him for saving an American general by killing an Afghan major in the middle of a joint military ceremony. But something was amiss. If the Army thought so highly of Stearne, why were his psychological evaluations redacted? Why did he have a slew of assessments after saving the general? Why did he leave the service to attend a culinary school? Even more puzzling, why did he graduate as a respected chef only to join Sabel Security the next day?

Yuri knew a thing or two about soldiers. When he thought about it, he didn't need the evaluations to piece it together. Stearne had cracked on his last deployment. Stress crushed the hero. The man came home shattered and tried to rebuild his life. He was probably struggling with his sanity on a daily basis. It was merely a matter of time before he went on a rampage. Stearne was the most dangerous of adversaries, a man so hooked on danger that his addiction transcended his survival instinct. He could explode at any moment and destroy any perceived threat… real or imagined.

"Something happened in France," Vasili's voice woke him from his thoughts. "There was an attack on Alan Sabel. Several Russian soldiers were shot or drugged."

"That can't be right." Yuri rolled his chair to Vasili's workstation and leaned over his shoulder. "We haven't deployed our men yet. We haven't even finished our intel—"

The two men looked at each other. Without a word, they understood the implication. Strangelove had put them in competition with another banda. The general had given them three weeks to complete the task and challenged someone else to do it in less. Had the other banda succeeded, Yuri's failure could have ended his career. It was only by luck that the other banda had failed.

"Should we put the Mexican project on hold?" Vasili asked.

Yuri's eyes never stopped scanning the report. "Nothing stops. Strangelove will not allow it. He's given us three tasks. I'm sure more are on the way. Any failure will not be accepted."

"He's setting us up to fail." Vasili's voice cracked. "He's looking for an excuse to have us executed."

"Calm down."

"I told you the keylogger was a bad—"

"There is no time for blame." Yuri's voice echoed in the empty office.

Vasili stood. "You don't care. You don't have any children."

Yuri rose to face him. "And neither will you if we don't focus on the problem."

"The problem is you. You never take responsibility. I have a wife and family. They are my responsibility."

"I understand." Yuri put his hand on Vasili's shoulder and pushed him back in his chair. "But we have to execute our missions."

Vasili looked up with fear and anger.

"If someone figured out where Sabel was going, so can we. What did we miss?" Yuri patted his junior officer. "He only travels on his jet."

"Private jets change flight paths all the time." Vasili shook his head. "They must have deployed the men there in advance."

"How did they know Alan Sabel was heading for this man's house in France? And who is he?"

Vasili drummed his fingers on the desk. "What if they tracked the tail number, the same way you can track a commercial flight?"

Yuri took his seat next to Vasili. "Pull them up. Where are they?"

Vasili tapped and checked and tapped some more.

Yuri rolled over to his workstation and checked his own sources. They stayed silent for a long time, clicking away in their searches.

"I found them." Vasili nearly jumped out of his chair and cast a glance at Yuri. "They landed in Malmö a few hours ago."

"Malmö?" Yuri looked up the map. "Are there Sabel offices?"

"Only Stockholm, Copenhagen, Helsinki, and Oslo."

"It couldn't be…" Yuri measured the distances and looked at the clock. "Would they be going to Svaneke?"

Vasili brought up the surveillance cameras on Svaneke. Yuri spun his chair behind the lieutenant. The dark landscape showed nothing. Dark gray on darker gray. Vasili adjusted the contrast and brightness until they could make out shapes. Waves rolled across a rock outcropping in front of the lighthouse tower. Tree leaves blew across an empty yard. The sliding glass door slid open. A ghostly shape darted inside.

"That's not Alan Sabel." Vasili tapped the screen. "But they were flying on Sabel's jet. Then it must be the other one, the favorite guard, Stearne."

"What luck." Yuri slapped Vasili's back. "They took the bait."

CHUCK ROCHE PADDED DOWN THE hall of the Hyatt Regency Pittsburgh in his best suit. He waved off the Secret Service agent following him and knocked on room 1068. No one answered. He knocked again.

The lock clacked, and David Watson's bloodshot eyes peered through a crack in the door.

Roche pushed it open and barged in. "What the hell took you so long? A thousand supporters are lining up for my rally hours before the doors even open. Those are dedicated people, Watson. But you—just look at you."

"Sorry, sir." Watson plopped on the crumpled bed and rubbed his face. "Ambassador Givens drove me to the Barcelona airport and put me on a redeye. Coach."

"Are they on to you?"

"Jacob has his suspicions, but that's all they are. There's no way the Russians talked."

"I don't care about her serfs." Roche stormed to the window, his hands behind his back. "What about Pia?"

"I never saw her. I don't know what she thinks."

"I'll handle her." He faced Watson. "Listen up. Things are moving quickly. There's a damn good chance we can pull this off. My new campaign manager rehabilitated a Third-World dictator and got him reelected. This guy is good."

"What do you need, sir?"

"Alan Sabel is trying to ruin me. He's traveling the world, looking for proof of my ties to Santalum. You need to find some dirt on that guy and make him spend the election defending his reputation instead of attacking mine."

Chuck Roche turned back to the window and opened the curtains. A hundred reporters and crew meandered in the parking lot. He stepped back.

"How do you know what Sabel is doing?" Watson's voice sounded like a wounded animal. "I'm working there, and I have no idea what they're up to."

"Why not?" Roche glanced at Watson. "Haven't you worked your way inside?"

"Why even worry about the Sabels?" Air travel is dehydrating. Watson stared at the last bottle of water on the dresser as if he were thirsty. "I mean, shouldn't you be focused on the campaign?"

Roche grabbed the water bottle and held it between them. When he caught Watson's gaze, he ripped the cap off and took a sip. "Don't tell me how to run my business, boy. You think I'm handing out trophies for participation? My success in business doesn't come from being the fastest guy in the race. It comes from destroying my enemies before they cross the finish line. You kneecap a guy, and everyone else hangs back like horrified little sissies."

"Sorry, boss. I'm jetlagged." Watson eyed the water in Roche's hand.

Roche walked near the window but stopped short of being seen. He craned over his shoulder. "Jetlagged enough to check in with your real name?"

"No sir." Watson's parched lips rubbed against each other like sandpaper as he spoke. "What do you need done?"

"Find some dirt on that guy." Roche took another sip. "If you can't find it, make some."

Watson watched the hypnotic bottle, his tongue clicking in a mouth as dry as a sand dune in the desert. "What do you have in mind? Bribery or drunk driving?"

"Hell no." Roche's anger exploded. "Think big. He adopted a little girl. Why? Why did he build a multibillion-dollar company and just give it to her? Is that why she never filed charges?"

Watson looked confused. "Are there any facts or evidence to support—"

"You don't need any goddamn evidence. You're not in the FBI anymore. All you need to do is ask the question." Roche looked out the window. "If you accuse, you need evidence. If you suggest, all you need are imaginative listeners."

"You're a genius, sir." Watson swallowed hard. Then he stared at the wall. "Where's your cane, sir? You might be seen without it."

"I broke it. Don't worry about who took the blow. It'll be fixed in an hour." Roche's face turned crimson. "Get your mind in the game, damn it. You have work to do. Get one of Sabel's maids to say something you can use. Get moving."

Watson shrank back.

"What's the matter with you?" Roche leaned over, letting half the bottle spill on the floor.

"It's just that..." Watson swallowed again and looked at the remaining water.

"What is it? Speak up, boy."

"She's a tiger, sir. She'll—"

"I love tigers!" Roche spun around with excitement. "Especially in chains."

CHAPTER 24

AN HOUR BEFORE LANDING IN DC, Pia rubbed her tired eyes. Hours of staring at Pozdeeva's clues made her hazy. Then a noise erupted at the back of the jet.

Agent Tania was in Olivier's face.

"Sure." Tania's shrill voice pierced the cabin. "In sci-fi, the traitor who t-t-turned the good guys over to the evil empire is inexplicably redeemed, b-b-but that's not how it goes down in my hood."

Pia took her friend by the shoulders and swapped places in the aisle.

"The way I p-play the game," Tania continued shouting while leaning around Pia's back, "the traitor gets tossed out the c-c-cargo door!"

Pia faced her friend. "Back off."

Tania shook her head and marched to a seat farther forward.

Pia returned her attention to Olivier, who sat at a table facing Alan. Behind them, on the sofa, Olivier's three teenagers looked scared and cold. She joined the men at the table.

"You really have to get Tania under control," Dad said.

"TBI increases agitation, Dad." She looked at Olivier. "While I agree with her in principle, no one's getting tossed out of the jet."

Olivier shot his cuffs and looked out the windows. "Where are we going?"

"Wherever you stashed the documents Dad requested."

He glanced her way. "It's not that I don't appreciate your 'personal guarantee of security', but I'd rather take my chances with the Russians."

Alan pounded the table. "I trusted you. I need those documents—"

"And I trusted you!" Olivier pulled his jacket tight around him and twisted away.

Neither of the Sabels could respond. They looked at each other with pained expressions. The decision to withdraw protection for the Jallet family made sense at the time. Olivier had not pleaded for more and had hired his own. The death of his wife was not a Sabel problem. But pointing that out was a fruitless argument.

"You can't beat them." Olivier turned back to them, his face red, eyes bulging. "You think you're safe, sitting in your American towers. It's true you're safe from terrorists and gangs and criminals. Have you ever taken on a government? There are layers upon layers. You can't get to Popov until you've disposed of Strangelove and the GRU."

Pia tried to inject a calm voice. "I took on the Chinese government—"

"Please." Olivier's shredded voice strained with contempt. "The pandas of international intrigue. You know nothing. You surround yourself with veterans because you can afford them. What was I to do? Do I have the same resources? Was the company you built with your hands ripped from your fingers? Did the woman you love bleed to death before you signed everything over to Santalum?"

The three of them sat in silence, each lost in their own contemplation.

Pia wondered what the scene was like for Olivier. His children would have been next if he didn't agree. She knew the horror and powerlessness of an attack like that—and the seed of hatred it left behind. For Pia, it had been a driving force in her life. But she never had to worry about children. Certainly, Popov and Strangelove would have sent repeated reminders that his family was still vulnerable.

"I know who we're up against." Pia met Olivier's gaze. "We believe Strangelove orchestrated #HuntersFail for political gain. I'm not going to let him get away with it."

"Easy to say."

Pia tapped her finger on the table. "I'm going to take Popov down."

"He will ruin you." Olivier sneered. "He's been wrecking lives for forty years."

"Where do I find him?"

"You don't. He lives behind a façade of embassies."

"He must have a home somewhere."

"If I knew, I would never tell you," Olivier said.

She leaned back in her seat. Maybe Tania had the right idea; the ungrateful bastard should be tossed out the cargo door. She tried to hide her anger but could feel Dad watching her. He knew her too well.

He nosed up the aisle. Pia took his hint and met him three rows forward.

"Let him think about it for a while." Alan sounded as frustrated as she felt. "I'll work on him."

"Popov and Strangelove tried to kill us, Dad. We don't have the luxury of time. They could strike again any second."

"You're right." Dad gave her an appreciative nod. "We'll focus on Strangelove. No one's going to vote for Chuck Roche. He just announced he's going to give everyone the best healthcare. He's making promises he can't possibly deliver. The voters will never fall for his bullshit."

He turned to leave, then stopped and stared at his phone. He tapped her shoulder. "Remember this?"

He held his phone between them. Displayed was an old picture taken in middle school. Her team carried young Pia on their shoulders. She looked a little uncertain about the stability of her ride. In the background, Dad held a massive trophy. She felt a strong fondness for those days in the warmth of a loving home and community. Alan Sabel—Dad—had been a critical supporter of her success. He spared no expense to find the best coaches in the world. Most important, he'd always been there. Every game. He'd done more than anyone could expect of a father.

She smiled at him. "Those were good times, Dad."

She took the seat facing Tania. Her friend had taken to meditating. With her eyes closed, her earbuds in, she noticed nothing around her.

Emily and Sylvia chatted across the aisle. Sylvia had eagerly accepted Pia's invitation to Washington after Pia donated ten times what Sylvia hoped to raise for her charity. Pia wanted to hear more about the foster kids in Monaco, sure. But she wanted to see Jacob happy as well, and Sylvia seemed genuinely interested in him. Which made Sylvia a rare woman.

Emily paused their conversation and turned to Pia. "Is there anything that will confirm Jacob's claim that the Russians in Barcelona are working with Watson? Or anything that links Watson and Roche?"

Pia shook her head.

"Then I don't have a story. Roche's campaign manager denies any connection. They claim the Russians were probably scammers trying to shake down your dad for money." She paused. "I'll assume you don't want Jacob's adventures in Barcelona going to print?"

"I appreciate keeping that confidential. Thank you. But we're meeting Roche when we get back. You can join us."

Emily's eyebrows rose. "Thanks! That would be a scoop."

Emily and Sylvia resumed their conversation.

Pia took out her phone and looked up another trauma-injured family: Stefan and his adopted children Emma and Ethan.

The children's biological father had smuggled a band of terrorists into the country before losing his life in a gun battle with Jacob. Stefan, choking down guilt for his father's part in the plot, adopted the children as his way of paying for the sins of his father. An act much like Alan Sabel's adoption of Pia after he unwittingly aided the killers of her parents. But where Alan built an international conglomerate for Pia, Stefan had given away nearly all of his family fortune to charity.

She opened Instagram and found Stefan's profile. Hundreds of pictures rolled by. She started with the oldest snapshots. Stefan forced a smile at his camera with an arm wrapped tightly around two children in front of the Eiffel Tower. In the next, blank-faced kids slurped ice cream with the Rock of Gibraltar in the background. Several more pictures showed pained expressions of a family in front of iconic tourist destinations. Then something changed. One selfie was the dividing line between three awkward tourists and a family.

In the pivotal pic, Stefan, wrapped in a robe, cuddled two small, wet children in towels while reading a book. It looked familiar. She zoomed in and realized it was *Falling Up* by Shel Silverstein. In the next picture, the three of them stood in the rain looking at something. Pia zoomed in and discovered it was a graveyard. Emma held a small bouquet in her hand. Yet another showed them outside Stefan's former family mansion, shuttered. They appeared to be throwing rocks.

They were saying goodbye to their past. Letting go of their tragedies and moving on.

The next series of snapshots showed Stefan, his lanky frame dwarfing the little ones, reading and singing and dancing and playing. In the most recent series of photos, they were laughing. Interspersed with the fun pictures were more pictures of quiet reflections: in the woods, at a monastery, in a meadow. You never let go of the worst moments, but you can give them air once in a while and continue living.

She missed him.

She missed having a family. She missed those days so long ago when she would wake up in the middle of the night screaming. The great Alan Sabel, a self-made billionaire, would lie in bed with her, holding her firmly against his soft nightshirt. She could feel his heartbeat, soothing and calm. Back then, Dad could make the scary world feel safe.

She clicked hearts on all Stefan's pictures and sent him a text. "I love you. I miss you."

In a couple weeks, he would return from his journey of self-discovery, and they could reignite their romance.

She hoped.

That's what Dad was fighting for, the right of Pia and Stefan to live and love in a free democracy. It's what America stood for. Family values as any individual wanted to define them. The right to a free press, religious freedom, freedom from fear and oppression, freedom from want. Dad was right to pursue Strangelove's intrusions into our free elections. He was right to risk their lives to connect with Olivier Jallet. Strangelove and Popov were a form of evil whose connection to Roche threatened everything Americans cherished.

She glanced up at Olivier and his children. A handful of French citizens represented her future with Stefan in that moment. They had suffered at the hands of these beasts.

Families need someone to keep them safe from the monsters in the world. How many lives had Viktor Popov destroyed? And Strangelove?

Pia rose and walked back to where Alan and Olivier held a tense discussion. They looked up at her.

"I don't think you understood me." Her voice loud and strong. "I'm not going to bring Strangelove and Popov to justice. I'm going to kill them."

CHAPTER 25

MIGUEL TRIED THE GLASS DOOR. It slid open easily. I wasn't surprised. We were on the kind of remote Baltic island where locals never lock their doors. The few tourists had left with the last warm days of summer.

I ran around the front of the red-brick house and planted a wireless video camera. I checked the feed on my helmet visor: the small square in the upper right corner gave me a fair look at the front door, the yard behind the stone wall, and the village lane. I ran back to my cozy bush on the opposite side and let Miguel know I had him covered. He was free to check the place.

Watching a quiet building at three in the morning on a cloudy night is boring. Our part of the island didn't even have a barking dog.

My thoughts turned to Sylvia. There was something eternally sexy about her. Is sexy a good basis for love? Sure. But I had bigger questions to ponder: who wears a bright red cocktail dress at lunchtime? And who shows up hours later, in the same outfit, at your hotel? And what did Mercury mean about the past-lives thing? The Romans didn't believe in that stuff. As far as I knew. I never read any of the books he keeps making me buy.

Was he serious that I would kill such a beauty in however-many-lives ago it was? Impossible. I would never kill a woman. On the flip side, how could such a lovely young lady kill me? What was I in that past life anyway, some kind gutless powder puff? Or was I such a stud that she killed me out of jealousy? Yeah. Must have been jealousy. I was probably a king with a harem, and she wanted to be first wife.

Mercury's hand waved in front of my face. *What're you smoking, Willis? If your soul moves on to a new body, you step up in the world.*

Since you ain't no kind of king now, you can calculate the odds: you were no higher up than a DMV water boy handing out licenses to pimply-faced teens.

I said, *But what about this love-thing with Sylvia?*

Mercury said, *Oh my brutha, is that what you think she is? Love?*

He started laughing so hard, his head went back and his mouth opened wide. He covered his thin toga at the belly. *Dawg, that's a good one. I said she killed you and you think that means she loves you? See, that's why humans are all sick.*

But you said we knew each other in past lives.

Mercury bent over laughing with his hands on his thighs. *Dude, when you're young, love is all about sex. When you're middle-age, love is all about family. When you're old, love is all about partners. But some people mistake a power struggle for love. That's where you and Sylvia come in. You've never been in love. You two are like those couples who are married for two years but take five years to get divorced and ten years after that, they still rant about each other. You two don't love each other. You want to own, control, dominate, and destroy each other. You're not in love with that girl—you're in eternal bondage.*

Why did his explanation have such a familiar feel to it?

Still, there was something really sexy about that woman. I pictured her in my mind.

The smile.

Those eyes.

That walk.

I looked around at the bushes and trees. Something was making an electronic squawk.

It was coming from my earbud.

"Jacob? You there?" Miguel's voice was more urgent than usual.

"Roger."

"A little help."

The visual clues of the last few seconds replayed in my head. Dark figures had flitted between shadows, hopped the stone wall, and slid into the house.

I'd been distracted by a beautiful woman.

Again.

"Clearing the courtyard," I lied. "There in a second."

I ran into the yard, leapt the wall, opened the kitchen door and let off a three-round burst at the ceiling. The muzzle flash would blind anyone with regular night vision goggles while our Sabel visors muted bright light. I ducked back out and ran for the sliding glass door.

My first adversary was a seasoned veteran. As soon as I rolled inside, I felt one of three bullets glance off my body armor. It hurt like hell. I rose to one knee and found the guy peering over the kitchen counter. My first round knocked off his helmet. Before I could take advantage with a kill-shot, two of three rounds bounced off my ribs. My shots were knocked off target and clanked into the hanging copper pots. The window shattered. The guy behind the counter vanished.

I rolled and spun behind a couch. Stuffing exploded out of the furniture, and the sliding glass door collapsed in a waterfall of shards the size of daggers.

"I'm pinned in the living room." My warning to Miguel that I would not be arriving anytime soon to save his ass.

"Nice. Three in here, pushing me up the lighthouse stairs."

A scratching noise drew my attention to the corner of the room. With one big leap, I cleared the sofa's back and landed on the seat. I sprayed lead at knee level across the room.

Most armies issue body armor that reaches from the family jewels to the neck. Top that with a helmet, and you're as good as it gets in the twentieth century. But Sabel armor is twenty-first century stuff and made of liquid Kevlar. It's more flexible and covers us from the turtleneck to elbows and knees. Even with such great coverage, a bullet in the neck chokes your breathing for several minutes.

After the bullet hit me, I thought I would suffocate before my trachea reopened. The only bright side was the guy who fired the shot lay on the floor, bleeding out.

Miguel's firefight streamed into my ear. Channeling the ancient ways of his people, Miguel had become a skinwalker, the ancient warrior-wizard who could change physical forms for battle. Miguel chose to become a bear, befitting his large frame and broad shoulders. The transformation from man to bear involved a war whoop of such volume and intensity that it alone destroyed most adversaries. At that moment, as it live-streamed through my earbud, his battle cry destroyed my ability to hear the bad guy from the kitchen launch his assault.

Only my standard tactic of never staying stationary in a firefight saved me. I was in the process of doing a summersault when he opened fire and shredded the couch. I saw his muzzle flash and aimed, but my rifle was off by thirty degrees when I pulled the trigger. Luckily, my errant aim had taken out a guy.

Mercury smiled and let go of the off-target barrel. *Who's got your six, brutha?*

I said, *Why didn't you warn me they were coming?*

Mercury said, *Dude, I was warning you of the greater danger: Sylvia.*

The guy behind the counter mistook the thud for me dying and poked his head up. I took his helmet off with a bullet again. While he scrambled to find it, I slid across the counter and fired Sabel Darts over the edge, hoping to hit exposed skin. It took four shots, but I heard the telltale exhale and slump.

Miguel yelled again, his voice echoing not only in my ear but through the building. The distinctive thump of a falling body followed.

"Clear," he said in a calm tea-and-crumpets voice. "You?"

"Affirmative. Did you find the docs?"

"Naturally." He appeared in the doorway. "Only five of these guys?"

"You don't look like a bear."

He shrugged and kicked one of the bodies. "Interesting. AK-105 with sound suppressors."

He referred to the newer Kalashnikov, cousin of the famed AK-47 but lighter, stronger, with a folding stock and shorter barrel. With both sides using sound suppressors, the only noises came from the things we destroyed. And there was enough of that to wake the nearby village.

Something flashed in my video feed from the front of the house. Three shadows swept around the lighthouse, fanning out to enter our little brick sanctuary.

"Three or more coming."

Before I could explain directions, Miguel raised his MP5-SD under my nose and squeezed off a shot. A dark figure fell face-first outside the broken glass door. I turned to see what happened. Miguel turned the opposite direction. We pressed our backs against each other. We both lit up the night firing on full-auto in opposite directions.

I shot the man in the courtyard. He was wounded but still trying to work his rifle. I let him struggle while I checked the grounds for stragglers. In the trees beyond, two heat signatures emerged. They looked left and right, scanning the area. Their night vision couldn't see us inside the dark house.

Miguel fired through the wall into the other room. Artwork and glass clattered and cracked and fell.

His muzzle flashes gave the guys outside a target. They raised their weapons. I took them out, finished off the guy on the ground, then swapped magazines. Miguel pushed off my back and jumped through the doorway to the other room.

I backed to the brick wall and checked outside. No one else. I ran to cover Miguel.

He aimed at a light flashing around outside but held his fire.

The light flashed on a body, then followed the trail of blood and destruction to the house.

"Locals," Miguel said. "Let's go."

"I darted a guy." I pointed to my catch behind the kitchen counter. "Carry him."

Miguel huffed his displeasure at being my beast of burden but hoisted the body to his shoulder anyway. We set off across the courtyard, trying to sneak out before the cops came. It was doubtful the Danes would be fond of having a war erupt on their idyllic little island.

We slipped through the woods, heading for our boat. A glint of reflected light caught my eye. Something in the tree. I reached up and yanked a wireless video camera from its perch. There was a USB port on it, so I connected it to my phone and uploaded an image of the hardware to Bianca's team. Most internet-connected devices keep a record of what they're doing and for whom. We upload a copy of those records, called an image, to our techies. Bianca's people could trace the signal to whoever had been watching the house. That might tell us where to find more Russians. Maybe another ambush, if we're lucky.

A beam of light crossed us. We looked up to find an old man in a bathrobe with a flashlight. He gasped. With body armor, helmets, and video-augmented visors, we looked like space aliens.

"Keep calm and call the police," I said.

He trembled.

"Russians," Miguel said, pointing behind us.

The old man followed Miguel's finger with his flashlight beam. As much as I hated to do it, I darted him. We took off jogging for the boat a half-mile down the coast.

We cast off and went around the southern tip of the island, hoping to avoid any of Denmark's finest. Once we reached the open seas, I relaxed.

"Are you any relation to Changing Woman?" I asked the big guy.

He eyed me suspiciously. "Why?"

"Heard a rumor about you being her son, Monster Slayer."

He leaned back and didn't speak for a long time. Many Native Americans are not interested in sharing their spiritual beliefs for a host of reasons. Despite having fought together for the better part of a decade, he wasn't sure I was worthy. Seeing as how I spent half my time talking to a figment of my imagination, I wasn't so sure either.

Finally, he sighed. "When the Dineh—Navajo to you—left the third world and came to the Glittering World, it was infested with foreign gods. These monster gods killed people and destroyed villages. Changing Woman gave birth to twin boys. The stronger twin was called Monster Slayer, and the other was called Born for Water. Monster Slayer killed the foreign gods and drove the demons from our land."

I looked at Mercury.

My forced-into-retirement god shrugged. *What can I say, bro? After the Romans turned Christian on me, the dark ages descended across Europe. It was a libertarian wet dream: illiterate people, plagues, wars, ignorance, and filth. The aqueducts hadn't been cleaned in a thousand years. Just imagine the stench. Like the rest of the gods Christianity chucked out, I went for a stroll in the Americas. It was like how y'all go to the Caribbean for some R&R, ya know what I'm sayin? Had me a good time smiting people, too. Until that damn Monster Slayer showed up. He wiped out all the Celtic and Mesopotamian gods like he was mowing the lawn. 'S why you never hear about them anymore. Dude, I barely got out alive.*

I said, *You were killing people?*

Mercury fisted my shoulder. *Bro, you don't know what a good laugh is until you talk a bighorn ram into headbutting a guy off the side of a mesa.*

I let out a long and sorrowful sigh. Miguel nodded in sympathy as if he'd heard my god's confession.

Back in our sweaters and wool caps, we returned the boat in Ystad at dawn. The owner helped us get our Russian friend, drunk as he was, into the rental car. Before long we were back on the road to Malmö.

We were loading our sleeping Russian into the jet when Bianca called. "The camera was monitored by a Russian cybersecurity company based in Stavanger."

CHAPTER 26

WHEN HE ARRIVED AT THE office that morning, Yuri could barely concentrate for thinking about his impending lunch date with Andrine. He felt like a teenager. How could she have such power over him that he counted the minutes remaining until he would see her again? He smiled to himself then reminded himself of his workload.

He brought up a news feed with clips of the American debates from the night before. There would be snippets in there they might use for new memes. It was an open-floor debate, each candidate casually addressing the audience. Veronica Hunter dominated the topics. Chuck Roche, on the other hand, loved his silver-handled cane. He didn't need it for any medical reasons; he thought it made him look like Fred Astaire. And that obviously mattered to him. He wandered the stage while the other two candidates spoke. He walked with his cane barely touching the ground. He twirled it and examined its intricate elephant head in sterling silver. When Veronica Hunter dropped a zinger on him, he referred to an unproven conspiracy theory about her, saying, "If I win, I am going to instruct my attorney general to get a special prosecutor to look into your real estate investments." He held his cane by the shaft and slapped the weighted head in his other hand. "You should be in jail."

Hunter looked at him as if he'd given a compliment. Something had gone horribly wrong in America. But that wasn't his problem.

There were other things to do. Yuri pulled up last night's surveillance video from Svaneke and fast-forwarded it until he saw muzzle flashes and falling bodies. The dropping bodies were the wrong ones. Yuri felt himself stop breathing as the shocking duo dispatched a platoon of his countrymen. Impossible. He backed it up to check. Sure enough, it was the Americans leaving the scene. A hand reached up in front of the camera. Then the feed blinked offline. Jacob Stearne and his big friend had dispatched Strangelove's ambush with inhuman and ruthless precision.

Were he not an atheist, he would have thought the gods had intervened on Stearne's behalf.

A vision of Strangelove's strategy appeared in his head like jigsaw pieces. The banda that attacked the Sabels in France must've planned that attack for weeks. Yet Yuri was given the same Sabel assignment just days before the attack. The package in Zurich was devoid of anything useful. Yet Strangelove had ordered Yuri to monitor the remote location personally. What was Strangelove's game?

Yuri felt himself leaning over his desk, his nose just inches from the screen. His heart raced as he moved the pieces into place. The old man had never liked Yuri's psychological warfare. He preferred physical operations. But—like assassinating Kennedy—overt acts required a scapegoat to prevent the incident from igniting a war between two nuclear powers. Strangelove had expected the Americans to track down Yuri's banda and arrest or kill them.

When that didn't happen, he stabbed Yuri. Was that act planned? Or was the general's frustration boiling over? Then the orders to kill Sabel. The old man had expected Yuri to die in the attack on the Sabels. Now the orders to monitor Svaneke. What was that about?

The answer cut him like a knife.

Strangelove had played a brilliant endgame. When #HuntersFail was traced, the evil mastermind of the terrorist attack—Yuri Belenov—would already be dead. No further leads would be pursued. Strangelove and Popov would drink a toast to the fallen heroes of the Federation and go on to the next task.

Yuri would have to move fast to stay alive. There were new logistics to handle now. His timeline for going rogue jumped from *soon* to forty-eight hours. Maybe. Barely enough time to get the banda packed up and dispersed. Many gigabytes of tools and scripts would need to be copied to anonymous storage sites. A ton of high-end computers, carefully rigged to mask their work through the hacked computers of housewives and civil servants and executives, would be shipped to—to where?

And all of it had to be done under Vasili's patriotic nose.

One word leaked to Strangelove, and they were dead in an hour.

Which meant it was time to separate the allies from the enemies. He glanced over at his lieutenant, who hunched over his laptop. They had worked together for two years. He had been a loyal officer. Vasili deserved one more chance. After all, the lieutenant had a family.

Vasili could feel the major's cold stare and glanced over his shoulder.

Yuri pointed at his screen. "Did you see that?"

"Svaneke?" Vasili was white. "Ten men ambushed them, and Stearne walked away."

Yuri tapped on his screen with a finger. "What kind of camera was that?"

"Axis PTZ, remote controlled."

"Logs and diagnostics software onboard?"

"Of course."

"Who has those logs now?" Yuri turned his chair to face Vasili. He leaned forward as his lieutenant realized the problem.

Vasili said, "But we spoofed the IP addresses."

"How long will it take Stearne to trace the camera's live-stream back to Istanbul? Then Paris? And finally, Stavanger? Six levels of spoofed IP addresses might fool the average geek, but Stearne has Sabel Technology behind him. How long do we have?"

"Three days," Vasili's voice shook. "Or two."

"Time for an executive decision, Vasili." Yuri lowered to a whisper. "Do we stand and fight—or run?"

"We stand and fight." Vasili's eyes opened wide. "It is our duty."

Yuri flicked a glance over his shoulder to their fifteen hackers. Some had rifle training at one time or another. None of them had weapons that weren't plugged in. Yuri and his lieutenant had five firearms between them. None were automatic, and only one was semi-auto. When they moved operations here, they never expected Stavanger to become a war zone.

Vasili rubbed his face. "We must report this."

"Ask yourself a question first. Why did Strangelove set up an ambush?"

"To eliminate the threat."

"And why have us monitor it?"

Vasili thought for a long time. Yuri waited patiently.

"You think he did it to expose us." Vasili looked up. "You're saying he purposely turned us over to the Americans? No, no. He would never do that. Besides, he doesn't know where we are. By design, he doesn't even know we're in Norway. Complete deniability. We're an autonomous company with no visible ties to Russia or the GRU." Vasili bit his knuckle as the realization came to him. "And that's why he used a camera with logs. In case his ambush failed, he knew Stearne would trace it to us, the men monitoring the island. There is no connection between Moscow and us. Strangelove is sacrificing us."

Yuri nodded.

"Why?" Vasili asked.

"Americans are smart and methodical. It's not a matter of 'if' the Americans trace #HuntersFail back to us, it's when. At some point, they will follow tiny clues back to this room. What will they find?"

"Our dead bodies. Or, if we survive Stearne, rogue operators who worked alone. No ties to Russia." Vasili accepted his Avos' and slumped in his chair.

"We have an option." Yuri studied the lieutenant's face.

Vasili sat up and glanced at the others, then back at Yuri. "You mean, those crazy ideas about going rogue? Of becoming stateless? Abandon our posts?" Vasili turned back to his workstation. "I must report this, immediately."

Yuri grabbed his lieutenant's arm and pulled him back, face to face.

"Don't jump to conclusions." He watched as his man softened. "These are my orders: tactical retreat. We bug out now, each man to a different location. We lay low for a week. We reconnect and set up in a new location. We will not abandon our posts. Imagine the surprise on Strangelove's face when we report for duty."

Yuri studied the lieutenant's reaction carefully. Vasili appeared to like that option.

"Those are my orders," Yuri said.

"With all due respect, sir, we should stay. Strangelove is testing us. I'm sure of it. He probably has a better ambush planned. For all we know, there could be another banda outside, waiting for them."

The New Soviet Man indeed. Vasili had more faith in Strangelove than the Pope had in Jesus. Under other circumstances, it would've been comical, but Yuri nearly snapped. He fought his rising rage. "Those are my orders. Say nothing to Kaliningrad until we arrive at our destination."

"Yes, sir." Vasili saluted.

Yuri smiled and patted Vasili's shoulder. "Did you find a criminally insane Mexican in New York?"

Vasili didn't answer.

The New York mission was critical to Yuri's escape plan. Strangelove must get regular updates on the current workload, or he would crash their party.

"There are half a million Latinos there," Yuri said. "In any population of that size, there should be ten thousand criminals. Of those, there would be hundreds of mentally ill candidates."

"Yes, I found them. And I narrowed the list to three loners who rant online against the city and state."

"Prepare a report I can take with me." Yuri tried to smile. "We must complete our assignments even on the run."

Vasili smiled at that order.

Yuri gathered the men in a semi-circle around him. He opened with a joke, then cited each man's accomplishments. Everyone had made a tremendous effort creating a news storm out of the smallest local provocations. Anything involving a Mexican immigrant, legal or not, had been elevated to national attention with subtle racism and a lot of hyperbole. Roman's project had reaped the biggest banners. His story was the banner on several news sites.

Then he explained the compromised video feed that required a tactical retreat. "I'm sorry we have to uproot your lives again."

"Don't be." Igor crossed his arms. "We don't need Russia. Russia needs us. But see how they pay us? We should leave and keep going—on our own."

"We don't need the old men who used to run our country." Roman shook his fist. "They do nothing for us. They know nothing about the new economy."

In his peripheral vision, Yuri saw Vasili gasp.

Another voice added, "They made us crash the airliners. The Americans will have our heads when they find out it wasn't #HuntersFail."

And another, "We owe the general nothing. I say we strike out on our own."

"This is insubordination," Vasili shouted above them all.

Yuri held up his hands to quell the uprising. "Easy, gentlemen. There will be no rebellion, no insubordination. We are Russians. I am working on a plan to keep us out of American hands." He gave everyone a stern look. "We have a lot to do. Get to work."

The faces of insurrection remained as they lowered their voices. The group broke up, chatting in smaller groups before returning to their tasks.

He caught Roman's gaze and gave the man a see-me-later nod.

Yuri turned to Vasili, putting his face to the lieutenant's ear. "Let them think whatever they want. I have methods to ensure they answer when I call them."

Vasili's lips formed the first syllable of a protest. Yuri cut him off. "Do not challenge my authority." He lowered his voice. "We must be gone before Stearne gets here. Work on getting the office ready to ship out. I want to see significant progress by the time I return from lunch."

Yuri trotted down the stairs and stepped into an alcove to wait. Three minutes later, Roman came down the stairs. Yuri grabbed him. "Tell the men to keep their mouths shut. One more word in front of Vasili and we're in a Moscow prison by dinner time."

Roman's eyebrows shot up. "Then we're really—"

"Make sure there is a copy of all our tools where Strangelove can find it. And another he will never see. I'll address the men later. As soon as I can shake Vasili."

Roman ducked his head and bounded back up the stairs.

Yuri floated up the street to a French bistro. It was early for lunch, with only two other tables taken. He sat, spreading his arms in a grand style. He felt like the tsar expecting his servants to wait on him. Andrine lit up the room a few seconds later.

They both ordered soup. After all the pleasantries of weather and family were exhausted, he leaned over the table and held her gaze.

"I am going to New York tomorrow for a business trip. My associate fell ill and cannot go. His room is already paid for, and his first-class flight is non-refundable. It is waiting for a beautiful young lady who wants to see the world but also wants to come home again. Will you go with me?"

Andrine's mouth fell open. Her sparkling eyes widened. Her slender hand covered her face for just a moment before a breathless laugh escaped. She gasped twice before she could speak. "Do you mean it? Just the two of us?"

He nodded. "But you would have your own room and—"

She nearly knocked the table over when she wrapped her arms around him. She hugged him with the most satisfying embrace he'd ever felt in his life. In that moment, he felt happier than he'd ever dreamed possible.

She sat back in her chair, gushing her thanks over and over. He plied her with the details. They conjured up trips to MoMA and the Statue of Liberty. They planned a stroll in Central Park. They considered if visiting the 9/11 Memorial would be too depressing. They wondered if they could find tickets to the latest musicals or if they should settle for an old standard instead. In all, they planned a hundred days' worth of excursions for their seven-day trip.

The waiter brought their soups and looked at Yuri for a moment. He said, "Excuse me, but it was your friend who was murdered on the waterfront a couple months ago, right?"

"Yes." Yuri took a sip of soup and looked up at the man.

"I was sorry to hear they overturned the conviction of those drug addicts."

Yuri said, "They should have given them the death penalty right away."

Andrine's eyes flashed as she grabbed his wrist. "Surely you don't support capital punishment."

CHAPTER 27

PIA SAT AT THE TABLE with Olivier and Dad as her jet neared Washington DC. Time was running out to expose Roche and his Russian connections, but the Frenchman had yet to help them.

"Jacob broke into the Russian Embassy when Popov stole his dog." Pia leaned across the table. "And you saw what we did to the Russians at your farm. How can you doubt my ability to keep you safe?"

Olivier crossed his arms and stared out the window as the early morning sunlight spread gold across the cloud tops below them.

Pia glanced at his children, huddled on the couch at the back of the jet. One was asleep. The other two were watching her tense interrogation of their father. She needed answers, and there was little time left. But would she be as harsh on Stefan? Would she berate him in front of his children?

Alan leaned into Olivier's space. "You betrayed us. Why should we give you sanctuary? Why shouldn't we put you on a flight back to France as soon as we land?"

Olivier shrugged.

The oldest boy spoke to his father in French. His words were foreign, but his angry tone was easy enough to translate.

At another table, Tania, Emily, and the new girl, Sylvia, huddled together in conspiratorial conversation. Tania said, "Another thing to w-w-watch out for with Jacob is…"

Which was not a conversation Pia was interested in. She drummed her fingernails on the table impatiently. Was there a way to overcome the Frenchman's fears? Was it worth the effort?

"Forget him, Dad." She nodded at Olivier. "We need to figure out what Pozdeeva wanted. His files are full of things we don't understand. Have you looked at the microdot inventory?"

"There are thousands." Alan shook his head. "You're still looking for the needle in that haystack?"

"It must be in there." Pia pulled up the inventory Bianca's team put together. She pushed her tablet between them. In unison, they sighed when faced with the monumental task of looking through forty thousand documents and files. First stop: a glance through the pivot table showing types of documents: invoices, handwritten notes, deeds, recordings, bank statements, financial filings, photographs, and miscellaneous.

"Let's check the notes first," Dad said.

Olivier's son got up from the couch and engaged his father in the impatient and petulant tone only teenagers can voice. His father responded in the universal tone of fathers: louder and deeper and angrier.

Pia and Alan glanced at them for a second before looking at each other. They had been like those two in the past. They felt the antagonism between parent and child like an age-old song they used to sing. If felt like years since their conversations escalated too quickly. They gave each other a knowing smile. They were glad to be beyond that stage now.

Not counting yesterday.

They turned their attention back to the screen. They noted a few promising items and pulled up the translator's notes with the original scan. After twenty entries, nothing jumped out at them. They kept looking.

Olivier's argument with his son grew to the shouting stage. Olivier stood, his face red, his fists clenched. The boy's arm pointed at Pia as he shouted something in French. Olivier slapped his hand away. The boy made a fist.

Alan stepped between them. His large build intimidated them into silence. He pushed them apart with a stern scowl.

For a full minute, Alan stood with a hand on the chest of both Frenchmen. Their heated breathing and snorting began to subside. The boy lowered his fist, then his chin. The father sucked his teeth and let out an exasperated sigh.

Olivier calmed his breathing and rattled off what sounded like a concession to his son.

They retook their seats.

Olivier turned to Pia. "Please accept my apologies. My son said, '*Chacun voit midi à sa porte.*' Everyone sees noon at his door. It means, we care only about our own interests. He is right. I have been looking out for my family, ignoring the danger you are in." He folded his hands in front of him, penitent. "It is useless to argue. You have proven yourself capable against these men, albeit in small numbers."

"You'll be safe at Sabel Gardens," Alan said.

"I appreciate your generosity." Olivier held up a hand. "We cannot stay there forever, but when we leave, I will take full responsibility for my family's safety. Blaming you for my wife's murder—" he bowed his head "—was not right."

Pia nodded. "What can you tell us about Dad's cache of documents?"

"Strangelove's men got to Barcelona ahead of you. They found the trail and discovered Eleni's cache. Strangelove came to me in person the day after you wiped out his men in Cyprus. He didn't know if you'd left anything with me, but he suspected it. He threatened my son. I told him about the boxes you left in my care. He took everything and left instructions with more threats if I didn't comply. We called him minutes after you called me." He choked and took a moment to compose himself. "I am truly sorry."

"We're past that," Pia said.

"What are you looking for?" Olivier asked.

"Dad documented transactions between Roche's companies and the Russian company, Santalum. It was a long time ago, but we believe it proves money laundering. Our agents in Singapore and Bogotá have retrieved caches, and we have the documents from Zurich." She sighed. "When we get to Washington, we'll sort through it."

"We went to the FBI," Alan said, "but they need some tangible evidence before they can open an investigation. They called me a conspiracy theorist."

"Did you know Pozdeeva?" Pia asked.

"Not personally." Olivier scratched his chin. "I heard his name. But I can tell he was reasonably important because he was never in any official photographs."

"That's it." Pia looked back and forth at the men. "The Russian way."

"What?" Dad asked.

"What's *not* in the Pozdeeva files?" Pia asked. "What's missing?"

Alan grabbed the list and scanned it. With his eyes glued to the screen, he scrolled patiently, checking each line like a near-sighted entomologist counting insect eggs. After several quiet minutes, he looked over the edge of the tablet at Pia, then set it on the table.

"There's nothing about me."

"Did they have kompromat on you?"

"Their auditors were in our satellite facilities." He nodded with his mouth drawn tight. "They photographed and analyzed satellites we were building for the Defense Department."

"Is that bad?" Pia asked. She prayed for a positive answer and knew there wasn't one.

Olivier picked up Alan's tablet and scrolled through the data.

"Espionage is treason." Dad clenched his fist. "They had pictures and videos of them looking over the software and the codes in our facilities. It was proof that they'd had access to top-secret technology. Reporting them would've destroyed my reputation in the industry. Not reporting it implied that I allowed it. That's how Strangelove and Roche kept me from going after them. I would've gone to jail."

"Mutually assured destruction." Pia reached for his hand and held it. It was a difficult secret for him to keep all these years. He'd been played by the financiers, but he never revealed the extent of his security breach to the government. "How badly did they compromise US intelligence operations?"

"If we had launched those satellites, they would've had a front-row seat at the CIA." He met her gaze. "I made excuses and found a way to rebuild them using ternary systems instead of binary. Where binary has off/on operators, everything is either zero or one, ternary has off/on/maybe."

"But that's what makes our system impossible to hack. That's a good thing."

"Yes, our system is rock-solid in security." He shook his head. "The

Russians have never hacked a Sabel system to this day. But I should've told the Feds. Lying by omission is still lying. It would've been the end of Sabel Industries, so I kept it a secret."

"It's been years. Nothing bad happened. We can come clean now."

"You're right. I should. Even if they ban us. It's the right thing to do."

Olivier coughed. "Are you done with your confession?"

Pia and Alan looked at him.

"This is a picture of Ilya Pozdeeva standing at CIA headquarters in Langley." He pointed at a corner of the picture. "Barely visible in the background is Kryptos, the famous sculpture containing the Vingère cipher. There is another picture of him standing at the Hirshhorn. If you're familiar with the sculpture museum's grounds, you'll notice he's standing to the left of Antipodes, the second cipher by Jim Sanborn, who made Kryptos. He gave you this clue because everyone knows Popov detests art. He thinks it's a waste of time. Pozdeeva left you a code."

"You need a key to decode a Vingère cipher." Pia grabbed the tablet and looked at it. "I'll get Bianca's people on it right away. Thank you, Olivier."

"What would he have left for a key to the cipher?" Dad asked. "Something you don't write down but is easy to find. Like a calendar or a famous quote or a name."

They retreated into their thoughts for a minute before deciding it could be anything.

"One more thing." Olivier pointed to a file on the tablet. "This is the deed to Popov's dacha. The very house where he murdered my wife."

CHAPTER 28

WE LANDED IN STAVANGER ON a chilly yet sunny November morning. Neither of us had a clue what to do with our captured Russian soldier. Miguel had advocated for pinning a confession to the murders in Svaneke on his chest and dropping him off at airport security. Mercury backed that plan. My idea to keep him around prevailed. You never know when a sedated Russian might come in handy.

The pilot lowered the airstair. I handed him a pistol full of Sabel Darts.

"What am I supposed to do with this?" he asked.

"In case our guest wakes up."

"I'm not taking part in your kidnapping."

"Let's get our roles straight." I patted his shoulder. "I'm the kidnapper, which makes me a fugitive. You're aiding and abetting a fugitive's flight from justice after his participation in the biggest Danish slaughter since King Christian II murdered a hundred and fifty Swedish leaders in the Stockholm Bloodbath of 1520."

The pilot pinched the bridge of his nose. "Stockholm is not in Denmark."

"That's what the Swedes were telling King Christian—" I lowered my voice to a whisper "—and look where that got 'em."

Miguel shouldered him aside, and we left.

The nice thing about flying on your own jet while looking, acting, and dressing like the ground crew—because that is your true socioeconomic brotherhood—is that no one expects you to walk into customs. We skipped it and went straight to the rental counter, where the only car left was an Audi S5 hot rod.

We drove the short distance to NATO's Joint Warfare Center. That's where big-brain guys plan the genocide of certain political or ethnic groups who might piss them off someday. It's also the biggest collection of brass outside the Pentagon and about as useful. Luckily, we didn't need to break into the base. The carrier-class routers we were looking for were outside the perimeter. Carrier-class routers are the kind that internet suppliers use to drop a megahuge-bandwidth connection to operations like your local cable company or the biggest military co-op on the planet.

The little camera on Bornholm had sent its video feed to a spoofed IP address. Until Bianca explained it to me, I had no idea that hackers could pretend, or spoof, the physical location of their computer. Now that she explained it to me, I still don't get it. All I needed to know was that to find the guy, we had to find where he plugs into the internet. She traced him to a switching station near NATO's JWC.

We walked into the unattended station, an innocent looking building about the size of a school gym, in broad daylight with our balaclavas on. I smiled and waved at the video-attendant who sat in Oslo. Probably. She waved awkwardly and frowned and spoke through the intercom in Norwegian with a certain amount of surprise and strain in her voice. *"Hvem faen er du?"*

"Air Conditioning."

"You are English?"

I shrugged. "OK."

"Some ID please."

"Hang on a sec." I raised my rifle butt and smashed the camera.

Miguel had the door open. We circled into our target: the router room. It was about the size of a basketball court and filled with server racks. It was geek heaven. Each rack was bolted to the next, rows and rows of them. Power and networking cables cascaded from a wiring harness above our heads.

Bianca's team had prepped us with complete how-to's. We installed two devices, a dummy that was easy to spot and another they wouldn't notice for days. We had them wired into the right ports and were out of the building in two and a half minutes.

Balaclavas off and scooting through the neighborhood, we thought we had gotten away with it.

Mercury leaned in from the backseat. *'Sup dude? Getting on the wrong side of NATO just for fun? Didn't Changing Woman talk your boy out of this?*

We're good, I said. *Down the road and gone.*

Mercury laughed. Another voice laughed with him.

I looked over my shoulder to see one hot blonde with a cat in her lap. *What the fuck? You promised not to bring your friends around. You know I can't handle it. I need my meds.*

Mercury squeezed my shoulder in a patronizing manner that made me want to break his hand off. *Chillax, bro. You're in her hood, show some respect. This here's Freyja, goddess of love and battle. The Norse knew those two things are inextricably connected. Anyway, I was hanging at her crib, Sessrumnir, where she keeps her warriors. You should drop in sometime. You'd love it. Your kind of people, homes. Anyway, her MVP for Viking of the Year is driving that cop car.*

I said, *What cop car?*

Miguel turned around to look out the back window at the same time I looked in the mirror. Three seconds later, a VW Passat with *Militaerpoliti* written on the hood crested the hill, lights blazing.

"How did you know they were coming?" Miguel asked.

"I get messages." I shrugged.

"I hate NATO cops," Miguel said. "Always act like they're in charge of the free world."

I put the hammer down. The Audi doubled the speed limit. We pulled away from the Passat, but traffic—and my reluctance to endanger the nice people of Stavanger—worked against us. Miguel worked the phones and maps, asking the Sabel Security help desk for good escape routes. Between the sources, Miguel pointed me in the right direction.

Norway never got the memo on autobahns from their German friends. Everything was a two-lane road. Making matters worse, the major streets were half bicycle lanes. Skirting traffic that stopped because of the sirens and lights, we screeched against guard rails and sent a couple cyclists wobbling off the shoulder.

We took a wrong turn heading for a ferry dock, which seemed to be the destination for every road that wasn't heading up a mountain. Not that there were any options. I threw it into a four-wheel drift and spun around with the cop on our heels. He never took Ms. Sabel's aggressive-driving course and couldn't make the turn. We were heading up the hill, watching him in the mirror, as he tried to get his car turned around in a crowded ferry-ramp.

Mercury leaned forward. *Did I mention Freyja has money on that guy? Don't get cocky now. Look out for the school bus over the hill.*

We crested the hill with enough speed to get some air under all four tires. When we came down, the brakes were already slammed to the floor.

Three kids looked into my eyes, frozen with fear. They stood in the street next to a bus as I slid sideways. We stopped with a foot between Miguel's door and the kids. The engine stalled.

Miguel zipped his window down. "Hammersåk?"

Two of them blinked. One pointed to the left.

The engine fired up. I slipped into gear.

Mr. Viking flew over the hill, slammed on his brakes, slid sideways. I kept my foot on the brake to protect the kids. He squealed his way down the slope and bumped the side of my rental. The impact wasn't enough to set off the airbags, but we were stuck to each other.

He started yelling in Norwegian over the loudspeaker. He was using one hand to hold the mic and the other to open his door. He had one foot on the ground.

I tossed up my hands and shrugged apologetically. At the same time, I stomped the accelerator. Metal screeched against metal as I extracted my Audi from his VW. With all four tires pouring smoke, I pulled away, slowly at first, then gaining speed until the last shred separated. The cop stood there with his mouth open.

He had no idea what to do. Apparently, most Norwegians respect authority.

Miguel waved goodbye to the kids. They waved back.

We flew down the side street, tires shrieking as we drifted onto the next big road. It took us into a dark tunnel. "Where does this lead?"

"We're on our way to Trolltunga. Troll's Tongue." Miguel pulled a pouch of pistachios from his pocket. "It's a big, thin piece of rock that sticks out over the fjord. It's two thousand feet high. An iconic piece of Precambrian bedrock. Like the Norwegian version of Monument Valley."

Crossing the yellow lines in the dark tunnel, I passed a truck and two cars like they were standing still. "Why there?"

"I've never seen the fjords."

"Miguel."

"You know," he said while munching a nut, "whenever I travel with you, I get shot at, arrested, chased, shipwrecked—all kinds of bad things. Can't we do some sightseeing once?"

"We've never been shipwrecked."

"Hurricane Dolly."

"Yeah. OK. Not the ship though. Just the landing craft. I'll give you 'Zodiac-wrecked' on that one."

A mile behind me, the cop's flashing lights lit up the tunnel like Christmas. We flew through the three-mile-long tunnel, seven hundred feet below Byfjord, otherwise known as the Atlantic Ocean. I passed two more cars and squeezed back into my lane to the sound of everyone else slamming on their brakes.

Finally, I broke the silence. "Has Bianca found the bad guys' lair?"

"Not yet. Soon as we're out of the tunnel, take the first right. Should be a nice view while we wait for her team to get back to us." Miguel finished his pistachios without sharing. "Since you're no fun."

We sped up the incline leading from the bowels of the earth and turned onto a small ribbon of pavement. The damn cop was behind us, only half a mile. Our fenders clicked across the fence posts, and our tires whined around every hairpin turn. We reached the scenic overlook and slowed.

Miguel rolled out.

I pulled to a stop, got out, and leaned my butt against the hood. Miguel was right. It was a nice view.

The cop screeched to halt behind me. He got out and claimed to have a weapon in his hand. I couldn't take my eyes off the scenery. He kept ordering me to do things in different languages. I presumed they were instructions for getting on the ground. I get that a lot. Police always want me face-down on the ground.

I turned slowly and faced him and waved with a wry smile.

He had a funny look on his face when Miguel darted him from behind.

Mercury said, *Thanks, homeboy. You won me some money off the local goddess. Unfortunately, she's pissed off, and you're in her sights.*

I said, *What does that mean?*

Don't get too close to the cliff.

I started walking forward.

"Bianca has their office located." Miguel picked up the knocked-out cop and put him in the driver's seat of our trashed rental.

We climbed in the cop car, and turned off the lights, sirens, and radios, and headed back to town.

CHAPTER 29

"YOUR ATTENTION," YURI STEPPED UP on a packing crate in the center of the office in Stavanger. "I've sent Vasili on an errand for a reason."

The men stopped packing their monitors and computers for a moment and faced him. "Igor and Roman were right. The Americans will kill us if they find us. And worse, Russia will let them. You know it's true. Only we can protect ourselves."

"It's time you realized that!" Roman shouted.

"We can thrive if we work together." Yuri looked each man over, one at a time. "But not if we remain within Strangelove's reach. That means we need to travel a good deal. Moving as much as possible. To help with that, I've transferred a hundred thousand euros to each of your accounts."

A round of applause was quickly followed by murmurs.

"It is not the Motherland's money." Yuri held up a hand. "This is from my own account, saved for just this kind of emergency." He felt no reason to tell them it was Alexi's money. "Travel to your favorite country, take a few passports and identities with you, relax for a few days. In a week's time, we will reconvene as stateless entrepreneurs."

A big cheer went up.

"We've been anonymous drones for Russia. What will we do in the future?" asked Igor.

"We will form our own cyber-collective, like Cicada 3301." The legendary, secretive hackers posted puzzles scattered online for several years starting in 2012. Cicada 3301 claimed they intended to recruit highly intelligent individuals. As a player solved each puzzle, a new puzzle or cipher was revealed, each increasingly difficult and individualized. While a few anonymous individuals claim to have won, the organization has never revealed any results. Rumors have surfaced that the NSA or CIA was the sponsor, while others believe it to be a criminal syndicate.

Yuri said, "We will call ourselves, the Stateless Hacktivist and Resistance Collective, SHaRC."

Another round of applause and smiles.

"What about #HuntersFail?" one of the men asked. "The Americans are still tracking the source."

"If they crack the spoofed IP addresses—" Yuri waved his hand around the room "—this is what they'll find."

"How do we contact each other?" Alexandr held up his smartphone. "We should burn these."

"Throw those in the boxes we're going to let Strangelove find." Yuri smiled. "I have set up a secure video-chat server. We can ring each other or conference the whole group. Because we're going to be hunted, you can force open the video link to anyone should he not answer. That way you can tell if he's being coerced or detained."

"You hear that, Petr?" Igor called out. "Now we can catch you having sex with monkeys."

Yuri allowed a good laugh at Petr's expense.

"When I find a new location, I will send for you, and we will wipe these systems clean. We will make a fresh start."

The men talked amongst themselves with a good deal of excitement. Most of them held no allegiance to their nation. From hours spent online, they felt more European than Russian. None of them had been happy with their assignments. Killing Americans seemed pointless when they were so easily robbed. No idea pleased them more than escaping the military oversight to work for themselves.

Everyone went back to work.

Half an hour later, Vasili returned. The lieutenant handed Yuri two burner phones in bubble wrap. His expression was sour. "You cannot escape Strangelove."

Yuri stared long and hard at his right-hand man, hoping to determine if it was a guess or real knowledge. He could not tell.

"Look at your bank account." He patted Vasili's shoulder. "You now have enough money to take your wife anywhere she'd like. Croatia by the sea, where they film *Game of Thrones*. Your family would have a wonderful—"

"It might take days," Vasili hissed, "maybe years, but he will never let us go."

"The Mediterranean, then. Your wife will make love to you if you take her to Valletta on Malta."

"He tracks things we never thought of." Vasili shook with anger. "We will never rest while he's alive because he will never let us."

"There's a nice bed and breakfast near the Barrakka Gardens." He patted Vasili's shoulder. "Have a vacation, relax."

Vasili turned away and packed a crate.

If there was one thing Yuri had learned in his career, it was that those who voice fears have already given in to them. He made his decision without regret. He'd given Vasili a chance to join them. That's all he could do. Nietzsche was right when he said, *Nothing burns one up faster than the effects of resentment.*

Yuri glanced at his system, the last computer still plugged in. "Damn. Stearne landed in Stavanger an hour ago. We must get moving."

He turned to his men. "Step it up. The shippers close in an hour. Get these boxes down there. Then clear out your apartments and go. Before long, you will be sipping champagne at your dacha in Santorini with beautiful women hanging on your arm."

The men laughed and picked up boxes of computers and monitors. They carried them out. Within ten minutes, the office was empty save the two officers and their personal gear.

Vasili stared at Yuri.

"Get moving." Yuri pushed the air between them.

Vasili scowled and made a fist he didn't raise.

"Wait." Yuri reopened his packed backpack. "Let's take a selfie before we part. In a few months, we will be promoted, and I will show you this picture of you—with such a sad face."

Vasili frowned.

Yuri popped his new burner from the packaging and held it up, wrapping his arm around his lieutenant. Then he frowned at the phone and pulled it in close to examine the screen. "Fuzzy. A brand-new phone and the lens is smudged already. Hold on just one more second."

Yuri reached into his backpack and pulled out a spray bottle that looked like glass cleaner. He looked at the camera, held it between them, and sprayed Vasili in the face. "Oops. Sorry."

He handed the young father a tissue and watched his handpicked confidant wipe the Novichok VX-Y agent into his skin. A variant of the deadly VX nerve agent developed by the British for the Cold War, his was designed by the Soviets to have the same effect without leaving any trace behind. In an hour, Vasili would die.

"Forget it," Vasili scoffed, tossing the tissue in a trash can.

Yuri shrugged and put his poison and phone back in his pack. "Do you have a destination planned?"

"My family will meet me here in the morning." Vasili turned away. "We enrolled our children in school here. We were going to make Stavanger our home."

"I see." Yuri nodded thoughtfully. "That still might work. But take her to Malta for a vacation anyway. Or Morocco. Have you been?"

Vasili shot him a disgusted look, picked up his laptop, and trudged out.

Yuri watched his screen display the five cameras he had hacked in the city. He flipped back and forth until he found what he was looking for: Jacob Stearne and his Indian friend had already destroyed the camera feeds from the data center outside NATO's JWC. They were making quick work of his spoofed IP addresses. He estimated he would have half an hour to get out of town.

His new phone rang with Strangelove's caller ID.

Which should not have happened.

He had not yet given the number to anyone. All his men had gone out to buy their own burners. A simple security measure. His video-chat system made old-fashioned phone numbers unnecessary.

Except that Vasili had bought his burner. Traitor. Yuri's anger burned through his stomach to the wound in his ribs.

He answered the call. "General, how are you this evening?"

"Congratulations, young man. You've created your own nation in an afternoon, SHaRC. I like it." Strangelove chuckled. "Vasili left an open Skype session on his laptop. I watched your declaration of independence—live."

The pain in Yuri's side exploded. He could feel the old man's hands reaching through the phone to stab him again.

"General, you told me to leave the package at the lighthouse, and you would take care of it. You failed. Now Stearne is in Stavanger. My executive decision was in Russia's best interests. We—"

"Coward! You have been given the mission to eliminate Stearne. Instead, you are deserting."

"We are through with you, Strangelove." Yuri took a deep breath. "You no longer own us."

"I will call you tomorrow," the general growled, "after you've had time to think things over."

Strangelove clicked off.

Yuri hurled his phone against the wall. It shattered.

Immediately, he realized his mistake. He couldn't leave a scrap of anything behind. He scrambled to pick up the pieces and put them in the last trash bag with Vasili's tissue.

The whole time, his mind boiled over with hatred for the general. Who did the old man think he was? Turning perfectly good lieutenants into informants against their superiors. It had been Vasili who told Strangelove about the keylogger. Had to be. It was Vasili who gave the old man his new phone number. Had to be. Which made killing the young man Strangelove's fault.

The general had put Vasili up to it. Probably threatened his wife and children in the beginning. One way or another, he would make Strangelove pay for forcing Vasili's murder. And Alexi for that matter. And the others before that.

Yuri felt the hate and anger on his face. He was hot. People don't think straight when they're angry. That's why athletes trash-talk. Which was exactly what Strangelove was doing to him now. He stood up straight and took a deep breath.

Strangelove would not win this round.

He calmed himself. There were many good things in life to occupy his mind. Andrine waited for him. That was something to look forward to.

Andrine. Just the memory of her pretty face smiling at him lifted his spirits. Could he have picked a better hotel than the Andaz on 5th Avenue? Would she love the restaurant he'd chosen? Was a candlelit dinner on the roof too much? Would she suspect his intentions when she discovered they had adjoining rooms? Why was he so nervous?

He took another moment to calm himself and think clearly. One more check of the office. Everything looked clean. He dropped the laptop in his backpack, swung it over his shoulder, grabbed the trash bag, and left.

As he floated down the stairs, he plugged in his earbuds. Miles Davis, *'Round Midnight*, streamed into his ears like a drug. Bopping his head, his shoulders twisting with the rhythm, he kept his head down.

Three blocks up the street, police shuffled a crowd of people into his path. An ambulance pulled up behind him, locking him in. He jostled to see what was happening. A policeman pushed him back and barked at him to stay on the sidewalk.

He pulled his earbuds out and asked bystanders what had happened. No one was certain. A man had collapsed on the sidewalk. Yuri pushed his way forward and stood on his tiptoes. As he feared, it was Vasili. Too much nerve agent. The lieutenant should've been across town before he dropped.

Yuri's thoughts were interrupted by a tall man standing in his personal space, pressing uncomfortably close. In English, the man said, "Whoa, is that Miles Davis?"

Yuri felt a grin spreading. Running into someone who could identify Miles was rare. He looked up at his new companion.

Jacob Stearne.

The man who'd wiped out Strangelove's ambush.

He wore jeans and a leather jacket over a t-shirt with the silhouette of a soldier aiming a rifle directly at Yuri. It read, *US Army: If you're not behind us—start running*.

Yuri hunched his shoulders to mask his shock. "You're a fan?"

"He's OK." Stearne leaned over the lady in front of them to look at Vasili. "Innovative, but not as pleasing to the ear as Louis Armstrong and nothing as powerful as Trombone Shorty."

Yuri looked around the crowd to find Stearne's companion. The big Indian's eyes were glued to Yuri as he circled through the crowd thirty yards away. The two worked like wolves, one in front of you, keeping your attention, the other sneaking around behind you. Yuri admired his adversary for a moment. He was lucky there were only two of them.

They would never attack in a crowd with so many police officers and witnesses. Stavanger was a ridiculously peaceful town. Every civil servant in uniform had turned out to help the fallen foreigner. But the same rule applied to Yuri—there was nothing he could do either. They stood there, side by side, tensed and ready but unable to fight.

"Where can I find Strangelove?" Stearne asked.

"I beg your pardon?"

"Tell me where he is, and I'll let you go."

"Give me any trouble, and I'll give the authorities a video of you slaughtering ten men on Bornholm."

Stearne snapped a look at Yuri.

Stearne's were cold, dead eyes. A good deal of madness lay in them. He was a man who thought of human beings in stark black-and-white. If he deemed you worthy, he would sacrifice his life to save yours. If Stearne deemed you unworthy, he would snap your neck in line at Starbucks and order a latte over your carcass without so much as a dropped syllable.

"Don't worry." A crude smile tugged at one corner of Stearne's mouth. "I'll take the video off your corpse before I leave town."

The Indian had nearly completed his circle. In a matter of seconds, the two Sabel agents could drag him off. It was time for a tactical retreat. They would meet again, and next time, he would be prepared.

Yuri backed up a step.

The emergency team pushed through the crowd like an icebreaker in the Arctic. Outstretched arms created a corridor between the bystanders with Stearne and the Indian on one side—and Yuri on the other.

He waved goodbye.

"You forgot something," Stearne called.

The stretcher bearing Vasili's body traveled up the narrow space between them. Stearne tossed a small object across the gap. Yuri caught it without looking and backed up, letting the bodies of strangers fill in around him. He turned and walked quickly around a corner.

He moved briskly for a block before looking at the object.

Suddenly, he couldn't breathe.

He couldn't believe he'd been so careless. In his anger at Strangelove, he had indeed made a mistake. He'd left one last traceable object in the office. The wireless router with the logs of every internet connection the banda had ever made.

CHAPTER 30

PIA FROZE WITH THE LIMO'S door handle pulled halfway. Outside her window, a freezing rain fell on the main house at Sabel Gardens. She took another look at Dad, then started to speak.

He cut her off. "Don't worry. I'll have Olivier and his family settled in the guest house before you're done. And I'll be sure Jacob's girlfriend gets a room in the guest wing." He paused a beat. "You're stalling. Like it or not, Chuck Roche is the candidate for a major party and—if he's elected—will have sweeping powers that could make or break Sabel Industries in an afternoon."

"He's working with the Russians."

"Don't let on about that." Dad gave her his stern look. "Right now, he doesn't know what we're doing. Keep the conversation about money. Nothing else."

"But Roche is such a little bi—"

"So was President Hunter. We don't have any proof of his involvement in #HuntersFail. We will get him. Or. We may never get him. Justice is an uneven thing. Either way, we have to play the hand we're dealt. That takes us back to the standard operating procedure: kowtow to the powers that be. Party and ideology might change but we must kneel before presidents, or we'll wind up laying off tens of thousands of employees. Go in there and kowtow. That means: press your forehead to the floor."

"Thanks, Dad. I needed the visual." She nosed at the other limos lined up behind them. "Do you trust Olivier about Popov's dacha?"

"You're stalling." Dad shook his head and pointed at the house. "Kowtow."

She blew a frustrated breath and finished pulling the lever. The driver took the signal, opened the door for her, and stepped aside. She strode up the grand staircase with Tania and Emily a step behind. The *Post's* embedded journalist looked eager for her exclusive.

The trio marched into the main library. Chuck Roche leaned on his silver-handled cane in front of the giant globe. His white hair was neatly combed, his paper-thin skin revealing the network of veins beneath. Two aides, one tan and the other pale, stood near a side table, staring at her Gutenberg Bible. The book was displayed under a sealed glass bell.

Despite three women entering with heels that clicked on the hardwood floors, Roche pretended not to notice Pia's arrival. She turned to his aides at the bible. "Number Fourteen, formerly of Leipzig University."

The pale man's shocked expression gave away his understanding. The tan man's blank expression enticed her to explain. "There are only twenty-one complete Gutenbergs today. This is number fourteen, one of the vellum editions. That's why we keep it under the crystal dome."

She glanced at Roche, who continued his pretense.

"How did you…" The pale man looked too embarrassed to finish.

"I was in Leipzig with the National Team when I heard they needed to raise funds. I bought the book with the promise to loan it back on demand. Surely your boss told you this story."

Everyone looked across the room at Chuck Roche. Dwarfed by the globe, the small man gave it a push with one finger. It spun on silent bearings.

One of the suits coughed.

Pia shook her head at Roche's power play. She faced his assistants. "Since the candidate doesn't care to greet me, perhaps one of you could explain why he wanted a meeting with me."

The pale man blanched with embarrassment; the tan man reddened with anger at her impertinence. The pale one said, "Sir. Ms. Sabel is here."

"Is that right?" He turned with a big smile but didn't move. "How are you, my dear?"

"You called this meeting."

"And so I did." He smiled and stretched out his arms.

Pia stood still.

With an awkward glance at the others, he lowered his arms and crossed the room. He gestured to a nearby photograph of the National Team hoisting a trophy with Pia in the center. "You know how to win. We want to fill the new administration with winners."

"The election is days away."

"I'm going to win." He smiled. "We're very close. Thousands of voters attend my rallies. They're like rock concerts. You need to be on board so you can bask in my victory."

Pia stopped herself from voicing a slew of snarky responses that popped into her head. Kowtow was not in her vocabulary, but she could keep calm. For Dad. "What do you want from me?"

"For starters, no reporters." He pointed his cane at Emily, then moved it to Tania. "And no hotheads."

"Who you c-c-calling hothead, asshole? You wanna g-g-go a—" Tania stopped when she caught Pia's icy gaze. With a sheepish shrug, she took Emily's elbow. "C'mon girlfriend. Let's g-g-get away from that creepy old m-m-man."

"I promised her an exclusive," Pia said.

"I said—" Roche glared at Emily "—no reporters."

"Journalist," Emily said. She exchanged apologetic glances with Pia. Then she and Tania left.

"My men stay." Roche tapped his cane on the floor.

"If they were anything to worry about—" she looked the men over with contempt "—they would be on the ground right now." She crossed her arms. "Is there something you want from me?"

"A more important question is," Roche said, "what do you need out of the USA? You can have anything you want: fewer competitors, more federal contracts, inside—"

"Sabel Industries competes in the fair market. It's called capitalism."

"You can't be that dumb." Roche leaned back, twisting his cane impatiently. "Alan didn't grow a multibillion-dollar business without stacking the deck to win deals. Hell, I've leveraged overanxious governors to build out pipelines, eliminate regulations, and toss me tax breaks right out of public funds."

"Isn't that socialism?"

"Don't get cute." Roche looked her over, looking for a way to reset the conversation. "C'mon, join the winning team, Pia. What do you want? You could be the next Secretary of Education."

The men in suits coughed. The pale one muttered. "You promised that to Betsy Renard, sir."

"Did I? Well, hell, she did bring $200 million to the party. You're not going to let Betsy be a bigger donor than you, are you?"

Pia bristled at the name of the billionaire socialite who occasionally traveled in Dad's circles. The woman wasn't qualified to teach kindergarten, much less take responsibility for future generations of American children. Anger built like a volcano inside of her. Roche's campaign rhetoric had echoed unsubstantiated tales of corruption, and here he was, selling cabinet posts.

But. Kowtow. For Dad.

"How about those children you're always talking about. The kids with lousy families." Roche's grin spread slowly.

She felt confused for a moment until she deciphered his words. "You mean foster care?"

"Yeah, them. You could help them as the..." He turned to his assistants and snapped his fingers.

The pale man said, "Foster care is under Health and Human Services, sir."

"That." Roche pointed at his man. "Think about all those kids you could cure as the Secretary of Healthy Humans."

The pale man cringed. "Health and Human Services, sir."

The tan man crossed his arms and grinned like his team was winning a big game.

Words formed in Pia's head explaining that foster care was not a disease, but the futility overwhelmed her after the first tentative syllable left her lips.

Kowtow. For Dad.

Pia took a deep breath. She pulled a less-aggressive face. "Why would a successful businessman like you want to be president, Chuck? I mean, Mr. Roche."

He smiled at her flattery and pivoted his cane. "Haven't you been paying attention?" His voice rose with excitement. "Those damn fools like Veronica are all corrupt. They tax success, for God's sake. They hold back business with ridiculous regulations. They—"

"Bear Stearns, Lehman Brothers, Washington Mutual, AIG. They were deregulated, and it cost taxpayers several trillion dollars. Deregulation sounds great but never ends—"

"Don't argue with me." Roche flushed. He looked around the room, tugged his jacket and looked up at Pia. "You're a young, idealistic girl. Think of your future. Imagine the immense power available to people like you and me." He clenched his fist and shook it between them as he spoke. "People who know how to win at any cost. People who always succeed no matter who's in the way. It's the power I deserve. It's out there, and I can grab it. I can fix everything."

"But why you?"

"You've heard my slogan: *Make America Rule!* Oh, and by the way, I thought it up, you know. No one helped me. That's all me." He looked disappointed when Pia didn't respond. "Everywhere I go, huge crowds are cheering for me. Big audiences, huge rallies, all cheering—me— because they want me to rule America. You should come and hear them. They love me." He twirled his cane. "You remember what that's like, right? You used to be pretty good at soccer. They cheer for me the way they used to cheer for you, only louder and harder. I deserve that respect. I deserve that power. Stand on the podium with me, endorse me, and you can hear those crowds cheering for me. It's intoxicating."

"Crowds did not cheer for me." She stepped close and looked down at him. "They cheered for the team. Coaches, trainers, players, assistants— we worked together to achieve our common goal. The fans knew the training we'd put in and the effort we'd extended and the pain we'd endured. They honored our hard work."

"Oh, I see what you're doing." He shook a finger at her and grinned. "You're trying to make me lose my temper. It's not going to work, little lady. Think about who we are. After thirty years of tax cuts designed specifically to benefit this country's best owners, about a thousand people now own more of America than the rest of them combined. We were entrusted with this legacy for a reason—because we know how to use it. We're sponsoring Super PACs across the country. We're putting our candidates in offices in every state at every level. I'm the crowning achievement of everything we've been working for all these years. People like you and me are going to rule, Pia. I am going to rule everything. And you can rule too." He leaned back and giggled. "At least, rule over Health and Human Servants."

"Just go with HHS," the pale man whispered.

Deep breath. Kowtow. For Dad.

She strolled around him, making him twist. "It took years to earn a spot on the National Team. Talent is trained, not born. I have no qualifications—other than being rich—for a cabinet position. You don't have any qualifications at all for—"

"Be an ambassador if you want to be all high and mighty then. England, France, Germania, whatever you—"

"Not England, sir." The pale man looked paler.

"Don't be a fool." Roche snarled at his man. "She can give ten times what Goldstein paid for that."

"Goldman, sir. And, yessir."

As a history major in college, she'd learned about the wheeling and dealing attending all campaigns and legislation. The crass cynicism of Roche's offer enraged her.

Pia's dream-memory resurfaced. She felt herself on a cliff as tons of water assaulted the rock, shooting high in the air above her. Every drop fell back, and the ebb dragged out to sea. A calm and placid pool of blue-green ocean lay below her. She jumped into the water's warm embrace and felt at one with Mother Nature. Then the waves pounded back in, relentlessly roaring toward the stone, shocking her back to the present.

She said, "What if I say no?"

Roche flushed with anger, his skin turned scarlet.

"No one survives saying 'no' to me." Spittle flew from his lips; his blood vessels pulsed to the surface of his thin skin. "I'll cancel Sabel Satellite's federal contracts. You'll close the division in a week. I'll regulate Sabel Capital into oblivion." He stepped toe-to-toe with Pia, his wild, angry eyes flashing up at her. "I'll have the FBI investigate your little security company. Sabel Tech will roil under NSA scrutiny. You'll be ruined."

Behind him, the pale man palmed his face. The tan man crossed his arms and gloated.

Kowtow. For Dad. Pia softened. "Those are serious abuses of power. I should be careful."

"Damn straight." Roche gave her a venal smile. "I'll put you down for a hundred million for starters. We have a lot of work to fix this mess. There are a lot of simple solutions to things like healthcare and—"

She just couldn't do it.

She said, "Simple answers to complex problems only work in simple minds."

Dad would have to do his own kowtowing.

"How dare you?" Roche hoisted his cane and held it in one hand like a club. "You're making an enemy—"

"My enemy is Strangelove." She watched his eyes flare at the mention. "He's playing you."

"No, he's … ehm, who did you say?"

Pia held her phone up with a picture of the Russian agents in Jacob's hotel room. "These men said they arranged secret meetings for Watson and Strangelove."

"Everybody out." Roche glared at his men. They scurried away, their fancy shoes slipping on hardwood floors like dogs on wet tile.

"Watson works for you." Roche backed up a yard from her.

"Weekdays, but he works for you on the weekends. You'll issue him an IRS 1099 for consulting work at the end of the year, so don't try to deny it." She crossed her arms. "We have Strangelove's handwritten notes about #HuntersFail."

Blood pumped blue and red beneath Roche's colorless skin like an anatomical animation. She could almost see his synapses firing as he struggled to find an answer. Then he relaxed and came back. "You have nothing. If you did, you would've given it to that lügenpresse bitch of yours." He pointed his cane at the door through which Emily had left earlier. "You're young and petulant. I'll overlook everything you've said—if you sign on now. This is your last chance. Want in?"

"No."

"You're just as stupid as your old man." Roche turned on his cane. He marched halfway to the door, then stopped. "By the way, that little stunt with your Zurich files was clever. Too bad none of those companies exist anymore."

"What will Viktor Popov say about you?"

"You're going to tangle with him?" Roche strode out, tapping his cane with each step. "He'll save me the trouble of dealing with you."

CHAPTER 31

WE ARRIVED IN DC AN hour before dawn. The Russian we'd captured in Denmark was turning into an albatross. We had no idea how to explain his presence to Homeland Security. The pilot wouldn't touch him. So, I came up with a plan.

Miguel and I went through Customs and came back to drag the guy from the cargo hold to Miguel's G63.

We pulled around behind the car barn at Sabel Gardens and deposited the sleeping Russian. After pumping six Sabel Darts into the guy over the last twenty-four hours, we were slightly worried he might overdose on snake venom. Then we remembered he was one of the guys who tried to kill us in an unsportsmanlike ambush. The few lucid moments we had with him, he stuck to name (Pavel), rank (corporal), and serial number. All of which made himself a worthless hostage.

We propped him against a tree in some soft grass.

Miguel drove around to the front. "Was all this crap really necessary?"

"Detective CJ is after my ass. If I show up with a kidnap victim slung over my shoulder, he's going to think I had something to do with it."

"You had everything to do with it." He parked by the grand staircase. "I still say we should pin a note on him and drop him at Viktor's crib."

Mercury leaned between the front seats. *That's why Pia-Caesar-Sabel likes you better than Monster Slayer here. He's always thinking about fun things to do with your victims. That's just tactical thinking. You're smart, you listen to my strategic thinking. Keep on that road, my brutha.*

I said, *Frankly, I don't get what's so strategic about it.*

Holy Mother of Bellona, dude. I gotta explain everything to you—

twice. Your people find the guy and turn him into the cops for B and E. The cops are going ask the Russian Embassy about him. Viktor Popov will have to explain how this man got in the country. Why he wasn't listed on the diplomatic manifests. What job he has in the Embassy, shit like that. Even if Viktor is a hands-off boss, he's gonna know who the guy is and who brought him to the States.

I said, *You sure this is going to work? I mean the part about pissing off Popov so he's off-balance?*

Mercury said, *Have I ever steered you wrong?*

A whole series of bad ideas came to mind—but I let it go. You can't blame an out-of-work god for losing track of advances in morality. Which is why I rejected his first idea: give the Russian a cardboard sword and let him fight Miguel to the death. *Gladiatoria munera* is not considered a sport anymore. Legally, anyway.

As we went inside to report to the boss, she came up the path on her morning 10K in full Olympian mode. She barreled toward us like a cheetah chasing down dinner. Every muscle rippled beneath her spandex. I stepped back. She slowed just before impact and met us at the back door.

"Your girlfriend is nice," she said between pants.

"I'm glad you had a chance to talk to her."

"I didn't really," she said. "But Tania and Emily don't like her, so she must be nice. Oh, and, she's visiting for the weekend."

"Wait, what? Didn't she have to go to Milan in a big hurry?"

"Monaco. Fund-raiser for foster kids. My foundation sent enough to keep them going another year. Which gave her time to visit with us." Ms. Sabel smiled and squeezed my arm.

Mercury stepped up behind her. *You should mention that you don't even know her last name, homie.*

I said, *What's in a name? That which we call a rose by any other—*

Mercury said, *Don't even.*

"Why doesn't Tania like her?" I asked.

"Jealous." She turned and went inside. We followed. "I'm sure you want to spend some time with her, so take a couple days and show her the city."

"She'd be target practice for Viktor Popov," Miguel said. "That Belenov dude knew us on sight. They've been studying our profiles."

She cringed at the reminder that we were the subjects of intense Russian scrutiny. We stopped in the vestibule between her gymnasium and the main house. Ms. Sabel grabbed a towel from the rack by the door and wiped her face.

Sylvia wandered in looking like someone trying to get out of a maze. She was still wearing her red dress.

"Time zones always get me turned around." She looked at the three of us, then checked the time on her phone. She pointed an elegant finger around us and offered a tentative guess. "You too?"

"You have a keen eye for fashion," Ms. Sabel said to her. "Would you do me a favor and take Jacob to New York for a makeover? We can't take him anywhere dressed like that."

I looked down at my t-shirt. *US Army Rangers/Because even SEALs need heroes.*

Sylvia gave me the once-over. "Sure. When?"

"Now." Ms. Sabel and I said in unison.

We gave each other an embarrassed glance for sounding too eager. We were both anxious to get her out of there. Neither of us felt the need to explain the danger.

Ms. Sabel faced me. "I need you to meet with Kasey Earl. He's been calling and texting non-stop. By then Bianca's team should have some leads from Stavanger for you."

"Hours? I thought you said I could have a couple days."

"Days, hours, minutes, whatever." She shrugged. "We have to expose the connection between Roche and Strangelove since it doesn't look like we'll crack the Pozdeeva code in time. Oh, and Watson lands on a commercial flight later, but I'll handle that one." She leaned in and whispered. "Show her a good time, buy her a few outfits and whatever else she needs. Expense it. Take the jet."

She exchanged it's-been-funs with Sylvia and trotted down the hall. Miguel did the same and left in the opposite direction.

Which left Sylvia, designer dress and all, with me in an odd corner of a mansion the size of a stadium. It was the first time we'd been alone since our first meeting. She clutched her clutch and twisted her feet and looked around, her gaze finally coming back to me. She pointed at the space Ms. Sabel left. "She's amazing. Knows all the statistics about foster care. There are so many kids who never get a stable home, just shuffled from one house to the next every few weeks. When they turn eighteen, society forgets about them."

I just stared, transfixed by those eyes. And that smile. And those—

Mercury said, *Yo, Casanova, try talking to her. I hear women like that a whole lot more than being gawked at like a sex object.*

"Uh," I said eloquently. "Hungry?"

"Famished." She gave me that electric smile.

I led the way to the kitchen. The staff was busy making breakfast for the security team. Since Viktor made his threat, we'd quadrupled the guards at all Sabel locations. Which meant Chef was working around-the-clock to feed everyone. Not wanting to bother her, I grabbed a mixing bowl, buttermilk, flour, malt, and the other ingredients and stirred it up. I added walnuts and blueberries to the batter and let it sit while I whipped egg whites into a fine meringue. I gingerly folded in the meringue to boost the fluff-factor. Just before pouring it into the waffle iron, I drizzled in melted butter. Sylvia watched me work but said nothing. She didn't have to. I'm impressive in the kitchen.

We took our finished waffles to the nook, where I topped them with whipped cream and syrup. She stared at the plate, speechless.

I sliced the first bite and held the fork up. Her gaze locked on mine while she enveloped the offering with her lips and drew back. She chewed and swallowed and didn't think it odd that I had a second bite ready and waiting for her. She took in five more mouthfuls before I could stop staring into her pale blue eyes.

We managed to finish eating without having to "get a room"—as some of the kitchen staff suggested.

We took Sabel Three to New York City and watched dawn break across the Appalachians on the way.

We walked through Central Park while waiting for the stores to open. She resisted getting a new wardrobe until I explained that Ms. Sabel felt bad about whisking her away without giving her time to pack. I added a personal guarantee: no strings attached, which did the trick. When the first boutiques opened, she slowly warmed to the idea of shopping on Ms. Sabel's dime and eagerly picked out a few modest things.

We traipsed from Barneys New York to MTTM to Acne Studios, none of which I'd ever heard of before. She picked out several outfits for me that looked like they came from the Feed and Farm Store a few miles up the road from my folk's place in Donnellson, Iowa—at fifty times the price. Fashion appeared to be rich people spending a fortune to look like edgy poor people. If taking down bad guys doesn't work out, I can always make a living smuggling threads from back home.

She picked up some lacy personal items and asked if she needed to model them for me. I figured she was testing my no-strings guarantee and declined. She looked disappointed. When it comes to reading women, I never get it right.

After lunch at a trendy place, I left her to shop on her own and went to meet Kasey Earl.

On entering the café, the strong smell of freshly ground beans and all-American nectar floated my way. Patrons ordered in voices raised above the chatter of the remoras who operate out of American coffee shops armed with phones and laptops. Kasey sat midway down the row with his back to both the entrance and the window. A good indicator of why I always got the drop on him. I patted him on the back and swung into the chair opposite him.

He looked up and sneered at my fashion statement. "You coming out of the closet?"

I glanced at my chic outfit. "New girlfriend."

He nodded his understanding of the myriad humiliations a man must face to spark a fire.

He pushed the phone I'd given him across the table. "Ain't gonna need this no more."

"What's up, big boy?" I grinned. "We're not friends?"

"You ain't taking me seriously, Jacob."

"Sorry, buddy." I nudged the phone back in his direction but not across the halfway line. "We've been a little busy. The Russians invaded—"

"Think I give a shit about your bromance with Popov?"

The fact that he knew the name took me by surprise. Then I realized what it meant. Watson had found a way to communicate with Roche Security people after I stripped him of his personal phone.

"You haven't given us a reason to meet," I said. "Ms. Sabel's a busy woman."

"What I gotta do with you? I told you she'd pay big for what I got. Get real, or we're done."

I felt my temper building up. Who did this subterranean weasel think he was?

Mercury waved a hand behind Kasey's head. *Listen to the man, dawg. Pia-Caesar-Sabel told you to find out what he wants, and you're picking a fight. So think: what does he want even more than money?*

I said, *Sex?*

Mercury rolled his eyes. *Duh, but even more than sex?*

I shrugged, *I'm lost.*

What does everyone want?

Sex.

Mercury clenched his fists. *Other than... Aside from... In order to get...*

Then it hit me. Sometimes my tarnished god comes through.

"Kasey, if we aren't showing you the *respect* you deserve, it might have something to do with your many attempts—"

"Can we just get over that shit? OK? We agreed that trying to kill her was just business." Kasey glared and squeezed his paper cup hard enough to pop the plastic lid off. "You don't make her call me—I take this to the press."

"Two hundred people want to meet with her every day." I pushed the phone a little farther across the table. "Most of those people have an ounce of credibility. And all of them give her a reason."

"I got credibility."

"I know that." I tried to catch his wandering gaze. "But give me something. Anything."

Kasey looked over his shoulder then leaned across the table and looked me straight in the eye. "I know who killed her dad."

I was stunned. I couldn't speak.

Twenty-two years ago, when she was a toddler, two men broke into her home. At the tender age of four, Pia Sabel killed one intruder, Leroy Johnson. The other man shot her father and fled. He was never found.

"Don't fuck with me on this one, Jacob." Kasey grabbed my forearm and squeezed hard. "Don't try to guess. Don't try none of them tricks you play. And don't ask that Greek god of yours neither."

Mercury stomped between the small tables. *Greek? Who the fuck is he calling Greek? Shoot the squirmy little motherfucker, right now. Greek! You're not going to let him dis me like that and walk away, are you?*

I said, *I'll kill him later. I need to get a name out of him.*

C'mon now, bro. Zeus is my bitch! I wouldn't let Aphrodite give me a lap dance. Fuck the Greeks. Show him who's boss. Right here, right now.

"A lot of time has passed, Kasey." I tried to look skeptical. "Is this guy still alive?"

"You ain't getting nothing from me." He crossed his arms and leaned back. "I come across a clue and worked it. I put a lot of time and effort into this. And I come up with a lot more than you ever got." He leaned forward again to emphasize his point. "I got what's coming to me."

Mercury pointed out the window. *Hey now—looky here, homie. Who dat?*

I glanced outside. Multitudes of anonymous people passed by.

Kasey kept staring at my eyes while he waited for me to say something.

One of the faces outside looked familiar. But it couldn't be. Thousands of miles and many millions of people separated us.

"Jacob, you spacing out on me or something?" Kasey snapped his fingers in front of my face. "You gonna get me that meeting?"

I looked back at Kasey as the face outside registered in my brain. "Yeah, my brother. I gotcha on this one." I stood and grabbed my jacket off the chair. "She'll talk to you. Keep the phone. I'll be in touch. But you better have some evidence to back it up, or she'll rip you in half."

I patted his shoulder and strode out quickly.

When I reached the street, I looked in the direction I'd last seen the man. Sometimes, the most random things in life just happen. Sometimes the gods make them happen. Knowing Mercury, I was leaning toward random. The man I was looking for was disappearing down the sidewalk with a hot blonde on his arm. He had a reddish beard that conjured the word 'beatnik' while his darting dark eyes invoked high intelligence with the morals of a rattlesnake.

The Russian from Stavanger. Yuri Belenov.

CHAPTER 32

YURI FELT SO GIDDY, HE wanted to laugh. Everything was going right. He was free of Strangelove and Russia. It was risky and premature, but it was done. Life was beautiful on a sunny autumn day in New York City. And he had the finest young lady he could imagine by his side. He'd always scoffed at romantic clichés about floating on clouds and fluttering hearts, yet here he was holding hands with Andrine. He floated down the sidewalk, and his heart fluttered like mad.

Their outing to MoMA had turned into an education for him. She explained the exhibits, and he listened—and loved every minute of it. They walked soundlessly through Saint Patrick's Cathedral in awe of the stunning architecture and meticulous details in every corner. Even as an avowed atheist, he could appreciate the intricate work involved in building the church.

Everything he saw, he saw as if it were brand-new. Freedom had opened his eyes and allowed him to drink in everything with a new attitude. No longer observing the USA as a hostile environment, he could sense the excitement of it. No longer looking for opportunities to exploit, he could see Americans as they were: free to be good or bad, smart or dumb, kind or mean.

On their way to the famous New York Public Library, he glanced at Andrine. She sensed his gaze and smiled back and squeezed his hand.

They walked another block in pure bliss, but something began to bother him. He felt as if a spider were crawling on his back. It was an odd sensation. Yuri Belenov was used to being in charge, giving orders, bestowing medals, and having everyone else watch his back.

Then the pain in his ribs stung a warning and his phone rang.

Glancing at the screen, he knew the country code immediately. His reverie collapsed.

Strangelove.

"Excuse me," he said to Andrine. "I need only a minute."

He turned from her, faced the nearest storefront, and took a moment to compose himself. How had Strangelove tracked him down? They had all new identities courtesy of an alcoholic at the Estonian Embassy. He'd crushed the phone Vasili bought. He grabbed a new one when he reached America. The money and credit cards came from Alexi's account and had been washed through the Caymans and Luxembourg and Panama. Vasili died without even asking Yuri's destination. How did Strangelove find him?

In the windows of the giant H&M store, he saw Andrine's reflection.

She watched people walking by, innocent and unaware of the dangers so close at hand. Strangelove had located them by tracing her passport to New York. Which could mean only one thing: Vasili had betrayed Yuri's love for the girl knowing full well it could lead to her torture and death. It was a good thing he'd killed the bastard. A man who would stoop so low deserved to die. Hate filled the space between his ears. He raised the phone.

"You are having a good time?" Strangelove chuckled.

"Until your call. What do you want?"

"I understand your girl has beautiful legs." Strangelove's voice grew louder with each word. "It would be a shame if they were destroyed in a trash compactor."

Yuri gripped the phone and felt his soul collapse. "What must happen to prevent that?"

"Vasili gave you the name of a troubled Mexican. You were going to talk him into mass murder. That was a very good plan. You should do that right after you kill Jacob Stearne."

"Where is Stearne? How do I find him?"

"Others have done your work for you. They traced him back to Washington, DC. He has a home in Bethesda."

"What about Alan Sabel? Where can I find—"

"You've proven ineffective at multitasking. I've made other

arrangements."

Strangelove clicked off.

Yuri looked up at Andrine's reflection in the window.

She was giving directions to a stranger.

The conversation consumed him. He had to protect Andrine at all costs. She was everything, Strangelove was nothing. Yet Strangelove had leverage. Yuri was not free. Not yet.

He refocused on the reflection and took a closer look at the familiar-looking man talking to his girl.

In that instant, Yuri stopped being an atheist. He was suddenly filled with proof of God's existence and His divine hatred of Yuri Belenov. First Strangelove and now his new nemesis. Dressed more like a New Yorker than a soldier, Jacob Stearne chatted with Andrine. What had he done to deserve such a wretched fate?

It didn't matter. He would not accept his Avos'. Not this time.

Yuri reached for the pistol he always carried beneath his jacket—and found nothing. It was in the hotel safe because Andrine was an avowed pacifist who hated guns and violence.

Time for brains over brawn.

He sucked in a deep breath and faced the Sabel agent. "Mr. Stearne?"

Andrine looked surprised that they knew each other. If Stearne was stunned, it didn't show. The man was tall and muscular. He stared with an insane intensity. He looked directly into your cornea, but off by a millimeter to the upper left, as if staring three kilometers beyond.

"How ya been, Yuri?" Stearne grinned like a bear watching salmon come upstream. He stuck out a hand.

"Quite well, thank you, Jacob." Yuri found himself shaking hands with a forced smile plastered on his face. "May I call you Jacob?"

"I always honor a man's last request."

Yuri's adrenaline flowed, and his heart rate skyrocketed. He could not believe the man was standing there less than twenty-four hours after meeting him in Stavanger. Where did he come from? How did he find them? Did he know who killed Vasili? Or Alexi? What about the airline crash? Stearne wasn't calling the police, so he didn't know everything. There was no need to panic or give in to hysteria just because the man turned up on a random sidewalk in the biggest city in America.

Yuri nodded at Stearne, grabbed Andrine's arm a little harder than he intended, and continued their walk to the library.

He leaned to her ear. "He is a business associate of mine. I must speak to him privately. You don't mind wandering a little, do you? I'll find you when we're done."

Only mildly perturbed, she nodded as they passed the stone lions marking the entrance. The three of them trotted up the steps. Yuri slyly tossed his phone in a trash can as they entered. Andrine excused herself and headed for the main reading room.

Jacob pointed to one side and led the way up some crowded stairs. "How did a nice girl like her end up with a jerk like you?"

Yuri laughed it off and followed. He considered several ways to kill the man should he find the opportunity. The movies always make it look easy to stab a man with a pen or some other trivial object. In real life, the precision needed would require the victim to hold still while the pen was delivered at extreme velocity. The taller, stronger Stearne would not be easy. Yuri ran his fingers over his razor-sharp belt buckle knife. With the element of surprise, he could slice the man's throat. Maybe. A switchblade would be better.

Stearne snapped a glance over his shoulder as if he'd heard Yuri thinking. His gaze dropped to Yuri's buckle. A remorseless killer rose behind the American's eyes.

Not a chance he could take the man in public.

Then an idea came to him. One that should've come to him days ago.

"You appear quite hostile, Mr. Stearne," Yuri said as they climbed. "I am not your enemy. Why follow me around the world?"

"Why live-stream a lighthouse on a remote Danish island?"

"Do you want the official story?"

"I can guess. You're a security company guarding a client site."

Yuri smiled. They were both professionals; there was no need to lie.

They arrived in the McGraw Rotunda. Stearne leaned against a Corinthian walnut pilaster, ignoring the exquisite artwork surrounding them. The seventeen-foot barrel ceiling sheltered them with a fresco and intricate carvings.

Yuri marveled at the woodwork and murals. He looked up at the fantastic painting centered in the ceiling. "Why harbor a grudge about soldiers doing their master's bidding?"

"Why run from me in Stavanger?" Stearne faced him with his death stare; every muscle in his face devoid of normal, everyday tension.

"Why search for Strangelove?" Yuri asked.

"Why so many questions?"

"Because we have a common enemy." Yuri looked at the murals again, projecting his fearlessness.

Stearne tilted his head. "Are you applying for political asylum?"

Stearne's sarcastic answer proved one thing: they hadn't traced the airliners to him. Yet. It was only a matter of time. When they did, his life was over. The Americans would stop at nothing to kill him and everyone in the banda. They invaded Iraq, killing hundreds of thousands because of their frustration at losing Osama bin Laden in Afghanistan's mountains. They were an imperial wrecking machine, capable of destroying any person or nation that stood in their path. They would come for him, and they would never stop.

He had hours to change Andrine's identity and get lost among the anonymous hordes of Big Apple tourists. He held Stearne's gaze long enough for the soldier to take him seriously.

"You saying your enemy is Strangelove?" Stearne asked.

"He is my general." Yuri nodded. "I am a major in his unit. He asks too much. He violates the Geneva Convention worse than Dick Cheney."

"You don't like your boss," Stearne said. "Big leap from that to betrayal. Keep going."

"Why did Strangelove order me to kill you?" Yuri turned back to the paintings.

"They were painted by Edward Laning," Stearne said. "Under the Works Progress Administration during the Great Depression. They depict the history of the written word."

Yuri couldn't hide his surprise that a soldier from Iowa, stationed in Washington, would know details about a library in New York.

Stearne checked his curiosity with a nod at a plaque on the wall.

"Quit gawking and talk."

Americans. Always business, never appreciating everyday wonders surrounding them.

"Who are you to Strangelove?" Yuri asked. "Why does he care about an obscure soldier working for an American billionaire?"

"My problem. You think I trust you? Why do you want to turn on him? Why don't I just end your miserable vacation and call it a day?"

Yuri clenched his jaw and regarded the man. "He threatened my girlfriend."

Stearne might not appreciate art, but he appreciated beauty. That much was evident when he pursed his lips and nodded slowly. They had found common ground. Andrine was not a pawn to be sacrificed at the whim of political powers far away. Not in Yuri's world. And certainly not in Stearne's.

"And he orchestrated the ambush on Bornholm." Yuri sighed. "My part was only to monitor the video. After the other platoon failed, he's ordered me to kill you. He threatened her life for yours."

"Let's pretend I believe you for a minute."

"Ask him yourself." Yuri stared hard. "I'll tell you where to find him."

Yuri grabbed a passing college student and asked for pen and paper. He drew a crude map of an apartment building and a nearby office tower in Kaliningrad. He listed the streets and the landmarks. He tore the page from the spiral notebook and gave it to Stearne.

The next few seconds were critical. Everything hinged on getting Stearne off his back long enough to walk out of New York alive. Strangelove thought Stearne was in DC. He was in the clear for a few hours, perhaps as long as a day.

If Stearne killed Strangelove, great. If not, Yuri would work Strangelove's projects until he could get clear. His priorities were obvious: incite the mad Mexican to go on a rampage, find a new passport for Andrine, then flee the city. Wait for the news of who won the war between Strangelove and Stearne.

Handing the drawing to Stearne, he said, "Strangelove's home and office. One hundred twelve soldiers at the office. None in the apartment building. You take care of him, and I will be forever in your debt. I give you my word, soldier-to-soldier."

CHAPTER 33

PIA SAT AT A LARGE reading table in the downstairs library at Sabel Gardens, scrolling through the thousands of documents from Pozdeeva's drive. Across the table, Tania and Alan did the same. Around the world, a hundred Sabel employees toiled to discover the cipher key. In the midst of scattered pages on the floor nearby, Emily read through the information from Alan's Zurich files. Pacing the floor with a tablet in his hand, Olivier also tried to unravel the mystery of what a dead man so desperately wanted to tell them.

Veronica Hunter's caller ID showed up on Pia's phone.

When she answered, the President said, "I got your message. I'd love to have your financial support, but I'm not sure I understand what you meant about not making the same mistakes as Alan."

"You made promises, and he was generous. After the election, none of your promises materialized."

"There is no quid pro quo." The President used her in-no-uncertain-terms voice. "You give to the candidate of your choice because you believe in the platform. Separately, I listen to the advice of people like you and your dad. When that advice is in the best interests of the country—"

"Roche offered me HHS." Pia paused. "Or Ambassador to England, my choice."

"He's, um, inexperienced, Pia. Don't hold it against him." Hunter huffed. "What do you want?"

Pia explained several executive orders that would benefit Sabel Industries which in turn would benefit the country and the economy. Separately, Pia agreed that the donation once promised to Marty Maddox before his death might be released to the current candidate of the NEXT USA party. Since there were no guarantees that Hunter would win, the executive orders would be executed immediately. But, they agreed, there was no connection between the orders and any possible donation in the future. Pia clicked off.

Several people looked up, expecting an explanation. She didn't offer any.

"I'm sorry, Pia." Emily scooped up her pile of Zurich papers. "There's nothing in here."

"But it shows his companies receiving millions in financing from Russia."

"Ten, twenty years ago." Emily shook her head. "Most of the loans were paid back, the accounts were closed, and the companies were sold off or dissolved. If it's money laundering, the proof is still in Russia. There's no smoking gun here."

"Then why did they kill Eleni? Why did they send a squad after us in France?"

Emily shrugged. "The bigger question is: what was Pozdeeva doing at CIA headquarters? And what does the cipher tell us?"

"Unfortunately," Pia said, "CIA records are sealed. No surprise. And Bianca says if there is a Vigenère cipher buried in here, we need to know which documents hold the ciphertext and the key. The many pages in Latin are candidates, but they could be just calligraphy sheets. We just don't know. We're still working on it."

"You've tried his family, names, dates, anniversaries?"

"Ages ago. Nothing easy. We've tried the streets between his office and home, his favorite sports teams, cities he's visited. We're running out of ideas."

"He would've used something easy to explain," Emily said as if thinking out loud. "Which could be anything. It's maddening."

Olivier paced between them, muttering to himself.

"News from the local cops." Dad held up his phone. "The Russians disavowed the guy Jacob brought back. Now the guy's asked for asylum and wants my help. Claims he can help us in return. The FBI has a bunch of questions." Alan looked at Pia. "You have to face facts, Pia. Jacob's mental health issues put us in—"

"He's fine." She glared. "He tried to unsettle Popov. It was a good strategy. But, it didn't work."

"I've been summoned to discuss this." Alan stood, his voice rising fast and his face glowing red. "We have to stop Roche as soon as possible. But. Now I have to get an attorney and learn about the intricacies of asylum. Tell Jacob—"

"Let it go, Dad. He pulled your ass off a bomb in Germany."

"Yeah. Well." Alan tried to contain himself. "If you want to keep him around, bear in mind that sooner or later we're going to regret—"

"He stays."

"You need to listen to me."

"Enough, Dad." Pia glared at him. "I'm not a little girl anymore. I can handle everything just fine without your help."

He ran his fingers through his hair, turned away, then back, and let out an exasperated breath. Then he stepped in, kissed her forehead, and left.

Olivier paced faster, his route growing to cover the length of the library.

Pia's butler came in to announce the arrival of David Watson. As a mobile executive, Pia kept her sensitive correspondence on her phone and laptop. The secrets she wanted to keep from Roche were in the library, scattered around her. She instructed the butler to park her double agent in her home office down the hall.

Bianca entered and stepped around the butler.

She approached Pia and froze mid-step when she saw Emily. "I didn't know you were back."

"Just got here." Emily looked away. "A few hours ago."

The only sound in the room came from Olivier's pacing. Tania glanced over her shoulder, then buried her face in her tablet.

"I have to get back to the office." Emily faced Pia. "Thanks for taking me on your adventures."

Pia nodded. Emily left.

Bianca turned to watch her leave then slowly returned her gaze to Pia.

Pia patted her friend's shoulder gingerly. "Give her time."

"It's not easy, *mi parcera*." Bianca wrung her hands and looked over her shoulder at the empty space Emily left behind. She sniffled quietly, took a deep breath, then turned back. "Jacob has a lead on Strangelove's home and office."

"I saw his text. Could it be a trap?"

"Trust is the most difficult part of the spy business." Bianca took another deep breath, forcing herself to stay focused on the job. "Jacob's source claimed he was the guy charged with monitoring Bornholm. It's plausible that Strangelove would have a direct-report do it on his behalf to maintain a deniable distance. But the guy is an army major, which is pretty high-level for watching an empty lighthouse. That part bothers me. Jacob uploaded the guy's router logs yesterday. We thought it was low priority, but I've put the team on it now. The net is: we have no idea. Yet."

"What does Jacob want to do?" Pia asked.

"Swoop in, kill them all, sort through the rubble."

"What do you recommend?"

"Research and confirm the source first."

"I'll tell Jacob to chill for now. But I don't want to be on the bench if this is real." Pia sent a text to Jacob telling him to enjoy the weekend in NYC and that she'd get back to him when she was ready to make a move.

Bianca was about to say something when Olivier thrust his tablet between them. "I have something. Maybe."

Pia looked at several rows of thumbnails lined up on his screen.

"These are all the photographs taken in one office or another. It looks like an FSB office judging from the background. Soviet architecture covered the gray-and-bland spectrum. The pictures show Pozdeeva's friends, never him. Possibly, he is the photographer. But this one, and only this one shows him with the older woman who is not his wife or mother. Behind them, looking the other way is Viktor Popov—the man who killed my wife. This is the only picture of Popov. And it's the only one of Pozdeeva inside the FSB offices. I think it is the message to us. This woman is important."

Pia rolled Olivier's comment about Popov around in her mind for a second. Popov was wrecking the American election. Popov was enabling Roche. And Popov was a murderous bastard. It's a shame Jacob hadn't eliminated him when he had the chance. Popov was fast becoming her highest priority.

"I found a series of random documents." Pia reached for her tablet. "Hundreds of them. Unnecessary documents for Pozdeeva to include. Bills of lading for coal. Transfers of paper. Personnel requisitions. Many of them from the Soviet era. The only thing they have in common: they were requested by Olesya Sochneva." She looked at him. "Do you know who she is?"

Olivier shook his head. "No idea."

"Hang on." Bianca typed furiously on her phone. "How is it spelled in Cyrillic?"

Pia showed her the stamped documents.

Bianca searched for photos of Olesya and came up with hundreds of young Russian women including a movie star. Toward the bottom of the thumbnails was one old lady. They compared it to the photo Olivier found. The same woman.

Bianca dialed her assistant, spoke for a moment, then pulled the phone down. "Popov's secretary for thirty years."

Pia cocked her head. "Why her?"

"Secondary or tertiary contact," Bianca said. "Pozdeeva knew they would try to kill him. In case they succeeded, he needed a backup plan. You theorized they already found his co-conspirator—that's how they learned about the microdots. This woman must be the last resort. We know Popov is an evil man. In the Soviet Union, people were assigned jobs. If you weren't happy, there weren't a lot of options. It's possible Ms. Sochneva loathed him and willingly helped Pozdeeva."

"It's a stretch." Pia and Bianca looked at each other. "But what else do we have? Find her."

She marched out of the room and down the hallway to her home office.

Watson stood at her bookshelf, reading the titles. It was not a small bookcase. Filled mostly with her second-favorite subject, history, it also held many memoirs by soccer legends.

He glanced up at her. "Have you read all of these?"

"Why do Russians in Barcelona know you?" She pointed to a chair in front of her massive walnut desk.

"Your boy, Jacob, left me in a crack house in Barcelona." Watson saw her glare. He shrugged and took his assigned seat. "My profile was pretty high in Moscow. After all, I was the Senior Agent in Charge of Counterintelligence."

Pia rounded the desk and stood with her forearms on the executive chair's back. "When you interviewed for this job, you said Hunter only told me half the story of my parent's murders. You determined how much she told me by who was left alive. Tell me, who should be dead?"

"I never advocate killing."

"Sophistry. Who did you expect me to kill if I knew the whole story?" Watson squirmed in his chair.

"You offered to help investigate the murders." Pia pulled the chair back and sat. "What help can you provide?"

"I may have been too anxious for the job."

"Why have you traveled to Barcelona several times on your days off?"

"It's a great town." Watson tried to smile. "Messi plays there."

"What do you think the Russians told Jacob about you?"

"I have no idea." Watson pouted and shook his head. "Whatever they put in my dossier, I would guess."

"Did you travel to Barcelona and visit with Russian intelligence officers on behalf of Chuck Roche's campaign?"

"No, ma'am." Watson leaned back, pressed his hand over his heart. "I swear—"

"Chuck Roche admitted you are on his payroll."

"Not on behalf of the campaign."

"Have you seen this before?" She held a photo on her phone for him to see.

Strangelove's handwritten note defining #HuntersFail stared at him.

"Never." Sweat broke out on his forehead. "What is it?"

"You need to make a choice, Mr. Watson. Right here, right now. Who do you work for, me, Roche, or Strangelove?"

"Ms. Sabel, I don't know what those people told Jacob. I don't know what you hear or from whom, but I am loyal to you one hundred percent."

Pia stared hard in a silence that stretched long enough for him to stroke his gray crew cut, adjust his position in the chair, and re-cross his legs.

"Remind me," Pia said, "where did you go to college?"

"University of Wisconsin." He smiled. "Madison."

She nodded in thought. She sat up and leaned forward. "Well, your word is good enough for me."

He smiled, looking greatly relieved.

"See Agent Marty for your next assignment. Close the door on your way out."

She turned her chair away and texted Bianca. Behind her, she heard Watson hesitate, decide not to protest, then leave.

Bianca texted back two seconds before walking in.

"I have her on the line—Olesya." Bianca handed her phone to Pia. "She will speak only to you."

Pia took the phone, put it on speaker, and said hello.

"What Alan Sabel weared for funeral of your mother?" The woman on the other end of the line spoke with a heavy accent in a rough, aged voice.

"A polo shirt under a sport coat," Pia said.

"Why?"

"Because he was a poor grad student and hadn't picked up his dry cleaning."

"Those questions; Ilya tell me only you know answers." She paused. "You tell to his daughter when she ask for autograph."

Pia remembered the meeting. At a crowded restaurant in Leipzig, a father led his bashful teenager through the crowd to meet Pia.

"You were Viktor Popov's secretary?"

Pia heard the distinct sound of the woman spitting before she answered. "Only to feed children and grandchildren. Not good man."

"We agree. What was Ilya Pozdeeva trying to tell me with all this?"

"Poor wife. FSB put in jail. She knows only about microdots. I know the thing that is big."

Pia jotted a note to get the State Department to push for Ms. Pozdeeva's release. "What things do you know?"

"Ilya destroy all Viktor's kompromat on Alan."

"That's good!" Pia looked at Bianca. "Very generous of him."

"He do this thing for reason." The old woman sighed. "He want Alan get kompromat on Viktor, turn him in. Put him in jail."

"We would love to do that. But how can I get kompromat on Viktor Popov?"

Olesya took a deep breath and spoke quietly as if someone were listening to her. "Ilya have it. He—oh, how you say—hide in plain sight."

Pia and Bianca raised their brows at each other.

"The deed," Bianca whispered. "The dacha?"

Pia grabbed a pen and jotted on a pad of paper. *Get dacha location. Tell Tania + Dhanpal we go in 20.*

Bianca nodded and left.

"I want different thing." The woman's voice strengthened and rose. "You kill Viktor."

"Uh." Pia imagined the international incident that murdering a Russian leader might kick up. Jacob's incursion into the Embassy and his other Russian escapades had landed them in plenty of trouble already. Sabel Security was the focus of several ongoing investigations by everyone from Homeland to the FBI to the State Department. "That might be difficult. He's surrounded by—"

"Popov kill my granddaughter." Another sound of spitting came through. "Ilya tell me you are strong woman. Stronger than me. Do this for Ilya's ghost. Do this for my Tatyana. Do this for Bridgette Jallet. Do this for your mother."

CHAPTER 34

MEETING YURI BELENOV IN PERSON was a stroke of luck beyond the powers of Mercury and his band of deadbeat deities. Naturally, that didn't stop him from claiming it was his will. Gods are like that—taking credit for every leaf that blows your way. I considered thanking a more current holy one, but I never know what kind of reaction I might get. My lifestyle as a security specialist/international assassin doesn't fit the admonition of today's dominant deity to "love thy neighbor." Given my recent narrow escapes from death, I thought it best to heed the old proverb: dance with the god who brung ya.

After texting the boss and Bianca, I pocketed my phone and cut over to Madison Avenue. I peered through the crowd, hoping to catch a glimpse of Sylvia. She stepped out of Tom Ford just as I neared the store. I saw her before she saw me. My jaw dropped. An emerald green dress wrapped her exquisite form and made her auburn hair glow. Matching shoes, clutch, and jeweled barrette rounded out the outfit. She turned my way when we were still twenty yards apart. I wolf-whistled.

Several women walking by scowled at me. I ignored them.

Sylvia threw her shopping-bag-laden hands out and twirled.

Every male trekking the sidewalk rubbernecked and bumped into each other. One nearly ran into me, looked me up and down, made the connection, and muttered, "Lucky bastard."

Mercury stepped out from behind her with his arms folded across his chest. *You haven't heard a Jupiter-damn thing I've said, have you, horn-dog?*

Without taking my eyes off Sylvia, I said, *Whaaa?*

Mercury said, *They're going to empty the trash in ten minutes, homie.*

You gotta to move.

I said, *So?*

Sylvia smiled. Her pale blue eyes zapped me like tractor beams. I continued moving straight toward her under her spell.

"Do we have dinner reservations?" she asked. "Cause if you haven't made plans, I made reservations at Zenkichi. They say it's so private you can make love at your table. Do you like Japanese?"

Mercury stepped around my personal beauty queen and leaned into my face. *Dude! Yuri dropped his burner in the trash at the library. You can dig it out and get the confirmation Pia-Caesar-Sabel and Bianca are about to waste the weekend looking for. If Roche wins because you were too love-struck to grab a Russian phone when you had the chance, you're toast.*

Two statements snaked through my thick skull at the same instant. *Yuri's phone* and *make love at your table.*

I froze in midstride, still two steps short of Sylvia. She looked surprised at my sudden lack of enthusiasm.

There is no decision more difficult in a man's life than the choice between imminent sex and doing something for his career. In a nanosecond, I weighed the importance of my future with Sylvia against my future with Sabel Security. Ms. Sabel wanted Strangelove. I wanted Sylvia. Sylvia wanted me. But there was a chance Sylvia would still want me on Monday while Strangelove could be armored up with tanks in a matter of hours.

I said, "Ken Cheesy sounds fine."

"Zenkichi." She frowned.

I tossed a thumb over my shoulder, pointing about a mile down Madison Avenue in the general direction of the NYPL. "I forgot something at the library. I gotta get it real quick. Be right back."

"The library?" Her tone of voice bordered on incredulous. One more wrong word and she would go ballistic.

"Yeah. Take me a couple minutes. Wait right here." I looked at the Tom Ford store. The only thing I know about fashion is that Tom Ford is fashionista speak for you-can't-afford-it-farm-boy. Then I remembered I left her with my company AMEX Centurion card. It's black, made of titanium, and has no spending limit. At all. I looked at her.

She was pretty. I could trust her. Probably.

Cabs in New York are as elusive as trout back home. Sometimes you raise your hand and a cab stops. Sometimes two hundred of them roll by without tapping the brakes. Uber and Lyft would take longer to arrange than the five minutes for a sprint. I took off running.

A few steps away, I gave Sylvia a glance over my shoulder. She stood curbside, an elegant finger in the air for a cab. Sometimes you have to leave things to fate. Or kismet. Or whatever the Romans called it.

I crossed to 5th Avenue on 41st Street and rounded the lion statue at full gallop and saw the trash can at the top of the stairs. According to my memory, it was the only one Yuri neared during our meeting.

I stuck my arm in the restricting hole. Odd gooey sensations slithered over my hand, wrist, and arm. Junk food containers spilled open as I thrashed around in the muck. Then I felt something rectangular and solid, not Styrofoam. I pulled it out.

An unscratched smartphone sheathed in a Hello Kitty case stared back at me. I was confused. The design elements didn't strike me as Russian military-esque.

A twelve-year-old girl in braces snatched it out of my hand and yelled over her shoulder, "Ethan, I'm gonna kill you!" She turned back to me. "Thanks."

She ran into the crowd.

I stuck my hand back in the swamp.

"Dumpster diving is not my idea of a good first date." Sylvia's strained voice assaulted my ears.

I reached and clawed deeper, nearly crawling into the can. Few things in life are as disgusting as squeezing half-eaten junk food covered in ketchup. I persevered while trying to think up a witty reply. Before I came up with one, I came up with the phone. I extracted my prize from the narrow opening and observed it. It was black, cheap, and disposable. Definitely the right one because there was no way two jerk-brothers would trash a little sister's phone on the same day.

I faced my angel. "Found it."

Mustard dripped off the left corner. Her lip curled.

"Hang on a sec." I held a finger between us and called Bianca from my phone. She instructed me to have a courier deliver it to her right away without touching the fingerprint reader or any buttons. Yuri was a techie and would've set it to self-destruct at any unauthorized attempt. She would handle it at Sabel Tech. We disconnected.

"That's more important than dinner?" Sylvia sneered at the phone.

"The future of Russian-American relations depends on this phone." I took a breath after seeing her extremely negative facial expression. "As soon as I ship this out, I'll be ready for dinner."

She stared at the filth running down my right arm.

Mercury paraded behind her looking smug. *Now you with me, bro? Do you see why she ends up killing you every time? Cause you suck. Dump her right now, get it over with. Nothing lost. You don't even know her last name.*

I hid my grimy arm behind my back. When I asked, a passing mom pushing a stroller gave up a couple diaper wipes for my sponge bath. She didn't think anything of it because New York.

I took the shopping bags from Sylvia as we made our way down the steps to the street. I pulled the only purchase I made for myself on our little shopping spree, a t-shirt that read, *75th Rangers, Dangerous When Provoked.* Sylvia was not amused. She grabbed the t-shirt and replaced it with a shirt that set Ms. Sabel back $600.

I didn't see any difference. Except it had a collar. And long sleeves. And a pattern like the designer tried to do a plaid while tripping on acid.

I changed on the spot, trying to impress her with my abs. The daily sit-ups paid off. She grinned and bit her lip and blushed and looked away.

We walked up 5th Ave toward Central Park. I glanced over at her. "What's your last name?"

She shrugged.

"How is it you speak French, Spanish, and English without any accents?"

She looked at me sideways as we walked. "I was born in France, moved to LA when I was ten, moved back to France when I was eighteen. The Spaniards think I have a horrible accent."

"What took you back to icy France from LA?"

"A woman is waving at you." She pointed across the Zoo to the Delacorte Clock.

Agent Kayla from the local office met us. I gave her the phone and told her she could take the jet to DC if she promised to bring it right back. Kayla took off running.

Sylvia rolled her eyes. "You don't need to impress me with the jet-thing."

Damn. If I couldn't impress her with Ms. Sabel's wealth, my looks and charm were going to fall short. And I had only one impressive thing left in my arsenal.

We decided the zoo was too crowded and strolled through the park. We talked about interesting things, like how history was largely defined by wars until the nineteenth century when the dates of inventions and milestones in science grabbed more headlines. We pondered whether that was a good sign for civilization or just an anomaly. We discussed the importance of classical music training in childhood since we both abandoned stringed instruments as soon as our parents would allow. I had continued with the saxophone and Sylvia still played the trumpet.

As the sun set, the creeping evening chill allowed me to wrap an arm around Sylvia on our carriage ride. She snuggled in, and we rode in silence.

It was dark when the cab dropped us at Zenkichi in Brooklyn. The curtained tables were not quite as private as Sylvia imagined—unless she was more of an exhibitionist than I thought. We opted for the Autumn *Omakase*, a Japanese word meaning, "I leave it to you," or chef's choice.

We were on the second of eight courses—persimmon and watercress and tofu and goji berries—when Kayla texted me that she'd returned and left the pilots in the ignition. The Zenkichi staff explained each course and the ingredients when serving them. The third and fourth courses— maguro in vinegar with Tosa soy sauce followed by scallop in ponzu dashi broth—were equally life-enhancing experiences.

Then Bianca called. "You have to get down here right away. Assemble a team. You have to go after Yuri Belenov."

I turned away from the best date I'd ever had. "Why? What's

wrong?"

"We traced the router." Bianca took a deep, nervous breath. "I think he's the one who crashed the airliners. I'm working with the NSA and the FAA and Homeland, but the Feds will take time. You need to catch that guy right now."

"I don't know where to find Yuri, but I know where to find his boss."

"We haven't confirmed his map yet. But, yeah, that would be a good place to start."

My gaze wandered unfocused beyond the gauze curtains as my hand reached for the service button. I signaled for the check. Bianca kept talking about IP addresses and connections to FAA locations in rural Ohio, which sounded very high-tech and convincing but was way outside my field of expertise. I felt Sylvia's cold stare. Bianca finished up and clicked off.

I paid the bill, and we left in a cab. Sylvia responded to my apologies with the silent treatment. Not a hostile treatment. More of a one-step-short-of-hostile treatment. She was trying hard to fall in love with me—which was exactly what I wanted—but I was running off on a mission I couldn't talk about. Her aggravation was understandable.

Mercury turned around from the cab's passenger seat. *Toldya, bro. She's not going to be happy with you. You're not ideal boyfriend material. The only place your abs are going to get you is a modeling gig for the covers of cheap romance novels. Chest only, no face.*

I said, *Why didn't you tell me about Yuri?*

Mercury said, *Whatdya want from me? You expect me to follow all those little bits and bites you guys call communication these days? Those are for the new gods.*

Which gods? I need gods who can help me in the modern age.

They haven't formed yet. But there's a guy named Derrick, works out of George Lucas's garage, who's working on it. May the fulcrum be with you. Until then, I'm all you get. Before you get cocky, don't forget about that meteor we've got with your name on it. Have you even started on that shrine?

I made phone calls to assemble my team. Dhanpal and Tania were nowhere to be found. No one had seen them since Ms. Sabel's last text to me around noon. Miguel had just conquered jet lag and was ready for anything that involved shooting Russians. Only Emily and Alan Sabel were at the Gardens. I kept dialing to round up personnel.

We transferred to Sabel Three and roared into the night skies. I kept working the phones.

Sylvia read a book called *Death and the Damned* by some clown I'd never heard of.

We landed and went straight to the Gardens. The company was stretched thin. Our successes under Ms. Sabel's management had every employee fully deployed. Add to that the fact that everyone had been pulling double duty since I pissed off Viktor Popov and the result was: no extra personnel to go after Yuri and Strangelove.

The butler showed Sylvia to the guest wing while I walked into the library. Emily looked up from a table strewn with papers and tablets.

"Where is everybody?"

She shrugged.

"Have you seen Ms. Sabel?" I asked.

"She took Tania and Dhanpal to Lithuania." She stood and stretched. "They're going to sneak across the border to Riga in Latvia and tear apart Popov's dacha."

Before I could ask why David Watson strode in like he owned the place.

Mercury thumbed over his shoulder at our in-house assassin. *Hey bro, take this guy on your quest. You can make him walk point and get him killed.*

I said, *We don't just kill people.*

Mercury said, *Zat so? Let me put it in the Judeo-Christian vernacular for you: King David did it to Bathsheba's husband so he could have the man's woman. Oh. Hold up. You don't get Watson's woman. Ima have to think about this. I'll get back to you.*

Watson said, "Hey, Agent Marty told me to report to you. Can I have the day off? I've not slept since we left for Barcelona."

"No."

Behind him, Sylvia hovered at the doorway. Unwilling to come in, and unable to leave, she bit her lip. I wanted to say something. She wanted to say something. Neither of us knew what.

Alan Sabel pushed around her, dragging a familiar-looking Russian soldier. "Jacob, this is Pavel. You brought him here and now he's requesting asylum."

I shot a peeved glance at Mercury. *That was some strategic plan you had.*

Mercury ducked his head in shame and snuck away.

My phone rang. Bianca said, "Yuri's last incoming call originated from the office building on that map he gave you. It's in Kaliningrad. I have high confidence that this confirms Strangelove's location. Working with the NSA, we have a hypothesis that Strangelove ordered Yuri to crash the airliners."

"That makes Strangelove the priority over Yuri."

"Exactly. Here's the good part: we're getting intel from the CIA. They'll support us as long as we don't get caught. If we do, they'll—"

"Disavow our existence and let the Russians kill us. Been there, done that. Send me the coordinates. I'm on my way." I clicked off and stared at Watson.

"What?" Watson asked.

Alan Sabel took a call.

"I've got an assignment for you," I said. "How's your Russian?"

"Counterintelligence against the FSB for fifteen years. How do you think?"

"Good. Translate for Pavel here. I want to make sure we're on the same page. And don't try anything dumb. Pavel knows enough English to know if you're slanting it." I turned to my would-be assassin from Russia by way of Bornholm. "Word is you're looking for asylum. I've got just the thing to help you prove you're worth it. We're going after the GRU general who calls himself Strangelove. We know where he lives. Have you been there?"

Watson hesitated, beads of sweat breaking out on his forehead. He looked me over cautiously before he translated.

Pavel had been stationed at the *Informatsionny Tsentr* building for several months. He knew—and hated—Strangelove. He even drew a map of the area that looked a lot like Yuri's.

Watson's skin grew gray and clammy. A shiver crawled over him.

Miguel walked in and clanked a bag full of weaponry on the table. "Ready to die. Who wants in?"

I pointed at Pavel and Watson.

Miguel looked like I'd passed gas in front of the Queen. He leaned close to my ear. "A guy who tried to kill us and a guy who's planning to kill us?"

I shrugged.

"Anyone else?" Miguel asked.

Emily raised a hand. I began to shake my head because the last thing we needed was a reporter. I mean, journalist.

Miguel stopped me with a why-not shrug. "She shot a guy in the—"

"Yeah. I was there."

"IMPOSSIBLE! You can't be—" Alan Sabel's voice exploded in rage on his call. He clicked off and stormed straight at me like a linebacker going after the quarterback. "Pia's jet was forced down over Kaliningrad."

CHAPTER 35

Nothing ever went right for Yuri Belenov. The crazy Mexican wasn't so crazy after all. He'd screamed at Yuri and called the cops. Approaching sirens had forced Yuri to exit quickly. He ran down one alley after another, ducking through stores, pushing through restaurants to get away. He stole a windbreaker from a shop and traded it for another two blocks later. It was an hour before the patrols gave up and moved on to their next crisis.

He made his way across town, bought a new phone, and found a cab. He rode in silence, thinking through his next move. Failure would never fly with Strangelove. He had to run. With a little luck and the help of his banda—now SHaRC, he reminded himself—he could get away.

Strangelove could find him by tracking Andrine's phone. Simple enough solution: dump her phone. The next problem would be getting her to leave the hotel using a different passport. After thinking through several ideas, his Montreal plan was the only one worth trying. There were historical sites to see. He could tell her he was testing the TSA passport control and needed someone unknown to use a fake. Andrine would want to please him. It might work.

Yuri's banda contained the best hackers Russia had ever produced. Their skill was the only reason the old general was pretending to forgive him. Strangelove had found Yuri, but not the others. The old man still needed Yuri to bring them back. That made Yuri's next step clear: keep the SHaRCs loyal to him.

From his phone, he logged into Reddit using the anonymous username and joined the anonymous forum to communicate with his people. He left a post inquiring about the weather in Singapore a few hours ahead. It was code for the time of their anonymous video session on the H.234 system they'd set up. It was designed to avoid US and Russian surveillance and could force itself to live-stream on each user's phone in case of emergency.

The cab arrived at the Andaz and dropped him at the corner. When he opened his suite, the adjoining room doors stood open. Perfect.

Andrine stood in her suite in a bathrobe, looking through her suitcase. She looked up. "How did your meeting go?"

"Not as planned." He grinned at her casual attire. "I have to test the TSA at the Canadian border."

"Now?" She looked up with a pained expression. "I was about to shower for dinner."

"No, later." He mentally checked off the objects in the room and found her phone charging on the bureau next to him. "I'm looking forward to dinner."

She found her makeup kit and faced him.

They gazed into each other's eyes for a moment. Yuri felt something he'd never felt before. It was beyond the infatuation, anticipation, and eroticism he'd felt so many other times. It was a real desire to hold her, protect her, provide for her, cherish her.

Love.

"Someone called for you earlier." She dug back through her case looking for another item. "A general you used to work for."

Yuri's heart stopped. His blood ran cold.

"He said he'd call you later. I don't know how he got my number."

"Did he leave his?" He picked up her phone. It was Strangelove's connection to them and had to be disposed of.

Yuri's stone-cold voice had resonated in the room like a killer's. She stared at him. He needed to warm it up, mask the situation.

"Our phones look almost identical." He held up his third burner of the day and placed it next to hers.

She crossed to him. Her hands holding her bath-gear between them. She tilted her face up and rose on her tiptoes and kissed him on the lips. She looked into his eyes for a fleeting second, smiled mischievously, then disappeared into the bathroom and shut the door.

He stared at the bland, featureless door for a full minute. His astonishment remained unbroken until the shower splashed on. He shook himself into action. He unplugged her phone, thought for a moment, and replaced it with his. If she stepped out of the shower while he disposed of her phone, there should be a familiar looking object where she left it. As long as she didn't try to use it, he would be fine. That would give him time to hide her phone and throw Strangelove off their trail long enough to get away. With a little luck, they would be truly free by morning.

Pocketing her phone, he ran for the elevator. He'd have to use different identities and new hotels. That would take a lot of explaining. The elevator chimed open, and he entered the universal meditative state for the ride down.

How dare Strangelove call her? Yuri's heart ached. His head pounded with rage. The fat bastard deserved to die. What did Yuri—or SHaRC—care about Mexicans or Sabel Security? Why should they kill any more innocent people for Strangelove's sake? No. It would stop. He could beat the master at his own game.

Seething with hate by the time he reached the ground floor, he ignored the bellman and hailed his own cab. He rode north toward Central Park and walked into the darkness from there. But there was no darkness in the park. The ambient light from the city that never sleeps bathed the walkways with more light than a full moon. Yuri wondered if Americans ever knew what darkness really was. Maybe someday he would show them.

He laid Andrine's phone in the footwell of a horse carriage as he marched by.

His mind raced with hatred for Strangelove. But when he remembered Andrine, his heart rose and fluttered away. She had kissed him. They would consummate their love after dinner. It was her message. Nothing could be better. He'd played his cards just right with her. Not too much, not too soon—not too little either. And now he would reap the benefits of being a good, decent man. He smiled. It felt good to be a good man to a good woman.

Checking his watch, he realized he'd paced more distance than he'd planned. He felt his pocket for his phone. Which he'd left behind on purpose. It was time for the call with SHaRC, and he was on the wrong end of a large city. He raced for the park's exit. Cabs swirled by, filled with theater-goers and tourists and locals. None open for a man out of time and desperate to get back to his phone. Roman or Igor would initiate the call if he didn't. When he failed to join, they would force the video feed open to check on him. He had to be there.

He walked and hailed and walked and hailed from 85th Street to 72nd Street before a cab picked him up. Ten minutes wasted—and he was already ten minutes late. He bolted through the lobby and raced up the stairs, preferring not to wait for an excruciatingly slow lift.

He threw open his door and saw her through the open adjoining doors.

Andrine sat on the edge of the bed, a towel around her body, another around her hair.

Her skin was gray. Her mouth was slack, her features devoid of any pretense. In her hand was Yuri's phone. Roman's face displayed on it.

Yuri stared at her. Then looked at Roman and realized his man was talking.

Andrine's face rose to his. Tears streamed down her cheeks. "You did this? You killed all those people? The airliners—"

Her mouth fell open. She dropped the phone.

Yuri picked it up and yelled at Roman. "What did you say?"

"We could see nothing but the ceiling, we thought you were off camera. We were speaking in Russian, but somehow she understood—"

"Her mother is Russian, you fool. Why were you talking at all? The reason we use video—"

"How it happened doesn't matter." Roman was shouting. "Listen. Something came up. We think Sabel turned us in. The FBI, Interpol, everyone is looking for us. They have your picture. Sabel traced our router logs—"

"I believed you were a good—" Andrine burst into loud sobs.

"Yuri! You have to act." Roman's words rang in Yuri's head. "She heard too much."

His mind exploded. Ten minutes ago, he was in love. Ten minutes ago, his life was on the path to freedom. Ten minutes changed everything.

Now he had no choice. There was no other option.

Her eyes were locked on his, pleading. Her head shook silently back and forth, no.

She screamed.

His hands closed around her throat. Her face turned red. She tried to pry his hands away.

There was no other way. Not for the girl whose dream career was working for Amnesty International. Not for the girl who berated him for advocating the death penalty. She would never let him walk away from his complicity in #HuntersFail. It had to be done.

The movies make it look quick, easy, and quiet. Strangulation is none of those things. It takes tremendous strength and several agonizing minutes to choke a person to death.

He watched her through watery eyes. His whole future and all his dreams were dying with her. Tears dripped down his cheeks and fell on hers. They mingled together and ran like a river off her pretty face. She gurgled and thrashed and pleaded with animalistic grunts. She clawed at his wrists, her fingernails digging into his flesh. Her eyes bulged wide open, connected to his, begging for air. He squeezed harder, hoping to end her struggle quickly in a vain effort to relieve his own pain.

Alexi had been drunk. He gave up right away. Andrine was in love and clung to life with misplaced hope. He pushed her over and leaned his weight into his grip. It was best to end it quickly.

She began to lose consciousness, her eyes rolling without control. But that was only the halfway mark. Mother Nature gave life a tenacious hold in the powerful human mind. Where all rational hope to extend existence ended, the highly evolved brain retreated inward to preserve itself until the brutality passed. Her heartbeat and breathing could revive her body after several airless minutes.

"I'm sorry, Yuri." The phone lay next to him, Roman's face still on it. "It has to be done. You know that."

"Shut up." Yuri spat at the phone. "Shut up! Shut up! Shut up!"

Her eyes focused on him once more at the sound of the voices. "Help—"

Yuri pushed down and squeezed harder. He felt blood vessels breaking. Her windpipe collapsed under his thumbs. For a long time, he pushed and squeezed. As life drained out of her, an equal weight of humanity left him.

Then he felt it. Every muscle in her body relaxed forever. Andrine's life force was gone.

Yuri slid to the floor and wept.

CHAPTER 36

ONE OF PIA'S EYES OPENED after a concentrated effort. It swept a dark, barren room. Concrete. Light seeped in from a door left open an inch. A dank smell. A basement. Her arms hurt. Her feet hurt. Her weight was suspended from her wrists and propped on her ankles. Her body ached. She was stretched on a giant X.

She tried to speak but bit her lip. Still groggy.

She tried to recall her last waking moments. It came in bits and pieces.

All communications on the jet had been jammed by strong radio interference coming from the Russian fighters that forced them down in Kaliningrad. The soldiers on the tarmac had given her no explanation. No apologies. No answers of any kind. She'd been stripped of her electronics and weapons at gunpoint. She'd been escorted to a customs room at the terminal. Tania, Dhanpal, and the pilots were taken to other rooms. She never saw who hit her. She had felt only the powerful blow followed by the needle in her arm.

There was only darkness and the thin sliver of light from the door. A round knob. Not a lever. Not a bolt. This was not a dungeon. Not a cell. It was a room pressed into service. Hasty arrangements had been made. Her arrival had not been planned.

A swirling black cloud approached from the far end of the room. It morphed into Pozdeeva's poisoned face, yellow bile still dripping from his chin. "Comfy?" he asked.

Her head lolled and snapped back up. Had she fallen asleep again? She couldn't tell. Her lips and tongue still felt disconnected. Her muscles barely responded. Her weight burned her wrists and ankles. Did she hear voices?

"Alan. Could I get you some tea?" Eleni asked. Her dead body staggered across the room, then fell in a heap.

Her eyes closed. She heard Olesya's voice on the phone: *Do it for your mother.* What did she mean by that? How did she know anything about Pia's mother? Why didn't Pia ask her? She was too stunned at the woman's brutal request to commit murder on her behalf. Pia was no murderer. But if there were a man who should be killed, Viktor Popov was a prime candidate. But why do it for my mother?

A familiar priest opened the door, dragging a chair behind her. A sturdy, middle-aged woman, she wore a collar and a dark pantsuit. She stopped next to Eleni's collapsed form and sat and sipped from a cup and read a paper.

"Why doesn't God help me?" Pia asked.

"Why do you think it's about you?" the priest asked without looking up. "Why do you think you're the one who needs help?"

"Because I'm hanging from a cross. I've been drugged. I'm in pain. I don't know what they want."

"That's really the issue, isn't it? Not knowing what the future holds." The woman folded her paper. "Imagine being a young man who gave up his future to care for a four-year-old girl. He didn't know what she wanted. He didn't know what the future held. Are you praying for his salvation—or just yours?"

Pia felt nothing but pain. Her shoulders, her rib cage, her shins, everything reported agony to her brain.

"Why is everything a riddle to you people?" Pia's voice echoed in the closed space. "Priests, rabbis, gurus, monks, spirit guides—every answer is another question."

"You think I'm a priest?"

"You were the Episcopal priest who presided over Carmen's funeral."

"You used to think I was your mother." The woman dragged her chair into the dark. "Now you accuse me of representing God."

"It's all bullshit. You don't exist."

Pia felt the ice water dripping off her face. Her right eye opened. The left managed no more than a blurry slit. The door was open a foot. An old, sloppy man in a uniform with stars on the shoulders stood next to a young man with no insignia on his drab uniform. The young man held an empty bucket in his hand.

The old man said something in Russian. The young man saluted and left.

"I assure you," the old man said, "I do exist."

Pia looked down at her drenched athletic wear. A shiver rippled across her skin, traveling deep into her bones. Her teeth rattled. "Where are Tania and Dhanpal?"

"Any questions asked will be asked by me." He folded his hands behind his back and paced to the right. "Let's start with the easiest one. Where were you going?"

"Kaliningrad to kill someone named Strangelove. Know him?" It was Tania's idea when the fighters first appeared alongside the jet. Say nothing about Popov. Give them no reason to search the dacha.

The old man chuckled. "He does not exist."

"My father left a calling card on him. A scar down his neck."

Strangelove sneered and scratched his scar.

Her bravado didn't help. She was in deeper trouble than she expected. Dad's words came back to her. *They're the people who murdered Pozdeeva—and they're the people who invited you to St. Petersburg.*

And now she'd delivered herself to them.

Strangelove paced a few feet away and stopped. The end of the room on the right. Pia counted six steps. Twelve feet because of his slow, deliberate stride. He twisted something with a metallic sound. Window latch? Doorknob? It squeaked, but he didn't open it. He was testing to make sure it was locked.

"You have heard this name from the CIA?" he asked on his slow path back.

"Read it in the paper."

"Your father taught you bad manners." He laughed. "We do not tolerate bad manners."

"What do you want from me?"

He stopped and looked her over. His gaze was a tactical observation, not sexual, not predatory; he was simply assessing her strength and capability. His glance ended with a casualness that telegraphed his internal report: she was nothing to worry about.

"Where is Jacob Stearne?" he asked.

"On his way to kill you, Strangelove."

"Call me what you want." He shrugged. "This news about Stearne is convenient. I did not wish to track him down. And your father, the great Alan Sabel, where is he?"

"Safe inside Sabel Gardens."

The old man turned to her, tilted his head looking her over again. He turned to the doorway and called out in Russian.

A moment later, the young man came in with a large, hardwood cane and handed it to Strangelove. His furtive glance at Pia conveyed a heartfelt sympathy. He rushed out and closed the door. The room was completely dark.

She heard the whoosh of the stick an instant before it sent bolts of pain up from her shin. Another whoosh and more stinging agony from her ribs. Again, a whoosh and jolts from her left shoulder. Another and another, her knee, her breast, her stomach, her feet.

The desire to give up and die began to overwhelm her. The pain was almost too much to bear. Everyone told her it was bound to happen one day—and this was the day. She'd gone too far. Rushing off without a comprehensive plan. Running fearlessly into the unknown, flouting danger, expecting too much.

As she wrenched one way and the other, trying to defend herself, she felt something on her ankle. A chink of some kind. Concentrating, she wriggled her left ankle and felt it again. The chain links holding her down were open links, not welded. There was a chance one could bend. Maybe enough to break. When there was a chance, Pia screwed up her determination. She wrenched it harder and harder, throwing her weight to that side.

The blows were coming faster in shorter swings. He was tiring. Again and again, the stick rained down on her neck and head and thigh and calf.

He stopped.

She heard his breathing, ragged and winded. The cane clattered to the floor.

A flash blinded her. In the illuminated second, she imagined he'd taken a picture with his phone. She couldn't be sure.

He stepped away, toward the door. The sliver of light enlarged and he stepped through.

"What do you want to know?" she called out.

He stopped, a silhouette in the open door's narrow space. He shrugged. "Nothing."

"Why are you doing this to me?"

"Why do you think this's about you?" Strangelove asked without looking back.

"What are you doing?"

He turned to face her. "Making sure your slow and painful death summons Alan Sabel."

The door closed.

Pia took a deep breath. Her promise to Olivier was no idle threat. Strangelove and his boss, Popov, will die. Theirs were the deaths she looked forward to with unanticipated joy. She had to get out of there and get back to her people. They would storm the fortress and lay waste to this maniac. Nothing had filled her with more desire in her life. She wanted them dead.

The swelling began immediately. Every inch of her skin on the front of her body screamed in pain. No stranger to injuries—sports injuries, at least—she recalled how she persevered through each one and eventually healed. This was much greater pain, but ignoring it was her only option. She had to get out of there and free her friends. Their peril was her fault.

She twisted her left ankle. The chink in the chain revealed itself. She held it taut against the anchor and pulled with all her strength. Nothing gave. She relaxed and caught her breath. Once again, she moved the chain link to the right place, twisted it at just the right angle, and this time used her heel for leverage against the cross. The link snapped. Its noise echoed through the room. The link pinged off a wall in the dark.

She had a method. Therefore, she had hope. Her pain subsided for a second.

Ignoring the agony as it rushed back, she worked her wrists and ankles. The throbbing grew, her joints swelled, her muscles ached. She continued twisting, leveraging any angle she could find to free herself. It took the better part of an hour. When her feet hit the floor, she wanted to jump for joy.

The pain racking her body dissuaded her.

She fought off exhaustion and tiptoed to the right. She found the wall. Feeling her way in total darkness, she discovered a window and traced its edge to a latch. The latch was padlocked. Farther down she found empty shelves and bare concrete walls. At the corner, more wall. Another corner, more wall. Then, the door.

The aching and swelling made her woozy. Holding the doorknob for stability, she took a moment to gather her strength.

Backing from the door, she felt the floor with her feet until she found the hardwood cane. With a deep breath, she powered through the pain in her bones and marched forward.

Armed with one piece of wood, she pressed her ear to the door and listened. Nothing. But that meant nothing. She smacked the door with the stick and stepped back.

A second later, the door opened, the young man stepped through, his back illuminated by the light in the hall.

Pia brought the cane down with all her might on his skull. He thumped on the cement floor.

It was time to run. Make her break.

She took a deep breath and tried to move.

Her vision swirled. Her knees buckled. Her world went black.

She landed on top of him.

CHAPTER 37

Miguel, Pavel, and the Major pored over maps and adjusted the battle plan at the front of Alan Sabel's jet. We were on our way to a tiny target area in the Baltic. Watson slumped in the back, unloved. I never told anyone why he was unloved; they just picked up on my vibe and ignored him.

Alan Sabel sat across the aisle from me. He'd spent the first two hours of flight yelling at anyone he could get on the phone. *How did the Russians force her down? How could NATO let that happen? Where was the US Air Force? Why? How? When? Who?* He spent the next two hours of the flight yelling at everyone in the Sabel empire. *How did they know she was coming? Who told them which jet she took? How could the pilots let themselves be taken? Who is responsible, damn it?* The Major took the brunt of his anger.

Always the alpha-executive, giving orders and demanding actions, he eventually slumped in defeat. Then he was lost in his guilt-ridden thoughts about how he managed to get Ms. Sabel's parents killed over two decades ago. He stared at the photograph Strangelove had sent him of her bruised and beaten body.

The Major worked around his demands to assemble a team. Alan Sabel refused to let anyone from the other Sabel offices undertake saving his daughter. Even though the Oslo, Stockholm, and Warsaw offices were closer—he had to be there. He wanted only the best, most trusted operatives—Miguel, the Major, and me—on the team.

I was lost in my own problems. Sylvia's face wouldn't leave me. When I told her the Russians were holding Ms. Sabel for ransom, I expected her to wish me well. A hero's sendoff. But her negative reaction took me by surprise. She was afraid of falling in love with the kind of man who might come home in a casket. It spoke volumes about why I wasn't married and never would be until I left this death-defying job. No mother would want to wait for the father of her children to come home in a coffin. The soldier's wife is a terrible job held only by saints.

Our brief, but unconsummated, flirtation had been in utter denial of our careers. She assumed I was a well-paid lackey to a billionaire, fetching lost sunglasses and tongue-lashing servants as needed. Instead, I was off to invade a lonely corner of Russia, fighting a nuclear power with no tangible support from the USA. A suicide mission.

I had no idea what she did for a living.

Mercury tapped me on the shoulder. *Did it occur to you, my brutha, that a girl who wears a tight, red dress before lunch and willingly flees the Iberian Peninsula, might not be Mother Teresa? Or maybe she does a different kind of social work—*

I said, *Can we focus on Ms. Sabel for a moment?*

No need to get salty, bro. You got my 4-1-1: Pavel's legit; Watson walks point; and Strangelove is outside his mandate, so he can't command the resources he needs until Popov calls him back.

I asked, *Where is Popov?*

Surgery. You did a number on him, dawg. He's having another leg reconstruction. When he comes out of the ether, he'll be coming for you. And he won't be Mr. Happy.

Mr. Sabel held his phone across the aisle and pointed at the picture of Ms. Sabel crucified. "We can't let this guy live. You hear me?"

She was splayed out like a pinned insect. The wall behind her was smooth, gray cement. Beneath her, the same. In the picture's corner, a high, short window painted black.

I grabbed the phone out of his hand and deleted the picture. "He's trying to get inside your head. You're letting him. Sit tight. We've got this."

Mercury said, *You damn well better have this, young blood. You mess this up, we're through. The Dii Concentes is unanimous on this one. You can't build a shrine big enough to make up for losing Pia-Caesar-Sabel.*

I said, *I'd kill myself if I lost her.*

Suicide? None of this do-it-yourself bullshit, homie. Anything short of success and we'll have Strangelove peel your skin with a letter opener. With those things, only the pointy-end is sharp enough—

I said, *Yeah, I get it.*

Miguel and the Major trooped back to the cargo hold and opened the door. Pavel joined them. Watson and Emily were the only ones without parachute experience. Pavel had been in the KSO—Russian special ops—and knew how to jump. Miguel would tandem with Watson, I would carry Emily. We suited up with Sabel Liquid Armor, helmets, visors, parachutes, and emergency life vests.

Miguel leaned close to me. "Tell me again why I'm trusting my life to a Russian who tried to kill me?"

"Mercury vouched for him."

He gave me a long, solemn look.

I looked at Pavel. His face was white, his forehead clammy. If Mercury pulled a "just kidding" on this one, my next stop would be to sign up at the nearest synagogue.

Alan trudged into our cramped space. "Where's my gear?"

I waited for the Major to speak up. She turned away. I faced him. "You're not coming."

"The hell I'm not. I own this outfit—"

"You're not qualified. You'd be a huge liability. Your presence would jeopardize the mission. Not a discussion. Sir."

"Jonelle!" He stared at the back of the Major's head. He was the only one who used her first name.

"He's right." She kept her back to him. "If you come, Pia isn't the only one who would die tonight."

"What are you saying?"

The Major turned and grabbed his arms with tears in her eyes. "You have to come to grips with reality: she's already dead."

"You can't believe that."

"If you start with false hope, you can only fail."

Miguel and I glanced at each other. She was lying, but we could guess why. Strangelove would keep Ms. Sabel alive until Alan showed up. Then he would kill her in front of him to get what he wanted. Just like

Bridgette Jallet. That's why Alan couldn't come with us. We were setting him up for a second chance. If we failed, he could try again.

Alan stormed away, raging in loud profanities.

The jet had been dropping and slowing. We screwed in our earbuds and put on our helmets. The pilot put the jet in a tight, slow circle a few hundred feet over the Baltic. A Gulfstream is the opposite of an ideal jump plane, but our pilot was a master craftsman and held it a touch above stall speed. On his signal, we opened the cargo hold and rolled out into the darkness.

With Mercury's guidance, Emily and I landed like a seagull on the waiting stealth-Zodiac. The others floundered in the surf until they were picked up by the other three craft waiting in the dark. The six agents from the Sabel Stockholm office brought a good deal of firepower. When we were all aboard, they fired up the assault boats and we flew across the frigid black waters toward the Pregolya River in Kaliningrad.

We covered most of the distance on gas power, then switched to electric when we neared Russian patrol areas. It took a long time to get there because we valued stealth over speed. We beached on the river banks just below the building Belenov had identified as Strangelove's.

Pavel swore there were too many guards, regulations, and logs for Strangelove to conduct a covert operation inside the building. But next to it stood a stout brick structure that once housed a coal generator in the days when Kaliningrad was the part of Prussia called Königsberg. It was the most likely site for his trap.

The street was quiet, a business district buttoned up for the night. We deployed our team. Three Swedes with silent drones would monitor our perimeter; the other three joined my team as we crept from the river bank.

The generator building was an empty warehouse with a warren of rooms and chambers in various states of decay. Pavel suggested we start with the ground floor offices. A few boarded-up windows leaked faint light from inside. We formed up, ready for the assault.

Mercury said, *Where you going, homie? There's a coal chute covered in weeds on the other side. Strangelove has no idea it's even there.*

"Hold up." I waited until the team gave me the WTF? look. "I've got a better idea. This was a coal-fired plant. It has to have a coal chute."

I took off for the far side and whacked through waist-high plant life, heading to the spot where my deadbeat god said it would be. The team looked impressed. Miguel saluted his appreciation for my divine intervention.

We sent Watson down first. As expected, he wasn't happy about being my mine-canary. He used his initial report to complain—once again—about having a Sabel Dart gun instead of a real weapon. I saw no reason to tell him they weren't even darts, just blanks.

I let him rant, then came after him. Once I arrived down the lengthy spillway, I gut-punched him. As he doubled over in pain, I whispered, "Mission-critical chatter only."

The ruse with Watson was completely unnecessary, but it felt good.

The coal room was at least two levels below ground. Sabel Visors gave me an infrared look in the pitch black. The brick walls were coated with ancient coal dust. Otherwise, the chamber was barren. The team dropped down, assembled, and we took two stairs on opposite sides of the giant room.

The next floor up had one large empty space and several smaller rooms. One of the rooms held Tania and Dhanpal. Both were drugged and tied to iron pipes.

Dhanpal is a former SEAL. They're a short, wiry, indestructible breed. He once ran a 100-mile race on a bet and came in third. His condition in that dark generator station was unrecognizable. His head lolled when I whispered to him. He knew it was me and wanted to respond but couldn't. Tania was in the same state. We got them to their feet and sent them staggering back to the boats with Emily.

Mercury floated down from the ceiling. *Six on the roof, bro. They still think you're coming in from above. Four on the ground floor, hiding in offices. Bad news, though. I can't find Pia-Caesar-Sabel.*

I said, *Why not? Do they have a better god on their side?*

Whoa now. Mercury leaned back like I'd slapped him. *No need to get nasty up in here. They got no gods. They're holding back, waiting to see Alan-Caesar-Sabel in the flesh.*

He didn't come with us.

Dude. Do you think he's the kind of guy who sits around waiting for you to bring his daughter home? He's on his way.

I shuddered at the thought. Mr. Sabel was the kind of guy who would rent a helicopter and fly into the hornet's nest on the roof. But I didn't know what I could do about it.

Miguel handed out Sabel Darts-on-a-stick, handheld darts for silent operation. I moved the team into position below the stairs leading to the ground floor.

Pushing Watson in front, we entered the main gallery. It was a large empty space. On one side were two doors, slightly ajar; opposite were four doors, slightly ajar. They could take down waves of assault teams from their positions, each man taking a turn should the first man fail.

I slammed a dart into Watson's butt and kicked him forward. He crashed face-first on the oak floor with a satisfying thud.

It was not the noise expected in the Russian playbook. They were waiting for the definitive signs of special-ops soldiers: nearly-silent footfalls rushing to a point, then stopping. After a specified interval without danger, a second soldier would advance. The sounds would softly repeat until our entire squad was exposed in the central space. Only then would the Russians launch their counterattack. Once we engaged with the first soldier, the second and third would join in a crossfire. The fourth man would stay in reserve. Conceivably, a Russian squad could take out an invading platoon.

But none of that happened because the noise they heard was a loud bump. No scurrying boots. No pause before the next invader joined the first. Which presented a problem for the Russians. They had to investigate. It could be a vagrant or a raccoon or an enemy. Someone had to find out.

He opened his door just enough to poke his head around. He had standard night vision goggles, the kind that needs a hint of light to operate. There wasn't any. Turning on his flashlight for a split-second was his first and last mistake. I darted him.

The Sabel Dart is interchangeable with a regular 9mm bullet but, because the dart is twice the length of a standard projectile, there is far less gunpowder in the body. It makes a subtle bang, one entirely unfamiliar to a soldier. Which raised the curiosity factor exponentially for those waiting for a scouting report. Which brought out the second soldier across the way. It was a silent game of death. The first one to make a mistake would die. I darted the second soldier.

But I missed.

And that's when the firefight erupted.

Russian number two fired blindly in the direction of my muzzle flash. My standard procedure being fire, move, fire, move—his bullets hit the wall.

I ducked into the storeroom of the first man I darted as Miguel came out of the stairwell firing on full-auto. One of our Stockholm boys came out of the other stairwell and joined in. I fired my H&K MP5SD through the plaster wall into the storeroom next to mine and heard a Russian die.

Three seconds later, the Major called a cease-fire and inspected the damage. Three of the four Russians were bleeding out. One was sleeping off the dart. Watson was out cold but, unfortunately, unhurt.

Our automatic weapons were sound-suppressed, making only a spitting noise. The Russians were less interested in subtlety, firing long and loud. The ambush team on the roof heard the staccato pops and read them like a telegraph. We heard their boots pounding down the old wooden stairs.

Our Swedes ran to positions below the staircases. Pavel, still wearing his Russian-issued gear, including his Russian infrared ID beacon, strode into the center. He gave his former teammates the all clear signal. They let down their guard—and lost the battle. Four of the six went down in a heap. The last two dropped their weapons and put up their hands.

I hate when they surrender. Because then you have to take care of them. You're supposed to remember the Geneva Convention. Make them comfortable. Cut them a slice of cake.

"Larsson reporting." The voice of our west side Swedish observer cut into my comm link. "Car coming. Five kilometers out. Single occupant. Driving fast toward your location."

It was the third report from our perimeter observers. We could operate until Russian reinforcements came, so Larsson and Norfeldt were critical to our operations.

Pavel sauntered up to one of our POWs and berated him in Russian. It was pretty easy to understand his issues. It happens in every army from time to time. When an officer sends men on a mission ill-prepared and undermanned, as Pavel had been on Bornholm, he will face hell from the survivors. The young Russian's defection was easy to appreciate. He was getting back at his superiors for losing his brothers-in-arms to Miguel and me.

Miguel let Pavel rant for a minute, then stabbed the officer with a dart. He did the same for the other prisoner. No Geneva rules about putting your captives to sleep. Saves on cake.

"Let's search the building," the Major ordered.

"She's not here." I stopped everyone in their tracks. "This building is all brick. She was in a concrete room with a half-window up high. Khrushchev-era concrete, smooth and ultra-gray."

Pavel looked at me with a blank expression. His English was weak but he understood and began nodding and gesturing. In a thick Slavic accent, he said, "*Da, podval, kladovka.* Ehm, basement in *Informatsionny Tsentr.*"

We looked at each other. We were seven soldiers who knew what that meant. Strangelove had played us. Did he know we were relying on Pavel? Was Pavel in on it? Had they expected us to follow secret GPS locators to find Tania and Dhanpal? It didn't matter. Ms. Sabel was in the heavily fortified building next door. They were waiting for us.

With grim determination, we shouldered our weapons and filed out.

CHAPTER 38

A VINE-AND-WEED COVERED FENCE SEPARATED the generator building from the Information Center. We peered through leaves while our two perimeter observers sent their drones around for a look at the roof and upper-story windows. They reported back dead quiet. Which was scary as hell.

Mercury tugged my sleeve. *Every office on the ground floor has a Russian in it. The weakest link is third window on the right. It's an all-or-nothing play on Strangelove's part, no one in the floors above.*

I gave everyone instructions and ran to crouch below the specified window. When everyone was in place, I smashed a rock through the glass and emptied a magazine over the wall. There was no need to aim; they were small offices. After spraying left to right, I peeked over the sill. One scared, young soldier scrambled to bring his muzzle up. I shook my head. He took my warning and raised his hands instead of his rifle.

I gave the others the signal. The main door and six windows were breached by flashbangs, which are hell on Russian night vision goggles. My whole team entered the building at once.

I pulled the kid up by his collar, keeping my pistol hard against his eye socket. "Do you speak English?"

"*Angliyskiy? Da.* Yes."

"Where is Strangelove?"

He froze in fear. Answering the question was a capital crime.

"Three … two," I pushed the barrel harder, "one…"

"*Pogreb, podval.*" He stammered for the word in English. "Cellar? One floor down."

I stabbed him with a dart.

"Nordfeldt reporting." Our east side Swedish observer reported in. "Police barracks mobilizing."

It was the report we feared most. He calculated ten to twelve minutes for them to form up and travel the distance. Not much time for a rescue.

We met up in the lobby. There was only one set of stairs going down. The first man would have no chance of survival. We stared at the door. No one spoke. After a moment of silence, Pavel raised his hand.

"I go first." He took a deep breath. "Uniform could trick them. Da?"

The US Army and Sabel Security are not the only organizations to keep a live comm link for fire teams. The Russians we'd subdued were all wearing them. And that meant everyone in his former unit heard Pavel berate his captain. But Pavel knew he was the guy who led us into the generator station, blowing our element of surprise, which allowed Strangelove to ready his final snare. It was Pavel's act of redemption.

Pavel's a good man, not to mention brave. Mercury shook his head. *Hey, homie, there is one unmanned basement window. Follow me.*

I split the team. Pavel and the Swedes mounted the frontal assault. Miguel, the Major, and I went through a thick rose bush and found the basement window. On my signal, Pavel dropped a flashbang down the steps inside. We slid into the window opening.

"What is that smell?" Miguel asked when our noses were assaulted on the first intake of breath.

Mercury said, *Russians love gardening. And that means they also like to compost. Why do you think no one checked the window in this room?*

I glanced around. We stood ankle deep in someone's composting project.

"Larsson reporting." Our outside observer alerted us. "Car has arrived. Passenger is entering the building. Unarmed."

The last detail was all I needed to know to discard the information.

To the sounds of open warfare close by, we mucked our way to the hallway. Around a corner, a large open area lit up with muzzle flashes, mostly from the Russians. Pavel lay on the steps, his contorted body resting on his face. Mercury was right—he had been a brave man. The Swedes fired from the landing above. Six soldiers poured ammo into the cement, its soft composition minimizing ricochets.

What was missing bothered me. No commander. No general directing his men. That could only mean one thing.

Behind me, Miguel opened fire down the hall. With only a glance for communication, the Major and I rolled into the main room. We opened fire on the Russians from behind. The Swedes instinctively knew the drill and dropped down the stairs.

We won the battle. But. We were in Strangelove's grip.

The Major looked at me. I pointed down the hall. Miguel had been firing at something but hadn't joined us in the main room. We snuck a look out the door and saw Miguel pointing to a closed door. Two other doors stood open near him. He slid into one.

"Larsson reporting." The lookout's voice cut into my comm link again. "Identified car occupant from rental papers: Alan Sabel. He's in your building."

In unison, Miguel, the Major, and I said, "Shit."

"Let's get this done before he gets here," the Major said.

The Major and I took up positions on either side of the door. Our Swedes carried a dead Russian for a battering ram. We gave them a count, they smashed through and tossed the body inside. No one fired. The Major and I ran in, crouching and aiming. The Swedes stood at the door frame, covering us.

Strangelove sat at the far wall scratching a long scar on his neck with a pistol. Next to him, Ms. Sabel was bound at the ankles and wrists. A gag was tied tight in her mouth. One of her eyes was wild with anger. The other, swollen shut. Her face and body were bruised and swollen. Behind her, on the left, was the giant X where she'd been tortured.

Positioned around the room were eight Russians. One in each corner, two next to the door, and two behind Strangelove. Some had the look of well-trained veterans, but they couldn't take their eyes off the body of their comrade. Our brutality shocked them.

Nervous soldiers with loaded weapons are not a good thing.

"Lay down your weapons," Strangelove said.

"Why?" the Major asked.

"So we can wait for Alan Sabel in peace."

"We forgot to bring him."

We were in the worst of all battlefields: an enclosed space with too many weapons. Twelve automatic rifles in a space the size of a living room. Any gunfire was as likely to take out one of our own as one of them. The same was true for the Russians. Which made them even more nervous.

I trained my sights on one of the soldiers. The Major kept her barrel focused on the general. The Swedes had picked out one each as well. Even with Miguel, our secret weapon in the room next door awaiting his cue, we were several rifles short of a winning combination.

Mercury said, *Good news, my man. The Swede watching the boats was a medic. He realized the Russians gave Tania and Dhanpal heroin. He always keeps Naloxone, the antidote, with him. They're going to come through that blacked-out window in five minutes. Nobody pulls a trigger til they get here. You got this, bro.*

Normally, that would've been reassuring, but tension rippled through the room like static before a lightning strike. We were in a deadly game of chicken. The first one to blink would lose.

"I'm here." Alan Sabel's baritone boomed angrily behind me. He stepped around the Swedes and into the room. Still in his business suit, he strode to the center and faced Strangelove. "What the hell do you think you're doing?"

"Alan, get out of here." The Major smacked his shoulder.

Strangelove gave Alan a sick grin and scratched his scar.

The soldier at the back corner trained his weapon on Alan. Sweat ran down the boy's forehead into his eyes. He wiped his face on his shoulder. Way too nervous. My Russian, the one in my sights, moved his aim from the Major to Alan and back. He was calm. A guy who'd seen action a time or two.

In my peripheral vision, I could see two Russians beginning to quiver. They knew how close we were to mutual annihilation.

I moved my sights to the edgy kid aiming at Alan. Sweat coated his upper lip.

I was cold. Adrenaline cold. I had ice in my veins.

He was boiling over. He was young. New. Untested.

I knew how the kid felt, every shiver and quake. Any time I wanted, I could instantly recall being the jumpy teenager in his first firefight. It's not something you can forget. Scared and lonely, I had been seven thousand miles from Iowa surrounded by hundreds of strangers trying to kill me before I killed them. Adrenaline had amped me up to the point where my body felt like it was in a paint-shaker. All the sounds in the world had stopped. The only thing I could hear was the last sentence I'd laughed to my mom: *I promise, I won't get killed.* A lie. A big, huge ugly lie that only revealed itself the instant the first rifle cracked. I could die. Snap. Just like that.

It took many missions and an idle god to harness my adrenaline. To get cold.

This kid was on his first mission and had no gods at all.

"My demands are simple." Strangelove chambered a round in his pistol and took the safety off. "Your kompromat on Viktor."

"I don't have any. Pozdeeva gave us reams of information, none of it relevant."

"Why did you clean out your caches?" Strangelove asked.

"For kompromat on Chuck Roche. He's the only one I'm worried about."

"You lie."

In my ear came an update from Nordfeldt, our observer on the east side. "Sixty police, armored vehicles, leaving their compound."

"Let my daughter go," Alan yelled. "Take me instead."

"Nyet." Strangelove scowled and waved his pistol around. "You commit suicide. Then they go."

"Not falling for that trick." Alan leaned forward, aggressive and steaming. "Let her go, or my people open fire."

"Go ahead." Strangelove shrugged. "Give orders."

A ripple of anxious glances circled the Russians, each man looking to his buddy. I prayed to Jupiter for calm. Our team had all served in war zones. Half the Russians were well-trained but untested. The adrenaline rush felt like an old friend to me. It made the Russian's hands shake, and their fingers twitch on the trigger. Their vision narrowed to a tunnel that fixated on the target. Their minds raced through a thousand scenarios. None of them good.

One trigger pull would light the fuse.

Mercury said, *Dude! You gotta get everyone to chill out here. Tania and Dhanpal will storm those windows, but not for another three minutes. Two at best. Say something.*

I racked my brain for something relevant to say that wouldn't sound like "fire" in Russian. Nothing came to mind since I didn't speak Russian. I stole a glance at the Major and could see the same search for words going on in her head.

Pia Sabel's face shook from side to side. Angry and horrified at the same time.

Mr. Sabel remained under the delusion he could save his little girl. In the world of fatherhood, there is no calling as sacred as saving your child. That calling pulled a magnitude harder for him. He swayed with indecision. Call the Russian bluff or light the candle?

"You saved little girl once." Strangelove raised his pistol to Ms. Sabel's temple with a sick grin on his face. "Now you watch her die."

Alan leapt at him.

The twitchy soldier pulled the trigger. His bullet pierced Alan Sabel's head just above the eyebrow. A palm-sized piece of his skull opened like a hinged lid. A chunk of brains flew out with a spray of blood. Snap. Just like that. He was dead before his body hit the floor.

Pia Sabel screamed through her gag.

The Major put a bullet between Strangelove's eyes. His head cracked open like a melon.

I put down the nervous soldier.

Miguel heard the shots fired and burst through the wall. All Russian eyes turned to the crashing plaster and batting. The perfect distraction: we opened fire on the Russians.

Two basement windows opened. Tania, Dhanpal, and Emily dropped in from outside. An instant later, the Russians were dead and dying.

One of our Swedes was wounded.

The Major had a bullet hole in her thigh.

I gave the order. "To the boats."

Ms. Sabel had not stopped screaming since watching her father's head fall apart.

I couldn't stand to see her in agony.

I ran to her, stabbed her with my last Sable Dart. Her eyes fixed on me the instant before the paralysis set in. There's a minute or two of lucid awareness before the sleep medication takes over; the victim knows what's going on but can't do anything about it. In those moments, her eyes filled with grief before rolling slowly back in her head.

Maybe it was the wrong thing to do. But it was done.

Miguel picked up Alan's body.

I put a shoulder under Ms. Sabel and hoisted her up.

Tania helped the Swedes carry their man out. Emily and Dhanpal helped the Major make her way. There was no time left to retrieve Watson.

We ran for the boats on the river's edge as police searchlights lit up the building behind us. I handed Ms. Sabel to the man on the boat and climbed in. The boats pushed off and ran silently away from shore on electric power. As soon as we cleared the city limits, they cranked up the outboard motors and ran full throttle out to sea.

I looked into the crisp, cloudless sky at the infinite array of stars. When I brought my gaze down, it landed on Mercury, sitting on the pontoon.

I jumped up and pounded on him with my fists. *How the hell could you let that happen?*

CHAPTER 39

Four hours after Jacob knocked her out, Pia Sabel sat up in bed on her yacht, *Asteria*. Her good eye watched the Major's. "No. You're wrong. He can't be."

The Major sat in a wheelchair with her bandaged leg propped on a pillow and shook her head.

"Check again." Pia trembled and spun away in her sheets, ignoring the pain in her ribs. "Make sure before you say things like that."

She turned to Jacob who sat in a chair on the other side. He held her gaze for a moment, then looked at the floor.

The Major's hand stroked her shoulder. It felt like a knife ripping at her flesh.

It was impossible. God would never be so cruel.

Her good eye remained glued to Jacob but her mind didn't see him. It didn't register that his rugged face was swollen and red and streaked.

Captain Chamberlain came in and coughed politely. "If it pleases you, ma'am, I've a report on our dealings with the maritime authorities."

Pia turned over and stared at him without trying to reply.

The Major looked at her, then twisted to face Captain Chamberlain. "Go ahead."

"The Swedes and Finns have been kind enough to provide air cover. The Russian fighters have turned back. The authorities in Kaliningrad promised an international protest will be filed with the World Court and the United Nations. The American ambassador in Moscow has been summoned to the Kremlin. Maritime investigators in Gdańsk are awaiting our arrival there within the hour."

Pia felt her instincts kick in, pushing a reply out of her. "Are the best medical specialists waiting for us?"

"Yes, ma'am." He glanced at the Major. "You should know, I've ignored calls from the State Department and the FBI."

"Why?" Pia looked first to the Captain and then the Major.

"Air traffic control in the Baltics confirms your jet was forced down and seized. But the Russians are claiming you invaded. Our government appears to side with the Russians."

The Major turned to Captain Chamberlain, nodded and excused him.

Pia looked in Jacob's general direction. Her fingers ran across the soft sheets but felt nothing. She brought her fingertips to her face but felt nothing. She reached for the Major's hand but felt nothing. She looked at their intertwined fingers. Her pale hand contrasted against the Major's dark skin.

Without looking up, Pia asked, "Did we win?"

The Major said nothing.

"Would it matter if we won or lost?" Pia pulled the sheets to her chin. "Does anything matter? Why do we bother? We're nothing more than fools who think our struggles are important."

The Major squeezed her hand. A tear rolled down her cheek. "He's gone, Pia."

"They can do something in Gdańsk. I'm sure they can. They have to."

Jacob stood suddenly and crossed to the windows. He put his hands on the glass and leaned against it and looked at the Baltic. "I should've taken out that shaky kid. I knew he …"

His unfinished sentence hung in the air between them.

Pia sensed herself standing on her dream-cliff. The water swelled off the cove and came charging forward. She longed to jump in and let the surf crush her against the rock. She took a deep breath. Everyone was staring at her.

"Day after day, for as long as I can remember, he was there. Now. In an instant." Pia threw back the covers and glanced at her bruised arms and legs. "He can't be gone. He can't."

She stood on shaky legs, grabbed a cane, and looked at Jacob. "Where is he? I want to see him."

Jacob looked at the Major. They stared at each other and didn't answer.

"I want to see him." Pia grabbed Jacob's arm. "Now."

He considered her plea but couldn't look at her. "You're sure?"

"Now!"

He turned and led her out through the corridor. The Major followed, taking her wheelchair to the elevator. Pia hobbled on her beaten ankles, leaned on her cane, and edged down the steps to the ship's infirmary.

Tania sat inside, staring at the ceiling. Miguel leaned against the opposite wall.

Alan's body lay on the table under a sheet.

Pia waited, staring at Jacob. He started, then hesitated, then reached for the sheet. He pulled it back.

Alan Sabel, the energetic and gregarious founder, entrepreneur, industrialist—and father—was gray and still, his one eye tilted up and to the right. His shattered skull lay open, the broken shard of bone still connected by an inch of skin. The exposed brain looked like nothing more than a lump of fat. A good deal of it was missing.

She fell on his chest, her arms wrapped around him. A rabid wolverine tried to bite and claw its way out of her insides. She convulsed in pain and anguish.

Tania placed her open palm on Pia's shoulder.

"We killed Strangelove." Pia sobbed before continuing. "I'm going to kill Popov. He's next. Then I'm going for Roche."

She went silent. No one spoke or moved.

After a long time, Pia rose from the soulless cadaver and hugged Tania and cried.

Jacob pulled the sheet back over the big man's face. Then he fell into a chair and put his face in his hands.

The Major said, "I should've shot Strangelove right off."

"Why didn't you?" Jacob asked.

"We didn't have situational control." The Major snapped. "I thought one of them might have orders to shoot Pia."

"Stop." Pia straightened up and limped away and stopped in the doorway. "Popov and Roche and Watson did this. Not us."

She sensed her employees looking at each other with grave concern.

She glanced over at Tania. "Don't leave him alone."

Tania nodded and folded her hands.

Pia left, the three followed her, a silent entourage.

"It's all bullshit." Pia raged in the narrow hall. "Humans are nothing more than babbling idiots. We think we're so important, but it's meaningless. In one second, everything we've ever done, every championship won, every company built, is gone. Just gone. And for what? So we can think we're significant? Why become President? Why build an empire? Why win a trophy? So you can force your will on thousands when you're no better than the man who digs your grave."

She stopped at her bedroom window and watched the whitecaps on the dark sea rolling by. Heavy clouds blotted out the dawn. Her people filed in behind her, uncertain what to say or where to stand. Her closest friends in the world watched her, uncertain how to help.

How dare they stare at her?

"Get out." She turned and pointed her cane at the door.

Jacob looked at the Major. The Major looked at Miguel. Their eyes moved from one to another. They stood rooted in place.

"Get out! Get out! Get out!"

They filed out, hunched over, heads down.

She slammed the door. "Leave me alone."

CHAPTER 40

MS. SABEL'S VOICE RANG IN my head like the reverberations from a grenade in a small room. The door nearly smacked my heel as it banged against the jamb. I grabbed the wheelchair's handles and pushed the Major behind Miguel.

We trod in silence to the Major's room. I pushed her inside. She crawled from the chair to the bed and lay face-down on the pillow. She began to sob.

Few people had known about her decade-long affair with Alan Sabel. Fewer still knew of her many refusals to marry him. She'd once told me she had no intention of having ultra-rich women talk about her behind her back in the social circles of the elite. I couldn't argue with her. Race, age, and socioeconomic contrasts were fertile talking points for gossips. Especially for the insecure second and third wives in that circle.

She was in as much pain as any bereaved widow. More so because she could've taken out Strangelove in the beginning. A decision she'll turn over in her mind for the rest of her life.

Just as I would regret not shooting the shaky kid who'd killed Alan Sabel.

I withdrew quietly and closed the door.

Miguel followed me to my stateroom. I sat on the edge of the bed and stared out of the portal.

He leaned against the wall and gazed at the floor. "We've lost a lot of good friends over the years. Why does this one feel worse?"

I shook my head at his rhetorical question. He knew. I knew. Soldiers sign up to die. It's our gamble: come home a hero or a ghost. Alan Sabel never signed up. He was an executive. He told people what to do, and they did it. He told Strangelove to let his daughter go. He expected that would be it. What an idiot. Why didn't he see the danger? Why did he burst in? I told him to stay out. Dumbshit.

I should've shot the nervous kid. Alan Sabel was my responsibility. My boss. It was my job to protect him. That kid was the weakest link in the room—and I knew it. Now Alan's dead. My failure to act deprived Ms. Sabel of the only parent she had left. She'll never forgive me. She shouldn't. I don't deserve it.

Where was my god in all this? What good is it to know when Dhanpal will arrive? What I need from a god is practical intel: when to put the nervous kid down.

I looked around the room. No gods in sight.

Figures.

Outside, gray waves sloshed under gray clouds. None of the usual dawn-colors were present. The horizon was invisible to my untrained eye. I thought about Ms. Sabel alone, bereft, and desolate. A great way to destroy a human being is to cast her adrift in a cold and lonely world. Nothing can make up for even one lost family member. Losing them all was too much to contemplate.

Miguel pulled his phone out and dialed. Without looking at me, he turned and headed for the door. As he stepped into the hall, I heard his side of the conversation. "Dad? Did I wake you? Sorry, I forgot about all the time zones. I just wanted to say…"

Then he was gone.

The phone in my hand may as well have been a rock. Why couldn't I call my mom? Because Ms. Sabel didn't have a mom to call. Why should I have that luxury?

Not a single new thought crossed my mind. I lost track of time.

Emily came in and sat in the only chair. She sighed loudly.

Her presence made me realize what I should've done. I should've given Alan a pistol and a mission. That's what Ms. Sabel did on Cyprus. Something to keep his mind occupied, so he didn't have to wring his hands and invent bad ideas. I could've had him sit on Watson's sleeping butt to make sure the traitor didn't wake up early. I could've had him help Larsson with the recon. I could've put him in charge of the boats.

Anything to keep him from dreaming up a rescue plan that would never work. To his untrained mind, his plan sounded like a grand and heroic adventure.

Damn it.

"I'm trying to get eyeballs on our story." Emily sighed again. "The politicians are saying Pia's gone crazy. My story has been drowned out."

She put her elbow on her knee and plopped her chin on her palm. "Makes you think, you know?"

A few responses wandered into my mind, but I didn't say anything. I glanced her way before turning back to the gray waves.

"Who matters to you. Who you care about. What's important." She sat back and sighed again. "The girl I dated in high school committed suicide. She came out to her parents, but they were fundamentalist somethings. She couldn't live without their love. For the longest time, I didn't think I could live without hers."

A question crawled in my brain. I didn't speak for two minutes, but I longed for a distraction. "High school? I thought you weren't gay."

"You were the only guy I ever dated. I was trying to …" She sighed. "I didn't want to be gay. It's not all pride parades and porn-sex, you know."

She stared at the ceiling as if she were praying. Then she pulled her phone and dialed. As it rang, she gave me a glance and stood up to leave. When she stepped out, I heard another one-sided conversation. "Bianca, it's me." She started to cry. "Will you forgive me? I don't know why I didn't say yes…"

Then she too was gone.

The company attorney called me. I clicked on and found myself struggling to say hello.

"Jacob, you've got to own this." He was breathing hard as if he'd been running. "I tried to talk to Pia, but she's unable—well, understandably unable—to grasp the problem. The Major doesn't answer her phone. I need you to step up and make everyone understand: NO ONE TALKS TO THE COPS UNTIL I GET THERE."

His shout snapped my head back. "What? What cops?"

"Any cops. The FBI, Customs, Coast Guard, Maryland or Virginia.

Don't worry about Gdansk, I've got that covered. Wait, where do you guys land? Dulles Executive Terminal, right? Never mind. I'll have a team of attorneys meet you. Yeah. So. Nobody says a word without consulting a lawyer first."

I sat up straight. "Why?"

"You haven't seen the news?" He waited a second. "No, of course not. You are the news. You guys are everywhere. The Russians are calling it an act of war. The UN is holding an emergency session. President Hunter has called on the Attorney General and the FBI to make arrests for breaking the laws of a foreign country. They're talking about immediate extradition out of Gdansk. But don't worry about that, I'm making arrangements."

That's what Emily had been talking about. I thought about this for a long time.

He broke the silence. "If you haven't been watching the news, you haven't heard about the election. Chuck Roche won. Hunter conceded half an hour ago."

I made no reply.

The attorney, a stout guy who helped me beat some rush-to-judgment charges more than once, repeated my name several times. His voice came out of a cloud. "Jacob? Jacob?"

"Yeah," I said. "I'm here. I'll tell them."

I clicked off.

When I was in high school, my father announced that our farm was not big enough to support two heirs. When he retired, only one child would get the farm. With his midwestern sense of fair play, he tossed a coin to determine who would inherit his estate. My sister and I watched the coin spinning as it rose. When it came down, I snatched it out of the air. She loved farming. I didn't want to spend another hot summer day pulling weeds out of a combine. There was no need for fate to prevent her destiny from being fulfilled. My father was proud of me in that moment. I felt abandoned. We shoved our feelings into our back pockets and moved on with life. As avid pacifists, my family was shocked when I left Iowa State early in my sophomore year to join the Army. They never condemned my choice, but never embraced it either.

That wasn't why I avoided going home year after year. They loved me, even though I had chosen a warrior's life. It's just that, after visiting Tokyo, London, Istanbul, returning to Donnellson, Iowa held little interest. Why face the tired anecdotes, the perennial judgments, the endless familial rivalry? Mom's questions feel like razor blades. Dad's endless advice on how to marry Brianna Wagner so I can run her family farm. Uncle Marty's small-town jokes never end. Cousin Daryl's insecurities: "If I'd joined up with you I would've been a colonel by now." That from a guy who still flinches when I look at him.

God how I miss them.

CHAPTER 41

YURI STOOD ON THE RUE Sainte-Pierre in Montréal as evening sleet peppered him in early November. In his ears, Heather Nova sang the old Hungarian suicide song, *Gloomy Sunday*. He looked at his tracker app and looked back at the Hotel le Saint James. He gritted his teeth and waited under an awning. Luck got him across the border. Pure luck. Headlines scrolled across the bottom of every TV in every bar and restaurant from New York to Toronto. Every cop car that drove by put a lump in Yuri's throat. All of North America searched for the hackers who brought down Flight 1028. It was no longer known as #HuntersFail; they were calling it a terrorist attack. Rumors flew about Russians orchestrating the disaster. The American president had stressed that there was no definitive intelligence. Pictures of Yuri and his men had yet to surface. It was only a matter of time.

Half an hour went by before the man who looked like Yuri trotted down the front steps in a black raincoat and whistled as he walked down the street. Yuri turned up his collar, crossed the street, and trotted up the steps into the hotel.

He strode to the front desk, doing his best to feign a good mood, and caught the clerk's eye.

"Monsieur?" the clerk looked surprised to see him.

"I dropped my key in the storm drain," Yuri smiled and pointed outside.

"Ah. *Bien sûr*." The clerk grabbed a blank and ran a new key.

"*Merci beaucoup*." Yuri tapped the key to his forehead and turned around. He walked back into the night and headed for the café next door.

He took a table by the window and ordered a salad for dinner. He'd lost his appetite but knew he would need his strength. The next few hours would be as physically demanding as the last had been mentally. The salad arrived, topped with grilled salmon. He thanked the waiter and picked up his fork.

His wrists extended from inside his sleeves, revealing the deep gouges left by Andrine. The most difficult ten minutes of his life was not strangling her but removing his DNA from under her dead fingernails. Why did she have to be a peace-loving socialist? Why did she have to champion the unwashed masses? Why did she care about people? Why not be a passive farm girl who would trust her man to have reasons for his actions?

He laid the fork down and pulled his sleeves over his wrists.

Pushed the earbuds back in. Chet Atkins' *Almost Blue* fit his mood.

It was Strangelove's fault. Why had he done anything for the fat slob? He'd been such a fool. All those years he'd convinced himself he had an important career—but it was meaningless. In a hotel room in New York City, everything he'd ever wanted died. Everything was gone. Every promotion, every assignment, every medal was rendered pointless in that small space of time. Why had he worked so hard? Because he wanted to be a big man? Who are the important men? What good does it do them? So they can snap their fingers and have other men jump to do their bidding? Is Vladimir Medevtin any better a man than Yuri Belenov?

Damn Strangelove to hell. And all those who empowered him. If it was the last thing he did, he would kill them all. All the oligarchs, right up to Medevtin. He would do it for Andrine. She would not be sacrificed in vain. He would bring her death back to haunt the souls of those who toyed with the lives of others. Those responsible would die—and anyone who stood in his way.

Roman called from São Paulo, interrupting his meditation. "Strangelove is dead."

"Impossible."

"*Tass* is reporting it. Sabel Security invaded the *Tsentr*. Sabel has declared war on Russia."

Yuri took a bite of salmon and thought about it. An interesting development. How could they have snuck into Russia and taken down the king of assassins? Stearne proved one thing: Russia's officials were vulnerable. And that meant Andrine's death could be avenged.

"This Sabel operation is our enemy." Roman was talking as Yuri ate. "We are lucky they lost their leader in the fight."

Yuri nearly choked. "Who?"

"Alan Sabel, the founder. He was killed. One down and several more to go."

Yuri paused in thought. Then it came to him. In a flash like a summer storm. Medevtin was no better than Belenov. Belenov had manipulated Jacob Stearne into killing Strangelove for him. Ordering people killed was certainly a presidential privilege. Therefore, he was almost as powerful as Medevtin. With good men behind him, Yuri Belenov could be just as powerful. And SHaRC was full of good men. There was no reason they couldn't become powerful without a nation, just as Roman and Igor and the others always said.

Nationless was the twenty-first century Utopia. Nothing to tie you down. No old people to feed. No schools to build. No roads or armies. No place for your enemies to attack. Just a few smart men and a fast internet connection. He'd gone along with Roman and the others just to get out from under Strangelove. But now he understood what they were talking about. Genius. No more nations. No more bosses. No more living to please others. No more laws. No more *helping those less fortunate.* Fuck them all. Yuri would build SHaRC into a formidable force and reap the rewards.

They could bring the oligarchs to their knees.

He would do it for Andrine.

"You need a new perspective." Yuri sipped his glass of wine. "Sabel Security is the enemy of Russia. But, we are no longer Russians. We are SHaRC."

"Sabel hacked our logs and pinned #HuntersFail on us." Roman mulled it over. "They will come after us."

"I have negotiated with one of their men already. They are reasonable people. We can work with them."

"If you say so."

Yuri listened while Roman reported on his men and their travels. He was only mildly interested. Roman wanted to talk, and Yuri needed to eat. So, he listened. Igor had gone to South Africa. Someone else went to the Maldives. Another struggled with internet connections in Bali.

As Roman droned on, Yuri's mind wandered to Andrine's purple, swollen face pleading with him to stop.

He tossed his fork down again. He felt bile rising in the back of his throat.

Roman's voice came through a fog. "Have you heard from him?"

"I'm sorry. Who?"

"Vasili. He's the only one who's not checked in."

"My mind has been …" Yuri stopped himself from breaking down. He took a deep breath.

"Andrine. That was very hard for you, I know." Roman hesitated. "It had to be done. For the banda. I mean, SHaRC."

Yuri grunted an agreement.

"Do you want to talk about it?" Roman sounded unsure of himself. "Getting it out will make you feel better."

"In time, perhaps. Not now."

They listened to each other breathe, uncertain where the conversation should go next.

Finally, Roman broke the silence. "Will you miss your family?"

"My mother." Yuri sighed and left a long pause. "You?"

"My brothers, my father, grandparents. All of them."

"We will need to make enough money to bring them out of Russia." Yuri felt little enthusiasm. "We will trade stocks on hacked information. We can make a decent living from those."

"I did well in credit cards."

"You can make a million on those," Yuri said. "But when you hack merger contracts from a law firm and find out when Apple will buy Facebook, you can make billions."

"You are right." Roman's voice rose with excitement. "We can build our own private equity firm and buy up whole companies."

He heard Roman prattle his admiration for Yuri's wisdom. How important was he, really? What good did it do? Could he really bring down Viktor Popov? Money could buy them houses, ensure a little freedom. But #HuntersFail would always haunt them.

"You are still there, Yuri?" Roman's voice cracked.

"Sorry."

"You are still lost, my friend." Roman waited, but Yuri found nothing to say. "It was painful, no doubt. But, there are plenty more beautiful women in the world."

"There are not!" Yuri clicked off.

A few minutes later, the man who looked like Yuri skipped past the café window in the sleet, still whistling. Yuri threw too much cash on the table. He whisked through the hotel lobby and up the stairs, avoiding the elevators.

Opening the room with his new key, he surprised the occupant and hit him hard in the temple. The man crumpled.

Yuri pinned the man's arms with his knees. He needed no new scars on his wrists.

As he strangled the man who looked like him, he explained the situation. "Don't take it personally, Monsieur Babineau. You see, I need your passport and your identity. And I need to leave mine here with you. That way, the authorities will find the man who murdered my lovely Andrine. I know what you're going to say, that you have things to do and people who love you. The problem is, Andrine and I were going to do many things—and I loved her. A man you've never heard of, who goes by the name Strangelove, made me do bad things and she found out. So. I had to kill her. She had her whole life in front of her, but now she's dead. Just as you will be in a few minutes. All because of a man named Strangelove who lived far away and never met her. He never met you either, come to think of it. Do you want to know the ironic part? A friend of mine—no, not a friend. A new associate of mine killed Strangelove. The people responsible for your death have already been punished. Isn't that an odd twist of fate? Don't struggle, Monsieur Babineau, just relax and let go."

Yuri pressed his thumbs in harder and squeezed his fingers into the carotid arteries on both sides of the neck. The man's face turned purple, just as Andrine's had not so long ago.

Outside, the wind picked up and splashed raindrops hard against the window.

"Are you a Christian man, Babineau?" Yuri asked. "Oh. Don't answer that. Just know this: you are going to die for my sins. Isn't that nice?"

Yuri considered Babineau's bulging eyes. There was life left in them. He was fighting it. He had important things in mind, things he cared about, which made him hang on longer than necessary.

"Aren't you glad we had this little talk, Monsieur Babineau?" Yuri felt his heart beating harder as a rush of endorphins kicked in. "Talking about things makes us feel better. Don't you agree?"

CHAPTER 42

REFUSING A BOOT FOR HER smashed ankle, Pia leaned on her cane as she crossed from the main house at Sabel Gardens to the private chapel. The entire walkway was lined with well-wishers six to eight deep. Somber employees from all corners of Sabel Industries hung their heads. Tania walked on her left. Jacob on her right. The Major waited inside.

She did nothing to hide her extensive bruises. Her left eye was yellow and purple and swollen shut. She relied on Jacob's elbow and her cane for every step. She held her chin high and gave a morose nod to people as she passed.

A cacophony a few yards behind the line of mourners broke the muted gathering's decorum. Everyone turned left and right, looking for the source of the noise.

Raised voices shouted at the back of the chapel. Pia turned and pushed through the crowd until she found her oversized attorney shaking papers at two men in gray suits. Sensing her presence, he faced her.

"Is there a problem?" she asked.

"Fucking FBI wants his body for an autopsy." He turned back to the men in suits. "You're as low as they come, stinking maggots of the Stasi—"

"There's no need to escalate your language, sir." One of the men held his hands up. "We're just doing our job. I gave you the warrant."

"Why an autopsy?" Pia asked.

The two men glanced at each other. The quiet one spoke first. "President Hunter tasked the Bureau with discerning who shot him, ma'am. She's concerned it might have been friendly fire. I'd like to add that we were against the idea. But orders are …"

She felt her hand gripping the cane's handle too hard as the man's lame excuse trailed off. She fought the urge to beat him with it and turned her thoughts to how much she needed Dad. There was so much to tell him. So much advice she still wanted. Needed. How should she handle Hunter and Popov and Roche and Watson? Killing them was the only answer that came to her. He always had a different answer. She'd kept it secret that they were plotting to kill her. Instead of seeking his counsel, what were her last words? *I'm not a little girl anymore. I can handle everything just fine without your help.*

So wrong.

There should be many more years with him. Plenty of time for talking and confessions and apologies and appreciations. None of that would happen now. She'd squandered her time with him. The best time to be honest and thankful for loved ones is in the present. She knew that now. Too late.

The agents coughed.

"It should be simple enough." She looked at the men. "Sabel is standardized on 9mm while the Russians use a 5.45mm."

"It doesn't matter." The attorney turned beet-red. "The president doesn't have that authority. She's not a medical examiner, coroner, or judge. She has no right—"

"Let them have the body." She squeezed her attorney's arm.

Her head filled with rage at Roche and Hunter. And ultimately Viktor Popov, the man who somehow pulled their strings. They were to blame for far more than an autopsy.

"His body is an empty vessel." She thumped her chest with her fist. "He is with me."

She left them and entered the chapel. Jacob escorted her to a seat in the front pew next to the Major. Tania sat next to Jaz Jenkins across the center aisle.

An empty bier draped in flowers graced the front. A priest entered and raised her hand for silence. As the congregation quieted, a tall, handsome man stepped around the Major. Pia looked up to see Stefan Devoor, returned early from his travels. Stefan took her hand and looked into her eyes. Jacob moved over to give him room. He said nothing, but took the offered seat and kept her hand enveloped in his.

His contact was the only thing she'd felt since Kaliningrad.

The priest began the service with an invocation.

Pia observed the familiar woman who led the congregation in prayer. A tough-looking middle-aged cleric; Pia wondered if she was the same woman the cathedral had sent for previous funerals. The liturgy proceeded, but Pia heard nothing. Having been raised in the Episcopal Church, attending on those occasions when there wasn't a soccer tournament, she knew the rituals by heart. She knew when to stand and sit and kneel, cued by the rhythm of the rite. Little of it registered in her bereaved state except for a fragment of Psalm 90:8-9: *You have set our iniquities before you, our secret sins in the light of your countenance. For all our days pass away under your wrath; our years come to an end like a sigh.*

When it was over, she remained in her pew intending to pray and meditate. Instead, several people formed a line to express their condolences. Reluctantly, she stood to face them.

The eighth person was FBI Director Shikowitz. "You are in our prayers, Pia."

She recognized him through the fog of the day. He'd been a friend of Alan's for as long as she could remember. He'd helped her too many times to count. She said, "Tell your agents not to let up on their investigation because of the funeral. Getting this cleared up sooner rather than later is best for everyone."

He appraised her carefully and glanced over his shoulder before leaning in to whisper. "Hunter demanded the investigation, as did the Russians. But there was something uncovered by the investigators which would be improper to tell you. Therefore, I am not telling you this."

Pia cocked her head at his odd phrase.

"As Edward Snowden made everyone aware," Shikowitz continued, "the NSA monitors communications of many people overseas. Spies, terrorists, diplomats, and so on. They monitored Strangelove. Hours before you were forced down in Kaliningrad, they monitored a call from David Watson to Strangelove. Watson claimed he overheard you making plans to fly straight to Latvia." He paused and looked solemn. "I did not tell you this."

Shikowitz tugged her hand gently and patted it on top with his other hand. "I considered Alan my best friend, and consider you my third daughter. If it's not too much, I'd like to stop by tomorrow to help the Major with the mundane arrangements like paying the staff and finding…"

His voice continued, but Pia's mind went elsewhere. She'd expected Watson to shoot her, stab her, poison her. Treachery on this scale had never entered her mind. Jacob constantly complained that she charged ahead on missions without enough planning. She'd proven his point more than once. This time, her rash and impatient actions cost Dad his life. Should she blame herself? Or Watson? Or all of them? She felt the hot rush of anger rising up to her head. Which one should she kill first?

She sensed Shikowitz had asked her something that she hadn't answered. She didn't care.

"Who was Ilya Pozdeeva?" she asked.

Shikowitz hesitated. "Pia. There are national security issues involved there. I can't speak to—"

"Why did Pozdeeva visit CIA headquarters in the early '90s?" Her voice grew edgy.

"Friends don't ask friends to violate the rules of—"

She waved a dismissive hand and looked past him.

Shikowitz inhaled and formed a sentence that he decided not to speak. He smiled with understanding and left.

Bobby Jenkins came next. The friend who unwittingly saved Alan's life and career decades earlier. "I overheard your question." Bobby gave her a gentle hug. "All I know is that Veronica Hunter was Director of the CIA in the nineties."

"How does that fit in?" Pia squinted.

"No idea." He squeezed her hand. "I hope you will count on me the way your father did. I'd hate to lose that connection."

He reached up on tiptoes to kiss her cheek and left.

Jacob rose in front of the waiting line. He ushered them to the living room. It took a moment, but the line dispersed. Several stayed, whispering in small groups.

Pia's phone buzzed with a text from President Hunter, "I signed the orders you wanted. Sabel Industries is released from all Federal exclusive-use clauses. BTW: Campaign debt is crushing me, need help."

Pia texted back, "Dad's funeral in progress. Thanks for your thoughts and prayers."

Hunter's cursor indicated a reply in progress. Then it stopped. There was nothing Hunter could say now that wouldn't make it worse.

Stefan kissed her cheek. They sat in the pew. She leaned into him and felt his arm encircle her.

"Where are your children?" she asked.

"On the soccer field with your upstairs maid." Stefan sighed. "They've seen too many funerals."

"Sorry to interrupt." Emily knelt in front of Pia with a phone in her hand displaying a video. "President-Elect Roche is holding a press conference at the front gates. I thought you should know."

Pia stared blankly as the words rolled around in her head. Had she heard right? Roche stood outside? The man's insolence drove her beyond outrage. She shook with murderous intentions. Taking the phone from Emily, she turned up the volume. The Major leaned over her left shoulder, and Jacob leaned in with Stefan.

Chuck Roche stood a few feet in front of the gates, Sabel Gardens rising behind him, the turning circle filled with black limousines. He stood behind a temporary lectern festooned with microphones. "There will be those who question my motives for speaking at a funeral. Suffice it to say, I feel it's important to speak to you, the American people. You see, I knew Alan Sabel from the beginning. I gave him his start over two decades ago. I was the one who provided the connections and capital to launch his career. I did those things because he was my friend and I believed in him. So, why do I stand before his gates today to decry his actions? Because I believe in this country more.

"Alan Sabel invaded a sovereign nation, our Russian allies because he was rich and had the resources. He brought the United States of America—you and me—to the brink of war for nothing more than his ambition. His ego. His self-interest. Weighing the lives of a few against those of the country is something a leader must do every day. Would it be better to let one woman suffer or to endanger an entire nation?"

Chuck Roche looked at his notes and silently read a page. He looked back to the cameras.

"Can we stand by while unelected billionaires conduct their own foreign policy? Who here today believes that wealth dictates a moral imperative? Who believes that a rich person should decide when this nation goes to war—not because he should but because he can?"

Pia watched the small screen in her hand as the President-Elect paused to read more of his notes. Why was he so afraid of her? Strangelove's notes about #HuntersFail couldn't be tied to him directly. And what was Hunter afraid of that she needed an autopsy? What was it about Pia Sabel that drove them to such acts of desperation?

"Alan Sabel's accomplishments rise eighteen stories above the Bethesda skyline." Roche's voice rose to a shout. "Sabel Industries glows in bright neon from Sabel Towers, trumpeting his success. It's there to ensure every resident knows how great he is. Was. His treason against the United States of America should shine equally far. He brought his death upon himself. And we, the people of the United States of America, will have to pay for it. Well, I think that's wrong. The American taxpayers shouldn't have to fund their dangerous exploits. The Sabel Drone program has just been certified by the military. I will demand a reduction in price that will leave them no room for profit. I will drive them out of business."

Roche let the statement stand while he eyeballed every camera. Then he read his notes again.

"For now, I leave the survivors to mourn. Let them bury this traitor and say what they will. When the time for weeping is over, I, and I alone, will protect this country, not only from foreign retribution for Sabel's callous acts but also from his rogue mercenaries who endanger every American."

CHAPTER 43

I WAS OF A MIND to go out there and punch Chuck Roche in the nose.

After she heard Roche's rant, Ms. Sabel pushed off Stefan's shoulder and stormed for the exit. Her battered body didn't let her get three steps. I shoved my shoulder under hers while Emily grabbed her other elbow. We steadied her.

"You're not thinking about challenging him?" Emily asked with a quaking voice.

"Damn straight."

"That's just what he wants." Emily nearly shouted. "To provoke you, prove you don't care about Alan Sabel. He'll call you everything if you open the front door."

Mercury slapped my face. *You're gonna do this, bro. You go out there, open your mouth—I'll put words in it.*

I said, *Where the hell have you been?*

Mercury said, *Carrying you, homie. Now shut up and get out there.*

Are you going to make me say something stupid about the Capitoline—

Mercury gripped my shoulder hard. *I ain't doing shit for you. I'm doing this for Pia-Ceasar-Sabel. I'm the god of eloquence. Have some faith for once and do what I tell you.*

OK, OK, I said. *I'll do it.*

"What? Not you," Emily sneered. "We need someone with public speaking—"

"Jacob does it." Ms. Sabel's stern voice didn't leave room for discussion. "Bianca introduces him."

She turned to me. "It's not about me. Popov hijacked our democracy.

You have to do this for Dad and the USA."

She turned around, sat down between Stefan and the Major, and didn't look up.

In short order, I was following Bianca and Emily through the main house. Our indignant march pounded the marble floors.

We passed Sylvia in the foyer. She looked confused and out of place, embarrassed to be attending a funeral for a man she'd never spoken to. I'd been preoccupied, which left her to fend for herself. The press photographed everyone on the grounds at Sabel Gardens with telephoto lenses and drones overhead. And President-Elect Roche wasn't the only one saying bad things about us. Sylvia couldn't have come at a worse time. Our love affair had been grounded by life. She gave me a weak smile and a thumbs-up.

Outside, we headed for the gates. Reporters were packing up. Bianca ran ahead to the lectern when she saw someone reaching to pull a mic off it.

"A minute please," she said. "Sabel Security Agent Jacob Stearne was an Army Ranger who earned lots of medals in service to this country. We owe him the courtesy of listening for a few minutes."

She stepped back and looked at me.

No part of me wanted to move. I was rooted to the spot like an oak. I felt the eyes of a hundred reporters and the lenses of a hundred cameras turn to me. What the hell was I doing? Shooting people, no problem. Public speaking? No way. And this was not just public speaking. This was speaking to the entire nation about … what?

Mercury smacked my shoulder. *Move it, soldier. Don't stand there like an idiot. I told you I got this. Now get up there and open your mouth.*

I said, *Tell me I'm not going to be speaking in tongues.*

You're no coward. You're not afraid to speak in tongues or anything else I have in store for you. Think, dude, think. You've stood in the line of fire for these jackasses. No need to give a damn about them. Give a damn about Pia-Caesar-Sabel. You're going to set this straight. Right here. Right now.

Emily took a knee in the front row, her phone live-streaming. Bianca motioned expectantly for me to step forward.

I took the first step, then the second. Next thing I knew, I was tapping the microphones for some bizarre reason. I tossed my hands up, palms out to show I was unarmed. Force of habit. Hostile parleys in uncertain territories were common during my deployments. I opened my mouth.

"Friends, uh." My brain froze. I rocked back and forth. "Americans. World citizens. I'm just a soldier. Most of my adult life was spent ducking bullets and bombs in Iraq and Afghanistan. I never learned the finer points of speeching." I swallowed hard. "I mean, speech making. Oration. Whatever y'wanna call it."

Mercury punched me in the gut. *Speak from here. Make it bold.*

"I learned how to look a man in the eye—" my voice turned thunderous, "—and decide—the instant before pulling the trigger—whether he's friend or foe. Whether he was a man or coward, hero or terrorist. I don't know much about Chuck Roche. I never looked him in the eye. I never saw him in uniform. I don't know if he's even been on a battlefield. Some people voted for him, so I guess someone thought well of him."

I scratched my head and tried to think. "When a man dies, everyone remembers his sins. Richard Nixon was a crook, not the man who opened China. Today, Roche told you Alan Sabel was an egomaniac. If that's true, he paid the ultimate price for his hubris. I'll leave that for the Almighty to judge."

I took a deep breath and took a second to look at the camera lenses. They were big glass things, not like handheld cameras or phones. And there were a lot of them. I felt my gaze boring into them, through them, trying to see the people on the other side.

"I came out here to tell you about my boss, my friend, Alan Sabel." I paused and caught an encouraging smile from Emily. "He was good to me. He was good to everyone he met. He was good to this community. His philanthropy reached every corner of this region—and he didn't do it for glory. He did it because he cared. Is that treason? To feed the poor? To shelter the homeless? To comfort the afflicted? I should be so treasonous.

"Alan Sabel used to be our hero. He was an American success story. A grad student who adopted an orphaned girl and built an empire.

Everyone looked up to him." I paused again. I felt something welling up in my chest. A thickness in my nose and throat. "He was more than a success story to me. He was someone who gave a damn."

It caught up with me. I felt tears welling in my eyelids. No way would I let them see me cry. I turned away for a second. Bianca held a tissue out at a discreet level. I shook it off, took a deep breath, and turned back.

"Alan Sabel was a young man who witnessed his neighbors' murders and did not stand by. He did what no one else did. On the spot, he took responsibility for a child. Who among us has that kind of courage? We know the obligations, the sacrifices, the challenges—that's why foster care is full of discarded children. That didn't stop Alan Sabel. He stepped up and gave his home, his future, his life to a little girl.

"Compare his act to the elite who emotionally abandon their own flesh and blood after a divorce. Or those rich people who never bother to have children because they haven't the time. I'm sure the President-Elect has his reasons for his family situation. But who is he to judge a man like Alan Sabel?

"The real issue here isn't what Alan Sabel did. The real issue is: what would any responsible parent do? What would your father do if you were in trouble? What would you do for your son? Your daughter?"

I looked each reporter in the eye, one more time.

"What was Alan Sabel's crime? Was he any less a man than any politician? No. He was much more. What crime did he commit? What Roche said today was nothing but an aporia. When Alan Sabel's daughter was in danger, did he wait for the legal system to wend its way through a lengthy process? When a Russian general sent him this picture, did he wait for the State Department to file a complaint?"

Holding Alan Sabel's phone over my head for everyone to see, I wondered where the hell I'd found it. I glanced up at it. To my shock, the picture of Ms. Sabel, the one I know for a fact that I'd deleted, was in full view. Reporters squinted to see it and instantly recognized what it was. They began shouting for me to send them copies. I tossed the phone to Emily.

"Or did Alan Sabel do what any father would do—move heaven and earth to save his child? The very child he plucked from drowning in the river of obscurity? Would you do any less for your child? Is it treason to pull your daughter from death's door?"

I took a deep breath.

"For Alan Sabel, there was no border strong enough to hold him back. He saw no USA. He saw no Russia. No sovereign nation to be recognized—because certainly, no government is evil enough to shelter the criminals who attempted to murder his daughter. If there had been time, he knew Russia would've welcomed him; even helped him save her. But there was no time. He knew that Pia Sabel, this country's Olympic heroine, was in mortal danger and that he could—and therefore should—save her."

That one silenced them for a second.

"He was no rogue mercenary." I gave them my soldier stare and lowered my voice an octave and roared. "In my experience, heroism isn't something self-proclaimed, it's self-evident. I was there. I saw Alan Sabel in action. I served by his side. I looked him in the eye, and I saw it in his soul: Alan Sabel was an American hero."

I paused once again. When I spoke again, my voice was softer, quieter. "Sorry, I'm just a soldier. When I joined the Army, I swore to protect truth, justice, and the American way. And I've come close to giving my life for that oath many times. You know what I say to any civilian who dares to call Alan Sabel a traitor? Rot in hell, coward."

I turned on my heel and walked away to the cacophony of reporters barking questions. Bianca trotted alongside me.

Emily stayed behind to divvy up the photo of Ms. Sabel. Giving them that picture was a terrible idea. I don't know what I was thinking. Ms. Sabel would fire me for that one. The last thing a woman would want is having photos of her beaten body shared all over the internet.

"Do you know what aporia means?" Bianca asked as we paced across the driveway.

"What? Sure. It means … um … something. Why?"

"You used it back there."

"Oh." I kept up my stride. "Did I say it wrong?"

"No. It's just. That speech. It didn't sound like you. It sounded … more eloquent than I expected."

"Sorry."

"That's not what I meant. I—" She decided to quit while she was ahead. "You did great. Better than anything I could've thought up."

"Thanks."

Mercury strode alongside me. He didn't look at me. He didn't beg for props.

CHAPTER 44

YURI WAITED ON THE SIDEWALK of São Paulo's airport with his back to the nearest surveillance camera. Babineau's passport had served him well so far, but there was no reason to push his luck. Rain fell like a soft shower in the warm air, a welcome departure from Montréal's frozen streets.

When Roman arrived, it took Yuri a moment to recognize his friend. He opened the door, tossed his backpack in the back seat, and slid in. "What happened to you?"

"I have taken an oath for SHaRC." Roman scoffed. "Reconstructive surgery."

Yuri looked closely at his friend's bandaged face. "Orbital sockets, nose, and chin. You saved the smile. Facial recognition will not identify you. You are a dedicated man, Roman."

Roman nodded. "I've spoken to the others. They have committed to the same."

"You're taking on leadership responsibilities?" Yuri waited but Roman could find nothing to say. "You did well."

"I'm glad you approve." A trace of contempt colored Roman's words.

Yuri regarded him for a long time. "Are you challenging me, Roman? Are you worried about my leadership?"

Roman drove and bit the inside of his cheek and flexed his jaw. "We have discussed this and concluded that if we don't need nations, we don't need leaders."

They drove in silence for a few miles.

"I have bad news about Vasili, I'm afraid." Yuri took a deep breath. "He reported us to Strangelove. He gave the old man tracking information. Strangelove came close to having me killed in New York."

"He was Armenian. You can never trust them." Roman squeezed the steering wheel.

"He was from Novosibirsk."

"His great-grandfather was Armenian." Roman glanced at Yuri. "What did you do about it?"

"What would you have done?"

Roman thought it over. Yuri watched as his mind worked through several scenarios. For a hacker, Roman was a tough guy, but he was no killer.

"Eliminate the threat to SHaRC." Roman looked self-satisfied with his answer but kept his gaze on the road ahead.

"Roman, look at me." Yuri waited until his friend glanced his way. "If you and the others agreed SHaRC should be leaderless, then I am a liability. I know networks and routers, but I am no match for you or Igor, Petr, Alexandr, any of the others. My expertise is my leadership. If you don't need it, all that remains is a threat. I should be eliminated. You should stop right here and shoot me. Would you like a gun, Roman?"

Yuri pulled his pistol and offered it, grip first, to his man.

Roman worried the steering wheel, his gaze sliding to the weapon. Then he refocused on the highway.

When the GRU conscripted his hackers, Yuri had wanted to put them through KSO training, the Russian equivalent of American SEALs. Strangelove shot it down. The result was Roman: a man so easily intimidated he couldn't commit a simple murder when opportunity and need demanded.

"I killed Vasili." Yuri put his gun away. He turned in his seat to better face his driver. "I left his carcass in the streets of Stavanger. The lovely Norwegians were trying to revive him."

They drove on, a long and thoughtful silence settling on them.

"Three years I worked with Vasili as my lieutenant," Yuri said. "I've met his wife and children. I've spoken to his mother on the phone." Yuri opened a packet of Cocada he'd picked up in the airport. He offered one of the coconut, egg, and sugar confections to Roman. His friend shook it off. "He betrayed us. Strangelove located me in New York thanks to

Vasili." He finished a cookie and licked his fingers. "Tell me, Roman. Could you have done it? Could you kill Vasili? Could Petr? Igor?"

Roman tried to find words to say. He started and stopped a couple times. Yuri gave him as much time as he needed. The miles flew by, but Roman had nothing.

"I told you, plans need to be made." Yuri stuffed in another bite. "Some of those plans include eliminating threats to your men. Sometimes it means eliminating your friends. It's scary. It's dangerous. It's leadership."

"Like killine Andrine?" Roman glanced at the former major. "Would you kill me?"

Quick as a snake, Yuri pulled his pistol, chambered a round, and held it to Roman's temple. "If you threaten me, or my men, I will not hesitate. Even at 100 kph."

Beads of sweat formed on Roman's forehead. His breathing became shallow and rapid. Yuri remained unmoved until fear permeated every fiber of Roman's body.

Then Yuri put his weapon away. "You are a good man with nothing to fear because you are going to explain things to the others."

"What things?" Roman's voice cracked.

"That you are a group of peers—which works well in good times. But peer groups cannot make command decisions under duress. Peers cannot develop strategy. You will explain to them why leadership is important. You will do this because you are my new lieutenant." He waited a beat. "Don't worry, I will teach you how to kill."

Roman gathered his courage. "There is one thing you will have to do. They will not listen to anyone who has not taken the oath and made the commitment."

He pointed to his bandaged face.

Yuri shivered inside but nodded solemnly to Roman. "No one is more committed to SHaRC than I."

They drove for an hour before entering Santos, a beach town on São Paulo's coast. They changed the subject and talked about family and friends, and the remaining members of SHaRC. They discussed plans to hack money from the Americans and anyone else as soon as possible.

Then the conversation died down for a few miles.

"I've been contacted by Brad," Roman said. "He represents people who want to work with SHaRC."

"How did he find you?"

"Message boards," Roman answered quickly. "I swear. I did not compromise my brothers in SHaRC. You have to believe me."

Yuri observed him in silence. The trees and miles passed by. Then he said, "Who does Brad represent?"

"He didn't say. But he said Mikhail Yeschenko is involved—"

"Brad works for a company called Santalum." Yuri let his words sink in. "Viktor Popov was on the board until last year."

Roman snapped a glance at him. He returned his eyes to the road. They didn't speak again until they reached the city limits.

They arrived at Roman's apartment in a twenty-story building overlooking the beach. A bottle of vodka waited for them on his thin balcony. Below the railing, a curved stretch of sand. A soft rain fell, and waves rolled up.

"To SHaRC." Yuri clinked his glass against Roman's. "We will first need to rid the world of Viktor Popov if we want to succeed in our endeavors."

"The Americans are looking for us. They are our priority."

"This is why you need leadership," Yuri slapped his man on the shoulder. "The Americans are more dangerous. But they have no idea who or where we are. Popov has all our records. If you or the others were not careful transferring your money, he will find us in a matter of hours."

Yuri finished his drink one sip at a time.

"You win." Roman smiled and sipped his vodka. "We need leadership."

Talk is cheap, and Roman said all the right things. But Yuri wanted more. He needed something deeper from his new lieutenant. Especially in light of Roman's discussions with outsiders.

"Will you be loyal to me, Roman?" Yuri fingered the bottle of VX-Y spray in his pocket. "I have endured Strangelove's switchblade for you. Do you pledge your life to me?"

Yuri didn't want to kill any of his friends. Not any more than he already had. Not unless all other options had been exhausted.

Roman turned slowly to consider his leader.

Yuri could read the man's thoughts as they flashed across his face: no more rules, no more countries—we do not need leaders. Yet Yuri made a strong argument for having one. He kept them organized, saved them from Strangelove, financed SHaRC from his own accounts. Roman relaxed as he made up his mind.

The young man lowered his head. "I pledge my life to SHaRC."

"Not good enough, Roman. Do you pledge your life and your loyalty to me?"

Roman raised his chin and met his gaze. "I pledge my life to you before the others, Yuri."

"Then we understand each other." Yuri grabbed him by the shoulders and hugged him.

After they finished their vodkas, they joined a video discussion with the remaining members of SHaRC. They agreed on many things.

They listened to Roman's plea for leadership. They agreed they had to stick together or die facing Popov alone. They could make money together. They needed nothing but high-speed connectivity and their computer arrays. They liked Yuri's plan to infiltrate the stock market for profit.

Yuri promised to set up new offices in Brazil. The Stateless Hacktivist and Resistance Collective would open for business in a matter of days. In solemn tones, they pledged their loyalty to the collective. Yuri noted three who sounded uncertain. He would follow up with them later. It was best to make those determinations in person. He wrapped up the call on a lighter note, with a toast to their new world: SHaRC. Then they all clicked off.

With another shot of vodka, he and Roman talked about their personal lives and ambitions. Igor called before they could get very far.

"I have a friend in the FSB." Igor took a deep breath. "He sent word to my anonymous drop box that Viktor Popov has declared us enemies of the state. The Foreign Minister plans to hand us over to the Americans. Watch your backs, my friends."

Yuri clicked off. He stared out the window at the gentle rain falling on the beach far below. For a moment, he considered running to the balcony and taking a leap. Then he remembered Andrine. He would kill them all to avenge her death. What were his former masters after? Did he care? Viktor Popov, the spy of spies, gave the orders. He would simply kill that tired old fuck. If Jacob Stearne could steal a dog from under his nose, Yuri could strangle the bastard. He began to laugh.

Roman was pale. "What's gotten into you?"

"We have been 'sacrificed at the whim of political powers far away,' as Strangelove used to say."

"They sold us out." Roman topped up their drinks. "You think that's funny?"

"Ironic, actually." Yuri took his glass from his new lieutenant and slugged it back. "I met the man who shot Viktor Popov in the leg."

"Jacob Stearne?"

"You've heard the story?"

"Everyone's heard the story." Roman scoffed and refilled their drinks. "The Ghengis Khan of the SVR taken down by an American foot soldier. Rumor has it, Popov had the embassy's security chief beheaded."

"Sabel Security didn't attack Strangelove by accident." Yuri waited for Roman's gaze to meet his. "I met Stearne in New York. I was the one who gave him Strangelove's address in Kaliningrad. He attacked and killed Strangelove. Popov has discovered this. That's why he wants us killed."

"Impossible." Roman couldn't speak for several seconds. "You've declared war on the most powerful man in Russia. Are you mad?"

"Trust me, Roman. I have a plan." Yuri clinked glasses and downed his drink. "But before I take the first step, I will execute your plan."

Roman and Yuri shared a somber look. Then they rose. Roman retrieved a hammer. They took the elevator to the ground floor. They walked several blocks to a bad neighborhood. Yuri found an alley, dark and deserted. They took one more look at each other.

Roman ran out of the alley at full speed. He shouted for help. "They're killing him. Help!"

Yuri took a long look at the hammer. He took a deep breath and decided which of the four critical areas would be his starting point. He brought the hammer up quickly, smashing it hard into his right orbital socket.

CHAPTER 45

A LITTLE AFTER FOUR IN the morning, Pia fell into the chair at the breakfast table looking uncharacteristically disheveled. She dropped her swollen and bruised face in her hands. Chef set a cup of coffee in front of her. Pia mumbled thanks and warmed her hands on the sides while staring down into it.

"Did you get any sleep?" Tania looked at her phone.

Every minute since Dad's murder, her mind exploded with hate and anger. Closing her eyes became an exercise in visualizing vengeance. Her jaw tightened. "Are they done chopping up Dad's body?"

"Later today." Tania hesitated. "There's something you should know."

Pia looked up from her cup.

"David Watson came back from Russia. Jacob screwed up by taking him, and he screwed up by leaving him behind. Now Watson's spreading lies on all the cable shows going on about Kaliningrad."

Pia dropped back against the seat and closed her good eye. She sat motionless for a long time. "What is he claiming?"

"That you planned it. It was a calculated assault—just like Jacob's embassy attack. Pre-meditated murder."

"Let me guess: he's claiming inside knowledge because he was an employee of Sabel Security."

"Says you went crazy over Jacob's dog." Tania nodded. "That you're an egomaniac with her own army. That you abandoned him in Kaliningrad because you don't care about employees. Made himself a real victim."

Pia gripped her mug so tightly her knuckles turned white. "No one's going to believe it."

"The President-Elect held a news conference about it. Named Watson to his transition team—which legitimizes the man. Everyone in the country will wake up to this story."

Pia let out a long, sad sigh. "You're not stuttering."

"I'm focused now." Tania waited for a response.

"I'm focused on Popov," Pia said. "We lost the race to keep Roche out of the White House. If we take him out now, Popov will do it again with another narcissist. After we get Popov, then we go after Roche."

Tania nodded and drank her coffee.

After a couple minutes, Pia picked up her mug and sipped. "What does the Major say about Watson?"

"The nice way to put it: she was against hiring him in the first place." Tania drained her coffee. Chef appeared with a carafe for them. Tania poured herself another cup. "She'll be here at dawn. Bianca will be here at seven."

"What do you think we should do about Watson?"

"Say the word—" Tania held her gaze "—and he's dead by lunchtime."

Pia grabbed Tania's arm and raised her voice. "His message led to Dad's murder. My dad, not yours."

They stared at each other for a long time. Tania in sympathy, Pia embarrassed by her outburst. She let go.

"Popov is our top priority," she said. "He's not going to let us get away with annihilating his attack dog, Strangelove. And I'm not going to let him get away with pulling Roche's chain. Besides, there's nothing wrong with Watson looking over his shoulder for a few more days."

Tania sipped her coffee. "Popov could attack any minute."

Pia scrolled through the emails on her phone. "Anyone find a clue to Pozdeeva's cipher?"

"Not yet. Word games aren't my thing."

"Were they his?" Pia looked up quickly. "Did he play Scrabble or something like that? Olesya, the secretary, said he hid the kompromat in plain sight. Maybe he did the same with the cipher key."

Tania shrugged.

Pia checked the time: 11:00 AM in Moscow. She dialed Olesya's number and listened to it ring several times without going to voicemail. As she was about to click off, a sniffling woman said, "*Allo.*"

"Olesya?" Pia asked. The voice on the other end broke down in tears. "Olesya, is that you?"

"Nyet. Olesya…" the woman's voice broke down. After a long sob, a stream of Russian came out. The woman disconnected.

The only words Pia picked out were "*ubiystvo*" and "*mertva*". She used her phone to translate: murder and dead.

She couldn't believe it. The Russians were known to have phone monitoring capabilities. They must have been watching Olesya's phone. Her lungs crumpled. The old woman had waited for her call. She knew Viktor and the resources he commanded. She knew what he would do when he caught her. She had known talking to Pia was suicide. Olesya also knew Pia could not refuse her deathbed request: *Do this for Ilya's ghost. Do this for my Tatyana. Do this for Bridgette Jallet. Do this for your mother.*

Pia's breathing stopped as the last sentence struck her.

Your mother. That hadn't registered the first time. It was something she'd always known even though no one had said it before. Popov played a role in her parent's murders. How? Why?

Pia stared at the phone until Olesya's number showed up on an incoming call. She answered.

"You the American girl?" A different woman's voice, also anguished. "You do this to Olesya. They trace call. They come to house." The woman talking cried.

"I know. I'm sorry."

"Nyet. No good." The woman's voice trailed off as if she were putting the phone down.

"Wait." Pia took a moment to think how she could appeal to a stranger for help. "She told me to do something for Tatyana."

The line did not go dead. She could hear the woman breathing.

Pia said, "I need help."

"Nyet. No help you." The call disconnected.

Pia put the phone down.

Her very large attorney carried in a plate of pancakes smothered in whipped cream and syrup. When he sat, two chairs disappeared from view. He knifed two tablespoons of butter on top of his stack. After tucking a white napkin under his chin to protect his suit and tie, he dug in. "You have the best chef in town, you know that?"

He took an oversized forkful and filled his gaping mouth. Before he managed to chew any of it, he started talking. "First thing you need to do is get a blanket pardon out of Veronica Hunter. Lame-duck presidents need to fund their presidential libraries if you know what I mean. In my experience, a couple million should do the trick."

Bits of whipped cream and syrup spewed as he spoke. He didn't notice. Pia grabbed a napkin and pretended to fold it, using it as a barrier.

"Before we go that route—" he downed the load and refilled immediately "—you should get over to the Oval Office. As your dad used to say, you gotta kowtow to every president and candidate. With what they're saying about you, you'll need to do the full monty, pressing your forehead to the—"

"Not happening. Next subject."

"They were going to arrest you on the tarmac." He gave her the once-over while he speared another half-pound of pancake. "But my team kept the wolves at bay. We really came down hard on the Gestapo out there. Did you like that?"

Pia rolled her hand.

"They're going for all kinds of crazy." He stopped to swallow. As soon as the food cleared his gullet, he chugged orange juice. He reloaded his fork like a steam shovel. "We spent all day in court and bargained down to staying in the country. So, I need you and everyone who went to Kaliningrad to surrender your passports."

As the shovel entered his mouth, a tablespoon of whipped cream fell off. He commenced chewing and scooped the fallen dairy, adding it to the work in progress.

"What are the charges?"

"Multiple violations of the Neutrality Act of 1794 and all its updates and amendments."

She grabbed his plate and moved it out of reach. "A good lawyer wouldn't have taken all day to beat an outdated and misused law. When you go back to finish the work you should've done while you were racking up the billable hours, make sure the judge understands the extent of my US assets. I'm not a flight risk. Hunter's biggest problem isn't me leaving the country—it's if I stay."

He swallowed hard. He looked down at the repossessed pancakes as if they were a slain child. He removed the napkin from his chest, tossed it on the table, and left.

The lawyer's vacated seat was filled a few seconds later by Emily. She extended a tablet showing a document. "A draft of the President-Elect's press release going out this morning."

Pia glanced at it. "Short version?"

"The first executive order he plans to sign on January 20th is one that cancels all contracts with Sabel Industries except the drone program. He says that one's too important to national defense." Emily waited for a reaction. "He'll put you out of business."

"I owe you an exclusive," Pia said.

"Do you want to issue a statement?" Emily absently tapped a pen on the table.

"Roche is a terrible chess player." Pia sipped her coffee. "He can't see the moves in advance. Shooting from the hip might work in his refinery business, but it's disaster on the world stage. He revealed his strategy when he came here seeking my endorsement. When he left, I waved campaign contributions in front of Veronica Hunter and created an arsenal of responses for Roche."

Emily narrowed her eyes. "You made campaign contributions to Hunter in return for executive orders?"

"Never." Pia sipped her coffee. "She offered to help Sabel Industries and then, separately, asked for my support—which I promised but never gave."

"You lied to a politician?" Emily clapped her hands. "Someone finally did to one of them what they've been doing to us."

"It wasn't a lie," Pia said. "The situation changed."

Emily put out her fist. Pia bumped it.

"Here's your scoop," Pia said, "to be released half an hour before

Roche's press release: Sabel Aerospace is halting the drone program until the next president is elected. Management has deemed Chuck Roche too immature and irresponsible to have a weapon that advanced at his fingertips. Further, Sabel Satellite will open the world's most secure communication platform for commercial use beginning January 20th now that President Hunter has issued an executive order releasing us from exclusive use."

Emily smiled and gathered her things.

"If it's not my business, feel free to say so." Pia caught Emily's gaze. "How are things with Bianca?"

"Strained. I screwed up. But, I'm working on it." Emily slung her purse and left quickly.

Tania said, "A thousand companies would pay much more than the feds for bandwidth on your satellites. You're releasing that news just to make Roche shut up. You outmaneuvered him."

Pia sipped her coffee.

"Your dad would be proud."

"Thanks." Pia's face tightened.

Chef delivered a veggie omelet and scooped up the lawyer's unfinished plate.

Pia's phone vibrated with Kasey Earl's caller ID. She picked up.

"I want fifty million." His first words.

"You once strapped my father to a bomb." She let the words sink in. "Are you happy now that Strangelove finished your work?"

"Hey now." Kasey swallowed hard. "I got nothing to do with that. I'm sorry for your dad."

"I'm not paying fifty million, Kasey. I'll give you something if you have some kind of proof."

"I gotcha proof all right. Believe you me. Ten million."

"No."

"Five?"

"No."

"Why not?"

"I should turn you over to the police." Pia's fist tightened. "Withholding information is a crime."

"OK, send five mil, I'll send the file. But you're a bitch, you know that?"

"I'm not sending you money. You bring what you have to Sabel Gardens. We'll see."

"Send the jet for me."

"Get here tomorrow, or I'm calling the cops and reporting extortion." She clicked off.

Tania watched her. "The world doesn't even give you time to grieve."

Pia thought about the last two days of anguish. Was it any different from the first twenty-two years? Had she gone through all the stages of denial, anger, bargaining … what was next? She should have it memorized by now. The legions of therapists she'd seen over the years told her that grieving was an important part of moving forward with life. She saw it as an emotion that could cripple her if she let it.

She checked the time and wondered when Stefan would wake his children. He had been a calming force during the service. He knew her pain firsthand due to his own recent trauma. But she'd never dated a man with kids before. She'd spent a little time with them after the funeral. They were nice but distant. Did she have room in her heart for someone else's children?

A call interrupted her thoughts.

Pia checked the country code: Russia. She picked up. A professional voice on the other end asked, "Collect call originating in Moscow. Do you accept the charges?"

She did. A few clicks later and the voice of the woman who had called her back from Olesya's phone came on the line. She sounded as if she were talking through a culvert. The woman had gone to an old-fashioned pay phone in hopes of bypassing the FSB.

"What you do for Olesya?"

Pia considered her response carefully considering the Russians might still record it. "She asked me to destroy the person who killed Tatyana, Brigette Jallet, and my mother."

"You do these thing?"

"I will." She hoped her language would be ambiguous enough in court should it come to that.

"What help you need?"

"I need to know what word games Ilya Pozdeeva played."

"Every day, Ilya play crossword puzzle in *Izvestia*."

Pia thanked her and clicked off.

She dialed Bianca. "For Pozdeeva's cipher key: try *Izvestia's* crossword puzzle."

CHAPTER 46

EVERYONE HAS DIFFERENT TRADITIONS. MS. Sabel was intent on having a funeral service as soon as Alan's family could arrive in Washington. Some of us believe in old-fashioned wakes, the way we do them back in Iowa. Since we didn't have time beforehand, we decided to drink to his passing the day after. Two dozen agents gathered in one of the bars at Sabel Gardens. We played pool and told stories. Every now and then, someone would theorize about when and where Popov would strike.

Miguel, Tania, and I sat at the back bar and remembered Alan. Miguel remembered how he arrived either like a hurricane or a party animal, but he never entered unnoticed. Tania remembered how he was the sun in his own solar system, everyone orbited around him. But his star always turned in his daughter's galaxy. I remembered how he called the fully stocked bar we were in "the employee lounge". We all remembered how his booming laugh overpowered the mood in any room.

Every story ended with a hollow sigh.

Mercury stood next to me. *Yo, homes, he was the greatest Caesar of all time. Guys like him became gods back when we ran the show. Least y'all could do is name a planet after him. Uranus is the only planet named after a low-life Greek, you should make them change that to Planet Sabel.*

I said, *Thanks for helping me with the press.*

Mercury waved away my gratitude. *Did you know Alan-Caesar-Sabel used to read Shel Silverstein poems to Pia when she couldn't sleep?*

Who?

Silverstein. Dude who wrote A Light in the Attic *and* Where the

Sidewalk Ends. *Lots of them.*

I shrugged. Childhood seemed like light years ago.

Mercury said, *Hey, soon as we're all done drinking here, we're going after Popov, right?*

I said, *Can we prove he's connected to Alan's death?*

Mercury walked away, with one word over his shoulder. *Worse.*

The group talked and talked. But there was one thing none of us would talk about: how will Ms. Sabel cope?

Sylvia came in with a roller bag. She frowned and pursed her lips and tried to smile. I wove my way through the crowd to her. We stared at each other for a moment, neither of us knowing what to say. I know what I wanted to say, and maybe she wanted to say the same thing, but we didn't know each other well enough to open up. Yet. We inched close, nearly toe-to-toe.

She broke the tension. "I wish it had been more fun…"

I waited for her to put more thought into her statement, but she gave up.

She frowned. "Is what they're saying in the papers true? You left our dinner in New York to go kill all those people?"

Again, I waited for her to amend her question, but she didn't. "They were trying to kill me. I went to save—"

"I get that part. It's just … Those people have children. How can you kill them?"

"Some people overstay their welcome on the planet."

"You're judge and jury? You go to other countries and just walk in, guns blazing?" She waited for me to answer. I didn't. "I thought you were a good guy. Sensitive and vulnerable—"

"Every woman who's told me that crap ran away with the first bad boy who slung her on the back of his bike and roared off into the night."

"Really? Is that what you think of me?" She fisted her hips. "I'm looking for someone serious. Someone who wants a future. Maybe a family. I felt something serious in you."

That was a first for me. Aside from being the most beautiful woman I ever spent a couple days with, she was also the only woman who thought of me long-term. Hearing that felt like a cold slap. "I am serious about my future. And about you. But, I'm not going to stop protecting the world from the monsters among us."

"That might be fine for a young guy," she said. "Now that you're older, it's time to grow up. Find a serious career."

"Killing bad guys is serious."

"Is it a career?" The edge in her voice sliced like a knife.

"Who are you to throw around 'career'? What kind of job do you have that requires a short designer dress midday?"

Her jaw dropped. She grabbed the handle of her roller bag. She turned and started away.

"Wait. I'm sorry." I followed a step behind her. "I'll drive you."

"A Lyft is waiting outside. Thanks anyway."

"Where are you going?"

"Monaco." She quickened her pace.

I reached out to stop her. She sensed my move and twisted out of my grasp. She made a left into the hall.

Mercury stepped into my path and put a hand on my chest. Good thing he didn't say anything.

My heart cracked in half. A lonesome saxophone played in my head. I took her for granted. How much she affected me didn't sink in until she blew up at me. It instantly qualified as the worst breakup in my life—and we hadn't even kissed.

The room behind me was silent. No balls clacked on the pool table. No voices. No movements. I turned to see everyone staring at me. In unison, they looked away. Only Miguel held my gaze. The stoic Navajo lifted his chin a quarter inch. It felt like a warm hug.

Tania slipped behind the bar. She grabbed four shot glasses and slammed them down. A bottle of Casa Noble Añejo, Ms. Sabel's favorite tequila, appeared in her hand. She poured three glasses. The fourth, Miguel's, got a dose of pomegranate juice. He doesn't drink. I reached for my glass. Tania and Miguel took theirs.

Someone's hand patted my back before reaching for the last tequila.

"Here's to losing someone." Ms. Sabel's voice surprised me. She gave me an empathetic look through her not-as-swollen eye and hooked her cane on the bar. "Not all losses are permanent."

We tapped glasses and downed our drinks.

When the glasses landed back on the bar, no one spoke for a minute.

"She's an actress," Ms. Sabel said. "She has a supporting role in a French TV show. She has to be on set tomorrow."

I bit the inside of my cheek. Why didn't I know that before I said something stupid? Why didn't she tell me when I asked? Did I ask?

Ms. Sabel continued. "They had just wrapped a scene in Barcelona when a producer started grabbing her. She punched him in the nose and ended up on the garage floor looking up at you."

She could see the curiosity on my face. "We had breakfast this morning."

"So, I blew it?"

My three friends muttered their agreement in unison.

Ms. Sabel's phone chirped with a news alert. "Chuck Roche promoted David Watson from his transition team to Chief of Staff. The most important role in the administration."

Not wanting to discuss our illegal recording of Roche, Watson, and Hunter, I minimized my response to a knowing glance and a shrug. She let the others discuss the appointment and asked me to join her in a meeting. She grabbed her cane and limped away. I followed.

"Kasey Earl is here." She blew out an exasperated breath. "He wants to negotiate his fee."

Kasey Earl twisted around in a chair when we walked in. He wore a clean shirt with his hair slicked down like a dirt farmer going to church.

"Stand when a lady enters the room, Kasey." I kept a lid on my desire to punch him for his bad manners.

"Don't bother," Ms. Sabel said with a dismissive wave. "Do you have proof of my birth father's murderer?"

Kasey scowled, first at me, then at Ms. Sabel. "Wow, them Russians did a number on you."

Ignoring his comment, she rolled her hand. "What do you have?"

He pulled a thick folder out of his backpack and tossed it on her desk. "Check it out. Tell me whacha looking at."

He leaned back, crossed his legs, and plastered a smug look on his face.

We glanced through a stack of copies. Each one had been redacted with a black marker so juicy the ink had saturated clear through. Three on top were paper-clipped together. They were Roche Security payment records for contractor services. One of them was not redacted. It listed the payee as Leroy Johnson. Five thousand dollars had been paid the day before Ms. Sabel's parents were murdered. The service was listed as "pruning". The next stack had the name and social security number redacted. The second page listed the same amount and date, also for pruning. The last had an additional payment of $25,000 the day after the murders.

We looked at each other. She said, "Leroy didn't live long enough to get his second bonus. But the man who killed my father did. Is that what this is?"

We turned to Kasey.

"See what I been telling you?" He grinned and stuck a toothpick in his teeth. "Straight up, bitches."

Ms. Sabel started thumbing through the other copies. "What are these?"

"Authorizations and annual payments for pruning."

"Authorizations—you mean who hired them?"

"Yessiree, ma'am. And the project manager too. Ain't you proud of me now?"

I leaned against Ms. Sabel's desk and crossed my arms. "It has to be Chuck Roche since it's his company."

"Nah, I ain't falling for that." He shook his head. "I told you, none of your tricks. You don't know who it is. And there's three people involved anyhow."

"Kasey." Ms. Sabel thumbed through the stack. "These pages are two decades old. Companies like Roche Security don't keep records that long. They're only required to keep records for seven to ten years. Where did you get these?"

"I was doing me some research on a current issue. There was a kinda odd thing. A whattaya call it?"

"Anomaly?"

"Yeah, one of them." He leaned forward. "So, I kept digging back in the records looking for that same alomany. It come up every year like clockwork. But they only keep records back like you said. Then I asks one of the accounting ladies if there's any older shit. Pardon my language, ma'am. And she said there used to be a warehouse, but nobody goes there no more. They just shred the old stuff now. So, I go on down there. It took a week of pushing through dusty old boxes, but I done found it."

She dropped the papers on the desk. "What do you want for these?"

"Five million. Final offer."

"Years ago, I published a reward of $100,000."

Kasey started to shake his head.

"Kasey—" I interrupted his thinking "—we've known each other for a long time. That whole time, it's never been a secret that you're seven beers short of a six-pack. And you've always been aware that I graduated high school in my junior year and got a full-ride scholarship to Iowa State. Which doesn't make me a genius, but does make me a whole lot smarter than you. So, let me give you some free advice here. See, she can call the cops, tell them you have this information. The cops will go to your place with a warrant, take all this information for free, and charge you with attempted extortion. You'd go to jail."

"You sure about that?" Kasey's smug grin disappeared. "Hell. Don't matter none. They can't serve me no warrant."

Ms. Sabel and I shared a confused glance. She put her hands on the desk and leaned forward. "You don't have the documents?"

"They're safe. I can get to 'em when I want. Probably."

I palmed my face. "You left them in the warehouse. Let me guess, you bragged about what you found?"

"I didn't tell nobody nothing." Kasey swiveled his gaze between us. "I ain't stupid. But the accounting guy come around and asked me why I'm on the video down at the warehouse making copies." He fidgeted his fingers. "They done changed my access code. Now I gotta apply for another one."

I did some math in my head. A big company like Roche would have many layers of management. It would take time for one guy scratching his head to ask another guy higher up the ladder, "Do we have any incriminating information in storage section X:Y?" And the question would bubble up the food chain until it reached whoever authorized the checks. If he's still working there, Kasey was a dead man, and our chances of seeing the real box of documents would drop like a skydiver who forgot his chute.

Ms. Sabel did the same math and pinched the bridge of her nose with her fingers. "Look, Kasey, I'll give you $500,000 to bring the whole box down here. But tell me something. Roche has thousands of employees. This could've been a project by an aggressive VP looking to move up the ladder, or it could've been Roche. Do these records spell out exactly who's involved?"

"No, no, no." Kasey waved his index finger like a school teacher. "I ain't telling you shit until … pardon my language, ma'am. Let me just say this: you ain't gonna believe it til you see it."

We kicked him out. He promised to be back soon with the originals but stuck to his five-million price. The money wasn't a problem for her. What she hated was the principle of giving a slimeball like Kasey that much money.

I returned to the employees' wake. Ms. Sabel went elsewhere.

Miguel and I were shooting pool when the butler tapped me on the shoulder. "Could you spare a moment, sir? There is a man at the door from the US Senate. He insists on speaking to you or Ms. Sabel."

I followed him to the foyer, where a man dressed in a deep blue suit with a white shirt and a red tie stood at ease.

While my stride was still beating out a rhythm crossing the marble toward him, he started talking. "I'm Ivan D'Aquino from the Senate Foreign Relations Committee. Are you Jacob Stearne?"

He held up an official-looking ID card with his picture on it.

I said, "I am."

He whipped out an equally official looking folder and slapped it on my chest. "Are you the head of personal security for Pia Sabel?"

My hand slid to the folder and took it from him. I opened the folder to find some beautiful stationery with official-looking seals from the US Senate. "Yes, I have that responsibility."

"Will you be in contact with her today?"

"Most likely, why?"

"I expect you to give Ms. Sabel her copy." He slapped a second folder into my hands. "You are both hereby served with a summons to appear before the Senate. You will be compelled to give your sworn testimony about the Russian military personnel in Kaliningrad who you murdered."

CHAPTER 47

YURI AND ROMAN SAT ON the balcony overlooking the beach on a muggy afternoon in Santos, Brazil. They sipped beers and groaned about their bandages and whether taking the pain medication would be worthwhile. It might ease their agony, but they would lose their edge. Paranoia is a healthy thing for geeks when Viktor Popov is your sworn enemy.

Aleksandr was the third member of SHaRC to reach Roman's apartment in Santos. Roman led him to the balcony, where he gasped at Yuri's injuries. The three of them took their beers to the railing, leaned on it, and looked over the beach. Crowds had gathered. Many of Brazil's famously beautiful women sunned themselves just below them.

"That one is for you, Aleksandr." Roman pointed to a dark-skinned woman far below them.

"You can see with only one eye?" Aleksandr clinked Roman's bottle.

While Roman and Aleksandr chose future brides from the assembled throngs, Yuri looked down the beach with his good eye. An ominous feeling came over him. The sense of being watched. Rows of twenty-story apartments rose along the curved stretch of sand. Something along that row caught his eye: a blue glint. He scanned again, looking for something out of place. Then he saw it. A glint of sunlight on a spotter's scope.

It was on a building three hundred yards away. The blue coating of the lens reduced the sparkle but made it a unique signature to a major who started his career as a sniper.

A spotter and sniper were taking aim. He saw the puff of smoke.

Yuri felt like a man in a nightmare. He willed himself to move faster than the supersonic bullet could travel. It was an impossible task. He spun in place, reaching out with his arm. He shouted something. His extended arm hit Roman hard. The two of them went down. Roman's head hit the sliding glass door.

Aleksandr's head had already exploded. His body slumped against the wall.

Roman's eyes were on Yuri. He followed the major's gaze and realized what happened. He flipped over onto his hands and knees and scrambled inside. "Grab the laptops. Do you have your phone?"

"Right behind you." Yuri's head throbbed. None of his broken and reset bones were healed enough to handle the blood pumping hard throughout his body. "Do you have a safe room?"

They scrambled to their feet, grabbed the electronics. Outside, they could hear boots tramping up the stairwell.

"Better." Roman walked quietly and whispered. "Follow me."

They slid out of the apartment and down the hall. The pounding boots neared the corner. Yuri raced behind Roman to a nearby apartment. Roman unlocked it with trembling hands. He closed the door quietly and relocked it with an iron bar across the door.

Yuri looked around at the spartan accommodations. A TV monitored Roman's beachfront condo via streaming video. In the upper corner, Aleksandr's body remained in a heap. Roman made a call.

"Who are you calling?" Yuri asked.

"The police, of course."

Outside their escape room, the boots landed on their floor. Three crashing sounds later, they watched the live video as the attacking soldiers entered Roman's apartment. The men cleared the room and rifled through Roman's things. They tore open Yuri's backpack and found Babineau's passport. One of them began to make a call.

Sirens screamed in the streets below.

On the TV, the Russian soldiers in Roman's apartment looked at each other with alarm. They had not expected such a quick response. Packing up, they made a beeline for the exits and disappeared off camera.

Yuri grabbed Roman. "You did this! You spoke to that man … Brad."

"No." Roman shook his head furiously. "We never discussed

location. I would never divulge this place. This has always been my safe house. I planned on getting out of Stavanger months ago. I always used a spoofed IP phone. Brad hasn't contacted me since I left Paris. I swear."

Yuri pushed him away. Brad's tradecraft was superb. The American implied he was working against Strangelove and Popov, but trusting his words could be a fatal mistake. If Roman had allowed himself to be tracked, it could've easily been either party.

"Damn it." Yuri paced with his arms wrapped around himself. "He was just a kid. What the hell is wrong with these people?"

Roman watched him but didn't reply.

"They tracked him here." Yuri's pacing picked up speed. "No. He'd only been here a few minutes. They were in place on the rooftop. I saw the spotter quite by accident. Did they follow me? No. I used Babineau's passport and paid cash from Montreal all the way here. New phone, never turned on my laptop. They always follow money."

Yuri stopped and stared at his new lieutenant.

Roman dropped his shoulders. "I kept an account in Panama."

"They found it?"

"That's how I bought this." Roman waved his hands around. "When you conscripted me, you knew I was involved in the credit-card hack of Target. What you didn't know: I was also responsible for the Home Depot hack. My take was $3 million. It's been invested in Exxon Mobil, Amazon, and United Healthcare in America."

"I can't be angry." Yuri's head pounded with excruciating pain. "Your emergency system worked well for us."

Roman dropped to the sofa and gingerly held his bandaged face in his hands. "How did Popov find us so quickly?"

"Strangelove did the background on your accounts. He never told me about that one." Yuri paced again. He considered Alexi's accounts, the ones he'd used. Did Strangelove let everyone keep some outside money in case they made a break for it? Accounts he could track when he needed to? "We need to pool our money into new accounts. Yours and mine. I'll bet the others have an account here and there. We get the word out. Change phones, change IDs. Lay low."

Someone knocked on the door. Yuri drew his weapon. Roman waved him away and opened it. Uniformed Santos police officers stood in the hall. Behind them, three men were handcuffed and pressed against the wall.

One of the officers spoke to Roman in Portuguese. Roman responded in the native language, much to Yuri's surprise.

"They are offering us a look at Aleksandr's killers," Roman said in Russian. "The reason I came to Brazil—police protection is much cheaper here."

Yuri grasped his shoulder. "I have chosen my lieutenant wisely."

Roman replied with an impatient glance, telegraphing Yuri that his leadership would be short-lived if he didn't prove his value quickly.

They brought the Russian soldiers in one at a time and interrogated them. On the face of things, nothing came of it. But Yuri sensed a hesitation in one man's voice. A sign of weakness. They let the cops take all but the hesitant one away to be tried for murder. The cops let them know the coroner would retrieve Aleksandr's body soon.

When they were alone with their bound captive, Yuri dragged him to Aleksandr's body. He pushed the soldier to his knees in front of Alexandr's corpse. "You did this. You murdered my friend. Tell me who put you up to it."

The soldier offered no reply.

Yuri shoved the man's face into Alexandr's blood. They questioned him again. He showed signs of fear, but he didn't crack. Yuri pushed him to the floor and gave him one last chance to reveal his boss. The man refused.

He wrapped his hands around the man's neck and squeezed.

Roman pulled Aleksandr's phone from their dead friend's pocket and checked it. Then he grabbed two more beers from the fridge and sat nearby and watched.

When it was over, he handed Yuri a beer. "Do you want to talk about it?"

"Yes." Yuri rose to his feet and flexed his fingers. "You know, it takes a great deal more hand-strength than I ever imagined. I've been working my fingers with those grip strengtheners for a few days. I feel a remarkable improvement over the last two. One day, I will use these hands to strangle the life out of the oligarchs and the generals."

Roman nodded and sipped his beer.

"This was for Aleksandr." Yuri sat and took a sip of beer. "There. I feel better by talking about it."

"Popov sent them." Roman shrugged. "Brad is soft like an American. No Russian would take orders from him."

"Do you think Popov ran the operation himself? Or is there a new Strangelove? Whoever it is, we need to make him understand that coming after us is more difficult than leaving us alone."

"That is a noble undertaking for the man who would be king of the stateless."

Yuri nodded and smiled.

Then Aleksandr's phone rang.

Roman put it on speaker.

"We've never met, Yuri." The voice spoke in crisp, formal Russian. "I am Viktor Popov. I'm having the nicest lunchtime chat—with your mother."

CHAPTER 48

PIA LISTENED TO HER CORPULENT attorney from a facing couch in the library. He explained the intricacies of Senate investigations. She poured herself another cup of coffee.

"Promise me you'll plead the Fifth Amendment at the first sign of a loaded question." He took the last doughnut off the plate and stuffed a quarter of it in his mouth. "And keep your eye out for complex question fallacies. 'Who is the monarch of England?' is a legitimate question because it assumes there is an England and that it has a monarch. But 'Who is the King of France?' assumes two things at once, that there is a France and that it has a king. The former is true, the latter is not. Senators pull these questions all the time."

"Thank you." She blew across her mug. "I'm as ready as I can hope to be."

"In court, we can object to the judge when the prosecutor asks loaded questions. In the Senate, your only salvation is the Fifth. People may say 'ooh, you pleaded the Fifth,' but it's your right. Otherwise, a trick question can lead to perjury charges."

"I understand."

He rose, looked at the remaining pastry in his hand, and stuffed it in his pocket. He shook her hand and left.

As she wiped off the transferred powdered sugar, she looked up at the portrait of Alan Sabel on the wall. She suddenly felt as if she were treading water below the cliff while the ocean gathered a huge wave behind her. Why did he have to be the hero? Why couldn't he let the professionals take the risk? He'd done stupid things before—and the team always saved him. They gave him a false sense of invincibility.

Why Dad? Why have you abandoned me? I need you now. But that was the kind of man he'd always been: forever taking charge of everything around him. Blaming him was pointless.

She shook her head at the lifeless painting.

The real blame lay with those responsible for killing 365 Americans. Who gave the order? The same person responsible for so many other crimes. She needed to take care of Popov before his long reach found her.

She picked up her purse, pushed on her cane, and faced the giant globe before turning to the exit. The globe reminded her of Roche's visit. Why had he said, "You're just as stupid as your old man?" No one thought of Alan Sabel as stupid. Headstrong, driven, arrogant, but never stupid.

She strode toward the hall, barely using the cane. She set it on a table and took a few steps without it. Not quite yet. She retrieved it and took one more glance at the portrait.

It hit her like a punch in the gut.

Roche wasn't talking about Alan Sabel. He was talking about Lloyd Aston, her biological father. A man who made one fatal mistake: he found a way to break America's dependence on oil. A stupid decision in the eyes of Chuck Roche, the refinery tycoon. But how did Roche know Lloyd Aston? Had they met? Alan Sabel had never said a word about that. They'd once had a heart-to-heart about her parents' final days. And they had several lengthy discussions about Chuck Roche. Alan met Roche long after the killings. But if Kasey's information was real, the killers were paid by Roche Security.

Which could only mean: Alan had not known Roche was involved.

She turned on her cane and looked over her shoulder at his portrait. His smile beamed back at her.

If Chuck Roche paid the assassins, who was the project manager Kasey referred to? And who was the missing trigger man? Would either of them testify against Roche? Was Roche part of it? Could something like that happen inside his company without his knowledge or involvement?

Pia thought about Sabel Industries. Among 40,000 employees, were there people willing to commit murder for her? Statistically speaking, yes. Realistically speaking—she hoped not.

Kasey was right about one thing: she would pay to find out.

She dialed Kasey Earl. Her call went directly to Kasey's voicemail. "Kasey, I've considered your proposal. Five million will be transferred immediately upon delivery. I'll have Jacob work out the details."

STRIDING THROUGH THE SENATE WING of the US Capitol, Pia followed her guide to S-116, the Foreign Relations Committee room. Among the throngs of people lining the hallway, FBI Director Shikowitz appeared. He planted himself in her path.

"Pia, I'm here to wish you the best of luck today." Shikowitz grabbed her hand to shake it and pulled her in for a hug. When they were close, he whispered, "This is a Top Secret recording made by the NSA that you must have Bianca translate immediately. It's part of an ongoing investigation. Giving this to anyone is a violation of ethics, laws, and my own common sense. Therefore, you do not have it."

He pushed back from her and gave her a big, fake smile. His voice picked up loud enough for bystanders to hear. "I know you'll do well. You are a beacon of light and truth."

When he walked away, Pia palmed the SD card he'd pressed into her hand. She excused herself from the guide to find the restroom. Once there, she slid the card into her tablet and uploaded the file to Bianca with instructions.

She rejoined the guide and entered the imposing wood-paneled chambers that Foreign Relations had occupied since 1933.

Pia finished her opening statement to the Senate Committee. Photographers clicked and whirred, TV cameras loomed over her. A row of twenty old men and one middle-aged woman faced her with dour faces. The Committee Chairman made a statement about mercenaries for hire and citizens conducting foreign policy.

She tuned out.

Her thoughts turned to the President-Elect and his involvement in murder-for-hire. If Kasey's evidence held up and Roche was involved, should she release the taped conversation of Roche conspiring to kill her? She could think of a thousand charges the Feds could bring against her for having made it. It would be worth going to jail if she brought down Roche, but not if he managed to silence or discredit her first. And there were other futures to consider. Jacob and Bianca would be caught up in any investigation. She could only hope Kasey's documents would provide overwhelming evidence against him. Until then, she would need a better strategy.

Eventually, the Chairman said, "Isn't that right, Ms. Sabel?"

"I'm sorry, Mr. Chairman. TL;DR."

Everyone under forty laughed out loud. The sour-faced senators looked around the room. The Chairman banged his gavel. An aide leaned to his ear and explained, *Too Long; Didn't Read*. The internet shorthand for, *I couldn't wade through your boring drivel*.

"I said, we all want to get to the bottom of things. Is that right, Ms. Sabel?"

"I would rather stick to the truth."

A round of suppressed laughter rippled around the room.

The Chairman banged his gavel again and threatened to clear the room. He directed his attention back to her. "An apology for your impudence would be appropriate."

A long silence stretched. Not a single sound occurred in the room for thirty seconds.

"We can wait until hell freezes over, Mr. Chairman." Pia frowned. "I'm not going to apologize for insisting on the truth."

The room filled with the quiet noise of a thousand fingers clicking out tweets and texts on smartphones.

"My first question to you is, did you authorize your agent, Jacob Stearne, to attack the Russian Embassy?" The Senator pointed to a large poster being brought into the open space between her table and the dais. It depicted a silhouette slithering between buildings. Uniformed guards stood in the background looking and pointing in the wrong direction.

Her phone, laid out on the table next to her, displayed a text from her attorney: *Plead the 5th*.

"Your question is based on unfounded assumptions about who is in that grainy photo of yours. Nonetheless, I assure you, I never have and never would authorize my employees to break the laws of our country."

Her attorney's next text: *THE 5TH!*

"Do you deny the sworn testimony, heard before this committee, of Russian diplomat Viktor Popov, who stated, under oath, that Jacob Stearne entered onto Russian Embassy grounds and shot him in the leg to retrieve his dog?"

Her attorney: *5TH! 5TH! 5TH!*

Pia squinted. "Did I hear you right? A Russian diplomat testified that he kidnapped a decorated American veteran's puppy? I know about diplomatic immunity, but surely you expelled him from the country after that confession."

The voices in the room erupted, cameras clattered, the gavel banged again.

"Next question," the Chairman growled. "Did you fly to Kaliningrad with the express intent to kill Russian military personnel?"

Yet another text about the Fifth Amendment with a flurry of exclamation points popped up on her phone. She flipped the phone over, face down.

"I did not fly to Kaliningrad." She paused and lowered her volume, fighting her growing desire to leap up and throttle the bastard. "As Swedish, Finish, and Lithuanian air traffic controllers have already reported in the media, I was on a flight path to Klaipėda, Lithuania when Russian fighter jets forced my pilots—"

"What was your business in Lithuania?"

"My people have been tracing the criminals responsible for bringing down Flight 1028 and—"

"We are painfully aware of the outlandish claims you made to the media." The Chairman scowled, his jowls flushing with anger. "Do you have a shred of evidence that the good people of Norway were responsible for #HuntersFail?"

"I'm waiting for the Stavanger police to release public videos we can use for facial recognition of the men who—"

"Yes, the Committee has been in touch with authorities in Stavanger about your unsubstantiated claims. The router logs you claim originated in their fair city have been traced to Istanbul, not Norway. Tell us the truth, Ms. Sabel, you are way out of your league on this topic, are you not? Don't answer that. Just stick to soccer."

Pia shook her head. "Don't you get it? Viktor Popov has been meddling in the election—"

"You and your boy-toy—I mean, bodyguard—have a thing for this respected diplomat. You should be ashamed, Ms. Sabel. Ashamed."

The press corps erupted with laughs. Cameras clicked in rapid-fire succession and phones clicked with incoming and outgoing texts.

A text from Bianca came to Pia's phone, identified by a unique ping. She flipped her phone over and scanned her text: "Shikowitz's file is a recorded phone conversation between Popov and Strangelove minutes before Popov's surgery. He orders Strangelove to, 'kill the girl in front of Alan. Make him regret challenging us. Do not release him until he is compliant like Jallet. He will submit or die.'"

Pia bit the inside of her lip and felt rage building inside her. Strangelove paid the ultimate price for messing with America; now it was Popov's turn. As soon as she finished with the Senate.

The Chairman again banged his gavel. "Ms. Sabel, you are under oath and must respond truthfully to our questions." He remained silent to punctuate his demand. Then he continued. "Did you travel to Europe with the express intent to destroy a Russian general whose code name is Strangelove?"

"No."

The Chairman paused and stared at her until the room waited silently for his next word.

"Ms. Sabel, did you ever tell someone, and I quote, 'I'm not going to bring Strangelove and Popov to justice. I'm going to kill them'?"

CHAPTER 49

OUR ATTORNEY SPENT THE BREAK between Ms. Sabel's grilling and my testimony ranting about the Fifth Amendment. Bianca interrupted him with a better strategy. Since Sabel Technology was engaged in a national security contract and was actively tracing the responsible parties in the airline disaster, all our actions were covered. We could only testify in closed-door sessions. Since the proceedings were nothing but a publicity stunt for the Chairman, they would decline further questions. Probably.

I made my opening statement referring to the security issues. Which caused a lengthy delay. The press could see where this was heading and filed out to find some other gladiator in some other arena being torn to shreds. The Chairman's aide came to my table with a list of questions and asked me to strike the ones I would refuse to answer. I struck them all.

That didn't save me. They rolled out a big screen and played a video. In the low-contrast clip, a figure appeared to pole-vault the Russian Embassy's outer wall.

"Is that shadowy assassin you, Mr. Stearne?" the Chairman asked.

"No."

Mercury took a seat next to me. He wore a Brooks Brothers suit and a shiny red tie. *Yo, homie. Did Roger get you to confess to killing his mistress yet?*

No. I did a double-take. *Wait. Who?*

Mercury looked at me, incredulous. *The ugly dude up there. Roger. We used to be buds, he and I. Got him into Congress, first term, yo. But one day he ups and kills his pregnant mistress and blames me. Can you believe it? Mars, Diana, and I were going to roast him in a fire, but when we got to his crib, he'd already made a deal with Set.* Mercury straightened his tie. *And we had marshmallows and everything.*

A what kind of deal?

Not what, who. Set, the Egyptian god who killed his brother. Not a nice guy, dawg. Yeah, so Roger cuddles up with Set and the next thing you know the old guy gets kicked up to the Senate. Some poor homeless guy went to jail for the murder.

"Shall we watch the tape again, Mr. Stearne?"

I sat up straight. "Sure, but this time, can you roll it a few seconds longer?"

The video played. The part I was looking for happened. "Stop right there."

I gave thanks and praise to the *Dii Concentes*. When I launched the extra-large sandbag over the fence for a distraction, I remembered it breaking open on impact. The video caught the splat nicely. The white sand spilled out into a well-lit area. There was no mistaking what it was and what it was not.

"I'm sorry, Roger, did you think that sandbag was an assassin or something?" There was a lengthy pause while some of the senators tittered. "Do you need anything else from me? Or are you all *SET*—like an Egyptian?"

The Chairman squinted over his spectacles at me. He pursed his lips as we made a non-verbal connection. His eyes shifted to Mercury. He banged his gavel. "No further questions."

Twenty minutes later, I arrived back at Sabel Gardens.

Inside, Ms. Sabel yelled loud enough for a couple maids to listen in from the grand foyer. I shooed them away, only to find Tania standing with her back to the library doorjamb. I started to scold her for eavesdropping. She put a finger to her lips.

Olivier Jallet, the French dude, was pleading his case. He swore he never told anyone what she'd said to him on the flight back to Washington.

Tania held up her phone to show me the headlines. Ms. Sabel's swollen and bruised face, in full saturated color, graced the website under the banner, "Vigilante Princess or Rampage Killer?"

I rolled my eyes. Tania nodded.

I asked, "She hasn't seen it yet?"

Tania shook her head. "She knows her testimony started well but ended badly."

The shouting subsided. Tania hid her phone.

Ms. Sabel strode out, barely putting weight on her cane. She stopped in front of me. "Kasey texted back that he's ready. But I can't get him on the phone to make arrangements. See Cousin Elmer for your car and drive up to New York. Talk to Kasey. See what kind of game he's playing."

I went to the car barn where Ms. Sabel's Chief Auto Officer, also known as Cousin Elmer, leaned against a Ferrari 488 Spider. He said, "Miguel reminded her that a terrorist blew up your VW, so she's giving you this as a Thanksgiving gift."

It took me a few seconds to get my lungs working again. "Thank you."

"Don't thank me, thank her." Cousin Elmer tossed me the keys and walked away. "And don't do that until you see your insurance bill for driving it. She doesn't understand the economic strain. Fifty bucks says you'll put this baby on eBay by next week."

Screw him. I planned to drive the thing until my reality check bounced. Just in case he was right, I emailed my insurance agent and asked how much my rates would go up. He reported it would probably be more than my annual income, but he'd check and get back to me.

My new sled made the long drive up the Jersey Turnpike easy. Despite the freezing air, I kept the top down with the heat cranked up on full. A lot of young ladies did a double-take and gave me a smile. Which would've made my day if Sylvia hadn't walked off with my heart in her roller bag.

Mercury appeared in the passenger seat wearing a g-string of a toga. *Told you she's no good for you. What kind of a person walks out after a tragedy like that? You needed her.*

I said, *We barely knew each other, and I left her alone most of the time. Bad timing. Maybe she'll give me a second chance.*

Mercury said, *You don't need it. She's a narcissist. Worse, she's a pacifist. No future in their kind. They turn the other cheek, and—BAM!— they go down quicker than a sacked temple.*

I said, *Gandhi was a pacifist and he took down the British Empire.*

Fluke, dude. Just a fluke.

I made my way through the Lincoln Tunnel. Kasey's building was just off Tompkins Square. When I asked Google Maps where to park, it displayed a message I'd never seen before, "WTF I look like, a magician?" Even AI goes native in NYC. A few pedestrians eyed the Ferrari hungrily. I double-parked and ran in, trying to make it quick.

Naturally, Kasey lived on the fourth floor. No elevator.

I bolted up the stairs and stopped when I reached his landing. Something felt wrong. There were four apartments; one of the doors was ajar. I stood still and listened. A muffled TV played a floor down. Nothing else. Inching along, I did the math. The open door was definitely Kasey's. Amid the New York noise outside, I heard sirens approaching. With one last look around, I reached the door, pushed it wider with one finger, and peered in.

A loud bang echoed through the building.

To me, it sounded like a large book dropped flat on the hardwood floor. The average civilian would easily mistake it for a gunshot.

Kasey lay in a pool of black-red blood, dead center. He was hard to miss.

Blood had long since stopped flowing from the three holes in his body. One at center-chest, the second at the clavicle, the third in his forehead. Professional. The kitchenette's sink was filled with dirty dishes. His futon at the back had blood sprayed on the right side. A TV on the right wall also had some splatter. There was a bookshelf with some potted plants, Army Ranger memorabilia, and some Star Wars figurines. His lone medal—the Purple Heart he got after I sliced his ear off—lay on the coffee table. There were no boxes. No papers.

Mercury leaned over my shoulder. *Bro, you need to get to the super's apartment and grab a copy of the video.*

I said, *What video?*

Dude, the hallway camera. The cops are coming, and you're double-parked. So, move it.

Boots clumped into the lobby below us. Excited voices rose from downstairs. The boots hit the stairs at a run.

Mercury said, *Too late.*

I said, *Could you give me a little more notice? Like, y'know, enough time to make a clean getaway?*

Mercury said, *You need to get an attitude of gratitude, my brutha. You have god on your side, and all you do is complain.*

A cop's head came into view from the stairway at the end of the hall. She looked like a young version of the Major, a serious black woman with her hair pulled back in a tight bun. She stopped and drew her weapon. I raised my hands over my head in the airport scanning position.

"Identify yourself." She came up the steps slowly.

Her partner, a nervous-looking younger guy, came up behind her.

"Jacob Stearne, Sabel Security. ID's in my pocket. I have a pistol under my jacket."

She inched along. Her partner took nervous to DEFCON 1.

"Turn to the wall slowly." When I complied, she reached under my jacket and took my weapon. She sniffed it for recent firing. Then she pulled the wallet out of my pocket. "OK, Mr. Stearne, what are you doing here?"

"The victim claimed to have information about a cold case murder. My boss sent me here to collect it."

"Did you?"

"I've been here thirty seconds longer than you." I kept my hands raised and my face to the wall. The nervous guy still had his finger inside his trigger guard.

She turned to her partner. "Get that damn Ferrari towed before the EMTs get here."

"Wait! It's mine." I looked over my shoulder. "The keys are in my front pocket."

"Hang on a second." She peered at me. A decidedly unpleasant expression crossed her face. "Are you that guy who murdered all those Russians?"

CHAPTER 50

After the cameras and the lights left the Oval Office, the real meeting between President-Elect Chuck Roche and President Hunter began in earnest.

Roche twirled his cane with childlike giddiness and inspected the photos lined up on the Resolute Desk. "Why is your Chief of Staff still here?"

President Hunter snapped her fingers at her astonished aide. "I'll call for you when we need you again."

The door closed leaving Hunter, Roche, and Watson looking at each other like boxers before a fight.

Roche's cane launched a photo of Hunter shaking hands with the Prime Minister of Canada off the desk. It landed with a thump on the plush carpet. He said, "My program is working. She's completely discredited. Now all we need is another attack from a different angle and—"

"Get a grip on reality, Chuck." Hunter fisted her hips. "Pia Sabel is America's darling. She'll wriggle out of it. She always does."

Watson turned to the window. "I said all along we should've killed her right off."

"How did your plan work out, genius?" Roche pointed his cane at Watson. "I had to give you a job to cover your ass before they traced your calls to Russia."

"They already did." Hunter bit her thumbnail. "All seventeen intelligence agencies are investigating your campaign staff. They have recordings of—"

"What is this, East Germany?" Roche yelled. "They can't investigate me. I won."

"That's not how it works. The separation of—"

"You're still the goddamn president. Make them stop the investigation."

"I can't." Hunter turned away. "Presidents don't have that power."

"Fine, I'll do it when my Attorney General gets confirmed." Roche flicked a picture of Hunter shaking hands with the Queen of England off the desk. It hit the coffee table. The glass shattered.

"Watson, what new dirt did you find on Sabel?" Roche asked.

"Yeah, about that." Watson stared at Hunter.

"I told him to stand down, Chuck." Hunter faced Roche. "You don't know how thorough the press is. They track every rumor back to its origins. They'll debunk it like Pizzagate and Seth Rich. If you put some nasty story out there, they'll trace it back to Watson."

"Since when do my people take orders from you?" Roche swung his cane through the air between them. Hunter jumped.

"I asked for advice." Watson stepped in. "She's right. They trace it back to me, they'll hang you with it."

"But I had nothing to do with it!" Roche paced around the Resolute Desk. "I don't text. I don't email. They can't prove anything."

He stopped and tapped his cane against the side of Queen Victoria's gift to President Hayes. "First thing I'm going to do is get rid of this ugly desk. Where the hell did you find it, a garage sale?"

No one spoke. He caught Watson and Hunter sharing a pained glance.

"Fine," Roche said. "Get an expendable outsider. Find one of those brown-nosers who're dying to kiss my ring. Have one of them take the fall for it. Feed it to the conspiracy sites. Just get a goddamn story out there. We need to start a second fire before she can put out the first."

"Do what you want." Hunter tossed up her hands. "But long term, it won't work."

"Then we go with Watson's plan. Order a drone strike before you leave office. Don't leave your messes in my lap." Roche noticed the shocked look on his co-conspirators' faces. "OK, I'll bite, what's wrong with that idea?"

"You'll create a martyr and have a revolution." Hunter stroked his shoulder and spoke in a calming voice. "You can't touch her."

"If I can't touch her, Popov can. She already declared war on him. Watson, get General Krasny over to the Russian Embassy. We need to use their secure lines to have a conversation with Popov that our so-called *intelligence* agencies can't hear."

YURI TOOK HIS TURN AT the tripod-mounted field glasses. With care, he settled his bandaged nose between the lenses. His restructured orbital socket touched the eyecup, sending needles of pain through his head. He and Roman sat two feet back from the curtains, watching two white stucco motels across the river in Belo Horizonte, Brazil. It was their second day holed up in a city the size of Philadelphia—a city he'd never heard of before. They'd covered every conceivable topic to discuss. Except one. And now they were broaching it.

"You can let go of her like that?" Roman asked.

"Everyone loses a mother sooner or later." Yuri reached for another naan to hide his sigh. "Popov will hold our relatives over our heads. We can regret our choice. We can cry ourselves to sleep. What will change? Will Andrine come back to life? My mother? Your family? There is nothing we can do about it now. If we go back, they will either kill us or turn us over to the Americans."

He tossed the bread back in the box. Take-out Indian in the middle of Brazil did not taste the same as eating it in Mumbai. And talking about his mother was killing his appetite.

"We must shed everything." Yuri leaned to the binoculars. "Our families, our friends—any connection to Russia."

"You and I are made of steel." Roman finished his tandoori chicken. "Not everyone in SHaRC is so strong."

"To stay in SHaRC is to shed everything." Yuri stood and paced. "To leave SHaRC is to face death back home. To offer them a choice is to ask them to lie. We must test them."

"What kind of test?" Roman leaned forward and watched the motels. "Loyalty? Like gangs?"

"Such barbarism. How could you think such a thing? No. Investment tests."

"Where your money is, your heart will be also?" Roman craned over his shoulder to observe Yuri. "You think that's a stronger test than Strangelove's?"

"More honorable." Yuri picked up the discarded naan and took a large bite. "Do you have a better idea?"

Roman returned to his observations and remained silent for a long time. Finally, he leaned back. "If I am to be part of the leadership, I am glad to hear you will not use Strangelove's savagery. It should be as you say."

Yuri finished his chana masala and mopped up his lentil soup with the naan. He put the empty boxes in the trash can.

"They're here," Roman said.

Yuri moved to the window and raised his handheld binoculars. He checked their haircuts and their fashion sense and their movements. They were Russians. Not Americans like Brad. "I see three. No. five."

"Another car went around the back. There could be more."

"More than I expected." Yuri turned to Roman. "Which room are they swarming?"

Roman had rented a room with a credit card tied to his alias account. Yuri had done the same at the motel next door using his money. A test to determine which of them Popov had been following. Roman said, "Mine."

Yuri watched two thugs dressed in business casual exit the motel office. They nodded to men at the room door. The gangsters used a battering ram to break it open. The remaining men flooded into the room, guns drawn.

Yuri laughed. "It is like a circus car full of clowns."

"You think this is funny?" Roman jumped up. "This means they can lock down my account. I've lost everything."

"No. You've lost nothing. I will take care of it, Roman." Yuri gave him a hard stare. His voice lowered. "I have a plan in place. You will move all your money to my account."

"Me? But I …" His words failed him. He lost all his color.

"I will not have Popov follow SHaRC to the next destination. I will eliminate the threat. And right now, you are the threat. Popov is following you." Yuri pulled the pistol from his pocket and held it at his side. "You pledged your loyalty to me. It is time to put your heart into your loyalty oath. What was it you said? Where your money is, your heart will be also."

Yuri pointed to the laptops whirring away on the coffee table. "Sit down and transfer all your money to my account. It will be SHaRC's money."

He waited, but Roman remained rooted in place.

"I realize you've always thought of it as your safety net. Your getaway stash. But I am your safety now." He held the pistol to Roman's face. "Strangelove would kill you, forfeit your accounts, and leave. But I'm different. I'm going to give you a chance. But with a platoon of Popov's men across the street, time is running out. What will it be?"

They stood still for nearly a full minute.

"I'll do it." Roman rushed to the couch and touched the fingerprint reader on his laptop. "But won't he follow the transfer?"

"I have shell accounts in countries he'll expect. He'll find those. But then I will move it through Florida, Wyoming, and Nevada before bringing it back to the Caymans and Panama."

Roman relaxed and let a grin crease his face. "Exactly what the oligarchs did."

"I studied the Panama Papers." Yuri nodded. "I know how they operate. And I know their mistakes."

Roman brought up his accounts online.

"And move Aleksandr's accounts as well." Yuri checked the chamber in his pistol. "I saw you unlock his phone. I know you have his passwords."

CHAPTER 51

PIA ROLLED TO A STOP in a quiet Bethesda neighborhood in front of Stefan's modest home. She reminded herself not to rush. Don't look desperate. Don't expect too much. Thanksgiving is about family, not romance.

She'd been lucky to have him around in the days after Dad's murder. Stefan's friendship hit just the right note. Empathetic and quiet. He'd made no demands. He brought the children sometimes. Only when it was appropriate. He was a perfect gentleman. But. When she was ready to resume the intimate side of their relationship, he continued to be a perfect gentleman.

Maybe he was doing the right thing. She should trust him to make a move at the right time. After all, he'd dealt with being bereaved. He knew more about loss and recovery than she.

Or had he lost interest?

Maybe he considered her too emotionally damaged now. No one wanted a woman with so many problems. She had ghosts hanging on her family tree like grisly Christmas ornaments. Would she ever be anything more than a basket case to someone?

"Shit." She grabbed the flowers and orange juice off the McLaren's passenger seat. "It's just an orphans' Thanksgiving. Try not to over-analyze it."

She strode up the short walkway and rang the bell.

Stefan, Emma, and Ethan wrapped her in warm hugs and pulled her inside. The kids returned to their toy kitchen in the breakfast nook. Stefan showed Pia the bird in the oven. "Like you, I grew up with a chef. I'm just now learning. This is my first big meal. So, please, lower your expectations."

"I won't complain. I invited myself over."

"Nonsense." He rinsed a couple dishes in the sink. "I chickened out about five times before you called. I kept convincing myself you'd hold Alan's Uber-Thanksgiving at the Gardens. For some reason, I thought you'd continue his traditions."

She crossed her arms, leaned against the counter, and stared at the floor. "When you're a family of two but have a hundred people over for turkey … it's indescribably lonely." She felt a tear welling and turned around.

A stack of pamphlets greeted her. She tried not to pry, but the banner across the front caught her eye: "Since 1870, Georgetown Law has been an innovator in legal education." She picked it up and found an application guide underneath and the corner of a brochure about LSAT classes. She dropped the brochure and straightened the stack. When she turned back, he was right behind her.

"I've decided to pursue a law degree." He shrugged. "Family law, to protect orphans and foster children. But Georgetown is probably out of my academic league. Do community colleges have law schools?"

She smiled. He turned back to the stove. She glanced around.

There was a laptop on the counter next to the stove. A video was paused on a bowl of stuffing. She moved to it.

"What are your guests doing?" he asked.

"The Jallets are French. It's an unknown holiday to them. They're chilling in the guest house, anxious to see justice come to Popov."

"I'm glad you came." Stefan wiped his hands on a dishtowel. "Four is a good number."

She sensed him observing her. He reached around and pressed play on the laptop. A woman's voice spoke about the benefits of low-calorie stuffing. Stefan stood closer to her than they'd been in a long time. Their eyes connected in a way that felt electric to her. He moved in and kissed her on the lips. A genuine kiss. It was quick, not deep. Light, not intense.

But it had sparks.

"Eww," Ethan shouted from his mini-kitchen. "Not like Betty."

Pia pulled back. "Betty?"

"The babysitter." When her nose crinkled, Stefan's color rose. "No, no, no. Not what you're thinking. Betty brings her boyfriend over. They're teenagers. There might be more PDA in front of the children than I'd like, but it's hard to get good help."

Pia laughed. Schadenfreude at Stefan's expense felt good. It was the first time she'd laughed in a month. Even if it was an unimportant laugh, it was a step. There was relief too in knowing he cared enough to explain Betty. He poured them each a glass of orange juice.

"I squeezed it myself." She'd left the house with a different gift before realizing it would be in bad taste to bring a bottle of wine to a recovering alcoholic. She'd run back inside and looked around for something more appropriate. The first thing she saw was a bowl of oranges.

They clinked glasses and sipped. It was bitter with a strong taste of rind. She wondered if she'd over-juiced.

A timer rang. They pulled what looked like a sun-dried turkey from the oven. Burned beans and limp salad surrounded a cup of severely mashed potatoes. Neither of them could figure out how to make the gravy into a liquid again, so they left it. Empty carbs anyway.

They sat at the table and gave thanks for Pillsbury Crescent rolls. At least one thing came out right, albeit lopsided.

After dinner, they played soccer in the backyard with a ball the size of a grapefruit. Pia dazzled the children with her skills. She balanced a spinning ball on her knee before bouncing it to her forehead and rolling it down her back, down her leg to her heel, where she popped it over her head and caught it on her toe. She taught them how to pass the ball to each other. And then everyone was cold.

They went inside for hot chocolate and an animated movie. Stefan lit a fire.

Pia snuggled on the couch with him. It felt good to have his arm around her, to hear his heartbeat, to smell his cologne. Emma crawled in with them first. Ethan came a minute later and used Stefan's leg for a pillow. When the movie ended, Pia pulled out a worn copy of *Falling Up* by Shel Silverstein and read to them.

The children laughed at the poems, then fell asleep.

As they basked in the fire's dying glow, she marveled at Stefan's new life. In less than a year, he'd gone from spoiled scion to giving away his family fortune and adopting two children. Any professional psychologist would've predicted disaster. Yet he'd forged a family of three abandoned misfits. And she could easily become their missing mother-figure. It felt like destiny.

Almost.

She didn't feel herself committing to them. Not yet. He wasn't ready. The kids weren't ready. More importantly, she didn't know if she was ready. She understood Stefan's reticence to dive back into a hot-and-heavy relationship. Life with kids is complex.

After a long silence, she extricated herself from the tangled limbs and small bodies. She gave Stefan a kiss. "Can Betty babysit this weekend? Maybe we can catch dinner and a movie."

THE MCLAREN TOOK HER HOME to a strangely quiet Sabel Gardens. Her agents had staggered their family meals to keep a full rotation. They kept a low and quiet profile, the compound still in mourning. She parked and walked in through the family entrance.

In the dim marble side-foyer, she stopped and listened. The house was mostly silent. In one distant wing, an agent walked rounds, checking doors and rooms.

The foyer opened in many directions: the dark and empty kitchen; the dark and empty library; the dark and empty bar; the dark and empty formal rooms. She sensed the vastness of it. Tens of thousands of hollow square feet. Marble, oak, mahogany, ebony, and brass in every direction. Crystal chandeliers, sweeping staircases, double doors, furniture so heavy it took two people to move a chair.

What good was it?

Alan Sabel built it to impress her. To carve out a life in the woods. To make a cozy home for the two of them. To keep her safe. He did what he thought best to make them a family. He built big to make it better. While he was at it, to make sure everyone could see who was king of the hill. And who was his princess.

All she'd wanted was to curl up on the couch and fall asleep with Dad's leg for her pillow.

She looked left and right, half expecting his booming voice to echo down the halls any second, calling her name. His distinctive, confident march might round the corner at any second. She even ducked out of the drawing room to see if he were coming.

She wandered through the empty rooms, keenly aware of how Alan Sabel had filled the enormous space. People had come and gone every day. Business associates, executives, politicians, artists, and friends swirled through the rooms so often she couldn't remember being alone. But now, without him, the emptiness was overwhelming.

Wandering into the dark library, she reached for the light switch. Then changed her mind. She liked the dark. It fit. Besides, there was a small fire burning in the third fireplace.

Nearing the warm glow, she realized a woman sat in one of two wingbacks. Middle-aged, sturdy, the woman wore a clerical collar. She held a book in her lap and rested her feet on a coffee table.

"Excuse me, are you the priest from Dad's funeral?"

"Is that how you remember me?" She glanced over reading glasses.

"What are you doing here?"

"Reading a book, obviously." She held up a copy of Sophocles' tragedies.

"Can I tell you something, Reverend?" Pia eased around a matching chair and perched on the edge. "Once I stood on a cliff and watched the surf pounding against the basalt. A mountain of water pushed its way into the tiny cove, swelling the seas by ten feet. When the water pummeled into the bluff, it exploded skyward and fell back in tiny, frothy white bubbles. Then the momentum pulled the waters away from shore. The white foam broke away to reveal an ocean of infinite blue-green calm. I imagined myself jumping into the tranquil sea. In that moment, I felt connected to the entire ocean, from the shores of California to the Arctic Ice Shelf to sandy Caribbean beaches to the depths of the Mariana Trench. For just that instant, I felt the loving embrace of a universal creator and I understood how everyone on Earth is interdependent. I felt part of one great and cosmic plan for human beings to live well and love each other. Then the massive walls of water rose behind me and marched once again toward the land. The ocean carried me, helpless and flailing, toward the immovable cliff. Millions of tons of seawater would crush me against the jagged rock. I would explode skyward, to return again as nothing more than frothy red bubbles. I no longer felt connected. I was no longer in the presence of a loving creator. I was about to die at the whim of unimaginable power."

"You're not helpless in the ocean, Pia." The woman tucked a marker in the book and slapped it closed. "You're the rock."

"Then why has God abandoned me?"

"Is that what He's done?" She tilted her head. "You don't consider yourself lucky to have all these wonderful people in your life, even if it's not for as long as you'd like?"

"Excuse me? I'm supposed to be grateful that a monster murdered Dad?"

"My, how we like to complain." She motioned to the cavernous wood-paneled room. "Have you tried telling your problems to a Holocaust survivor? Perhaps you'd like to trade places with a Syrian or Sudanese?"

"I've lost my whole family." Pia edged into the chair and worried her hands. "I'm alone. And this is how you comfort me?"

Pia blew out an exasperated breath. She picked up her phone, ready to call security. Why listen to this interloper when she could have the woman ejected? Hesitation held her thumb over the panic button. She didn't press it. As rude and mean as this priest was, Pia found herself just forsaken enough to want the company.

"Do you really think you're so insignificant they aren't tracking you with live satellite feeds?" An ugly snarl dominated the woman's voice.

"What? I don't know what you—"

"You led Viktor Popov to Stefan's house." The woman's face hardened. Her eyes narrowed. "Popov won't hesitate to kill them. He'll start with Emma, then Ethan. He'll leave Stefan for last. Then you'll better understand why Olivier made his painful choices. And you sit here whining."

CHAPTER 52

NO ONE KNOWS WHAT GETS into Ms. Sabel sometimes. Some say it's the devil. Some say it's an angel. Some say it's the ghost of her mother. But when she gets a burr under her saddle, forty thousand employees jump. Even late on Thanksgiving night. Even if some of them bet on the Cowboys when it was tied in the fourth quarter. Even if they had more than their share of wine because they weren't planning on driving anywhere.

We hadn't been celebrating Thanksgiving all by itself. We were also celebrating Emily and Bianca's engagement. Some of us were celebrating extra hard, hoping to forget Alan Sabel died on my watch.

Which is why I was walking—in a fashion—an eight-block circle through Stefan's neighborhood. I fist-bumped the other Sabel agents when our patrols intersected. Every full circle I met Miguel. He let me know the Redskins were up by a touchdown. He considered the Redskins-Cowboys matchup a re-enactment of history and always bet on his people. Even if they have as much in common with Navajos as kangaroos.

Twelve of us circled around, weaving through alleys, using our Sabel Vision visors, and keeping in touch with our earbuds. Our mission: to keep Stefan protected—without him knowing we were outside.

The empty streets and alcohol gave me time to reflect on life. Since Alan's death, I felt as if I'd fallen down a deep well. Way up top, I could see the New Jersey cops talking to Detective CJ about Kasey's murder. Next to them, senators talked to the press about my role in the invasion of Kaliningrad. The fat lawyer called down to me about considering a plea deal. Less jail time.

But none of that bothered me as much as the sight of Sylvia walking out of Sabel Gardens after my implication that she was a woman of ill repute. In the history of cringe-memories, it was a new low for me. I'd never felt such a strong and instant bond with a woman before. I'd never blown it with so many megatons in such spectacular fashion in such a minuscule amount of time before, either. And, to top it off, Ms. Sabel was mad at me for doing poorly with a woman who helped foster kids.

All that thinking led me to contemplate those who had god on their side and how they firmly believed god would help them navigate treacherous times.

Mercury marched in step with me. *Have some faith, dawg. Don't you think I got you covered?*

I said, *Not really.*

Mercury said, *Oh yeah? Well. I still haven't seen a shrine under construction back at your crib, yo. When you gonna get on that?*

There was an argument I thought best to ignore.

Scenes of death played over and over in my head. Sylvia walking away. Alan's head blown apart. Kasey's body with three neat holes in it. I'd seen hundreds die. Most deserved it. A few were brothers in arms. But that night, it all weighed on me like never before.

Mercury never shuts up. *See, if y'all was down with the shrine thang, we could talk about the three Russians who got past your patrols on the main street.*

I said, *What? Where? Never mind.*

I barked into my comm link. "Yo, who has eyes on the front door?"

Three guys reported in.

I said, "Take cover and keep watch. You may have hostiles approaching."

I took off running.

Mercury floated alongside me. *And if you showed just one sign of respect, we could talk about the four Russians sneaking through the alley. Naturally, y'all know the front is a feint. They're going for the back door.*

My foot found a tree trunk and pushed off, allowing me a change of direction at full gallop.

"Who has eyes on the backyard?"

No one answered.

"Miguel, meet me in the alley."

I jumped a hedge and cut through someone's backyard. The next fence was easy to scale because they parked a table up against it. But the third house had a barking dog. They had a block wall that I grabbed onto at the same time the dog caught the hem of my jeans. He wouldn't let go and became the neighbor's dog when I finally shook him off. His confusion about the landscape saved me.

In the backyard next to Stefan's, I stood on the roof of a dollhouse and used my Sabel Visor to locate four heat signatures in the alley. They were waiting for a signal from the front door crew. As soon as Stefan went to answer the knock, they would sweep in the back and nab the kids. After that, Ms. Sabel's tall skinny boyfriend would be putty in their evil hands.

Miguel's large frame appeared on thermal imaging at the far end of the alley.

Two months earlier, Viktor Popov had been in a wheelchair. By now, he could be on crutches but not in a home invasion crew. Yet he didn't seem the type to stay at home and watch it on pay-per-view either. I scanned the area around me. Nothing else moved. No waiting cars with warm bodies in them.

My front yard crew reported they were in position and ready to move. Miguel signaled his readiness. We had the element of surprise, yet something bothered me.

Mercury said, *Dawg. If there was even the foundation for a shrine in your backyard, I would point out that they snuck through your patrols.*

Which meant we did not have the element of surprise. And that implied they were waiting for us to engage them.

The seconds ticked by while I thought it through. You can't keep special ops guys frosty for too long. One of them pinged me. "You giving the go, Jacob?"

"Hold off," Miguel said.

When you work with a guy long enough, you gain something of a telepathic connection. Miguel was a leader in action, never in words. He had the same problem with the scenario but was waiting for me to give the orders. Having too much pride to ask him for guidance over an open channel, I turned to my resident deity.

Mercury shrugged. *OK, homie, but this is the last freebie. Next time you want some advice, you better be buying some marble and have some plans drawn up. We clear?*

I said, *Absolutely. My word of honor.*

Word of what? Mercury did a full over-the-shoulder eye roll. *Metro Station, dude. Eight Russians showed up and got rolled by thirty Sabel agents. Think you're gonna fool Popov twice?*

"Shit." I used the open comm link. "Everyone fall back to Stefan's place. Make a visible defensive line behind the best available barricades. The guys we're looking at are the ones they want us to see."

Six of our guys jumped Stefan's fence and took up positions on his back porch. Reports came in from the front door as well. I saw Stefan pull back a curtain to check out the noise. As long as he didn't turn on a light, we were golden.

He turned on the lights.

His backyard lit up like daylight.

Miguel opened fire on the four in the alley. Even though he had no choice, it pretty much committed us to play right into the Russian ambush. I ran into the fray, firing Sabel Darts as I ran. Somewhere on the other side of the Russian crew, Miguel was coming at a dead run doing the same thing.

Our four targets hesitated a second, then jumped a fence and did a backyard tour parkour-style. We had to follow, even though it was a trap. If they got away from us, they could circle back and take Stefan's kids.

My buddy, the newly-displaced dog, had one Russian by the leg. I darted the soldier and carried the mutt back where he belonged. He gave me a second to escape before resuming his barking. I made it to another alley where Miguel had dropped a guy. At the corner, my friend stood holding up a hand.

He was listening.

Mercury said, *Congratulations, bro. You are officially boxed in by the enemy.*

"Miguel!" I whispered. "Over the wall."

In unison, we vaulted a chain-link fence obscured by a thick hedge and landed in someone's yard. On the other side, four new Russians ran up the alley to join their two remaining counterparts. Without Mercury's warning, we would've been Swiss cheese. Instead, we held our fire and wedged our way into vantage points in the bushes. When all six came into our field of fire, we put them down.

Behind us, a homeowner flipped on his lights and shouted about having a gun.

We were over the fence and down the alley in a heartbeat. There are too many well-intentioned-but-poorly-trained suburbanites who keep weapons handy. They shoot without regard to the trajectory and whether their neighbors might be in the line of fire. It was best not to make ourselves a target.

At the end of the alley, a bulletproof limo rolled by.

"Popov," I said. "Gotta be."

I ran to my car while Miguel went to the street to maintain visual contact. The Ferrari was not the best tactical vehicle due to its non-existent armor, but it excelled in pursuit. Miguel bailed into the passenger seat when I slowed near him.

He grabbed his .50 cal rifle out of his pack and assembled it.

I rounded a corner and saw the Russian limo three blocks ahead. I put my foot down. The Ferrari answered the call with a roar. Miguel stood up in the convertible, the wind buffeting his helmet. He aimed at the tires.

A Montgomery County Police Transport swerved out of a cross street. He slammed on his brakes. I slammed on my brakes. We skidded to a stop two inches from his back wheel.

Several barrels protruded through the transport's gun portals aimed at our heads.

CHAPTER 53

IT WAS A SAD GATHERING for the SHaRCs. Nearly in tears over being hunted by Popov, Yuri sat in a rented mansion. His unfocused gaze wandered down the slope where the lights on yachts bobbed on gentle sways in the cove. They were on Saint Barthélemy, commonly referred to as St. Barts, in the Caribbean. He felt worse than General Grachev at the Battle of Grozny. Gloom filled the sunny island air. He had failed them.

The other surviving members of SHaRC arrived, one at a time. They piled their bags and backpacks in the living room. Roman handed out room assignments, gave them instructions, and a glass of vodka. They milled about on the veranda, chatting with each other in low tones. They related their narrow escapes.

Yuri listened to their voices with a heavy heart. Their rash decision to become stateless was costing them far more than they had bargained for. But then, revolutions always require sacrifice.

Sodade by Césaria Évora, the saddest song in human history, streamed in his ears. The Brazilian singer sang of longing for something missing in life. While he could relate, he had to concentrate. He turned it off.

He had already committed his melancholy little speech to memory. All he needed to do was deliver it and hope it helped. Threatening Roman worked, but Roman was different. He had eagerly learned the grim things that must be done in desperate times. Yuri worked with him in Brazil, teaching him how to kill drug dealers for practice. The young man had come a long way. Now Roman was the kind of lieutenant who would execute orders without remorse. The others were still young and idealistic. The world had not yet jaded them.

Which led him to wonder why his men meant so much to Popov. Why commit such vast resources to hunt down a few hackers? It would make more sense to forget about them. His people were good, maybe the best, but no one is irreplaceable. Even if his men were that good, the reasonable solution would be to assign three bandas to the project. Popov had unlimited resources. They would never miss eleven young men and a major.

Unless Yuri possessed something he didn't fully appreciate.

Which must be the case.

Yuri observed his men across the pool through his open doors. What made them so special? Was it because he could tell the Americans who was behind #HuntersFail? Not without spending his life in jail. Popov knew they were on the run. That was better for everyone involved. So why kill Aleksandr on the balcony? Why send so many men to Belo Horizonte?

He looked at the pieces of the puzzle and realized his view was too limited. To a soldier like Yuri, Strangelove and Popov were as high up the food chain as he could see. But Popov was just a servant to someone else. Maybe several someone elses. Strangelove had alluded to being pushed around by strutting young peacocks.

Yuri thought back to the basic building blocks of modern Russia's economic and political structure: the oligarchy. It had risen from the ashes of the Soviet Union. At first, the oligarchy was in constant state of war inside Russia. Gang versus mob. Medevtin tamed them, but he never harnessed them as a team.

Yuri looked across the turquoise bay and put on his sunglasses to minimize the excessive sunshine. The glasses rubbed at his still-tender face.

Yeschenko, Prokhorov, Usmanov—in fact, all the Russian oligarchs—had gigantic egos. Their success in their given fields gave each man an unrealistic but resolute belief in his own omnipotence. They were vultures picking at the carcass of the global economy. They would tolerate each other, even work together to drive off competing species of scavengers. But they would peck the other's eye out if one of them felt disrespected. Yuri considered how the Americans—Roche, Ellison, Koch, Walton—were similar.

Each of these ultra-rich men had carved out his own slice of the world's pie. Each of them had convinced themselves he alone could run the world. All he needed was free rein.

As the world's twenty-first-century billionaires rose in power and stature, something parallel happened in politics. Globalization created a free market tightly governed by the politicians. And therein lay the billionaire's problem. When governments disagree, tycoons are often sacrificed at the whim of the officials.

Billionaires don't like to bow to bureaucrats. They don't bow to anyone.

A cool ocean breeze stroked Yuri's face.

He tapped a pen on his chin. Then what are the billionaires trying to accomplish? What do they want?

The eternal pursuit of all the money in the world.

That's where governments get in the way.

When Yuri earned his master's in American history, he was struck by the ferocity of postwar American national pride. The Great Generation knew that to overcome the Depression and the world at war, their best hope was selfless teamwork on a national scale. That same national commitment had glued the Soviet Union together for the second half of the twentieth century despite its obviously failed economic system. A population committed to a common goal was a powerful entity. Working together, they put men in space and cured diseases, built highways and schools, and achieved a higher standard of living for everyone.

After the Cold War, the world changed. The oligarchs didn't fight the regulations or the regulators. They fought the concept of regulations. They shredded the "United We Stand" idea, believing they could unleash unlimited growth if they were unfettered. Billionaires financed libertarian ideas. News organizations, owned by billionaires, challenged the federal model that had built the USA. Over the last thirty years, national pride transformed into a strange hatred of centralized government. Hatred of the very centralized government that saved them from the Great Depression, the savings and loan debacle of 1987, and the

Great Recession of 2008.

Most surprising about this American movement was that the American economy was the biggest, most productive economy in the history of civilization—yet politicians were campaigning to disrupt and dismantle what they called the "administrative state."

Why? Yuri scratched his head.

American billionaires, along with wealthy English and Germans and French, wanted to be more like their Russian counterparts. No holds barred. And the Russians wanted freedom from the arbitrary rules dropped on them by Western democracies.

The vultures had a common cause.

He laced his fingers behind his head and stared up at the ceiling. For twenty years, traditional governments like Russia, Germany, and the United Kingdom had tried to keep the billionaires in check. Enter Chuck Roche, America's President-Elect. He worked with Popov and Strangelove to disrupt governments that dared say no to his business interests. They had a common enemy: democracy. Russia wanted western governments that are too paralyzed to act. Regulations that, if not repealed, are ignored. Sanctions that can be disregarded. Dysfunctional governments.

Yuri's men had been bringing about that disrupted state with their relentless planting of fake news. They had been effective. Very effective. Soon, there would be no governments, no democracies, no sanctions— only oligarchs.

George Orwell had been wrong when he forecast the Oligarch Collective as the future political system. Their egos were too big to work together. Instead, the oligarchs were reverting to the Dark Ages. Each billionaire's corporation would fend for itself like an ancient fiefdom. Soon they would conscript their own armies to fight never-ending wars between city-state-corporations. Each oligarch could rule his corporate "nation" by decree.

Brilliant!

Yuri almost laughed out loud when he understood how far ahead of him they were. But there were three problems. First, he was not yet an oligarch. Second, Popov was trying to eliminate him. And third, the

Americans wanted him to answer for Flight 1028.

His Stateless Hacktivist and Resistance Collective wasn't just good at what it did—it was too good. Strangelove had been jealous, maybe even afraid. Popov also had that fear. If Yuri's men could disrupt an American election, they could easily expose Popov and his little machinations using the same methods.

Where did mysterious Brad fit in?

But there was a fourth faction in the mix. The useful-yet-dangerous Jacob Stearne and his boss, Pia Sabel. What did they want? They imagined themselves as the last defenders of a hopeless democracy. Fools. If SHaRC could sway an election, they could certainly take down a young woman and her mad soldier.

Yuri examined the young men milling about on the veranda and thought about where they were in the big picture. SHaRC was in a Hobbesian trap with Popov: they represented an escalating fear leading to pre-emptive strikes. Popov struck first by killing Alexandr.

And that was all he needed to know. Yuri knew how to win the war.

He rose and strolled around the pool to the veranda. The others stood in a big circle. Three of them, like Yuri and Roman, had bandage-wrapped faces. Those three were the first to commit to SHaRC in a visible way. He was proud of them.

The brilliant mathematician, Petr, was holding forth. "If we had ten thousand friends from Moscow to stand with us, then freedom from Viktor Popov might be more than a daydream."

Yuri patted Petr's shoulder and put his arm around him. "Petr, why wish for that? If we lose, then our sacrifice will be smaller in number and therefore better for the hacker community. But if we win, our brothers will revere us as gods—or even Jedi!"

A few men laughed sadly.

"No, my friends," Yuri raised his voice, "don't wish for one more man than stands with us here tonight. It's not about the money we can make. We can make money anytime we wish. This is about our freedom. This is about the respect of our peers. Think about it, gentlemen. When we win this war with Viktor Popov, we will bask in the admiration of every hacker from here to Moscow. We won't stop there. We'll wage war on the oligarchs. Our victories will be legendary. Why share the glory with any of them? No, I don't want more than the lot of you. You are the best."

He caught the gaze of each man in the circle.

"Not everyone agrees with me, I know." He waited while they looked from one to another. "It is a difficult journey. We've lost friends and family. It will get worse. I am a professional soldier while you are not. Nonetheless, I understand your anxiety. If you wish to go home, I will give you what you need: money, ID, whatever you want. Because." He tightened his mouth and lowered his voice. "I have no desire to die in the company of men who live in fear. If Popov wins, I have no intention of going out with a whimper. I'll fight to the end. And I'd be proud to die standing next to any of you."

Yuri felt Petr's arm lock around his shoulder. Petr said, "It sounds crazy, but—I'm with you."

A few others wrapped an arm around a comrade.

"You know what day this is in America?" Yuri asked. "Thanksgiving. On this day, Americans give thanks for all their riches. From this day forward, we will celebrate it as the day we were thankful to be in the company of real men. Brave men who resolved to fight the devil himself. Honorable men who chose not to run but to stand up to Viktor Popov. He is afraid of us because he knows what we can do. He is right to be afraid. We will not sit here and wait for Viktor to find us. We will do what he made us do to the Americans. We will hack through his security. We will find out where he lives. We will disrupt his life with fake emails and postings. We will find the evidence we need to convict him. And we will take him down."

Someone shouted, "Damn right!" Several others agreed.

The circle locked together, their arms grasping each other.

Yuri brought his voice to full-thunder. "We will kill Popov and anyone who wants to fill his chair. We will do it for all those who lost their lives to that beast. We will do it for Aleksandr. We will do it for Vasili. We will do it for Alexi!"

CHAPTER 54

PIA SQUEEZED THE PADDLE, DOWNSHIFTING her Lamborghini Centenario Roadster into a four-wheel drift that landed her on River Road. In the passenger seat, Tania buckled her seatbelt. Half a city ahead of her, the man who embodied evil. Popov was responsible for crashing two American airliners. He was meddling in her nation's election. And now, he was attempting to use Stefan as a pawn. All four tires found grip and vaulted them onto empty streets at two in the morning. Having not wasted time raising the top, she cranked up the heat.

Tania scanned maps on her phone. "Jacob stopped on Ewing Drive just north of Greentree Road."

"Jacob, do you still have eyes on them?" Pia asked in her comm link.

She slammed on her brakes approaching the intersection at the center of Potomac, Maryland. She looked both ways before running the red light. Vague noises came through the comm link in reply.

"Jacob, are you there?" The engine thundered them back up to speed.

A terse voice, speaking low through clenched teeth answered. "Can't talk. Police rifles aimed at me right now. Subject last seen heading south on Ewing."

Then she heard shouting, followed by Jacob and Miguel being thrown roughly to the ground.

"Those two are useless." Tania checked her extra magazines. "Bianca said we have live feeds from satellites just like the Russians. Can we get a view of Bradley Boulevard right now? Cause I'm thinking Popov's heading for his little hideout in the Embassy."

Pia shifted up, doubling the speed limit. "The Russians have theirs trained on Washington all the time, but mine are under contract to the intelligence community. No, we can't move them from Tehran or Mosul just to follow him."

"I know where he's headed," Tania spun the map around to show Pia. "We can cut him off at Little Falls Parkway."

Pia glanced but couldn't take her eyes off the road at speed. "How far?"

Tania checked. "Six miles."

Pia gave her a questioning glance.

"At your speed," Tania said, "that's under three minutes."

"It's a two-lane road." Pia shook her head.

They crested a rise and found a Toyota crawling along at the 45 mph speed limit. She crossed the double yellow line. The compressed air between the two cars boomed as she passed four startled teenagers. The little car bounced in her wake.

"What's the plan if we catch him?" Tania asked.

"Kill him."

"Bad idea. You're on record in the Senate. Everyone will know who did it."

"How do I stop him from threatening my friends and family?" Pia paused a moment. She wiped her eye. "Just friends at this point. I don't have any family left."

Tania stroked her shoulder. "Yes, you do."

The road widened into a four-lane parkway. She pushed the roadster up another notch. Wary of the residential neighborhood's ability to disgorge families heading home, her eyes scanned side streets for any sign of cars.

They flew over the I-495 overpass, getting a little air under all four tires. A comet-trail of sparks followed them when they landed. They stayed quiet and wove around a delivery van joining from the access ramp. Her turbulence rocked it from side to side.

"Make a dog-leg onto Mass Ave using Little Falls." Tania held up her phone-map for Pia to see, then pulled it down. "He's probably going for the embassy's secure entrance off Tunlaw. We might catch him."

Pia slid her wide, low car through narrow Westmoreland Circle, spewing smoke and tire squeals. The V12 bellowed down Massachusetts

Avenue. Over a rise, they could see the tail lights of one other car on the road. She wound it up higher, the note of the massive engine straining.

Tania pushed her feet into the floor, gripped the door handle with one hand, and the dashboard with the other. "We'll still catch 'em if you take it down a bit."

Pia kept her foot to the floor.

Without signaling or showing brake lights, their quarry turned right on a side street. Pia flew by. Grinding her tires to a stop, she held the clutch, wound up the revs, and let go. The tires broke loose. She spun it around in the narrow lane. She made it back to where Popov's limo disappeared and turned down the street. He was gone.

"Keep going down to New Mexico." Tania checked her phone. "He must've seen us. He's taking a shortcut through slower streets to scrub our speed advantage."

Pia drove as fast as she dared in the slender residential road lined with apartment buildings. When they rounded a bend, the limo was in sight for a fleeting moment. Pia slammed them into their seats as she pushed the chase to the limits.

They rounded the next bend. The limo turned into a blind drive behind a high wall.

She slowed as they reached the turning point. The barrier created a hiding place. Tania stood on her seat and aimed her assault rifle at the edge.

"Security gates," Tania said. "Protocol dictates that the occupants of the car have to get out, show themselves to the guards, proving there's no one holding them at gunpoint inside the car."

Rolling forward, their angle slowly exposed the limo. It sat imprisoned between the inner and outer gates to the compound. In Tania's theory, Popov would exit the car any second. Tania stood on her seat and took careful aim.

Brilliant white lights burst on them from a van parked nearby.

Tania dropped down, hiding her weapon. "Oh shit. Cops?"

Pia shielded her eyes. The van had a satellite dish on top and a big green square with RT America in the middle. Russia Today, the state-run news agency. A reporter ran toward them from the van with a microphone in her hand.

"Damn it." Pia dropped the clutch and smoked the exotic car around in reverse.

They headed up the lane at a good clip until the RT van disappeared in the distance behind them.

"Good thing I didn't shoot him right off." Tania stowed her rifle.

"You just told me not to kill him." Pia gave her friend a glare.

"Hey. You got friends here, OK?" Tania huffed. "You can go back to the Senate and say, 'I didn't kill Popov' and not perjure yourself. But we gotta do something quick before that guy gets some of our people."

The drive back to Sabel Gardens took significantly longer than the outbound trip.

Before they reached the gates, a horde of reporters ambushed her on her street. They stood in the road with cameras and lights.

A perfectly coiffed blonde was the first to reach her door. "Ms. Sabel, why did you try to murder a Russian diplomat in the street?"

Pia gripped the steering wheel and stared straight ahead.

"In your Senate testimony," the woman continued, "you pled the Fifth when asked if you swore to kill Viktor Popov. Is that what you were doing tonight?"

Pia let out an exasperated breath.

The reporter raised her voice. "Is it true you said, 'I'm not going to bring Strangelove and Popov to justice. I'm going to kill them'?"

Pia turned to the reporters. "Is it OK with you that Viktor Popov slit Bridgette Jallet's throat in front of her children? Did you know he murdered Olesya Sochneva, his personal secretary of thirty years? If those murders don't bother you because they took place far away, how about this? Sabel Technology tracked the hackers who killed 365 innocent Americans on flights 1028 and 31 to Viktor Popov's group. You tell me, what do you think should happen to him?"

She revved the engine and waited until the press jumped out of the lane before dropping the clutch.

They parked and walked to the main house. Pia's phone rang, showing a call from Stefan.

"Pia," he said without waiting for a response, "how could you bring your vendetta to my door? Have these innocent children not suffered enough? You've lost two fathers and a mother already. Where will it end? I beg you—do what I did. Renounce your wealth. Give everything to the poor. Walk away from the trappings of power and money. It does nothing but bring you grief and hatred and violence. Love can conquer everything, Pia. Mahatma Gandhi, Nelson Mandela, Martin Luther King changed the world without hurting people. You can do this. Leave it all behind and join me."

CHAPTER 55

MIGUEL HELPED ME PUSH THE marble slab onto the small foundation in my backyard. We got it squared up and level just before a familiar voice broke my moment of pride.

"You know, Jacob," Detective CJ said, "you're Montgomery County's public enemy number one."

He strolled into the backyard with a couple other guys in cheap suits.

Miguel picked up a shovel and held it like a baseball bat. He took a couple practice swings. Satisfied, he hoisted it to his shoulder and stared at the cops.

"Your bodyguard out front sent us back here." CJ thumbed over his shoulder. "Hope you don't mind."

"What did my attorney tell you last night?"

"We just have some simple questions on another matter. Nothing about your personal war with Viktor Popov." He pointed to the cheap suits. "These guys are from NYPD. They're concerned about the Kasey Earl murder."

I straightened up and faced them. "Gentlemen, I refuse to answer any questions without a lawyer present."

"We just have a couple easy things we've been wondering about since the video camera wasn't working." The bald guy put his hands out.

"I want a lawyer present." I gave him my soldier stare. He flinched.

"You see, there's no eyewitness," his buddy said, "but a lot of the residents said you were there when they heard a loud bang."

"L-A-W-Y-E-R."

"What're you building there?" CJ pointed to the slab.

Mercury stepped up behind the detectives. *Yeah, bro, what is that thing?*

I said, *It's a shrine. Obviously.*

Mercury scratched his head and stepped between the cops. *Shrine? Are you kidding me? This is a fucking dollhouse. Oh homie, I never should've trusted you. And to think, I came all the way here to tell you where to find the video the cops are saying doesn't exist.*

I said, *You know where the video is?*

Mercury folded his arms. *Shrine my ass.*

I looked at the work. *Uh. It's a model. Yeah. Scale model. I wasn't going big until … you know, I had some experience.*

Izzat right? Mercury grinned and walked around the mini-temple. *That throws a whole new light on things, bro. Yeah, tell the New Yawkas that the supervisor has a mirror copy on a cloud drive. The killer didn't know that when he erased it.*

"Shrine, huh?" CJ asked. "You mean like for Mother Mary?"

I processed the origins of the surname Czajkowski and figured it sounded Czech because it starts with the same two letters.

Mercury punched me in the shoulder. *Polish nobility, yo. Catholic. Descendant of the goddamned Vandals who trashed Rome. Feel free to kill him anytime now.*

"Virgin of Guadalupe?" I gave CJ a grin.

"You a man of the Church, Stearne? Or, are you making fun?"

"I was thinking about joining … you know, maybe."

He looked me over.

I suck at bullshitting.

"Looks more pagan if you ask me."

"Hey, guys, we drove for hours to get here." One of the NYPD guys stepped forward. "Can you just help us out a little bit?"

"You big city cops are smart, right?" I got in his face. "You looked at the building's cloud drive for a backup of that video, right? Because you know my attorney is going to subpoena that, right? And you know the cloud system is going to have timestamps for when it was recorded and—if it gets erased—when it got erased, right?"

"Yeah. Sure." The two looked at each other and backed up a step. "We've got a request in. But, uh, red tape and paperwork. We thought you could help us out. That's all."

Miguel gave his shovel a couple more practice swings.

"We had a call." They backed up another step, tossing nervous glances at Miguel. "Guy ID'd you by name. We had to check it out. You understand."

"Noted. I'm sure you've sent all the details about your tipster to my attorney." I watched them glance at each other, preparing to point fingers and spread blame. "Hey, I'll throw you a bone, guys: the shooter was left-handed. But you knew that from the splatter, right?"

They squinted at each other again. They gave me their cards, then turned and started to walk away.

CJ watched them for a minute. Then he stuck his finger in my face. "You're going to slip up one of these days, Stearne. You're going to make a mistake so big not even your whale-turned-lawyer can get you out of it."

He turned and trotted after the NYPD.

Mercury leaned on my shoulder. *Homie, you have my permission. Go ahead and put that dog out of his misery.*

I said, *Cop-killing is frowned upon these days.*

Mercury said, *The world's going to Orcus in a handbasket, yo.*

Miguel and I worked on the temple for the rest of the morning. The Corinthian columns went up easily. But the entablature was heavy. We had one in our hands when Ms. Sabel walked up without her cane.

She exchanged pleasantries then squinted at the shrine. "Is this for Mercury?"

My mouth opened but I was too embarrassed to say anything. I closed it.

"Yes," Miguel said. He gave me a look that said, *be honest about your faith.*

Easy for him. He grew up being a nonconformist in a Christian-dominated country. But he had friends and relatives who believed whatever it is that they believe out there in Monument Valley. I was a minority of one. Not counting a US Senator who turned to the Pharaohs for help.

"It's very nice." She walked around it. "Kind of small considering all he's done for you."

Mercury slapped me on the back. *Yeah huh, homie? Pia-Caesar-Sabel can see how badly you treat me and the Dii Concentes. Step it up, brutha.*

"It's a model." I sighed and pointed vaguely around my small yard. "If this looks right, I'll build a bigger one over there."

She surveyed the space. "When we get back, let's look for a spot at the Gardens. It would make a nice counterpoint to my chapel."

Mercury jumped in the air, pumping his fists. *I told you, dawg. Success is in the air. I knew she could see me. We are in! Hoo boy.*

I said, *I think you missed the vital part of her statement.*

"When we get back from where?" I asked. Experience had taught me to be wary of her impulsive missions.

"We're running out of options." She looked at the gray sky through the bare elms. "We thought the cipher was based on crosswords, but those aren't panning out. Bianca's team went through thousands."

"Where are we going before 'we get back'?"

"Without a keyword to break the code, it's the only clue Pozdeeva left us."

"When we get back from …" I let the question hang.

She didn't answer.

"Where did you even meet Pozdeeva, anyway?" I asked.

"Leipzig. His daughter was a fan looking for an autograph. She was too shy, so he stepped in and introduced us. I didn't have anything else to do, so we chatted for a while. Nice kid, nice dad. I don't remember the conversation, but I'm sure it was about soccer."

"Is that when you bought that fancy Latin bible?"

"Latin? The Gutenberg? Yeah." She stared at me funny for a long time. It got awkward. Then her jaw dropped. "Love your neighbor! Jacob, you're a genius."

She wrapped her arms around me and gave me a big hug. "Did you think of that or was it Mercury?"

Before I could answer, she started texting Bianca and turned around.

Mercury had the nicest looking toga I'd ever seen him in. Red trim with geometric patterns. *Hoo doggie. Did you hear that? She recognized my work. We are in, brutha! IN!*

I said, *The Gutenberg Bible thing? That was my idea. I thought that up on my own.*

Mercury said, *Where do you think all your good ideas come from?*

I said, *If that's the case, where do all my bad ideas come from?*

Mercury said, *Yeah. Well. It was still my idea. Least you could do is—*

I said, *Then what did it mean?*

Mercury said, *It, uh. Hey, I don't have to explain everything to you if I don't wanna. Mortal.*

She stopped thumbing and sent the text.

"But where are we going?" I asked point-blank.

"Latvia."

All my hopes that she would forget a small Latvian seaside resort called Jurmala faded. Sneaking into Popov's dacha was a bad idea even if it wasn't in a country that lives in fear of the neighboring behemoth with a bad habit of invading small republics. Not to mention what happened the last time she visited the Baltic.

She watched my unenthusiastic reaction. "I have a plan."

Which would have been a tremendous relief—if we were going to take on the Latvian soccer team. There's a big difference between strategists who spent a decade kicking a ball and strategists who spent a decade kicking Taliban ass. She told me her plan and my part in it. I didn't feel any better. My stomach felt like a gravel pit filled with excavating equipment.

"Instead of endangering others," I asked, "what if you used a disguise?"

"I hate crossdressing." She clenched her fists. "And for my size, nothing else works. Have you ever dressed as a woman?"

"Yes, an ill-advised Playboy Bunny Halloween costume. I'm never doing that again. Men are ... grabby."

"Yeah, well. I'm never dressing as a man again."

"Guess we're going with your plan then."

She play-punched my shoulder and left.

Miguel stood still.

I said, "Wonder what the whole Gutenberg deal was all about."

Miguel leaned on his shovel. "Before he died, Pozdeeva quoted a Bible passage, 'You will love your neighbor as yourself.' A ton of his files were in Renaissance Latin. That Bible verse—in Gutenberg's Latin—is the cipher key."

"Yeah." I ran my finger along one of the columns. "I knew that."

"Oh. You sounded like you were asking."

There were arrangements to be made. I pulled out my phone and dialed with less glee than if I were contemplating suicide.

It rang, and Sylvia answered.

"Hi, this is Jacob. Before you hang up, I have two things. First, I apologize. I spoke without thinking. I was angry—"

"You're forgiven." Her voice was flat. "It's the killing part that bothers me."

There isn't much a guy who spent more than a decade in the wars can say about extinguishing our nation's enemies. I didn't respond.

"But, is it true?" Her voice was quieter. "What Pia said when the reporter stuck a microphone in her car? That Russian guy really killed a woman in front of her children?"

"Yes."

"And when I joined her on the jet in Lyon—those were the kids? And the dad?"

"Yes."

"What was the second thing?"

I took a deep breath. Ms. Sabel's plan hinged on Sylvia agreeing to do something really, really stupid. "We're in need of a few actors for an insanely dangerous mission."

There was a long silence. I checked we were still connected.

"What's the film?"

"It's not actually a film." I paused. "Did you see the movie *Argo?*"

CHAPTER 56

CHUCK ROCHE LOOKED DOWN AT Central Park from his New York penthouse. A Secret Service agent announced Senator Jeff Sunderland. Roche kept his back to Sunderland, his attention fixed on the bundled people snaking every which way across the icy landscape far below.

Sunderland said, "Good morning, sir. Thank you for seeing me."

Roche sipped his coffee.

"I appreciate you considering me for Attorney General, sir."

Roche waved a few fingers at him. Sunderland approached and looked at the spectacular view.

"Look at that one." Roche laughed and pointed. "In the wheelchair. Ten bucks says he gets splashed by the garbage truck."

Sunderland looked at the President-Elect. "Excuse me?"

"Damn. He turned the corner. That would've been fun to see, right?" Roche looked up at Sunderland. "Poor dumb bastards down there. If they weren't so lazy, spending all their money on iPhones and avocado toast, they could save up, buy a hotel, and get out of the cold."

"Uh. I suppose that's true, sir."

"They tell me you want to be a general."

"Attorney General, yes. I spent my early career in Justice. I saw firsthand the travesty brought on by the Civil Rights Act—"

"Spare me the sales pitch, Senator." Roche pointed his cane at a pair of chairs near the fireplace. "What I need to know is: are you loyal?"

"Absolutely, sir." Sunderland gave him a serious look.

They took their seats. A silver coffee service waited on the table between them. A carafe, cups and saucers, sugars, milk, and spoons sparkled in the morning light. Roche watched Sunderland look at the coffee with a steely gaze.

Roche said, "You'll do what I need done?"

"Yes, sir."

"Even if I need something … special?"

"Yes, sir."

"What happens if one of those congressmen asks you about the things I need done?"

"At my age, sir," Sunderland gave him a grave nod, "I have difficulty remembering everything."

"Good man." Roche slapped Sunderland's knee and sipped his coffee. "Can you make this ridiculous investigation into Watson go away?"

Sunderland looked surprised. "I'd have to recuse myself. I had meetings—"

"Spare me the legal mumbo-jumbo. Can you shut it down? There has to be a way."

"Uh. Well." Sunderland smoothed the crease on his pants. "There are certain steps you could take. They would have repercussions, mind you. But, if Shikowitz won't drop it, there are steps you could take."

"Shikowitz?" Roche felt confused.

"FBI Director Shikowitz, sir." Sunderland paused. "The investigation is done by the FBI. If they believe there is wrongdoing involved, they would recommend the AG's office press charges. But you don't want it getting that far because there are people—deep-state people—who would run off and tell the *New York Times* about it. So, you would take steps with Shikowitz."

"Steps? You mean, have him killed? Do your people handle that, or is that CIA?"

"Uh." Sunderland swallowed hard. "I meant, you could build up a reason to fire him."

"Oh. Yeah. That's what I meant. Fire." Roche sipped his coffee. "You can fire him?"

"Or you can do it."

"I need to know, Jeff. If I make you a general, can I count on you?"

"Absolutely, sir."

Roche leaned back in his chair and sipped his coffee.

Sunderland said, "You know, I have some ideas about the Muslims and immigration—"

"I don't care about that shit. That's just what I said to get elected. Do whatever you want with those miserable wretches." Roche set his cup on the tray and poured coffee from the carafe. He savored the aroma, then picked up his cup. "Mmm. This is great coffee. Too bad you can't have any."

"Well, actually, I'd love to have—"

"What can you do about Pia Sabel?"

"I'm not sure I follow you, sir. What about her?"

"She's pissing me off." Roche's voice rose. "She's the one who should be investigated. She invaded Russia, for Christ's sake. She hasn't even been arrested."

"The Finns and Swedes confirmed her story—"

"Goddamn it, man." Roche smacked the table with his cane. "Why can't anyone just get rid of her for me?"

"That's not within the bounds of the Attorney—"

"Shut up." Roche slumped back in his chair and gulped the rest of his coffee.

He set the cup down and caught Sunderland's gaze. "You were one of the Cook Brothers' senators, right? They want me out of the way, don't they? Don't shake your head. I'm on to you. You want me to crash and burn. Then you can step in and take over."

"No, sir. As a point of order, if something happened to you, the Vice President would take over. Then the Speaker—"

"All of them, in league with the Cook Brothers!" Roche stood and pounded his cane on the floor. "You're one of them, aren't you? Admit it, damn it. I know you're just the kind of scum—"

"No, sir. They funded my Senate campaigns. Sure. But that was then. I'm loyal to you, sir. No one else. I swear it. I'll find a way to deal with Sabel. With a company that big, I'm sure she's done something."

Roche took a deep breath and calmed himself. He sat back down and poured himself another cup. "You do that, Jeff. You get out there and find something. I have another angle I'm working on with her. But, just in case it doesn't work out, you have something ready."

YURI TWISTED BETWEEN THE WORKSTATIONS squeezed into the living room. Working round the clock, his men slept only when exhaustion forced them. They were filled with the spirit of revolutionaries. Pride inflated his lungs. He patted Oleg's shoulder. Oleg was the most recent man to take the face-change challenge. His bandages were still clean and white, which reminded Yuri that he needed to change his own.

"I have a general!" Igor shouted. "General Zhirkov fell for the OZON rebate and clicked on it."

It was one of a hundred phishing hacks they'd sent past spam filters to officials across the Federation. It was too easy. OZON was favored by many online shoppers in Russia, but, like Amazon, never sent rebates via email. Yuri smiled and ran to look over Igor's shoulder. Could it be the win they needed?

Everyone else joined him, crowding around Igor and holding their breath.

"Who is he?" Yuri asked.

"Second in command of the FPS." The Russian Federal Protection Service, a group dedicated to protecting the Federation's most critical politicians and institutions. "An important man in an important service and directly connected to the President of the Russian Federation."

Yuri asked, "Who is on his contacts list?"

Igor looked over his shoulder with a smile. "Viktor Popov."

A cheer went up. The men bumped fists.

"Who else do we have?" Yuri checked the others. "We get one shot at this. We must have a coordinated attack. It has to be right."

The men grabbed their laptops and crowded around Igor's table. They shouted out names to check against General Zhirkov's contact list. Petr kept the list of matches. When they had a list of twelve ranking officers, they began constructing emails to send.

The first email from General Zhirkov was dated the day Yuri created SHaRC. It read, "I am happy to report that Major Belenov has begun the operation. Our first target was a Saudi bank. Gentlemen, you are now fifty-seven million rubles richer on paper. There are many hurdles to complete, but I have confidence in his group."

Igor sent it. Each man opened the hacked emails of an assigned recipient. They backdated the "receive" and "read" dates and filed the email in a new folder. Some made a reply-all, and others replied only to the general. In minutes, they'd created weeks of paper trails hidden from the hacked users.

Another email was created. It was dated a few days later when Yuri was threatened in New York. "Gentlemen, our Major Belenov has increased our shares by over one hundred fifty million rubles. But I have bad news. A certain group within the GRU, under the codename Strangelove, threatens our operation. We must support Major Belenov covertly. Make every contact you can to find Strangelove. Keep me informed."

Again, the hacked emails made fictitious replies with some good, some not-so-good information. The emails were backdated and filed. New emails flew between the fake co-conspirators. Then, they fired off the smoking gun: an email from Zhirkov to Pia Sabel telling her where and how to find Strangelove. Capping it off, an email from a captain went to a long chain of email addresses, including the apparently accidental inclusion of Popov. When the spymaster saw it, he would kick off an investigation. Within days, the planted emails would be unearthed, and a power struggle between Popov and Zhirkov would ensue.

Yuri amused himself weighing odds of who would win the fight between two powerful men. It didn't matter. It was a disruption that would buy him time. His most valuable resource.

Satisfied with a good day's work, they closed their computers. Roman poured shots of vodka. With a bellowed toast, they downed their glasses.

Yuri observed their smiling faces and compared them to that night in Stavanger when their revolution began. He should've refused the order to crash American aircraft. But he didn't. They all paid the price. Now he owed them a future. For the first time in weeks, he felt capable of delivering on that debt. He felt good.

Petr shouted for everyone's attention, then raised his refilled glass and pointed at Yuri. "Tell me something. Since you are the head SHaRC, how do we kill Viktor Popov? What happens if he worms his way out of it or kills Zhirkov? We are not like you. We do not know how to kill. He has thousands of soldiers at his command."

"Killing is so twentieth century, Petr." Yuri straightened up. "The twenty-first century belongs to those who can manipulate people without touching them. And that is what we do best. Who is smarter, the man who pulls the trigger or the man who convinces the killer it's the right thing to do? This is the first step. We will create confusion and animosity. We will make them loathe each other. Then, when they are at each other's throats, we will unleash a remote-controlled weapon that cannot be traced back to us."

The men turned to each other asking what he was talking about. He waited until their curiosity peaked.

"Brothers, friends, I swear to you—*I* did not kill Strangelove."

CHAPTER 57

BIG, JUICY SNOWFLAKES, THE KIND that melts on your skin, fluttered down to Pia's shoulders as she got out of the cab and checked her surroundings. Helsinki's Christmas Market filled Senate Square with laughing families, festive music, and bundled shoppers. Brightly lit, Helsingin Tuomiokirkko—Helsinki Cathedral—huddled over the scene. She watched the merry-go-round filled with children and winced as Stefan's words came back to her: *Love can conquer everything, Pia.*

Love didn't conquer Viktor Popov before he killed Bridgette Jallet. Love didn't save the people on Flight 1028. Love didn't stop Watson from turning her over to Strangelove. Love didn't save Dad. Her fists tightened until her fingernails dug into her skin. She took a deep breath.

In her peripheral vision, two men stepped off Tram 2.

She stared at the Restaurant Savotta for a second before heading in. With Tania two steps behind her, they joined two Sabel agents from the Helsinki office at a table by the back wall where they could see the window. Two more agents, a woman and a man, came from the kitchen and took a table near the door.

"The owner is onboard." Agent Kaspar nodded at the waitress to give them a minute. "So is the guard at City Hall. It would help if we understood the objectives better."

"I need to get from point A—" Pia tapped her finger on the table "—to point B without satellites or people tracking me."

Kaspar started to ask another question, but Tania cut him off. "That's all you need to know."

He put his hands up in surrender. "OK, since you can't talk, I'll talk. Thank you, Ms. Sabel, for letting me open Sabel K-9 Security. We have already selected several good dogs to start the program. Fifty people from around the world have applied to become handlers—and you haven't even made the official announcement yet."

"Your love of animals is infectious, Kaspar. I'm counting on you to make it a success."

"I have to. My children want to keep the dogs we have in training. I'll need to bring in hundreds before they'll let go of any."

The waitress approached and took their orders.

Pia asked the local agents about business in the Helsinki office while they ate. Halfway through, the couple seated next to them gave her a nod. Then they got up and made a show of putting on their coats in front of the window. Another window was blocked by the café staff.

"You sure you want us to stay behind?" Kaspar asked.

"Make it look like we're still here." She and Tania exited through the kitchen into a small, snow-covered courtyard.

This was it. Their last stop before boarding. They had to shake the tail to keep their destination secret. Time was running out, and their shadows were still following them.

They crossed through an alley to the back door of Helsinki City Hall, where a guard let them in. They padded through the marble halls and through a side door to Katariinankatu, Catherine Street.

Parked cars lined one side of the narrow cobblestone lane. Halfway down the block, a shadowy figure in a long coat approached them. On the other end, a motor scooter rounded the corner and accelerated.

"There's more of them than we thought," Pia said.

"Good thing we left our agents inside." Tania tensed and faced the lone man.

Pia stepped to the middle of the lane and reached for her Glock. She slipped it from the holster and held it to her side. The scooter revved up. A family with a stroller rounded the corner behind him. Taking a shot could produce casualties. The man on the scooter raised an arm holding something. Not a gun. As he got closer, she realized it was a Taser. She raised her pistol and aimed at him hoping to cause a flinch. He didn't flinch. Instead, he adjusted his aim.

Pia jumped to her left, into his path, as his Taser darts flew toward her. They missed by an inch but hit Tania's back. Pia twisted off her left foot. The bike sped by. She raised her arm, catching the rider under his helmet, knocking to the ground. She pumped a dart into him.

He writhed in pain and rolled away. The dart was stuck in his body armor. He reached for a pistol as his bike hit a parked car. At the top of the street, the Finnish mother screamed, and the father yelled something. Pia jumped on his outstretched arm and fired a dart in his lower leg. He exhaled and went limp.

Pia turned quickly to Tania to find the Taser's electrodes stuck in her friend's jacket. Tania held the man in the long coat pinned against the wall with her pistol.

"Who are you?" Tania asked.

Sirens wailed two blocks away. The Finnish family yelled at them again.

"No time." Pia raised her gun and darted the man. She spun around and rifled the biker's jacket for ID, grabbed it, and looked around for the best escape route.

The City Hall guard opened the side door and waved them in.

He pointed up a narrow staircase along the open meeting room. Shouting voices reached them from the back of City Hall. They ran up and found a closet at the end of a narrow balcony. Inside was a rack the size of a refrigerator filled with blinking electronic gear. They squeezed in behind it and listened.

From downstairs and outside, the sounds of police issuing orders floated up to them. A systematic search of the surrounding area was underway.

Bianca texted that she's sent Pia an email report on the Pozdeeva files. Pia pulled it up in the dark.

"We cracked Pozdeeva's code. The Latin documents make up a catalog of the companies involved in the rest of the files. There are ten thousand records of transactions between shell companies. This might be a paper trail proving Roche's involvement in money laundering. However, Emily says tracking down all the companies and tying them together could take years. We've copied the FBI on them. Among the decoded Latin documents, we found a personal letter from Pozdeeva to you. He calls it a confession. I've attached it here."

Pia took a moment to collect her thoughts and catch her breath before she opened the attachment:

In profound humility, I weep for all my sins. While my role in events was small, I am complicit in the murder of innocents. This has weighed on my soul since I met you. You probably will not remember, but my daughter was a fan of yours. She insisted on getting your autograph in a Leipzig café. You made a profound impression on me. You were gracious to strangers. You were accomplished despite your tragic childhood. And you had no idea who I was or what I had done. That night, I resolved to atone for my sins knowing it would take years.

Outside their small, warm closet, many voices echoed. Pia listened. They appeared to be conducting a search of the building. She went back to the email:

To accomplish this, I collected all the kompromat that Strangelove and Popov held against your adopted father, Alan Sabel. I destroyed all copies, electronic and paper. He is now free to seek justice on behalf of the families murdered and destroyed by these men. They have nothing to hold against him. The evidence he needs to convict them in the World Court is hidden in Popov's dacha in Jurmala, Latvia. In his library, one book stands out among the others. In it are all the documents Alan needs to convict these animals in the World Court.

No doubt you wonder why I do this. It is to unburden my heart. Hear my confession.

Pia's heart collapsed like a supernova. If only she'd been smart enough to decipher the code earlier, her father might have lived. All the trips Dad took to unearth outdated kompromat on Chuck Roche were unnecessary. Everything she had done for the last several months had been futile.

Outside their cramped space, voices approached. Boots ran up the stairs. Tania positioned herself behind the racks of computer equipment and peered between the servers. Pia squeezed in behind her. The door to their closet opened. Pia couldn't see past Tania, but she could sense someone peering into their dark space.

Tania held her Glock at the ready. They both held their breath.

Pia imagined her whole mission blown up by this lone incident. Just being called in for questioning by the local authorities would give her adversaries enough information to know what she was planning. The biker's identification burned a hole in her pocket. She longed to discover who came this close to her. But she couldn't move. The door remained open.

Their friendly guard spoke to the officer in Finnish, his tone explaining the closet's limited space.

Pia bent her knees and lowered herself to look through a gap. The officer was staring directly at her without seeing her in the dark.

The door closed. The voices trailed off into the distance.

They started breathing again.

Pia returned to Pozdeeva's confession:

In the early 1990s, Boris Yeltsin threw open the doors to a part of the KGB archives. He intended to discredit the Soviet regime and solidify his grip on power. It worked. But, a few years later, KGB officers closed those doors and wanted to assess how much of their operation had been compromised. Under the pretense of opening more archives to the CIA, I was dispatched to Washington as a personal liaison to then-CIA Director, Veronica Lodge Hunter.

The closet door opened again. The guard told them the police were gone and he'd sent for her agents. It was time to leave before anyone discovered them.

They wasted no time. Kaspar and the other agents waited at a door on the far side of the main hall. They held umbrellas to confuse satellite observation. The group exited the building together, each person immediately taking a different direction.

Pia and Tania strolled to the docks just a block away. They stood at the end of the pier and waited. Pia returned to reading:

Director Hunter never trusted the KGB or the FSB, much less my cover story, so she kept me at arm's length. She knew my real mission. I was a spy handler, developing and discovering new information for the Russian Federation. My tasks were difficult, but I executed them well. My successes brought me to the attention of Viktor Popov. He sent me on many clandestine missions. He only called me on the phone once. He told me to have a face-to-face meeting with Chuck Roche, the oil refining billionaire. He said that once I delivered the information, Roche would know what to do.

A Kilo-class submarine—rented for training exercises from a cash-strapped Baltic navy—rose silently from the ocean depths into the dark night. A crew member extended a gangplank. They walked onboard and climbed down a ladder to the cramped interior. Inside, a crew showed them to the galley. They sat on benches to wait out the long cruise.

Pia and Tania pulled the identity papers they'd taken from their pursuers in Helsinki. They'd snapped pictures and sent them to Bianca moments before the submarine dove. The sub was faster below the surface than above. The entire cruise would take place beneath the waves.

She went back to Pozdeeva's confession:

When I arranged the meeting with Chuck Roche, he insisted Hunter must join us. I was uneasy about including Hunter, it would expose my clandestine aims, but I could not risk contacting Popov again for instructions. Popov trusted Roche, so I assumed it was fine. It took a few days to align everyone's calendar. We met at a park south of Washington along the Potomac. I wasted no time when I arrived and got straight to the point. After I told them, neither Roche nor Hunter asked any questions. A week later, I read the news about your parents. I knew they had arranged the murders. The message I delivered was this: Lloyd Aston developed a metacapacitor technology that would destroy the oil business.

Pia didn't read the rest. Veronica Hunter. The woman had pretended to be a friend and mentor. All the while, complicit in the murders of her parents. No wonder Hunter was so quick to join Roche's conspiracy. Hunter had provided the killers, Leroy Johnson and his accomplice. Roche must've supplied the blood money. Pia's heart raced, her anger rose. How could she get revenge on a sitting president?

Her mind turned the revelations over. She recalled David Watson's claim when he applied for the job, that he could tell President Hunter had not told her the whole story about her parents' murders by "who was left alive." The implications were murky, layered, and deep.

Had anyone ever told her the truth? Alan Sabel? Veronica Hunter? Chuck Roche?

Her father's metacapacitor was an unproven technology that promised to store electricity a thousand times more efficiently than a battery in a fraction of the space. It could've saved the world from pollution. By killing her father and destroying his work, Popov, Hunter, and Roche had doomed the future of the planet.

She seethed with rising rage. The President and the President-Elect should die along with Popov, the man who gave the orders. Pia considered the downside: killing a president—past, present, or future—was bad for the nation. It would be a betrayal of democracy. She had to let the process work on them.

But Popov was wrecking American democracy. She had no qualms about killing him. After all, she'd made a promise to Olesya.

Then Stefan's words came to her. *Mahatma Gandhi, Nelson Mandela, Martin Luther King changed the world without hurting people.*

The faces of everyone who had died from Cyprus to France to Washington, and the untold numbers who might yet die, also came to her. Lives sacrificed at the whim of narcissistic sociopaths far away. She chewed the inside of her cheek until a crewman came for them.

The ship surfaced. They went topside and climbed aboard the electric-powered Zodiacs. Pia sat in the prow. Knives of sea salt stabbed at her cheeks as they sped toward a dark shore.

CHAPTER 58

SYLVIA AND HER TEAM IGNORED me by speaking to each other in French. Not just on the jet from Monaco, but on the drive from Vilnius, Lithuania to Riga, Latvia. Her cameraman was all over her, which she made sure I noticed. He wore tight Euro-clothes and shaved everywhere, including his eyebrows. Her sound girl, the last goth in black, chatted with the director, who had five-day stubble and a man bun. Supposedly they were a famous documentary crew from Paris or Milan or someplace.

The four of them sat across the aisle from me in facing seats. I had four chairs to myself as the train rolled off into the pre-dawn darkness.

Across the aisle, Mercury stood over Sylvia's shoulder and pointed at her. *See what I'm talking about, bro? This is how the woman treats you? That's disrespectful, that's what that is. I'm telling you, toss her off the train right now.*

I looked up. *And tell Ms. Sabel—what?*

He stepped into the aisle, working out kinks in his neck. *Yeah. I feel ya. Sure. You can toss her off the train on your way back. That's better. Just get her out of your life—soon as.*

I put my feet up and tried catching up on things, like Pozdeeva's confession. Ms. Sabel sent it to me just before she dove for the bottom of the Baltic. It blew me away. Everyone involved in her parents' murders were powerful people. And so far, they've gotten away with it.

The immediate question remained: who killed Kasey Earl? If it was one of Roche's people, they would've destroyed the box of records. If it wasn't Roche's people, who was it? Was Kasey dumb enough to brag to someone else about the documents? Knowing him, he was trying to sell it to the highest bidder.

Mercury sat next to me. *Yo, homie, you've seen Roche Security people. They're Sabel-rejects like Kasey. Most of them knew Kasey. You think they'd go after one of their own? C'mon, bro, keep thinking.*

I said, *Maybe Roche did it himself.*

Mercury put his feet up, his too-short toga barely covering him. *Dude, do you ever wonder what kind of ammo the killers used?*

I took out my phone and texted the NYPD cop about the ballistics. He texted back "5.45mm" and something about me owing him for waking him up in the middle of the night. My reply was, "Sleep is for the weak. Here's another tip for your troubles: the 5.45 is almost exclusively used in the AK-105. That rifle was built for the FSB's special forces. Which is run by a man named Viktor Popov."

Mercury nodded his approval. *That better be one damned big temple, you know what I'm saying, dawg?*

I said, *Why would Popov want dirt on Roche? Weren't they pals?*

Sylvia pushed my feet. I looked up and pulled them off the seat opposite me. She took the now-vacant chair.

"Are you going to tell us about the mission?" she asked.

I gave her my soldier stare. Not to be mean, but to make her understand we were not messing around here.

She flinched.

"How much help would you be if you accidentally—or under duress—told her adversaries the plan?" I waited for her to register the gravity of the situation.

She looked at her fingernails then glanced out the window, unable to figure out where she wanted to take the rest of the conversation.

"Put yourself in the bad guys' shoes." I leaned forward. "Picture yourself at a bank of monitors. You see two moms pushing strollers on the sidewalk and two dark figures sneaking through the bushes. Which group do you send your agents after?"

"We're the moms pushing strollers?" She almost smiled. "And you hide in the stroller. We're Plan B?"

"You and your team are naturals." I rubbed my palms together. "Don't worry. I've got the rest of this."

"Any advice for me?"

"Don't try to play the hero. Looks great in the movies, but it never ends well in real life."

Alan Sabel's last breath on Earth replayed in my head. I turned to the window.

Dawn spread blue and gold streaks across snow-covered fields and bare trees. It didn't last long. The sun disappeared behind the low, dark clouds covering the sky. Plenty of daylight made it through, though. I wished Ms. Sabel had listened to my advice to push it back eighteen hours. We own the night. It's always better to strike at 0300 than 0900.

The director of Latvia's National Film Centre met us at the station. He was a small man with thin gray-streaked hair combed straight back to a mini-ponytail. He bowed constantly. He spoke only to our director, which was fine with me. I shouldered a tripod and carried a case of Goth Girl's gear.

We tromped down sidewalks covered in fresh snow while knives of sea salt stabbed at our cheeks. The directors led the way, making grand gestures at every natural and architectural element we passed. Our director slapped their director on the back. They were getting along fine.

I pushed in my earbud and joined the comm link for Ms. Sabel and Tania. They updated me with an ETA. So far, so good.

Deep in a wooded lane, we came to a security gate. A big, serious-looking guy stepped from a guard shack, dressed like an extra for a documentary on the Battle of Stalingrad. He could go the winter living on nail sandwiches and gasoline. His heavy coat draped down to the tops of his thick boots. He wore a Ushanka hat with the earflaps down.

Any darts would have to be face-shots.

Our director, their director, and the guard gesticulated with ever-rising voices. Our director stepped around the shack, pointed at the sky, and started raving in French. The Latvian director did his best to calm him.

I calculated the time it would take to drop the gear and pull my Glock from the holster beneath my heavy jacket. I could do it before he could sound an alarm. But then my aim would have to be perfect. I had only a six-by-eight-inch moving target to hit. My problem was knowing how many more were inside the shack or out on rounds. On top of that, there was the Director of the Film Centre. He would freak in high C. I decided to let things ride.

I handed Sylvia five hundred euros, which she artfully offered Mr. Stalingrad for his troubles. That kind of money can buy a case of fresh morals in Latvia, a country with a quarter of the USA's average income. The guard palmed it and waved us through.

Sylvia turned to me, her eyes smiling. She wanted my approval. She'd done well, but the time for basking in glory was in the bar after the mission. If you survive. When she saw my blank expression, she looked disappointed.

Mercury stepped up behind me in his winter toga. *You done making eyes at your mariticidal future wife, bro? Because Pia-Caesar-Sabel is half a klick away, trudging through the snow in that forest over there. If you and Spielberg Junior aren't making a distraction, she will not be happy.*

"Can we set up now?" I asked our director. "This is getting heavy."

We set up in front of a nightmare of faux-rococo architecture. Everything that could be gilded on this vacation home had been. One day it would make a dandy whorehouse.

Sylvia peeled off her ten-pound overcoat to reveal a tastefully clingy dress adorned with bright sparrows and swans, topped by jacket covered in roses. She made several approaches and sound checks as they measured the light.

I counted six guards in the larger enclave, though there could have been twice that many. Only our burly friend, Mr. Stalingrad, stayed close. He wandered between us, staying out of the way, yet remained keenly interested in our operation. Or Sylvia. Every three or four minutes, he went back to the main guard shack by the road. Some of the other guards wandered in and out as well.

Ms. Sabel let me know they were in sight of the house. She waited.

I strolled over to our director as Mr. Stalingrad hovered a few yards away.

"The actress is freezing," I said. "Could we shoot some of the interior scenes now and come back for this stuff?"

The directors glanced at each other. Our director was on the ball. He insisted we get access to the nearest mini-mansion. The Latvian called the guard over. They discussed it. The negotiations weren't going well. No one was allowed inside.

Ms. Sabel pinged me for an update. Every minute she and Tania stood in the freezing cold was a minute closer to getting caught.

Sylvia picked up on the guard's reticence and joined the conversation, insisting they get some footage of her with the guards making his rounds inside. Any man who falls for money will also fall for beauty. I found her quick thinking impressive. We packed up and moved inside.

I alerted Ms. Sabel. She set up by a side door, ready with her slap-hammer. I gave her the go-ahead when the guard disabled the alarm system. She gave me a countdown.

We stood in a grand foyer that opened to a parlor on the right, dining room on the left, a hallway and stairs in front of us, kitchen and library beyond. On cue, I dropped the not-latched sound-gear case. Metal things clattered to the polished wood. At the back of the house, the lock took a whack.

Only two people in the room heard the second sound. One was me. The other was Mr. Stalingrad.

He pulled a SIG Sauer P239 from his holster. The film crew choked. He motioned for us to get behind him for protection. He kept his eyes and pistol facing the other direction.

I reached for my dart-filled Glock and kept it behind my back.

"Easy now," I said to the guard, hoping Ms. Sabel would hear me. "Put the gun away. We're fine here."

He looked over his shoulder at me. Then looked at the crew. Then back at me.

That's when I made a mistake.

I gave him my soldier stare.

He knew what it was and gave the same right back. He took a quick glance at Sylvia. She was a great actress but also an honest human being. Guilt creased her brow. In that instant, he put it all together. The five hundred euros. The desire to have him in the film. The need to get inside. He was big, but not stupid. His free hand reached for a button on his belt. Most likely a panic button. He was calling for help.

A split-second later, we both had our weapons trained on each other. Like two bears squaring off. Twelve feet of polished hardwood separated us. There was a good chance our bullets would hit in mid-air.

Behind him, Ms. Sabel and Tania slipped across the hallway.

In the tense silence, their footsteps were noticeable. His eyes swiveled.

Sylvia took two steps and kicked him. She knocked his pistol loose, lost her balance, and ended up in my line of fire. I kicked the gun down the hall, but the maneuver left my back to my adversary. I scrambled into the dining room to regroup. With my back to the wall, I checked out the windows for Russians. As I suspected, two were coming at full pace, fifty yards out. I ran through to the kitchen and checked the hall. My kick was fair. Mr. Stalingrad's SIG was within my reach.

I grabbed it and headed back to the foyer with a gun in each hand.

He had his back to me, with one arm around Sylvia's waist and another to her throat. He faced the film crew, who were ashen and shaking. Their eyes moved to me in unison, giving away my position. But Mr. Stalingrad didn't move. Which was tactically odd for a man of his experience.

Mercury said, *Dude, he's got his eye on them cause his pals are coming in the back.*

I spun in time to see two men enter the kitchen. Not the same two I saw from the dining room.

Even the most battle-hardened vets feel their blood pressure spike when the first bullet pops. Kaliningrad weighed on my mind. With civilians in the mix, I held my fire.

I slid to the side as one of the men barreled down the hallway yelling something in Russian. I held up my hands in surrender, my fingers still inside the trigger guards. He lacked the experience of Mr. Stalingrad. His focus shifted from attack to apprehend mode. A distraction just long enough for me to reacquire his face in my sights and pump a dart into his cheek.

I slid back into the kitchen, looking for his partner.

The front door opened, the other two guards ran in. Mr. Stalingrad barked orders. One of them ran up the stairs, the other came down the hall. The remaining back-door man held the dining room. I was trapped.

Across the hall, Ms. Sabel gave me a little wave. Using hand signals, I told her I was going for the dining room, she could cover the hall. She nodded. I pocketed Mr. Stalingrad's weapon and picked up a plate. I held it up in the open doorway that connected the kitchen and dining room. A bullet shattered it, giving away the shooter's position. I rolled into the room and fired three times.

None of my darts hit the poor kid, but they scared him enough. He crumpled into a ball behind a chair. Not a good shield. I darted him, then peered around the corner into the foyer. Sylvia and her freaked-beyond-belief crew looked like marble statues, gray and motionless.

Mr. Stalingrad hadn't yet moved. His confidence was disconcerting. He held a nasty looking stainless-steel knife to Sylvia's throat. I stepped through the open archway behind him, grabbed his coat collar, and pressed my Glock to the base of his neck.

Tension rose up inside him. Thousands of options went through his head in a second. He had nothing. He would have to surrender and we both knew it.

I said, "Let the lady go, and I'll—"

"Release Sergeant Tarasov or lady die." A shaky Slavic accent came from behind me.

Mercury said, *That Siberian cracker back there has a SIG Sauer aimed at Pia-Caesar-Sabel's head. You think you can save them both but you can't—and your little actress isn't worth it. You have a serious decision to make, homeboy. Unless you want to get stuffed in a bovem aeneum—a bull-shaped caldron that stews on a bonfire—save the right damsel in distress.*

CHAPTER 59

FROM THE TOP OF THE InterContinental Kansas City, Chuck Roche watched the cars twisting down the roads of Country Club Plaza. "They look like toys."

"Yessir." David Watson cleared the dining table and stacked the dishes on the room service cart.

"You should've gotten Arrowhead Stadium."

"It's not available, sir."

"CNN said I couldn't fill it." Roche turned around and faced his Chief of Staff. "I could fill Arrowhead."

"We filled the auditorium, sir." Watson pushed the cart into the suite's main room. "That's three thousand. They love you."

"They do, don't they?" Roche turned back to the window. "They really do."

Watson continued pushing the cart to the foyer, where he turned it over to a Secret Service agent and came back.

"Is Popov going to take care of Sabel once and for all?" Roche asked.

"Sir," Watson whispered. He looked over his shoulder at the agent's position by the door. The man was dealing with the cart out of earshot. "It's important to speak in the code we discussed. We have reason to believe the deep-state spies have infiltrated the Secret Service. Sir."

"Them too?" Roche scratched his head. "I thought the Secret Service was beyond politics."

Watson stepped closer to the President-Elect. "When talking about murder and foreign conspirators, assume everyone is deep state."

"No goddamn loyalty anymore, Watson. That's what's wrong with this country. No one understands loyalty." Roche grabbed his man's shoulder. "Except you. But then, you have good reason to fear what I might tell your former coworkers at the FBI."

Roche turned on his cane and crossed to the piano. "I could've been the greatest concert piano player in the world. I'm the best at anything I set my mind to. But I didn't pursue it because I don't like the piano. I had a teacher who kept telling me, 'practice makes the master' and all that crap."

Watson stood silently at ease.

"All right, we'll do it your way." He raised the keyboard cover and looked at the keys. "Is our old friend going to take care of the new problems that keep cropping up? He should. After all, she invaded his country."

Watson craned over his shoulder to see the agent retaking his position. "Use fewer identifiable—"

"Just answer the goddamn question."

"I've stayed out of the reporting loop, sir." Watson took one more glance over his shoulder and lowered his voice again. "Sabel has already linked me to our friends in Spain. We don't need another connection cropping up. Keep everything compartmentalized."

"This cloak-and-dagger bullshit is ridiculous, Watson." Roche shook his cane at the man. "Where is my National Security Advisor, General Krasny? Is he the *compartment* I need for a straight answer?"

"He's waiting downstairs."

Watson made a call, and a few minutes later a Secret Service agent ushered Krasny in.

The tall, thin retired general greeted the President-Elect. "Can't wait to hear your victory tour speech in person, Mr. President-Elect. They've been wonderful—"

Roche rolled his hand impatiently. "What happened with Ambassador Sadesky?"

Watson trotted out of the room and took up a casual conversation with the agent in the foyer.

Krasny glanced at Watson for a moment, then turned back. He softened his voice. "Communications were difficult."

"You did get to their NSA-proof room, right? Did you get hold of

Popov?"

"Well." General Krasny checked Watson and the agent again, assessing their ability to eavesdrop. "They did lend me their secure communications system. I was able to connect. But. Um. Sir. We have a problem with Popov."

"He got us into this mess. You better not have a problem with him."

"He's making demands." Krasny bowed his head. "He said, and I'm quoting directly here, 'Tell him I delivered the White House. If that is not enough to ensure his loyalty, tell him to check with Kasey Earl.' I don't know what that means, but he demanded the sanctions be dropped—"

"Goddamn it!" Roche's silver-handled cane landed on the nearest table lamp. The ceramic base exploded into tiny shards. "Watson! Popov has Kasey's payment records. How the hell did you let Kasey Earl get those? Damn it to hell."

He swung his cane across the piano, taking out the lid prop that held it open. The lid crashed onto the case with a resounding bang and splintered into pieces. "Can't anybody do what they're supposed to?" He struck the window repeatedly until he realized it would not give way. "Son of a goddamn bitch!" Breathing hard, Roche turned to another lamp and used his cane like a baseball bat. The lamp shattered against the wall. "I'm surrounded by fucking losers." With overhand blows, he pounded the silver handle into a painting on the wall, shattering the glass and leaving the handle embedded in the drywall. Roche tugged and tugged.

When Yuri returned from his last consultation with the reconstructive surgeon, he found the other SHaRCs in the living room watching the big screen.

It took Yuri a moment to register what held his men's attention. It was the view of the fake-house in Cartagena, Columbia. Six men ransacked it. Cartagena was a tripwire, an alarm to let them know when Popov was getting close.

And they'd just begun to like island life.

"Who are they?" Petr asked.

"Americans." Yuri scratched his smooth, beardless chin, which felt odd. "Sabel Security?"

"It doesn't matter," Roman said. "They're in the fake-house. For precaution, we leave here tonight. Next hideout is in—" he checked a list on his phone "—Durrës, Albania."

The group groaned in unison. Someone said, "For the winter?"

A phone alarm rang. Then another. Several men checked their phones.

"We're in!" Roman shouted. "Quick, pull it up on the big screen."

Someone clicked away on a laptop's keyboard. An email screen came up. An inbox with hundreds of emails.

Petr stepped to the front. "This is one of six email accounts used by Viktor Popov. Like dictators who move every night, Popov keeps opening and closing accounts. This is not his official email. But it's been in use for weeks."

"Send everyone a copy." Yuri raised his voice. "We can look through them on our long and painful flights to Albania."

They grumbled but went to their rooms to pack.

Yuri went to his, but the lure of looking through Popov's email was too strong a call to resist. He sat on the edge of his bed and started to look at his phone. Before he grabbed it, a nearby movement drew his attention. He reached for his gun and looked up quickly.

A stranger in the mirror stared back at him. He let go of the pistol and stared at himself. He sensed a new opportunity, a clean start with a new face. He resolved to do good deeds this time around. He would kill fewer people. If one of his men created trouble, he would try to work it out. He nodded at his reflection.

He did a quick scan of Popov's email. There were reports from Strangelove and other agents. They mentioned operations in Cyprus, Bornholm, France, and an interesting one in New York. It mentioned Yuri's newest acquaintance, Jacob Stearne. The agent reported he'd killed Kasey Earl and tried unsuccessfully to frame Stearne. In his reply, Popov requested information about "the package."

The field agent had replied, "Shipping via embassy courier. Summary: canceled checks signed by Chuck Roche. Correspondence about the murder of Lloyd Aston. Kompromat on the American President-Elect."

Yuri dropped his phone.

He couldn't believe it. Popov had something Sabel would want. He saw that as an opportunity. Changing his face had indeed changed his luck.

Roman appeared at his door. "Our man at the airport called. Eight men rented two cars."

The two men looked at each other and knew whoever their adversary was, they were in trouble.

"He called the police." Roman pounded a fist against the door jamb. "The men have been detained, but that only gives us an hour."

They both scrambled to finish packing. Twenty minutes later, every member of SHaRC was in a car or on a bike heading for an airport or a boat. Each man finding his own circuitous way back to Europe with new ID.

Yuri took his seat on the seaplane heading for Barbados, his laptop under his arm. His Avos' swung hot and cold. But he didn't believe in superstition. He knew his next move.

He called Sabel Security's main desk. Yuri said, "I need to speak to Jacob Stearne. Tell him, his friend from the New York Public Library is calling. He will want to speak with me."

CHAPTER 60

A THIRD GUARD HAD SNUCK in the back door behind Pia and taken her pistol. Her heart sank when she realized her mistake. Her battle-hardened agents would've been more careful. Thousands of options went through her head in a second. She had nothing. She would have to do as he asked and they both knew it.

Then Tania's voice came through her comm link. "You're in my line of fire. Drop on three."

Tania counted down.

Pia buckled her knees and dropped two vertical feet straight down. It's the least-expected move for a detainee. Her guard was ready for a sideways move or an elbow to the gut. He was surprised by her drop.

He fired. But his pistol was still aimed upward where her head had been. His bullet went into the ceiling. Tania's dart caught his heavy collar.

As she dropped, Pia worked out what he was thinking. He had to decide in a split-second whether to shoot Jacob or return fire. The first option would fulfill his duty. The second might save his life. He was a professional, which meant he would kill Jacob. When she reached the bottom of her deep squat, she powered back up at an angle. Her momentum thrust her shoulder into his extended arm an instant before he pulled the trigger.

His second shot went high.

Tania's second dart struck below his ear. He fell in a heap. Pia grabbed his pistol and hers, regained her balance and ran forward.

In the foyer, Jacob dropped the head guard. Sylvia screamed, her pent-up horror released. Two guards had come in the front door; one had gone upstairs. The other was in the process of aiming at Jacob.

Without time to level her weapon, she bolted at the guy, hoping to draw his aim. The man's eyes turned to her. He moved his pistol and fired. The round buzzed Pia's ear.

She drove toward him, wondering why she hadn't heard Jacob return fire. The Russian's second shot singed her hair. She launched herself and wrapped her arms around his waist, driving him into the umbrella stand. They slid across the polished floor and crashed into the front door. She rose and pounded her elbow into his jaw. He tried to fight back, but she kneed his groin then twisted back, landing her other elbow on his temple. His eyes rolled back in his head. Not out, but not present either.

Behind her, Jacob fired three shots in rapid succession. She looked back to see the last guard at the top of the stairs. Jacob's darts missed the man. He ducked away.

Tania's voice rang out from the dining room. "Three more, front side."

Jacob pushed the film crew under the stairs. Pia darted the man under her knees and rolled to a better position.

Upstairs, the last inside man peeked over the banister.

Jacob brushed him back with a couple darts. He shouted over his shoulder, "Did you find it yet?"

"Haven't had time," Pia said.

Tania joined her by the front door and checked the window.

"Now would be good."

She couldn't argue with that. She ran back to the library.

Pozdeeva's clue was vague: *In his library, one book stands out among the others.* She looked over the books on the shelves. Most were in Russian, a few in English, even fewer in French. They were ordered by look, not logic. Older, canvas-bound academic books lined the bottom shelves. Many worn titles filled the reachable range. Up high were more academic books. There were no photographs, no art, no families or loved ones.

The first book to catch her eye took her by surprise. The title was in Russian, which meant nothing to her. But the author was in English: Dale Carnegie. An old worn copy of *How to Win Friends and Influence*

People in Russian. Next to it, another recognizable author, Stephen R. Covey. Its title was also in Russian. The big 7 on the front led her to believe it was *7 Habits of Highly Effective People*. She stepped back and took another look at the shelves.

Behind her, Tania ran through the hall to the kitchen. "Two more in the back."

In front of her were many recognizable self-empowerment books. The bedrock of American business and management theory lined the shelves. The section next to it was filled with classic history books, from *Guns, Germs, and Steel* to de Tocqueville's 1835 classic, *Democracy in America*. One entire case was devoted to biographies of American presidents. Scattered throughout were essays and treatises on American politics. Some were rare and others bestsellers.

There were books on gerrymandering, the Civil Rights movement, American economics, unions, libertarians, religious minorities, and a host of books written by Americans about Russia. The Cold War, nuclear war theories, books by generals, books by CEOs, books by US Senators, virtually all written by American authors.

Viktor Popov knew more about America than most Americans. She felt a shiver run down her spine.

"Find it yet?" Tania ran back to the foyer. "We're at DEFCON 1 out here."

Pia scanned the room looking for what stood out.

On her third pass, she found it: *The Art of Happiness* by the Dali Lama.

It was not a large book. Not the coffee table-sized book stuffed full of papers she'd expected. She pulled it from a high shelf and opened it carefully. Between pages 112 and 163 a small square had been cut out with a razor. In it were hundreds of microdots.

She closed it. She searched the desk for rubber bands and secured the covers. She stuffed it in the lining of her coat, where she'd created hidden pockets in case they were stopped.

She raced back to the foyer. "Ready."

Tania tackled her, driving her to the ground. Shots rang out, coming from the upstairs landing. Tania spun on her back and fired a Russian assault rifle through the ceiling. The last Russian inside staggered to the stairs and rolled down.

Pia started to say thanks.

Tania said, "That's two. I save your life one more time, you owe me a vacation in Bali."

"Deal." Pia rose to her feet.

They bumped fists.

Jacob trained a confiscated Russian rifle through a broken window and fired a burst. The louder noise made by regular bullets escalated the tension in the air.

A reply of gunfire erupted outside. Shouting and more gunfire. Jacob counted off the adversaries. Tania confirmed. The three of them against six fresh Russians. Pia could only hope things were working the way she planned.

The Russian assault began with a barrage of bullets. Two charged the front, two crashed the back. Pia fired into the hallway, pinging bullets off the body armor of the attackers. They fell into the kitchen. Tania and Jacob dispatched the two in front then joined her, circling the two trapped in the kitchen.

The Russians emptied their magazines and swapped.

During the lull, Dhanpal snuck in from outside and surprised the Russians. Both soldiers surrendered. Tania darted them.

"Anyone home?" Miguel's voice came from out front.

"Mission objectives achieved." Pia gave each of her team a hug. They went about their cleanup chores, retrieving all darts and casings.

With Jacob by her side, she faced the cowering film crew. "Everything's going to be fine. We've cleared the immediate area, and now we're leaving."

The Latvian director pulled himself up. "Are you going to kill us too?"

She glanced at Jacob. He shrugged. He hadn't had time to explain.

Pia grabbed a fistful of the Latvian director's shirt and pulled him to his tiptoes. "I am not here. She is not here." She pointed at Tania, then Miguel and Dhanpal. "They are not here either." She waved her free hand around the room. "The guards had some kind of breakdown. Mass hysteria. Drugs. Probably. Who knows. This guy—" she pointed at Jacob "—saved you from them. Are we clear?"

"But you killed all those men!" Sylvia's shriek echoed off the walls. "They could have children who need them at—"

Pia grabbed her wrist, silencing the actress, then held up a dart and explained its function. The film people crowded around the tiny needle-tipped dart, then looked up at her in unison.

"We were not here." She pointed to her people again. "Tell me you understand."

The director nodded with an anxious rapidity. The rest followed suit.

Sylvia looked at Jacob, then pointed at Miguel and Dhanpal. "Who are they?"

Jacob glanced over his shoulder. "Plan C."

Pia didn't have time to ask what they were talking about. She said, "I have to go."

She shook hands with each and thanked them for their participation. A generous check for their performance would follow. In back of them, Jacob pulled something off a shelf and examined it. A small reproduction of the central fountain at the National Gallery of Art in Washington, DC: Mercury, winged messenger of the gods. They shared a glance, and she smiled her approval. He pocketed the hand-sized bronze.

She and Tania left the way they came, out the back and into the woods. Not far behind them, Miguel and Dhanpal left the building and picked up pine branches they'd positioned earlier.

Miguel called out to her. "Sure, leave it to the Indian to sweep up the tracks. Typical."

"Indians, plural," Dhanpal said.

"You're not an Indian." Miguel pushed the smaller man. "I'm an Indian."

"You're not an Indian." Dhanpal pushed back. "You're a Native American."

"Then you're a Mumbai ... ian."

"It's Mumbaikar."

"Mum biker?"

Their voices faded into the distance as Pia and Tania began running through the woods. Dogs began barking on the other side of the subdivision. As they picked up their pace, she thought about fate and the intricate web of life. The man trying to destroy her democracy was also the man who ordered her parent's murders. All three of them. She couldn't decide what that was. Synchronicity? Concurrency? Serendipity?

She settled on *convenient*.

A slow and painful death awaited Popov. He was nothing more than a rabid animal whose destruction would ensure the safety of everyone else on Earth.

Those thoughts surprised her. Was she losing it?

Stefan's voice came back to her: *Leave it all behind and join me.*

CHAPTER 61

WE HELD OUT OUR GLASSES and watched the Latvian director pour Riga Black Balsam from the liquor's iconic handmade ceramic flagon. He claimed the thick black syrup is a form of vodka infused with twenty-four different plants and herbs. Supposedly, it cured Catherine the Great of a deadly illness back in the day.

My phone buzzed with another call from Dhanpal. Then one from headquarters. The thing had been buzzing ever since the Latvian cops gave it back to me. I pressed ignore. Sometimes, you have to be present for the people whose lives you saved. It doesn't hurt if one of them has auburn hair, ice-blue eyes, and a smile that could cause a spontaneous mutiny on a battleship.

We toasted to the local lawyers who convinced the authorities that our story was true and that the Russians were lying. They may have inflamed some of the ethnic distrust between the native Latvian police and the Russian-born guards at Popov's dacha. Which was not cool—but was effective. We were free. Our last engagement before the long drive back to Vilnius and the Sabel jet was this celebration. Our Latvian host insisted on it. He'd never felt so invigorated in his life—although the invigoration came after he'd pissed himself. Apparently.

I hoisted my glass and held my breath because I've had drinks in foreign countries before. My French friends, including Sylvia, made the mistake of sniffing it. They gagged. I slugged my shot back like an oyster and collected a nod of approval from our host. The others tried to sip it and once again nearly gagged. It had the flavor of bad cough syrup with the aftertaste of dry fertilizer. Our Latvian laughed. On the bar next to us were five tall glasses filled with black currant juice on the rocks. He poured our second shot into the juice.

"All world's a stage," the Latvian said in his thick accent. "We do finest acting in whole lives today, yes?"

We clinked glasses and sipped more cautiously. The sweetness helped a little, but it was still clear why this was a regional drink and not taking global market share from rum or tequila.

Sylvia had warmed up to me since I saved her life. A little. She turned to me and smiled and waited for me to say something.

I smiled and gave her my sexy look. Which dove into epic awkward territory.

"So." I took another sip to change my expression. "Why are you so interested in foster children?"

"Don't you feel like the gods were smiling on us today?" She lit up that atomic smile of hers so I wouldn't mind that she dodged my question.

"Truth." I clinked glasses, held my breath, and took a sip. Something in the way she watched my reaction struck me as odd. "Which gods watch over you?"

"Aphrodite." She giggled.

BOOM!

All of Mercury's hatred for her came into focus. I faked a smile and turned away.

Mercury stood in my new line of sight. *You understand now, right, homes? This is some serious shit. You can't be hanging with no Juno-damn Greeks.*

I asked, *Is she Aphrodite? Or does she just talk to Aphrodite the way I talk to you?*

Mercury said, *Hey now, I know she's pretty and all that, but dawg, who's been watching over you all these years, huh? Besides, Venus is much hotter. You want babes—stick with Venus. Dude, they named body parts after Venus.*

I looked over his left shoulder, then his right. *Where's Venus been hiding then?*

Don't be playing with me, brutha. Mercury straightened up and smoothed his toga. *You're alive today because of me. Whereas Aphrodite figures killing you will spare a hundred future deaths. Never trust those Greeks. Especially if she starts talking wooden horses.*

Sylvia said, "Are you OK? You look like you're going to be sick."

"War wound." I winced and put my hand on my side. "Flares up now and then."

"You were a real hero today." She squeezed my bicep and turned her pale-blue eyes up at me. Electricity zinged up and down my spine. "None of us have to be back in Monaco tomorrow. We might take a day. Enjoy the scenery. Catch up on some sleep. You know?"

I felt my grin spread across my face like a zipper opening on a sleeping bag.

Before I could answer, my phone pinged. Again. Headquarters was now dinging me on auto-redial. I had to deal with it, but it was far too loud in the bar. I excused myself through the side door and stepped into the frigid night air.

"He's been calling the main switchboard all afternoon." Bianca was in a hurry. "He said he's the man from the NYPL. We ran a voice analysis and think it's your guy from Stavanger, Yuri Belenov. I need you to call him. I want to hijack his phone."

"Love you too, babe."

"In your dreams. Call the guy." She clicked off. The number appeared on a text.

The building next to the bar offered a nook that kept the icy wind off my neck. I screwed in my earbud and called him.

"I'm hurt," Yuri said when he clicked on. "You killed Strangelove—for which I, and all of humanity, thank you—but you never gave me credit."

"Three-hundred sixty-five Americans died on flights 1028 and 31."

"What does that have to do with me?" He huffed with contempt. "I can deliver Viktor Popov."

His boast almost made me listen to him. I said, "Turning yourself in would be better than waiting for me to find you."

"You're better than these little threats, Jacob." Yuri's voice was calm and smooth. "You're looking for bigger fish than me. Do you know who killed Kasey Earl? Do you know what they took from him?"

That took the wind out of my bravado. How the hell did he know about Kasey Earl? Was he the killer? "Do you know anything, or is that a name you heard on Twitter?"

Miguel called. I clicked ignore.

"You want to be your girlfriend's hero." His voice turned cocky. "You're looking for the people who ordered her parents' murders. I can lead you to the answers."

"She's not a girlfriend. More like a sister." Ms. Sabel had once referred to our relationship as siblings in madness.

"Whatever. Sister then." Yuri almost laughed. "She wants to know who these people are."

His words felt like an ice pick striking at the question that kept Ms. Sabel awake for over twenty years—which was the same as ice-picking me.

"Nothing you've said is a secret." I tried to sound calm. "What do you want?"

Two cars stopped side-by-side in the middle of the street near the bar. Both were loaded with men who spoke to each other through the partially lowered windows.

"Two things." He left a dramatic pause for me. "Popov dead—and an American pardon for my team."

"Your first demand is only a matter of time, with or without your help." I left a dramatic pause of my own. "The second is not my call. If it was, I'd lie to you, bring you in, and kill you in Times Square. They'd give me a medal."

"Talk to your girlfriend. She has friends in high places."

"Sister."

One of the two cars pulled to the curb. Four men got out and went into the bar. The other car sped off and turned the corner.

"Too tall for you, Jacob?" He laughed. "Do powerful women intimidate you?"

"If you think 'just following orders' is going to save you, read up on the Nuremberg Trials."

"You won't make this decision on your own." He hesitated a second. "I'll give you this much: A banker named Eleni collected evidence of

Chuck Roche laundering money in Cyprus. Popov's people beat Pia Sabel to it and destroyed it. She arrived five minutes too late. Tell her that, see if it moves her."

Cyprus was a story we kept inside Ms. Sabel's inner circle. We don't have leaks. Which meant he gleaned it from our enemies.

"Still not motivated?" Yuri asked. "I have the orders from Popov to Strangelove for her murder. He wanted Alan Sabel motivated like Jallet."

That tipped the scales pretty hard. "Let's pretend she's interested. How does your little fantasy play out?"

"You find something Popov needs, I broker a trade at a neutral location."

The second car full of goons was looking for the bar's back door. I knew something the goons didn't: there was no back door. The bar had a side door, and I was looking at it. The backup squad would be delayed. My window of opportunity was thirty seconds long.

"What good does a neutral location do me?" I pushed out of the nook and started for the bar.

"You get advance notice."

"You're a trustworthy man. Probably." If not for his accurate map of Strangelove's offices in Kaliningrad, he would've been listening to dial tone. "I'm not making any promises."

"You're a capable soldier. Your girlfriend—I mean soul sister—is a resourceful woman. I am a dangerous man. Figure something out."

He clicked off.

Bianca texted me. "He used an IP relay-phone. We only found his transfer point, a bar in Nicaragua."

Damn.

I slid back in through the side door and stood in the shadows. Mr. Stalingrad and three Russians stood near the front, searching the crowded room. While I watched, their eyes passed over Sylvia and her crew.

Sylvia saw me and waved. Which brought Mr. Stalingrad's attention to me. I smiled and nodded at him. Sylvia looked disappointed that I didn't acknowledge her first.

I wanted to fall in love with her. She wanted to fall in love with me. But the gods—and Mr. Stalingrad—were keeping us apart.

She crossed the short distance to me while my brand-new enemy tried to push through the bar's tangled partiers.

"Trouble." I nodded Sylvia toward the Russians. "They're after me. Go straight to the van and take it to Vilnius tonight. Have the pilots leave the minute you get there. Don't wait for me. Go right now."

I backed out with both Sylvia's, and Stalingrad's scowls fixed on me. Not the image I'd prefer to leave with, but I had no choice. I ran down the brick street looking for options.

Mr. Stalingrad took the bait. He was coming for me, not Sylvia. I could hear them a corner behind, tromping after me.

I ignored my ringing phone and looked for a way out. I try to be a good boy—until I'm facing eight-to-one odds. Then it's survival mode. No matter what you see in the movies, no one can take on eight men and win. Stealing a car was not out of the question.

I rounded a building and saw the proprietor of a small motorcycle dealership closing up. A few quick steps later, the muzzle of my Glock was hard against his neck. We did an awkward dance back inside. He relaxed when I whipped out my American Express Centurion Card. On seeing the black titanium, holding a gun to his head was easily forgiven.

In less than a minute, I was exiting his showroom on Sabel Security's newest company vehicle: a BMW R1200 RS sportbike.

I'm no stranger to motorcycles, but I was a bit rusty and nearly hit the building across the street. I walked it back and pushed off the sidewalk just in time to see a car full of big men in my mirror.

We were in old town Riga. The bike's navigation display, crisp and bright as it was, was written in Latvian. On my right was the *Sv. Petera baznica* ... whatever. It looked like a big old church to me. With a twist of the throttle, I pulled away and rounded a bend. I used a lane tight with traffic to weave my way clear of my pursuers.

One of the Russians was waiting for me on the other end. He stood calmly with a gun at his side while the pedestrians on the sidewalks pointed and screamed. I ducked down and zigged left before zagging right. I peeked over the handlebars. He wasn't intimidated or raising his weapon. He held a phone to his ear. I revved it up and aimed for him. He calmly stepped out of the way and let me by.

I could feel his pistol aiming for the back of my head.

The bike burned rubber nicely when I made my radical U-turn. I shot up the street, weaving between stalls hawking handmade Christmas gifts. The second car full of Russians rounded the bend ahead of me. My only option was to stay in the pedestrian lane. But it poured onto a busy street. I leaned the bike hard. My knee brushed the bricks as I swung in front of a small white delivery truck. The foot soldier ran after me. I left him in the dust. Or snow in this case.

Weaving through crowded plazas, I scraped a car here and there before finding a multi-lane bridge. I opened it up and flew across a wide river.

I whipped down an alley behind the national library, cut the lights, and called her.

"Did you get to the van?" I asked when Sylvia picked up.

"Yes, but …" There was an odd grunt and a strange mewling.

"Sylvia?"

Her voice came out hushed and strained. "Jacob—help!"

My soul collapsed like a soda can under a boot heel. Stalingrad was smart, I had to give him that. He'd left someone to watch my girl.

Mercury crossed his arms. *She and her buddies stayed to finish their drinks. That's what kind of girl she is. I'm telling you, bro, you don't need—*

I said, *I got this.*

I asked her. "Did he hurt you?"

"No. He says he's going to." She spoke to someone behind her in French. "He wants whatever you took."

"Let me talk to him."

An incoming call tried to reach me again. I ignored it.

"He doesn't speak English, only Russian and French." She spoke to him in the background again. "I suppose you're a one-language American like everyone else?"

"Arabic and Pashto, thank you very much. Saved my ass in the war." I reined in my harsh tone. I was mad at Mr. Stalingrad, not Sylvia. "Translate for me, word for word. I have what he wants. But I'm not dumb enough to walk into an ambush with it. We meet in neutral territory. Somewhere neither of us have been before. Like a warehouse with a big parking lot. I'll be in plain sight at a distance. When you and the crew are safely off the lot, I'll deliver the package."

She discussed something with him before coming back to me. "I know a place. Bialystok, Poland. We shot an indie film there. There's an abandoned warehouse on the far end of town. Farmland all the way around. He's never been to Poland."

"Perfect. I'll be there."

"Don't do it, Jacob." She choked, then whispered, "He's planning to kill you."

CHAPTER 62

AFTER HIS CALL WITH JACOB, Yuri rose from his pew in the empty airport chapel and joined the throngs of people moving through Roberts International Airport in Monrovia, Liberia. He spotted a young boy lagging behind his family. In a few quick steps, he was right behind the child. His burner slipped neatly into the boy's slightly open backpack. When the NSA and FSB tried to locate him, they would find a very surprised Liberian family vacationing in Paris. Yuri turned on his heel and joined Roman heading for the street.

"It went well?" Roman asked.

"We will see." Yuri marched to the curb to hail a cab. "Sabel is only half the battle. Popov will need motivation as well."

"You're sure this will work?"

"No." Yuri directed the cabbie to the hotel. "Everything in life is a gamble. We have forty-eight hours to put this together."

"While we're traveling?"

"When is the flight to Albania?"

"In the morning. First stop is Doha, then Athens." Roman calculated in his head. "Thirty-six hours before we're in Durrës."

"Then we have twelve hours left over." Yuri smacked his friend's knee. "Plenty of time."

"Perhaps we should reach out to Yeschenko." Roman's voice was weak with uncertainty. "His email showed he valued us. We could use an ally."

"You think the rich care about you, Roman?" Yuri glared at his man. "He would help us only if we dance for him—like his slave girls. And only then if the Kremlin approves. That means Popov."

Roman shrugged.

Salty, humid air blew from the beach across the Cape Hotel's tiled patio. They sat in the shade, sipping lemonade and working through the trove of Popov's emails. Reading such tomes of hastily-prepared communiqués was almost as bad as reading someone's tweets. But they pressed on in the growing heat.

In the third hour, as dusk became imminent, a boy struggled off the beach and walked below their terrace carrying a heavy box.

Yuri summoned him. "What do you sell?"

"Protection for da white man." The boy ripped open a big, bright smile.

"Do I need protection?"

"You—dangerous man." The boy looked him over. "Da big men think you da threat. They challenge you. Are you ready?"

Yuri and Roman exchanged amused glances.

"What should I do to be ready?" Yuri leaned forward and looked at the boy's wooden case.

"Have da blade." The boy dragged out the last word. He balanced his case on one knee and opened it like a magician doing a trick. He waved his hand in front of the knives encased in red velvet. "For you, da man expecting trouble: a ZDP-189 steel blade in a Harkins Triton."

His gesture stopped on a sleek-looking switchblade with a handle shaped like a coffin. Yuri and Roman shared another glance before leaning forward to get a closer look.

The boy picked it out of the case and handed it to Yuri.

It was heavy yet nimble and made him smile. A flick of the button slid the blade straight out of a titanium grip at high velocity. A second flick slid it straight back in. The action was smooth, powerful, enticing, almost erotic.

He grinned. "How much?"

"A thousand dollars. But for you, $995 US."

"No way." Yuri sat up straight and frowned.

"You're not worthy." The boy snatched the knife back and walked away. "You not dangerous at all."

Yuri could not believe the boy's impertinence. He had a mind to beat the boy and take the knife anyway. He looked at Roman for support but found his friend with a smile on his face.

Roman whistled to the boy. "Seven hundred."

The boy flipped him off without turning around.

"OK. A thousand dollars, American." Roman laughed.

"Are you crazy?" Yuri faced him.

"It is my gift to you. It made you smile, Yuri. You deserve it."

The boy came back. Roman peeled hundreds from his roll and made the exchange. As the boy turned to leave, Roman grabbed his arm. "If we meet any dangerous men looking for the rest of my money, you will discover we are not dangerous at all." He gave the boy his meanest glare. "We are deadly."

The boy tore away from him, threw his chin high, turned his back, and walked away.

"He's not easily intimidated." Yuri watched the boy disappear down the street. "Thank you, Roman. It is a tremendous gift."

"I left one very much like it in Brazil. They're handmade by Jeff Harkins. Look closely at the blade. He's engraved his signature on it."

Yuri examined it and found the signature. For the first time in ages, he felt an affinity for his new lieutenant that was difficult to express. He couldn't remember the last time someone had given him a significant gift. Especially one as personally bonding as a switchblade.

They enjoyed a dinner of questionable proteins and delicious drinks. Afterward, they returned to the hotel terrace and continued the laborious search through thousands of emails as dry and boring as the Gobi. Late in the evening, after an hour's silent toil, Roman burst out laughing.

"You'll want to see this." Roman pointed to his laptop screen and turned it to face Yuri.

It took a moment to register as he read the screen. "Popov is using the account in real time?"

"It's a different account." Roman could barely contain himself. "His passwords are simple variations of his original password. Petr cracked the code: add one letter or number to the end of the original password. Igor expects to get in all his accounts before we reach Albania. We might even crack his laptop camera."

"Our people are not just good hackers," Yuri said. "They are the best."

The two of them shared a snicker, one of boyish delight at their triumph and the defeat of a hated foe.

The latest incoming email came from a guard on Popov's personal property. Sabel agents had overwhelmed them unexpectedly and taken something small but unknown. The head guard, Sergeant Tarasov, reported only one item appeared to be missing from the house: a small statue of Mercury, winged messenger of the Roman gods. He closed with a vow to track down the thieves at any cost.

Roman pulled the laptop back. "What's our next move?"

Yuri sliced open a phone's clamshell packaging with his new knife. "This is it. We can broker a deal now."

For the next two hours, he tried to reach Jacob Stearne with no luck. He still had to go through the switchboard at Sabel HQ to find him but went straight to voicemail every time. As the evening wore on, and the drudgery of reading meaningless field reports in Popov's email became too much, he tried something on a whim. He called Sabel HQ and asked for Pia Sabel.

After waiting on hold, she answered with the sounds of a harbor behind her and the breathing cadence of a brisk walk.

"I apologize for the intrusion, Ms. Sabel, but I've tried getting hold of Jacob Stearne for—"

"He's busy, Major Belenov. I've been briefed on your proposal. The answer is no."

Yuri turned down the brightness on his laptop and let his eyes adjust to the night around him to better focus on Sabel. "I'm disappointed to hear that. I thought you'd be interested in getting Kasey Earl's trove of documents. The ones that bear Chuck Roche's signature on what amounts to your parents' death warrants."

The auditory clues on her end indicated she'd stopped walking.

A moment later, she said, "You have to answer for Flight 1028."

"If there is a God, I will answer someday. If there is no God, then nothing matters."

She said, "I make things matter."

He felt an unexpected chill despite the heat. Something rustled the bushes behind him. He snapped his fingers at Roman, but his lieutenant didn't understand.

Yuri had to focus on his conversation. "It was brave of you to take on Viktor Popov. I'm impressed by your valor."

"You know we're tracing this call. We will find you."

"I apologize in advance for your team's impending disappointment." Movement in the dark shadows caught Yuri's eye. "All you'll find is an innocent travel agent in Singapore."

"I just got out of a submarine, and I'm about to get on a jet. This call ends in thirty seconds." She paused. "Why did you call?"

"The question is not about me." He saw more movement in his peripheral vision and twisted in that direction. "Rather, the question should be: who do you want, Ms. Sabel? Viktor Popov or Chuck Roche?"

"I'll worry about them." From the background noise, it sounded as if she were on the move again.

He snapped his fingers at Roman and pointed into the dark. Roman rose and walked to the edge of the tiled terrace.

"What about both of them?" he asked. "You can have kompromat on both Popov and Roche."

"Bold claim. Prove you can deliver and you get another ten seconds."

"I'll throw in a bonus to help your legal team defend you against your own government: I have the email from Popov to Strangelove ordering your murder."

"My attorneys have that handled." She spoke with confidence but a hitch in her voice betrayed her interest.

From the edge of the lighted area, Roman shrugged. Behind him, another shadow moved. Paranoia? The Americans? The knife-boy returning with friends for the rest of Roman's cash?

"My people hacked Popov's email. I just read the field report about your daring adventure in Jurmala. Eight Russian soldiers subdued. A French film crew distracted them. So very clever. I'm in awe. But I'm dying to know, Ms. Sabel, what was on the shelf? What did you steal from Viktor?"

It was only a split-second of hesitation. He'd won her attention. Mission accomplished.

Sabel said, "What's your proposal?"

"I'll be in touch." He clicked off.

The shadows bothered him. Nothing good came out of flickering shadows. Yuri slapped his laptop closed. He rose and pushed Roman. He pointed inside and waved for his friend to follow. He strode quickly through the empty lobby. Roman grabbed his laptop and trotted to catch up.

Beyond the hotel's front door, on the street side, more shadows lurked. He turned and jogged through the kitchen.

"Wait, Yuri," Roman called from the lobby. "Where are you going?"

There had been times in his life when he had overreacted. There were other times, like this one, where he knew his doom was seconds away. He could feel it in his skin. His life depended on moving quickly.

He shoved his shoulder into the kitchen exit and stepped into the darkness. Two men ran toward him. He backed into the kitchen, grabbed a large iron pot, burst back into the night, and smashed it with all his might against a head. The man went down with a bleeding gash on his pale forehead.

His other adversary caught the backswing in his hands and fought for control of the cauldron. Yuri tried to pull it back, and when the tug-of-war reached full exertion, pushed it hard into the man's face. At the same time, he landed a swift kick to the man's groin. A second smash from the pot put the assassin on the ground.

Roman ran to the door and stopped in the opening.

"Popov found us." Yuri pointed as he panted. "Let's go."

"Why do you say Popov?" Roman stammered for his next word.

"Sabel had no idea where we were. If Americans knew our location, she would be the first to know. C'mon."

Roman didn't move.

Yuri squinted at him. Then events fell into place. Only the two of them knew they'd randomly chosen Liberia to change planes. They had been traced through Roman in Brazil. And now they were found in Africa. Blood boiled into his head.

"Hey, Yuri." Roman reacted to the fire building in Yuri's eyes and backed up a step. "It's not what you think."

Yuri reached for his VX-Y spray in his pocket. His hand found his new switchblade instead. He snapped it open. "Whore!"

He lunged at his friend and stabbed him between the ribs. For a moment, they looked into each other's eyes.

"Why, Roman?" Yuri's eyes flared. "We were so close to being free."

He pulled back and shoved Roman into a slump against the door jamb. Snatching Roman's laptop, he put it in his bag with his own.

Roman wheezed through his punctured lung, trying to ask for help. He reached a desperate hand toward his boss.

Yuri pulled a pistol from one of the unconscious assassins and ran to the street. A motorcycle came up the lane. He shot the rider, grabbed the bike, and fled into the night.

CHAPTER 63

AFTER PIA CLICKED OFF YURI'S call, she crossed the street from the wharf and ducked into a dark alley. Silence shrouded the city, every movement echoing through the dark and empty streets. Tania followed, her eyes on her phone.

"They were Russians," Tania said.

"Who?" Pia asked.

"The guys we beat up last time we were in Helsinki." Tania showed her a report on the IDs from Bianca's team. "Gotta be Popov's people, right?"

They stopped and listened to the telltale taps of shoes on Helsinki's ancient cobblestones. Whoever was following them was a hundred yards back.

Pia checked her pistol and kept watch over her shoulder. She'd suspected Roche Security, but his people couldn't have guessed she'd be there, much less put agents in place for her return. Unfortunately, she'd expended most of her darts in Jurmala. She pulled her mag and counted out three. Tania held up two fingers.

The first man following them walked past the alley without a glance. The second man turned the corner quickly. He stopped, silhouetted against the ambient street light.

Tania stepped out, gun drawn. "Hands up."

He hunched his shoulders, raising his collar. He reached for his gun. Tania wisely held her fire. Their pursuers knew about the Sable Darts and used their thick winter coats for protection. The first man returned, rounded the corner, and took up a position to back up his man. A split-second later, a bullet smashed Tania's armor. She landed on the ground.

Pia stepped out and fired at the shooter, catching his overcoat but surprising him. She ran for him at full bore only to take a bullet square in the chest. Armor or no armor, it hurt like hell. She kept running.

He fired again. Hitting her shoulder at the edge of the armor.

Pia threw her arms out as she launched herself, wrapping him up, neutralizing his gun, and pounding the back of his head onto the pavement.

Behind her, Tania sat up and fired her two darts at the other guy. One of them caught his neck. He slumped to the ground.

Pia pounded her full weight into her man's chest. Twisting for all she was worth, she slammed an elbow into the left side of his head. Then twisted back, connecting her other elbow with the right side of his head. He twitched and blinked and passed out.

"Tell me, boss—" Agent Kaspar's voice floated in from the street "—why the elbows?"

Pia stood, clutched her chest, and waited for the silver sparkles in her vision to pass. "If you hit someone hard enough to knock him out with your bare knuckles, you'll have at least three broken metacarpals. Use the heel of your hand or your elbow. Where were you?"

"Delayed by road construction. You left the pickup point before I could get there. So, I followed the sound of gunfire—and here you are." He pointed up the street. "I have a car."

"Do you have ammo?" Tania asked.

"Maybe a couple magazines." He led the way.

Bianca called, and Pia answered as they walked.

"Belenov lied," Bianca said. "He used a school teacher in Uruguay. He hijacks a different computer each time. His malware masks the incoming TCP/IP configuration and modifies the DHCP and DNS—"

"Spare me the tech speak. Is it safe to assume we didn't get him?"

"Short version, his program erases everything after the call, including itself. We can't trace him. He's smart."

"I noticed he didn't flinch when I mentioned it." Pia climbed in the backseat of Kaspar's Skoda sport wagon and brushed dog hair away from her. "What did you think of his proposal?"

"Tough call. I'm a math and science girl, I want to examine all the details."

Kaspar turned up a street blocked for roadwork. He backed up for a three-point turn. "You see? Everything in this town is under construction. They work all night."

Pia surveyed the workers before turning her attention back to the phone. "Belenov's not going to give us any details."

"I find that suspicious," Bianca said.

Pia could hear Dad's advice from years ago. *There is a time for caution and a time for risks; choosing wisely is what separates success and failure.* A lesson she'd proven in soccer for years. But where would the risk fall with Yuri Belenov? Who could she turn to for advice now? The Major had yet to pull out of her guilt-fueled grief. Tania voted to take the deal and get both Popov and Roche.

Pia asked Bianca, "What does Jacob say?"

"Last tracked going 100 miles per hour through southern Lithuania. He's not answering his phone." Bianca took a long breath. "Bottom line: Belenov's offering a deal with a devil that could lead you to a bigger devil."

"As much as I hate working with the man who killed 365 Americans," Pia said, "we have to take his deal."

From the front seat, Tania pumped her fist in the air. "That's right. We can kill Belenov after we kill the guys he serves up on a platter."

"One last thing." Bianca took a deep breath. "You need to know—Emily was the one who told the Senator about your intent to kill Popov and Strangelove."

"I figured that out after I yelled at Olivier." Pia paused. "She's a reporter. Exchanging information is what she does. I've forgiven her. I hope you will as well."

"I can't. I feel betrayed. I'm going to break off our engagement."

"If you want to get married and stay married, get used to forgiving. It works both ways. Or, so my grandmother tells me. She's been married over fifty years. So. Forgive Emily."

"I'll think about it."

They clicked off.

The car slowed again and turned down a narrow lane. At the far end:

more construction barricades.

Pia looked behind them. One large truck turned up the street. She tapped Kaspar's shoulder.

"I see him." Kaspar's eyes filled the mirror. He downshifted and powered forward.

Tania handed Pia two magazines of real bullets from her backpack.

Kaspar blew through the barricades, yanked the handbrake, and drifted sideways. He caught the slide and flew down a cross street. At the bottom, a motorcycle stopped. The rider raised an assault rifle. Kaspar cranked the wheel into a pedestrian lane. The vehicular barriers scraped the quarter panels with a heart-stopping screech. The biker rounded the corner. Kaspar broke free and burned rubber through a maze of plywood stalls, closed for the night.

The bike gave chase.

Pia pushed down a dog barrier and crabbed into the wagon's back space. She planted a foot on each side of the hatchback and released the fifth door. It popped open. She sighted down her barrel. The biker slammed on his brakes. He swerved, complicating her aim. He ducked behind a vendor's stall.

They quickly came to the end of the plaza. The truck had parked broadside to them. Two men with rifles opened fire, splintering the windscreen. Tania leaned out the window and brushed one gunman back.

Kaspar cranked the wheel and slammed on the brakes, drifting them into a U-turn. They smashed into three stalls, sending Christmas ornaments and wood flying in every direction. He stalled it on the turn and cursed.

Pia recovered from the violent spin and fired through the debris falling back to earth. A bullet whizzed through the air. Kaspar restarted his car. He revved the engine and dropped the clutch. She agreed with his strategy: run him down and hope the engine block caught most of his bullets.

Two men stepped out from behind the truck. She fired despite the jarring ride across cobblestones hundreds of years old. Making an effort to counter the bumps proved futile. She fired the rest of her mag and reloaded.

Kaspar shouted out in pain. He tore the wheel to the left, smashing hard into a stall. Pia turned around in the small space to examine her driver. Only his left hand remained on the wheel. His right shoulder bled profusely. Tania applied pressure to the wound.

Bullets tore through the quarter panel near her knee.

Pia looked for telltale gunsmoke and found it at the same time she saw fuel spilling from under the car. She fired carefully, preserving as much ammo as possible. Kaspar turned unexpectedly to the right, sideswiping a building. Shards of brick fell into the street behind them.

They swerved again. Pia held the roof as their fender caromed off a car going the other direction. The truck came out of a side street and stopped. The gunmen jumped from the cab. One held an RPG launcher.

She emptied her mag. Pia yelled, "Turn!"

"Nowhere to…" Kaspar groaned.

Pia looked over his shoulder. A straight street, long and narrow. High brick walls on either side.

She heard the whoosh. She saw the flash. It hit forward of the left front tire. The engine saved them from the brunt of the blast and the shrapnel. Pia held on with each foot and hand braced against a different panel of the car. The Skoda lifted in the air, rolled one and a half times, and landed on Kaspar's door.

Pia scrambled from the wreckage, black stars blinking in her peripheral vision. She aimed where she guessed her attackers were and hoped they were intimidated. Her free hand felt her empty pack in the vain hope of finding a new magazine.

Nothing.

An unnaturally bright light illuminated the street behind her.

She turned to the car. It lay on its side, the undercarriage facing her, her adversaries on the far side. No one was getting out. Flames licked the engine compartment at the front. At the back, fuel poured onto the road at an alarming rate. Three feet separated the flames from the growing spill.

Pia stepped on the axle, hoisted herself onto the car, and looked in the window. Tania struggled with her seatbelt. Pia grabbed the passenger door and tore it open only to have gravity slam it down on her back as she reached in. Twisting into the pain, she grabbed the belt and pulled slack from the B-pillar. Tania used it to unlatch the buckle. She fell on top of Kaspar.

Pia propped Tania's door open with her shoulder and reached inside.

Bullets chipped the brick wall behind her.

Tania's hand reached up from the smoke-filled cabin, holding a magazine. "Four left. Use them…"

Tania coughed.

Streamers of red and yellow flames snapped above the front tire. Pia grabbed the mag, reloaded, and fired three shots.

She reached back into the darkness, found flesh, latched onto it with all her strength and pulled Tania up by the forearm. She brought half her agent to the car's bodywork. From there, Tania scrambled between Pia's feet until she lay sprawled on the wreckage.

"Get clear!" Pia shouted at her. She reached back inside and felt nothing. She knelt, the car door still weighing on her back. Still nothing.

"Get out of there," Tania shouted back. "It's on fire."

"He's still in there." Pia reached again. "I'm not losing him."

A raft of bullets flew over her back. She tossed Tania the pistol as another round from the Russians blew out the door. Chunks of safety glass rained down on her back.

A flame erupted under the dash, lighting the interior. Kaspar lay slumped against the driver's door. His hand wavered weakly in the empty space. Limited consciousness. She reached in and touched his fingertips. The flame exploded upward, blasting her face with scorching heat. Her sleeve caught fire. She leaned back and felt another round of gunfire ripping through the bodywork. Flames filled the open door. The heat drove her back. The door slammed shut. She reached for the handle but felt the searing heat before she touched it.

"We gotta go." Tania held up her weapon.

Pia slammed her fist on the bodywork and felt the intense heat building inside. "No!"

Flame exploded out of the back door, flinging her to the ground. She looked skyward. "Goddamn it."

Tania ran to her, five yards behind the burning wreckage.

"Nothing you could do." Tania whipped off her jacket and wrapped it around Pia's arm.

The flames roared through the car's shot-out glass, reaching ever higher.

Tania pulled on Pia's arm. "We gotta go. It's going to blow."

They took off down the narrow lane with a piece of Pia's heart still in that flaming passenger compartment with Kaspar. As they ran, Pia heard Stefan's words ringing in her head. *It does nothing but bring you grief and hatred and violence.*

CHAPTER 64

SYLVIA FAILED TO MENTION THAT Bialystok is a damn long way from Riga. Riding a fast bike with a used god on the back gets boring after the first ten minutes. Especially since he passed the time by recalling the good old days chasing Christians around places like Corinth, Ephesus, and Galatia. Has-beens gotta brag. Then he started in on how I never listen to him. Just like my dad.

Mercury said, *Jesus has the same problem. None of y'all listen to him either. He says 'give all your money to the poor and follow me' and the first thing you do is vote for the richest guy running for president. I mean, huh?*

We were in southern Lithuania nearing the border when the sun, still beyond the horizon, turned the black night into dark blue.

My high-speed ride paid off. I was well ahead of them. I pulled onto the grounds of an abandoned manufacturing plant. A crust of snow covered a landscape so flat I could see Dubuque from there. Probably. Riding around the outside of the parking lot to avoid leaving a trail, I came to the backside of the structure.

I toured the ruined building. Pretty much an empty barn on steroids, made of thin bricks and corrugated sheet metal and broken glass. Not much existed in terms of hiding places. I parked the bike in a corner. Only an oil drum obscured it. I leaned my butt against the wall near the door and began the long wait.

Mercury stalked the empty room angrier than I'd ever seen him. He'd started haranguing me at the end of the ride, whipping himself into a frenzy. *Get woke, dude! I'm telling you. She stayed for one more round— cause that's how the Greeks be. No sense of responsibility. Doesn't care that danger's coming. You even pointed Stalingrad out to her, and she stayed to party. She's the kinda ho who loves making her hero save her, over and over.*

I pounded both hands into his chest, pushing him back three steps. *Don't call her a ho.*

Chill, bro. Mercury clenched his fists. *You don't want to be pushing a god around. I don't fight little mortals like you.*

He snapped his fingers.

Something in his voice told me I'd better let it go. But he was getting on my nerves. One more insult and I was going back on my meds. I rolled the bottle of pills around in my pocket.

Mercury disappeared for ten minutes, then reappeared with a brawny guy carrying a hammer. *I found Ukko hanging around outside. I'd introduce you, but he hates Christians, former or otherwise. They ripped off all his believers too.*

I said, *Who?*

Mercury looked to the skies with impatience. *You're trespassing on his block, and you don't know who he is? Ukko—sky god in these parts. You really should study up a bit before you travel.* Mercury turned his back to his pal and rolled his eyes and spoke in a whisper. *Ukko thinks he's up there with Jupiter. As if. You need a little time to be chilling down, you know what I'm saying, bro? So I'll be hanging with Ukko for a bit. Good luck with the Russians.*

Ukko put his arm around Mercury, and the two of them walked out.

Fine.

An hour later, a van pulled in from the highway. With the mile-long approach, it seemed like forever before they got to the expansive parking lot. The van stopped a long way back. They made a hard right and circled back toward the highway. There were no cars following them.

Half an hour later, she called.

Sylvia said, "He said you were there, waiting to ambush him."

"Does he want the package or not?"

"He found a different place, a couple miles up the road."

"Let me guess, it's just like this one, only with a difference." I thought for a moment how to phrase the question so her answer wouldn't give it away. Working with civilians presents challenges. "If there are any buildings inside a city block, but no farther than three blocks away, I want you to phrase it by telling me, 'nothing around here but a BLANK building really far away'. You fill in the blank. Now take a good look around and give me the answer."

She took a few seconds. "There's nothing around here but an old silo really far away."

"Hang tight, I'll have you rescued in an hour. I'm out of gas."

"Hurry. I don't like these guys."

"One last question." I couldn't stop myself. "Did you have one more drink before you left the bar in Riga?"

"Well. The Latvian director was so nice, and he looked so lonesome when I said we had to leave. He insisted we have one more round. And I didn't understand what you were telling me until it was too—"

I clicked off.

Nothing pisses me off more than finding out god was right.

I got on the bike and peeled out without waiting for him.

Ten minutes later, I found it. Sylvia failed to describe it in proper detail. It was a mid-century concrete silo with a flat roof. An ideal sniper's nest. But that didn't matter, because Stalingrad's sniper was lying next to me, out cold.

I took up his position and sighted his rifle. It was an SVLK-14 Sumrak, one of the most powerful rifles made and the only model I didn't have in my collection. I nodded thanks to the unconscious sniper and repositioned myself. Mr. Stalingrad and three of his friends paced impatiently around the van, rubbing their gloved hands for warmth. Inside it, the film crew cowered in the cramped space with a fourth Russian. That left three more Russians unaccounted for.

I searched the grounds for five minutes trying to find the missing men.

I was deep in the search when someone grabbed my ankle and dragged me backward three feet. Spinning over, I scrambled for my pistol before realizing it was Miguel. He crouched below Stalingrad's visual range with a shit-eating grin. The downside to having an American Indian best friend is that he lives the stereotype. He really can sneak up on you. He does that skinwalker thing, turning himself into a church mouse.

Dhanpal climbed the ladder and rolled onto the roof. "We could only get three of them without open warfare."

"You guys followed me?"

"Ms. Sabel sent us to help you back in Jurmala," Dhanpal said. "She figured you'd get in over your head sooner or later. We were the car following you when you bought the bike. We were trying to call you, tell you we were there to help."

"It's amazing how far you'll go to make your girl think you're a hero." Miguel punched my shoulder. "Bianca tracked you since you turned your phone off."

"Had to concentrate." I picked up the spotter's field glasses. "Can't talk and ride a bike at 200 kph."

"OK." Miguel shrugged. "Talk or shoot?"

He was asking which task I wanted. No sense in letting Stalingrad know the cavalry had arrived. Or, in this case, the Indians. I waved my phone at him and waited until he got dialed in on the sniper rifle. Dhanpal shimmied back down to the ground for his part.

Watching the Russians through spotter's binoculars, I called Sylvia.

"Hop out but don't stand within arm's reach of the guy." I hesitated. "He has a lot longer reach than you might think."

"Most men do." She got out, holding the phone to her ear. Stalingrad's attention turned to her. Before he could ask any questions, Miguel put a bullet into the pavement a quarter inch from each of his big toes.

Stalingrad shot a scowl my way. A light cloud of gunsmoke gave away our position.

I waved. "Tell him to line his men up against the wall, or they can die where they stand. That includes the guy in the van."

Sylvia relayed the message.

Stalingrad looked like he was having open-bowel surgery without a shot of vodka. Miguel put a round through his right shoulder pad. Stuffing and threads flew out. Stalingrad didn't flinch. He scowled and snapped his fingers. All four of them lined up against the wall. One guy thought we were going to execute him. He trembled like a leaf in an Iowa tornado.

Sylvia and the crew got in the van and left as fast as they dared on the icy road.

Dhanpal collected the Russians' weapons and gave Stalingrad my most beloved possession: a five-inch statue of Mercury. Stalingrad waved the statue at me. He believed he had what he came for. Which he did—until Popov figured out otherwise. I felt a little bit bad for lying to him. But not my problem. It would give us time to get back to the Sabel jet and out of the Baltics.

Dhanpal tied them up with duct tape while Miguel kept them from wiggling their way out. When we were done, I decided the sniper's rifle was a good trade for the little statue and slung it over my back for the ride.

In minutes, we were on the road back to Vilnius, about thirty minutes behind Sylvia. Back on my bike, I followed Miguel and Dhanpal in their rented Ford Edge. It was another long ride, and my butt was already sore.

It had been a long day. Halfway through, it was all I could do to stay awake.

The day was gray, visibility low, the landscape monotonous. My eyelids slumped, and my chin drooped. I almost missed the helicopter that flew parallel to the highway for a few hundred yards.

It stayed too far out to identify any markings. It hugged the ground, then rose, tilted forward, and zipped away into the foggy morning.

Dhanpal clicked me on the comm link. "Are you a wanted man in Poland too?"

"We crossed into Lithuania ten minutes ago."

"And nothing bad happened in Lithuania?"

"Not yet." I thought about it. "That's where we left the jet. We did a low-key entry into Latvia."

We drove on in silence for a minute before it hit me. If you're a Russian in search of military support, Medevtin's staunchest ally is Belarus. We were only twenty miles from the Belarus border, running parallel. I buzzed them back, but they didn't pick up.

I came over a small rise in time to see the white smoke trail from the anti-tank rocket heading from the helicopter straight to their car. Miguel had already burned the brakes; the nose of his ride was diving for the pavement. The rocket grazed the left-front fender and exploded two car lengths away. The shock wave blew their car five feet up in the air, spun it three times and dropped it on its side in a roadside marsh.

My bike skidded to a stop, like every other car on the highway. I jumped off and pulled my prized sniper rifle. I sighted the chopper through the scope: a Russian Mil Mi-25 attack helicopter with Belarus markings. It hovered at an altitude of fifty feet to keep him off local radar. It was wheeling its Yak-B Gatling gun into position to finish off my friends. I fired a round into the engine. Nothing happened. Armor. I tried another, watching my ammo because sniper rifles have small mags. The second cracked the pilot's windscreen and got his attention. The gunship turned toward me. I put a bullet into the rotor hub, a helicopter's most vulnerable part.

The SVLK's accuracy was amazing. So was its power. The bullet shattered the critical feathering hinge, causing the pitch links to fly off. The pilot no longer had control of the rotors that gives it lift and direction. He wisely shut down the power before the rotors turned him over and cartwheeled him across southern Lithuania. But his ship immediately became as aerodynamic as a rock. He fell straight to earth.

I ran for Miguel's crash site. Fuel poured out of the ruptured tank.

Miguel emerged from inside. He stood on the rear door, let out a war-whoop, and started jumping up and down on the edge. I thought he'd gone nuts until the car dropped onto its wheels with a splash in the inch-deep murky bog. As I arrived, he ripped the passenger door off and yanked on Dhanpal's torso. I lent a hand. With three tugs, we extracted our buddy from the tangled seatbelt and airbag remnants. Miguel stood him on his wobbly legs and checked him out.

Dhanpal took a second to do a systems check before giving us a big smile.

"Wahoo!" Miguel leaned back to shout. "What a ride! We should do that again."

Mercury came splashing through the weeds. *Get on that bike and get moving, dawg. You gotta get to Attu yesterday. All three of you. If you don't, Pia-Caesar-Sabel is going to die.*

I said, *Chill. We have a tradition of celebrating when we cheat death. Besides, I'm going to take Sylvia home.*

Mercury grabbed me by the shoulders. *Will you listen to me for once, dude? Sylvia's flying commercial. You're going to Attu.*

Behind me, Dhanpal said to Miguel, "Is he OK?"

And Miguel answered him, "He gets messages."

I said, *You're just jealous of Aphrodite and me. I don't care what you say, I'm in love with—*

Mercury shook me like a rag doll. *Are you listening to me? I'm a god, and I'm telling you to go to Attu. Holy Diana, you're as deaf as the goddamn Ayatollah.*

I said, *Is this like the deal with Noah? Go and build—*

A bolt of lightning struck the crashed chopper with an earsplitting crack followed by a deafening explosion. Ukko walked out of the fireball heading toward us. He pointed his hammer at me. I instinctively ducked.

I said, *Is he like Thor or something?*

Mercury said, *Regional cousins. Don't worry about it. Right now, he's covering your tracks because even he knows how important this is. You. Have. To. Go—*

I said, *Attu, OK. Why does that sound familiar? Is that like Valhalla?*

Mercury said, *Look it up.*

Behind me, Dhanpal asked, "Is he losing it?"

Miguel answered, "The guy just saved your life. Have faith."

Mercury's voice was rushed and angry. *Just get your squad moving. You need to leave right now.*

Ukko walked up, crossed his arms, and gave me one mean-ass glare. *You have god on your side, and you argue? Move it, or the next bolt is yours.*

Life is not going your way when two gods are yelling at you.

Or maybe it is. I'm never sure about these things.

I turned to my companions. "We gotta go."

Miguel struck out for the bike. Dhanpal reluctantly followed.

I stared at Mercury for a minute. When Ukko raised his hammer, I ran after my pals. A lightning bolt struck the Ford. The fireball singed my back.

We reached the highway shoulder. The three of us stopped and stared at the one-and-a-half seater BMW.

I said, "We need to call a cab."

Miguel said, "You just shot down an Eastern Bloc bird in a NATO country. You'll be answering questions until spring. Got time for that Inquisition?"

"We can't all ride that."

"You kidding me?" Dhanpal asked. "When I go back to visit the grandparents, I see whole families riding on smaller bikes than this in Mumbai."

Being small and lithe, he hopped on the gas tank. I got on behind him. Miguel, the size of a redwood, got on the back. Barely.

Awkward isn't the right word for it. I'll just skip ahead to the part where we arrived in Vilnius.

Sylvia and her crew were miffed about being relegated to commercial. They grabbed their gear and sneered their way to the waiting limo that Sabel Security's help desk arranged. All but Sylvia slid inside. The driver held the door for her. She stood there, waiting for an explanation from me.

There were no explanations that made sense. I was going on a mission because an unemployed god, who could be nothing more than a figment of my imagination, told me to. I wanted nothing more than to wrap my arms around her and tell her how madly I'd fallen in love with her. Her eyes told me she was waiting for me to say that. What her eyes weren't saying was how she would react. Given our many broken dates—and the fact that I was kicking her off a private jet for reasons I'd refused to explain—I didn't hold out much hope for our future.

We faced each other, not quite close enough for a kiss.

"Where are you going?" Sylvia asked.

"Somewhere." I sighed and looked across the apron to the main terminal.

"Are you going to kill people?"

My eyes snapped back to her with too much ferocity. She winced and backed up.

I took a deep breath. "Did we kill anyone in Jurmala?"

She nodded her understanding, but her eyes still avoided mine. "Someone shot down a helicopter. They grounded all the flights for a while. Was that you? Did you kill the people in that helicopter?"

"They fired a missile at Miguel—" my voice rose with my temper "—and were about to finish him off with a four-barrel Gatling gun that fires four thousand rounds a minute. Should I have let them?"

She turned, sniffled back some tears, and got in the limo.

I texted Ms. Sabel. "Don't worry. I'll be there."

CHAPTER 65

YURI RODE THROUGH RAIN ALL night, stopping only to find a trash bag to keep his backpack dry. He tried but couldn't listen to his treasured jazz playlists. Betrayal occupied every cycle of thought he had the entire way. Brutus betrayed his uncle Julius Caesar and was pardoned by Mark Antony only to be hunted down by Augustus. He ultimately committed suicide after losing the Battle of Philippi. Hitler betrayed Stalin when he ignored the Molotov–Ribbentrop Pact and launched Operation Barbarossa. He committed suicide when the Russians poured into Berlin. Julius and Ethel Rosenberg betrayed their country's nuclear secrets to the Soviet Union. The fact that all those traitors died in the end, gave him no solace. His hatred for Roman grew by the mile. Was he so desperate for a lieutenant that he overlooked warning signs? How could Roman have been so stupid?

He arrived in Freetown, Sierra Leone late the next morning. After risking breakfast from a street vendor, he found an ugly motel on the beach. An unfinished apartment building crouched next door, its rotting concrete, and crumbling support beams slowly sinking into the sand.

He had one last anonymous account which he used for the room. He took a shower and a nap.

It was a fitful sleep. When he woke up from dreaming about Alexi's splash into the Stavanger harbor, he fell back only to see Vasili's body on a stretcher being pushed beneath Jacob Stearne's judgmental nose. When that woke him, he closed his eyes again and saw Andrine. The worst ghost of them all. She didn't judge, she didn't beg, she just clawed at his wrists without mercy.

He sat up rubbing those wrists.

He needed a different topic to occupy his mind. He considered his plans. If Igor and Petr were not in this duplicity with Roman, he owed them a warning at least. Sierra Leone had little internet access outside the high-end hotel district. He walked to a phone store and bought a pair of Africell phones. He made a hotspot for his laptop with one and reserved the other for the call.

The assembly of hijacked computers around the world was still working. A few of them had been compromised, but plenty had survived. He logged on SHaRC's dark-web server. Several coded posts indicated the others were making progress. Some of the posts were mere minutes ago. He posted his warning that Roman had turned on them. He hesitated for a long time, considering whether to tell them of his harrowing escape. In the end, he decided against it. No need to worry them yet.

He had to act fast to have any chance of survival.

He dialed Viktor Popov and Pia Sabel and put them both in a phone conference.

When they were on the line, he started. "Each of you wants what the other has. I want immunity from both sides."

Pia spoke first. "Immunity, amnesty, pardons are the prerogative of my government. I have no influence over them. I will speak on your behalf about what you're attempting to do here. That's all I can give you."

Popov coughed. "We come back to subject later. First, I must know, why does Ms. Sabel want kompromat on Roche?"

"Many people in my country believe he intends to destroy democracy," she said. "The information you possess can answer that."

Popov scoffed. "You Americans think everything is either democracy or autocracy. You don't see real world. Become enlightened. It is a struggle between order and chaos. Medevtin brought order to Yeltsin's chaos. Roche will do same for USA."

"Democracy is always chaos." Pia huffed. "It's a terrible way to run a country—it's also the best."

"Yes. Do what you must. Do it without involving me."

"You are involved, Mr. Popov." She paused. "Until your country's oligarchs find out you've been siphoning off hundreds of millions from

Santalum. If I'm not mistaken, Santalum is their private company where they stash their billions."

"You talk nonsense like stupid girl."

"We're certain Medevtin and his friends are unaware of your personal fund. Pozdeeva left seven hundred microdots in your dacha. My people looked them over. We've verified a few of the accounts. In fact, just to test our theory, we took ten million US dollars from account 4929310-N and donated it to the Ukrainian Humanitarian Initiative in your name. They were ecstatic. Check your email."

Yuri muted his phone to hide his snickering. Then he thought about her chances. Brash as she was, Popov would most likely kill her. Either way, he stood to walk away clean if this went well. In the background, he and Ms. Sabel could hear Popov typing away on his keyboard. No doubt checking to see if he was down ten million.

"We have deal," Popov said nervously. "We meet in Sevastopol in four hours."

"In Russian-occupied Crimea?" Ms. Sabel asked. "Not a chance. Neutral territory."

"I have a plan," Yuri said. "I've devoted thought and resources to this. But I want immunity first."

"You make proposal," Popov said. "I promise not to kill your sister."

Yuri couldn't speak for a moment. His father told him they'd made it to Istanbul. "You son of a bitch!"

"American curses? You are a failed Russian. You get no immunity. Make your proposal, or you hear her die now."

Yuri took a deep breath. He would kill Popov and ask for immunity from Popov's replacement. But that would come later. Sabel had come through for him with Strangelove; there was a small chance she could pull it off against Popov. For Yuri, it was worth everything to take that chance.

"Socotra." He waited for Sabel and Popov to look it up. "You both arrive and park your airplanes at opposite ends of the airstrip. Come in person. You will be allowed one bodyguard. No weapons. You will walk to the opposing aircraft to be searched by guards from the opposition. You will then walk two kilometers perpendicular to the airstrip, curving toward each other, and make your exchange there."

"Socotra?" Ms. Sabel asked. "The World Heritage island?"

"The territory of Yemen," Yuri said. "No military installations. And none allowed."

"Acceptable," Popov said. "With one requirement for Ms. Sabel: You must prove there are no copies of microdots."

"We will be there at the appointed hour. There will be no proof." She clicked off.

"*Suka!*" The Russian word for bitch. Popov dropped the call.

Yuri sent the command to the remote computer to erase its malware and turned off both phones.

"*Blyad!*" He shouted into the lonely mist. He dialed his father's phone, his mind racing with questions about his sister. No answer. He hurled it against the wall and jumped up and down on the pieces.

The noise he made masked the approaching boots. He looked up in utter shock when three men burst into his room and pounded him to the floor. He stopped resisting when a rifle pressed against his nose.

"You're beaten, Yuri." A fourth man entered the room.

Yuri managed a strained glance over his shoulder to see the familiar voice.

Brad.

The camo-clad gunmen picked him up and shoved him in a chair. They duct-taped his arms and legs. The leader leaned into his visual range and looked him over.

"We're not here to hurt you, Mr. Belenov. You're in good hands. We only have you taped up because you keep running away. So, we good?"

Yuri nodded. One of the men ripped the tape off his mouth.

"What do you want?" he asked.

"You don't need to know—and you don't get to ask." Brad picked up Yuri's second phone and waved it. "Where did you set up the meeting?"

Yuri frowned. The fact that his captors didn't know had implications about who they were. They were definitely American. It showed in their military tactics and discipline.

Brad slapped him. "I said, we're not here to hurt you—but we will if you don't cooperate. So just be a good boy and answer my questions."

Yuri tried to stare the man down. Brad shrugged and nodded at one of his men. A pair of industrial side cutters crimped down on the last joint of his little finger.

"One knuckle for every hesitation. One finger for every lie. You can count, so do the math on how many chances you get before jerking off becomes a memory. One more time, where did you set the meeting?"

The side cutters pressured his finger and drew blood.

He started nodding involuntarily. "Socotra."

"What the fuck's that?"

"An island in the Arabian Sea."

Brad turned his back on Yuri and pulled a satellite phone from his pocket. Yuri could only hear the local side. "Yeah, won't work. Too close to Russia, forty thousand inhabitants, witnesses coming out your asshole. I need something of equal distance for both of 'em, preferably on American soil. Whatcha got?"

There was a long pause.

"Yeah, I like that one. How long for them to get there with no funny business? Ten hours. Perfect." The man clicked off his sat phone and turned back to Yuri.

He handed Yuri the second Africell phone. "Call both of them back, give them this updated location." He held his phone up with latitude and longitude displayed. "Abandoned base; nearest human inhabitants are two hundred miles away; runway is big enough for small jets and C-130s, but that's it. They're allowed one aircraft each. Anything looks out of place, they all die. This deal goes down clean. Both of them walk away unharmed. Got it?"

They sliced the tape off his right hand.

He took the phone and dialed the numbers. He delivered the instructions. After a few sharp and angry questions, Popov and Sabel were pissed but agreed to the change. Yuri handed the phone back.

"That wasn't so hard, was it?" Brad showed a sick smile. He nodded to someone behind Yuri.

A man stepped around and jabbed a needle into Yuri's arm. His lights went out.

CHAPTER 66

STANDING IN THE OPEN CARGO bay of a Russian Antonov An-12, Pia held her arms up and let the Russian soldier wand her coat. Nothing metal. The soldier pointed down the road a hundred yards where Tania waited. Pia pulled up her fur-lined hood and shoved her gloved hands into her pockets and turned into the icy gray mists.

Her long strides caught her up quickly.

"Any word from Jacob?" Pia asked.

"No Sabel Satellite coverage out here." Tania held up her phone to prove her point. "Besides, no one's heard from him since he declared war on Belarus. That was yesterday. Maybe he's dead."

"Don't joke like that." Pia walked in silence for fifty yards. "He said, 'Don't worry. I'll be there.' Where is 'there'? We didn't have the meeting set up at that point. And then we changed it."

"It's charming that you have faith in that guy." Tania shrugged. "I'll just point out—one more time—that one of your two most trusted agents is with you, right here and now."

Two inches of wet snow covered the ground. Flurries swirled in the air. They walked down an empty road lined with barren foundations. The original wooden houses that once stood on them had been left to the elements and disintegrated seventy years ago. They trudged on.

Pia's gut twisted into a knot. She was about to meet the man responsible for recently killing 365 Americans and the murder of her parents. Jacob had told her he felt cold and calm just before engaging in battles. Most people feel hot and scared when facing danger. For the first time, she felt icy. The rising adrenaline in her veins gave her chills. Whether she lived or died today no longer mattered. Only that she got to look in Popov's eyes and let him feel her rage.

Tania looked around. "I gotta say it again—I don't like the location change."

The ground-hugging fog obscured everything in front of them, but they could see vertically fairly well. In the near distance, snow-covered peaks rose into iron clouds. Closer to shore, more fog rolled in as if they were on the set of a horror movie.

"We're a thousand miles from North America," Pia said, "and five hundred miles from any sizable city. Popov didn't have any more time than we did, and we have some advantages here."

"What the hell is this place, anyway?" Tania asked.

"The site of the only WWII invasion to capture American soil." Pia gave her a glance. "Twenty-nine hundred Japanese invaded and held it for nearly a year. Fifteen thousand Americans descended on them and took it back in a vicious two-week battle. The Coast Guard kept a base here but packed it up in 2010."

"Well, thank you, Ms. History Major."

"You know what the worst part is?" Pia asked. "Only twenty-eight Japanese soldiers survived. The invasion was supposed to give them an air base they could use to disrupt American naval operations. They never built the base or resupplied the garrison because the Americans island-hopped in the South Pacific instead of directly attacking Japan. Colonel Yamasaki and his battalion were sacrificed at the whim of political powers far away. Their deaths were meaningless in the end."

"The inherent problem with war."

Her people had cleared Popov and one bodyguard but allowed them a golf cart because the old Russian's leg wasn't up to the walk. Eventually, they could make out the golf cart. As they came closer, they could see Popov, a crutch under his arm, thirty feet to the side of the cart. The big man from Jurmala stood next to him with a shredded shoulder pad on his overcoat. Both wore Ushanka hats with the ear flaps down.

Pia and Tania stopped twenty feet away.

"Hand over book." Popov's voice crackled with age.

Pia shook her head. "Where are my files?"

"In cart. Box too heavy for man with bad leg."

Tania started for the golf cart. The big Russian trotted up to her and grabbed her.

"Until you fulfill your part of bargain, no deals." Popov wagged his finger. "Where is book?"

"Nearby." Pia watched Tania and the big man return. "I have trust issues."

"What do you want?"

"Why did you kill my parents?" She waited until he started to speak before cutting him off with a wave of her hand. "I know, you didn't do it. You got Roche and Hunter to do it. Why?"

He leaned on his crutch and appraised her, head to foot. "I am not therapist. Get help from qualified person."

"You need those microdots." She closed the distance between them. "Answer me."

"You have no understanding." Popov scowled. "I save world from greatest depression ever. Your father invent new eco-friendly power storage. Sound great to tree-huggers but destroy industry that produce $400 billion of business every day."

"Democracy harnesses free enterprise. It would have worked out in free markets."

"No. Democracy is chaos. In 1927, John Deere company invent gasoline-powered combine. It changed farm economics overnight." Popov snapped his fingers. "One man takes care of land that once support five, ten families. In two years, depression around whole world. Human suffering go on for ten years. Millions starving, homeless, destitute. You see? Democracy, free enterprise, free market—all chaos. We chose orderly transition. Keep coal job, keep oil job, keep natural gas job; many millions of people work, take care of families. Your father would not listen. Stupid."

"Solar, wind, and nuclear provide better, higher-paying engineering jobs."

"Does not matter. Your mother and father are still dead. You lose. Where is package?"

She stared at him. He stared back, unrepentant.

The desire to punch him in the face nearly got the better of her.

"Here's how it's going down." Pia stepped to him and towered over him. "Tania is going to verify that what you brought are the originals. Then, I'll give you what you want."

"No. We leave box when—"

"I siphoned off another ten million and give it to a charity in Monaco. You need what I have more than I need your offering." She grabbed his lapel and shook him as her voice rose to a shout. "Take it or leave it."

Popov scowled and snapped his fingers at his guard. The big guy waved an arm at Tania like an usher.

Tania trotted over to the cart, inspected the box and contents. Then she stepped clear, set the box in the snow, and faced south. She made an odd sweeping gesture, like an aircraft director on a carrier, with her knees bent and her arms gesturing to the ground at her right. She held her pose for several seconds, then rose, picked up the box, and headed back.

"What is meaning of this?" Popov pointed a shaky finger at Tania.

Pia stayed silent.

A small black dot appeared out of the pewter sky and grew larger as it approached. A drone, half the size of a Predator, flew a nearly silent circle around them. It released a small parachute, banked its wings, then headed back into the pea-soup sky.

"This is against rules." Popov turned his bony finger to Pia.

She shrugged.

Tania ran for the package floating to the ground fifty yards away. The big Russian ran after her. He clubbed her with a meaty fist, sending her sprawling across the snow. He picked up the package, returned, and handed it to Popov.

"Such a gentleman." Pia glared at the guard.

The big man stared blankly.

"Are these originals?" Popov asked.

"You don't need to worry about copies," Pia said.

"I think you lie." Popov snapped his fingers.

His guard reached into his pocket and retrieved a Russian Grach, the standard Russian Army sidearm. He aimed at Pia's head.

"We have drone too," Popov said.

He turned and started limping on his crutch toward the golf cart.

Pia stared straight into the pistol's barrel and realized that this time she didn't have a backup plan.

His thumb flicked the safety off. She watched his finger slide inside the trigger guard. It located the proper pressure point and began to tighten. She looked into the Russian's eyes. He had the same distant, stress-free stare Jacob had when the pressure mounted.

Every fiber in her body tensed.

Pia said, "My drone has a thirty-millimeter chain gun and instructions to kill you if I fall to the ground for any reason."

"Too bad he speaks no English," Popov called over his shoulder.

Without warning, the padding on the Russian's left shoulder exploded. Stuffing and threads shredded outward in slow motion. The bang of a very loud weapon reached her ears in the next instant. He ducked and wheeled to his left, leading with his pistol. He relaxed and raised the barrel skyward, letting the weapon dangle by the trigger guard. He let out what Pia assumed was a Russian curse.

Pia followed his gaze to find Jacob, dirt and snow falling from his shoulders, sighting down a large, long-barreled rifle. To the left and right, Dhanpal and Miguel also rose from the ground, forming a triangle around them.

Dhanpal marched Viktor Popov back to face Pia.

"This is not agreement." Popov squinted with an angry face.

Jacob disarmed the large Russian and handed Pia the smuggled weapon.

She familiarized herself with the pistol, checked the action, the chamber, the safety.

Tania came at a full run, jumped in the air, and landed both feet in the guard's back. He fell face first on the ground. In anger, he spun around but checked himself at the sight of Jacob's rifle. Jacob walked up close, the barrel aimed straight at the guard's head. The man conceded defeat with raised palms and gave Tania an apologetic nod.

"Get the book." Pia nodded to Dhanpal.

He took the book and checked Popov for weapons. He gave Pia an all-clear sign, then backed away.

Popov's eyes darted left and right, looking, hoping, praying for a way out.

Pia stared at the old man and wondered how many of his victims had looked in every direction for salvation before he killed them. How many had begged for their lives? Had he given them time? Hatred multiplied in her stomach and rose with the taste of bile in her throat. She wanted to pull the trigger and avenge the hundreds of innocent lives he had destroyed in his career of evil.

Stefan's last words rang inside her head. *It does nothing but bring you grief and hatred and violence. Love can conquer everything. Mahatma Gandhi, Nelson Mandela, Martin Luther King changed the world without hurting people. You can do this. Leave it all behind and join me."*

"You live good life." Popov's defiant tone angered her. "You grew up rich, successful. Nothing to whine about. No reason to pull trigger."

Pia felt herself squeezing off the first shot as if someone else were pulling the trigger. Neither intentional or unintentional, it was more of a reaction with no regrets.

She hadn't aimed properly. The bullet passed through his left forearm. "That's for Flight 1028."

She aimed her second shot. It hit his right femur as planned. "That's for Tatyana Sochneva."

His crutch came out from under his arm. He snatched at the handle, caught it, and kept his weight on it. With his other hand, he grabbed at the bleeding hole in his leg. He looked up at her with pathetic tears streaming down his face.

"Do you remember her? She's the daughter of Olesya Sochneva." Pia fired the third round into his left femur. "That's for Olesya."

Popov's knees collapsed against each other, propping him up in horrific pain. His lips trembled. He tried to form words.

She watched him and waited. When he said nothing, she fired the fourth round into his abdomen, off-center to prevent hitting the spine. She didn't want him to lose feeling in his legs before he died. Popov crumpled at the waist, still propped up by his odd tripod of two dysfunctional legs and a crutch. "That's for Bridgette Jallet."

"Please." He gasped. "Mercy."

She shot him in the heart. "That's for Sandra Velocitane—Mom."

Popov fell to the ground, landing on his back. He groaned. He looked at his chest and saw the blood pumping out.

She stepped closer and leaned over, looking into his fading eyes. "This is for Lloyd Aston, my first dad."

She shot him in the right eye.

Popov died.

"This is for Alan Sabel, my second dad." She shot him in the left eye.

She stood for a full minute, staring silently at the gore. The gun dangled by her side. Then she said, "And this is for fucking with American democracy."

She emptied the magazine in his carcass.

CHAPTER 67

MR. STALINGRAD STARED AT ME with wide eyes and a face drained of color. He began shaking his head back and forth. Thankfully, he was man enough not to shit himself. His anxiety was understandable, but pretty far down my list of things to worry about. Ms. Sabel's sanity was right up there at the top. I raised my palms and tried to calm him. I wasn't getting anywhere because he didn't speak English. I turned him over to Miguel, who speaks French, and stepped quietly to Ms. Sabel.

I put an arm around her shoulders. She leaned into me.

"Want to talk about it?" I asked.

"No."

"OK." Hell, I'm no therapist.

The cold breeze picked up a notch and stung my ears. Watching her stare at Popov's carcass made me ache inside. I knew something she didn't: a cold-blooded killing haunts you for a long time. Even when you have a good reason, and the guy deserved it, you always know you had the option to take him in and let the rule of law run its course. Right now, there was nothing I could do or say to make it better. She was staring at him and thinking something dark and sinister about herself. My best course of action was to change the subject, keep her mind intact until we could get back to civilization and get some treatment from a real psychoanalyst.

I said, "I never heard your mom's name before."

"I've never said it out loud before."

"Sandra Velocitane sounds like a nice name. I'll bet she was—"

"Stop." She twisted out of my embrace. "I want to revel in this moment."

Mercury stood on the opposite side of me. *Hoo-doggy, that's some sick shit right there, homie. She could turn evil from here. You need to pull her out of it. I don't want another Caligula on my hands.*

I said, *Are you saying you turned Caligula evil?*

Mercury said, *Those were my drinking days, OK? I thought we were just messing around, but it got dark and sick real fast. I am not going there again, bro. Work on her.*

We stared at Popov for a long time. After a couple minutes, she reached out and took my hand.

"You did the right thing," I said softly. "You got the bad guy."

"Three more to go."

"Whoa." I faced her. "You can't kill the US President or the President-Elect. We are not—"

"No, I intend to destroy them."

The word *destroy* has different meanings depending on your life experience. For a soldier, destroy means to kill someone, pulverize the body, set the remnants on fire, and piss on the ashes. I was hoping a billionaire soccer star might have a kinder, gentler interpretation. "Um. Yeah. Do I want to know what you mean?"

"The worst thing you can do to a rich man is make him poor." She started walking away. "The worst thing you can do to a powerful man is make him powerless."

I caught up. Miguel pushed Stalingrad and followed a few paces behind us. Dhanpal and Tania commandeered the golf cart to carry Kasey's box and brought up the rear.

"Did you say three?" I asked her.

"Roche paid for the operation, Hunter found the assassins." She walked a few yards in silence. "Someone pulled the trigger."

"Who?"

"The pruner. Kasey Earl's files should hold the answer."

Mercury kept pace on my other side. *And that person was most likely not a president, dawg. Meaning, she's going to kill him. You gotta keep her from going off the deep end.*

I said, *You're the one always telling me to kill the bad guys.*

Mercury said, *That's you, though. You're just a grunt. Someone fries you on the electric chair, we can find another grunt. But she's different. She's royalty. Now, how would it look if a Caesar got the needle for murder? After Augustus died of natural causes, we went through seven assassinated emperors before Vespasian finally went out from old age. We can't be wasting that much time, dawg. We need stability in the Caesars. It's good for commerce. You gotta do something.*

I glanced over at her. "Just tell me who the third man is, and he's dead."

She met my gaze with a short smile. "Sometimes a woman takes care of her own problems."

She had an odd look in her eyes. A chill zipped down my spine.

"How did you end up here, on Attu Island?" she asked. "Did a messenger reach you?"

"Something like that." My mind raced through new subjects. Telling her Mercury was worried about her mental health was not where I wanted the conversation to go. "It was damn cold in those old foxholes."

"Do you have a plan for his temple?"

"Hiding in the dirt for hours left me pretty hungry. Is there food on the jet?"

"There are two famous temples to Mercury from ancient times. There's one in Rome that looks like the Parthenon. The other is outside Naples and has a dome. I like the dome idea. What do—"

Gunfire erupted on the runway ahead of us.

Ms. Sabel's jet sat on one end, the Russian transport on the other with over a mile of pavement between them. There were three Sabel agents and three Russians, plus two pilots from each plane. From the scope on my SVLK, it appeared both groups had left the airplanes and ventured a quarter of the mile-long runway toward each other. Neither group had rifles. Pistols with their short barrels aren't terribly accurate to begin with and, with a good distance remaining between them, hitting anything would be an accident. But flying bullets can be lethal, accident or not.

Mercury said, *I don't want anything that looks like the Parthenon, you hearing me, homes? Domes are Roman, whereas rectangles—even updated Corinthian columns instead of that lazy-ass Doric crap—are just so 5th Century BCE.*

I said, *We can talk about that later. What's going down out there?*

Mercury said, *They have field glasses, bro. They saw Pia-Caesar-Sabel execute Popov. They're not happy about that cause they're supposed to bring their guy home. They want retribution.*

We were roughly half a mile from the standoff, forming an equilateral triangle between us. My sniper rifle would have tipped the balance of power except that we were downhill from the others. A good sniper needs a prone or kneeling position to steady the heavy instrument. I gave it a try standing up without a shooting stick or bipod. Fail. The extra-long barrel swirled around too much.

Ms. Sabel grabbed my arm. "There's no reason to kill innocent soldiers. Let's come up with a plan that gets everyone home."

We faced each other. I shrugged. She crossed her arms and gave me her "try harder" look.

Which made me turn to god for an answer. Considering he recently encouraged me to shoot a police detective due to a millennia-old vendetta against the guy's ancestors, I had to be careful about asking him for help.

I said, *You said you didn't want her going off the deep end on the sanity thing. Well, here she is, looking for a way out of a deadly confrontation. What can we do?*

Mercury looked disappointed. *You already know the answer, my brutha. You figured out how to motivate the Russians in Barcelona, you can do it here too.*

I stared at him for a long time before it dawned on me.

I explained my idea to Stalingrad with Miguel translating into French for me. Stalingrad stood stone-faced for a long time. Then he said something in French.

Miguel said, "He brought something for you."

Stalingrad reached into his big overcoat and pulled out a large metal object. He held it out as an offering to me: the statue of Mercury.

Miguel said, "He was going to beat you to death with it because you made him look bad, but now that you've redeemed yourself, he's offering it as a gift."

I took it and handed him the book full of microdots detailing Popov's disloyalty to the Russian oligarchy. I checked his pistol to make sure it was empty and gave it back to him. Stalingrad and I took the golf cart, waving a white flag. His people were wary—even the pilots aimed at us. We stopped thirty yards short and shouted out. One of them approached, his muzzle aimed straight at my head.

Stalingrad got out, waved the book around, and walked back while his man held me at gunpoint. I'd let him take credit for killing Popov. With the evidence of Popov's crimes against the Federation, he could convince them they would all go home heroes. If they didn't buy it, his men might kill him on the tarmac. His problem.

Judging by the tone of voice, they were a skeptical group. It sounded like they were drawing lots for killing me. Uncertainty reigned until they started to warm to Stalingrad's idea. Eventually, he appeased his countrymen. Then we were all friends.

Stalingrad said something to me. One of his soldiers translated for him. "He says you are honorable soldier. Next time he has chance to kill you, he only wounds you out of respect."

Working with professionals is a welcome relief in the age of terrorists. We shook hands. He turned it into a Russian bear hug but thankfully skipped the kisses on both cheeks.

They regrouped, loaded up the golf cart, boarded their plane, and took off.

I made the long walk to Sabel One at the far end of the runway.

Halfway back, I heard another turboprop in the sky. It had a similar but different timbre from the Russian Antonov. I looked to the gray mists above and saw small specks floating in the air. At first, there were five or six, but more and more appeared. I counted fifteen before they became clear enough to identify: paratroopers.

Between them, one item fell faster than the men. I sighted it with the scope as it fell to earth. An American flag, weighted on the bottom, it had a small drogue chute at the top to keep it unfurled and identifiable at a distance. They were announcing themselves: US Army.

One by one, they landed like pros and took up tactical positions around Ms. Sabel's jet. I checked them over and recognized their lieutenant. He had been my last commanding officer before the Rangers turned me out. We'd been good friends and parted on good terms. We exchanged muted recognition in our steely gazes. This was business for him. No special considerations would be given.

I kept walking and joined Ms. Sabel and the others being held at gunpoint at the pointy end of the jet. Reluctantly, I surrendered my hard-won sniper rifle.

The C-130 they'd jumped from spiraled down from the skies and landed. It stopped nose-in to our position, blades spinning like a rotary guillotine. Then it turned around as if it were mooning us and lowered the ramp.

David Watson strode out.

CHAPTER 68

YURI GOT UP AND STAGGERED to the bathroom with only one eye functional, and that was blurry. He fell back in bed and marveled at the silk sheets before drifting off again. Some hours later, after a dream involving Andrine, alive and well and naked, he sensed someone in the room with him. He saw two silhouettes in suits discussing him in the third person, but he was out again before he could ask them anything.

A cool, wet washcloth slid across his forehead. He sat upright and grabbed the wrist that held it. A well-dressed man, attached to the hand, stared back. Yuri blinked and blinked again.

Brad.

"Ah, there you are Mr. Belenov." Brad wrenched his arm away. "Enough laziness. Time to get up. The tailor is here, and we mustn't keep him waiting."

Yuri looked across the expanse of perfect bedding to find a diminutive man with a tape measure around his neck, holding a rolling rack of men's suits.

"Who do you work for?" He looked back at Brad and his washcloth. "Where am I?"

"You are safe, Mr. Belenov. I assure you." Brad rose and backed up. "You're also behind schedule. First the suit, then the barber, then the final alterations. We have to get moving."

Yuri's strength was coming back but was still depleted beyond resistance. He crossed to the window. They were on a cliff, high above an ocean. The coast was rocky. Waves pounded solid black cliffs directly below him. Spray shot high into the air. He had no energy. He could barely stand. He had no choice.

"OK," Yuri said, "I'll go along."

The tailor held up different suits to Yuri's frame and picked a dark blue, slim-fit Zegna. Yuri slipped it on and fell in love with the feel. The tailor scurried around, marking this, tugging that, smoothing the back, and making more marks. Then he pulled the suit off Yuri and left.

For the first time, Yuri took a look around the room and realized he was in a first-class suite in a nice hotel. Brad watched him with part respect and part wariness, like a fighter squaring off in the ring.

Bottled water waited on the wet bar. Yuri grabbed one and chugged most of it. Then he turned to Brad. "I'm hungry."

"Too bad." Brad tossed him an apple from the bowl on the coffee table.

Yuri looked it over suspiciously before taking a big bite. Cool and sweet.

"Talk to me." Yuri dropped to the couch and put his feet on the table. "What is going on and where am I?"

"If I knew, I couldn't tell you. I'm a special ops guy on a mission. My employer paid me a lot of money to bring you here. It's a private island in the Azores. You're supposed to get a suit, manicure, hair, and shoes. Then you get delivered to cocktails at 1900. End of mission."

On cue, a knock at the door took Brad away. Yuri dug through his old clothes while Brad was occupied. He found his switchblade and hid it in the sheets. He bounced back to the couch and finished the apple.

A woman came in and gave him a manicure and pedicure. She was followed by a barber who gave him a great cut, trimmed his stubble to a three-day length, and shaved his neck. The tailor came back with the suit, which fit like a glove. He produced shiny shoes and the fanciful socks celebrities wore. When Yuri looked in the mirror, he saw someone who could easily be mistaken for an important man. He smiled at his reflection. When Brad turned away, he palmed the switchblade and stuffed it in his pocket.

His handler led him down an elevator, then to a banquet hall where he opened a large door, ushered Yuri inside, and announced his name loudly. "Presenting Major Yuri Belenov, President of SHaRC."

With that, Brad turned on his heel and exited, closing the door behind him.

A few stately women stood among the hundred or so men. Many of them turned slightly to acknowledge the newcomer with a minimal nod before returning to their conversations. They came from all over the world. Though predominantly white, most races and creeds were represented. They were immensely rich judging by their clothes, accessories, and attitudes. From their stiff conversations, he also surmised none of them were friends.

No one approached him. He continued observing the assembled crowd. After a few seconds, he began to recognize many of them. Two were wealthy Russians who had bought major soccer teams on a whim. Others were famous dictators or autocrats. He spotted an Arab prince who had just ascended the throne. A Swedish billionaire running for prime minister. A Chinese businessman who had just paid the highest price ever for a piece of art. More faces came to him as he completed his observations.

A hand squeezed his elbow. "Yuri, there you are."

He turned to find Chuck Roche, leaning on his silver-handled cane. "Mr. President-Elect, good evening."

"You must have a million questions, my boy. Walk with me."

They promenaded through the crowd, Roche nodding and speaking to the others who paid him no more than slight attention. They twisted their way to the balcony. When they exited the loud interior, Roche closed the door behind them. He pulled two cigars from his breast pocket and offered one up.

Yuri waved it off, wary of any offerings.

Roche lit his and puffed a few times. "You have to be the quickest thinker I've ever heard of. My people are quite good. They tell me you gave them the slip six times. Of course, they would've had you in Brazil if Popov hadn't meddled—against my wishes."

It could be a trick. It could be the truth. If there was one thing Roche was famous for, it was lying. Yuri didn't react.

"You're understandably cautious." Roche waved his cigar at the crowd inside. "Relax. Welcome to Regents United for the Legacy Eternal. RULE for short. It was originally named something in French. It sounded better. But our forefathers had to dump Napoleon after Waterloo, the anti-French contingent converted it to English. You've heard of our public facing think tank, Global Economic Development Institute?"

"Yes," Yuri said. "Are you a GEDI knight?"

Roche shook his cigar at him. "Don't get cute."

Yuri looked over Roche's shoulder at the people inside. Vultures.

Roche puffed his cigar.

"For centuries, this group worked through governments." Roche turned to the sea. "We've had puppets, we've had partners, kings, queens, princes, generals; we've had all kinds of arrangements. Then Teddy Roosevelt came along—quite by accident—and took democracy seriously. RULE shored things up with Harding and Coolidge, but the Depression swung the pendulum back to democracy. Took us another fifty years to get things back under control. It's been a long, expensive trip."

"My, how you've suffered." Yuri parked his butt on the balustrade and crossed his arms.

"That smart mouth won't get you very far." Roche puffed and blew out a big blue cloud.

Yuri wondered if they were going to kill him. Perhaps all the nice clothes and fair treatment was part of a killing sport devised by the rich to amuse themselves. But they wouldn't have bothered with a new suit and a manicure if that was the end game. They wanted something. He had a thousand questions about what RULE wanted, but he heeded his mother's proverb: *a fly will not get into a closed mouth.*

"Do you know Yeschenko?" Roche asked.

"What I've read in *Pravda*."

"He's a good man with a sharp eye. He called a special session of the board just to tell them that you'd formed Stateless Hackers ... whatever it is. Strangelove was going to kill you, he said."

Roche waited for Yuri's reaction like a vulture observing a mouse for signs of life.

After a second, Yuri responded. "Stateless Hacktivist and Resistance Collective, SHaRC."

"Awful name. A good consultant would've spared you the embarrassment."

"Says the man who belongs to RULE."

"Touché." Roche glared at him. "But don't get cocky. No matter what you call us, we own a quarter of the world."

Roche returned to his cigar and blew a cloud out over the abyss. "Your methods have proven valuable. We need good men like you and your SHaRCs."

Roche rested his forearms on the marble rail and watched the waves slam into the rocks.

After a minute of silence, Yuri sighed sarcastically. "The suspense is killing me."

Angry eyes swept back to him. Roche snarled and poked at him with his cigar. "My men could've killed you in that stinking hotel room. Is that the life you want to lead? Looking over your shoulder for Roche Security all the time? Hell, boy, I could snap my fingers and have you tossed over this railing."

A hot flash of rage overwhelmed him. He grabbed the President-Elect by the throat and pushed the old man over the marble until most of his weight tipped over the balancing point. He pulled the switchblade and snicked it open and held it to Roche's face. The miserable old man's life was literally in his hands.

The President-Elect's eyes went wild with fear.

Yuri said, "Never threaten a man who has nothing to lose."

He heard the clicks and rattles of weapons drawn. He could sense the Secret Service rifles pointed at him from a hundred yards away. He pushed Roche's weight farther over the edge. If anything happened to Yuri, Roche would die, and someone would have a whole lot of explaining to do.

"Drop him." Behind him, a calm voice spoke in Russian. "You'd be doing the world a favor."

Yuri considered his options but didn't want to test them. Not yet. He pulled Roche back from the brink, set him on his feet, and smacked the cane hard across his chest.

Roche grabbed the cane, glared at the newcomer, then at Yuri.

"Beat it," Yuri's benefactor said in English.

"You'll regret this," Roche hissed, his eyes sliding left and right. He hobbled away, trying to suppress his gasps.

"You've proven your own point—bluffing is stupid." Mikhail Yeschenko stepped out of the shadows and switched back to Russian. "The only thing he knows about your capture is what I've told him. You don't have to like him to join our group. No one does, and yet here we are."

"Join? I was kidnapped at gunpoint."

"My, how you've suffered." Yeschenko ran Yuri's lapel between his thumb and fingers.

"I must admit, it was not as bad as the Holocaust."

Both men fake-chuckled at his crude joke.

"Roche." Yeschenko put his palms on the railing and watched the roiling waves. "He's the most important man in the world. Just ask him. He'll be the first to tell you. We couldn't believe the Americans elected him, but we're not about to draw attention to the gift they've given us."

Yuri observed him closely. Years ago, Yeschenko walked away from the collapsing Soviet empire with the largest tracts of oil fields under his control. He managed to convert the oil rights to cash and the cash into shipping before the government took the oil fields back. He had proven himself a smart man capable of surviving tumultuous political landscapes.

"Do I have a choice about joining?" Yuri asked.

"Everyone has a choice." Yeschenko pointed at the sheer cliffs below. "You are being offered an opportunity to work for RULE."

"If I choose this work, do I become a billionaire?"

"You don't 'become' a billionaire." Yeschenko looked up quickly. "No one hands you billions. RULE is not a benevolent society. If you want money, you take it."

"What is it?" Yuri glanced back at the party inside. "Some kind of secret society?"

"Secret?" Yeschenko scoffed. "Hardly. We've been around forever. We will be around forever. Ours is a natural formation. We seek each other out. We always have. We always will. We make no secret of who we are. As a distraction, we plant stories about secret societies and conspiracies like the Tri-Lateral Commission, the Rothschilds, the Illuminati, the Deep State. But we remain in the light. We drive Lamborghinis, buy football clubs, race yachts, build palaces. The people know us and admire us for our success. They even vote for us where that's allowed. Nothing secret at all."

Yuri watched him in silence.

"You've been seeking us out," Yeschenko said, "and you don't even know it. When you formed SHaRC, you were seeking us."

"I formed SHaRC because people like you made me crash two American airliners. It was the only thing we could do to survive. You ruined our lives. I've had to kill people to escape the Americans. They will hunt us down and—"

"Don't whine to me about that little incident." Yeschenko sneered, waving away Yuri's complaint. "In a matter of days, Roche will prove Sabel Technology wrong by bringing in the perpetrators. I've not decided who did it yet. Puerto Rican separatists? Chechen rebels? Neo-Nazis? Maybe a resurgent FARC faction? Who do you prefer?"

"Not ISIS?"

"Passé."

"Puerto Ricans then. They opened fire in the American Congress sixty years ago." Yuri observed his benefactor carefully. "But can I trust the Americans?"

"You saw the man who runs America now." Yeschenko put a patronizing hand on his shoulder. "Are you worried?"

"How can I trust you?" Yuri stepped back.

"The airline disaster was Roche, Popov, and Strangelove. Their methods were great thirty years ago, but now they're pointless. Roche came up with a plan for RULE to take over the USA and Popov bought into it. All Roche cares about is leading the parade of his worshippers. He doesn't care about where they're going or how to get there. Within a year, he'll be in for a rude awakening. He promised jobs and healthcare and tax cuts without any idea how to produce results."

"Then why are you happy he was elected?"

"We aren't interested in making Roche look good." Yeschenko

spread his hands. "We want the same thing you want, Yuri. We want the stateless, nationless world. A world without regulations, without sanctions. A world where you can be free to pursue your business interests without being forced to compensate every worthless farmer who lives downstream."

Yuri took a moment to roll the words around in his head. "Strangelove helped Roche by creating disasters to fit Roche's campaign. Then what did I do that you liked? The planted news stories?"

"Ah! Yes. Those were my ideas." Yeschenko smiled. "You didn't know it, but you had help from our friends at Cambridge Analysis Group. They matched voter registrations at the precinct level to five thousand publicly available data points on each person in the USA. You created thousands of bizarre news stories targeting the specific hot-button for each American voter."

"Just like we did for Brexit." Yuri stroked the stubble on his chin. "We fed anti-Hungarian stories to the man who hates Hungarians, we sent anti-union stories his union-hating wife, free-trade stories to his anti-globalization sister."

"Don't forget the truly unbelievable stories like the candidate who ran a pedophile ring in a pizza parlor."

"In chaos," Yuri began to nod, "there is opportunity."

"Opportunity exists when my house is in order, and the other guy is in chaos. Roche wasn't an alternative candidate, he's a chaos candidate. He can never stop us because he has no idea how to govern." Yeschenko turned to the ocean, his hands on the balustrade. "You have already been doing everything we need done. We need SHaRC to weaponize distrust around the world. We need to keep governments paralyzed. This is a new century and a new paradigm." Yeschenko waved dismissively over the cliff. "Nations and governments are so twentieth century."

Yuri pursed his lips and squinted. "No Russia? No Britain? No Germany?"

"USA and NATO and the EU," Yeschenko said, "are just self-righteous thugs who want to dictate what's right and wrong. They use terms like regulation, sanctions, international trade law, but it always works in someone else's favor. Never in mine. And never in yours. Your work in Georgia, Brexit, and the USA was perfect. The future belongs to those who can wreck the trust that people place in mythological institutions like the free press, the FBI, political parties, Interpol, CIA, the World Trade Organization."

"And when they no longer trust their establishment, you can control any markets you want."

Yeschenko bowed with feigned humility. "Right now, they don't believe their scientists. They don't believe their news organizations. They don't believe their institutions. It's working."

"How does SHaRC make billions doing that?" Yuri asked.

"You successfully financed your exit from Stavanger by reading emails from international companies and placing bets on their stock performance. Your work was so impressive that the people in the room behind us have coughed up seed capital for a new private equity company. We expect big returns. Only the American SEC stands in your way. They're one of the institutions you can cripple with the help of Roche."

A grin grew across Yuri's face. "He pledged to deregulate the financial industry."

"And you can help him by planting stories about how the SEC is hobbling jobs in America." Yeschenko patted his shoulder. "Now you see why we tolerate him?"

The duplicity in every concept streaming from Yeschenko's mind alarmed Yuri. How could he ever trust a man who propagated distrust? For now, he would play along and make sure not to object.

"I like working with RULE." Yuri straightened up, ready to salute.

"Don't worry, you've already been hired. There's no ceremony. We will give you instructions. You do your part. I will be your contact. Our friends will accommodate you anywhere you want to set up." Yeschenko leaned in conspiratorially. "I hope you don't plan to stay in Albania. Terrible food and the women are mean."

"We liked St. Barts. Or maybe Brazil."

"The French police are too sophisticated. Go for Brazil." Yeschenko shook his hand. "By the way, you have a few messes to clean up before you start. You can't leave people walking around knowing who you are and what you can do. They might hunt you down and wreck our plans. For that, Brad is at your beck and call."

"Doesn't Brad work for Roche Security?"

"He does. But I am the customer who hires Brad's team for missions like contacting you in Stavanger and bringing you in when you didn't trust me."

Yuri squinted in confusion. "Why not just start your own security company?"

"Yuri, you disappoint me." Yeschenko leaned back. "When they get caught, who do they work for?"

"They work for Roche, but he can't divulge his client without losing credibility with the rest of his customers. Your anonymity is guaranteed." Yuri nodded as he thought. "Brilliant."

"As I said, clean up your messes. Brad is at your command." Yeschenko walked away. He stopped after a couple yards and faced Yuri and wagged a finger. "But don't tell Chuck."

CHAPTER 69

WATCHING DAVID WATSON CROSS THE runway brought Pia's temper to a boil. She kept her clenched fists in her pockets and a blank look on her face. The soldiers finished disarming her team and carefully stacked the Sabel weapons just out of reach.

Watson stood off sixty yards. After everything was secured and the lieutenant gave him an all-clear sign, Watson came forward like a meerkat approaching a tiger. Twenty yards away, he stopped with an I'm-close-enough look.

The wind blew, sleet peppered them, and for a long time, no one spoke.

"This is your rodeo, Watson," Pia said. "If you have a question, ask it. If not, we'll be on our way."

"What are you doing out here?"

"Counting polar bears." She saw the lieutenant smirk before catching himself and returning to his soldier stare.

"No, you're not." Watson closed the gap by five yards. "You're meeting Viktor Popov."

"Not much of a meeting. His escort shot him for stealing from the Federation. Check it out. His body is out there in the snow full of Russian bullets."

Watson looked out across the white into the mist. He had the look of a conflicted man. Conflicted by the choice of confirming her story firsthand the way a career FBI man would do it, or bluffing his way through the rest of the encounter.

"Did he give you a box?" Watson asked.

"You mean the box of records Kasey Earl took from Roche

Industries' warehouse? Yes. He did give me those. And Tania is inside the jet uploading photographs of them to the cloud as we speak."

"Nice bluff. Sabel Satellites don't cover this island." Watson gave her a tight, smug smile and braved five more yards. "Did you give Viktor the Pozdeeva files?"

"His sergeant took them." She pointed to the sky. "Moscow needs the evidence."

Watson snapped his fingers at the lieutenant. The officer dispatched two soldiers to the jet. A few minutes later, a scuffle could be heard inside the aircraft.

The lieutenant dispatched another pair.

Pia noticed the lieutenant and Jacob staring each other down in some kind of silent communication. After a minute, the lieutenant shrugged and mouthed, *orders.*

A short time later, a soldier with a bleeding nose descended the airstair with a box in his hands. Two more bruised soldiers came next holding a writhing Tania by the arms and legs. They deposited her next to Pia, then retreated to whisper something to their lieutenant. He rolled his eyes, nodded, and the pair ran back into the jet. They returned supporting one of their own who walked with great difficulty.

Tania leaned close to Pia and whispered, "Leroy Johnson's accomplice was Watson."

A soldier pushed Tania back.

Pia felt her anger rising. Her eyes swept the tarmac, calculating her odds for killing the bastard where he stood and getting away with it. With a platoon of paratroopers behind him, it was a short calculation. Her powerlessness infuriated her even more. She swore to herself the man would die. Soon.

Watson narrowed his eyes to slits.

The soldier with the box handed it off to Watson and rejoined his platoon. Watson rifled through it for a few seconds.

The wind stopped. Every other sound was absorbed in the fog's cold embrace.

"For your information—" Watson said loud enough for everyone to hear "—President Hunter has determined these documents to be classified Top Secret. Divulging their existence or their contents to anyone would be a violation of the Espionage Act of 1917, punishable by death. There is a list of people who the president has authorized to see them. No one here is on that list. Anyone who has seen them and leaks their contents will be prosecuted."

"You will answer for the downing of Flight 1028, Watson." Pia's voice echoed around them. "We have Strangelove's notes. We know he did it to help get Roche elected. We know you were there—you're the *Badger*."

"He's a great man. You can't make unfounded charges against him. Roche didn't know anything. I never told him about it. How was I supposed to know Strangelove would do it? I thought he was joking."

"The crime scene report indicated Lloyd Aston's suicide was staged." Pia crossed her arms. "They pointed out that the gunshot residue covered only the top of his wrist and not the fingers, as if someone had put a hand on top of his and pulled the trigger for him."

"So?" Watson sneered.

"I know it was you, Watson. Your name is on those canceled checks."

"Lieutenant—" Watson turned to the soldiers and pointed at Pia "—kill them all."

The soldiers looked to their officer. He stared at Watson.

"You heard me, soldier." Watson's voice strained. "That's an order."

"With all due respect, sir." The lieutenant's mouth opened and closed a couple times before he found the words. "If that was an order—which it is not—it would be an illegal order. You're nobody. If he's sworn in, you'll be the president's chief of staff, but that's a few weeks away. Even when the transition takes place, you still won't be in my chain of command."

The soldiers squared off against Watson.

Watson and the lieutenant had a staring contest.

"Fuck you, then." Watson dropped the box and crossed to Pia.

He pulled up two yards away, out of her reach.

"Who cares?" He leaned forward, up on his tiptoes, as he shouted. "There's nothing you can do about it. Your daddy's dead. Nothing in that box will see the light of day. Any pictures you might have taken are Top

Secret and must be destroyed. If you don't comply with that order, you will face the death penalty."

"Not if the president is a criminal—" she lowered her voice to a growl "—involved in a conspiracy to commit murder."

Pia produced her phone, pulled up a file, and pressed play. The distinct voices of Watson and Roche echoed in the frozen silence.

Watson: "You guys are underestimating her. She'll never stop coming after us. Our only option is to infiltrate Sabel Security and kill her—now."

Roche: "How many times do I have to tell you two? I'm bringing her inside the campaign. She'll come around. But, just in case, you need to be close to her."

A silence fell over the group for a long time. A white-tailed eagle screeched overhead.

"Did you really think we're that dumb?" Pia's killer stare made Watson step back.

Watson looked over the rest of her team and found no sympathy, no one receptive to an excuse. He turned to the lieutenant and his soldiers to find the same glaring hatred.

"Doesn't matter!" Watson stepped close to her and lowered his volume so only the two of them could hear. "You can't touch me. You want to know what happened? Roche paid for it. Hunter assigned McCarty to hire a crew. He pulled Leroy Johnson and me. I was an intern that summer and starving. They promised me cash every year for the rest of my life and a career at the FBI. I took it. If I had to do it all over again—I'd do it all over again. Roche is a genius. He's a giant among little men. Whatever he wants, I get it for him. You blew it. You had a chance. You turned him down. Well, news flash, bitch: we won. He's president, and you're not. Want to hear something that's going to make you really sick? They gave me a pardon."

Pia's gloved fist slammed into his jaw.

He never saw it coming. He fell backward.

Sitting up on his elbows, he rubbed his chin, then looked up at her. "It's a pardon for anything and everything, and there's no date on it. I can kill you, then fill it in anytime I want. So—fuck you."

She kicked him in the ribs while he was down. "It won't stick. He's not even in office yet."

"Hunter pardoned me. He's going to pardon her. There's no recourse on presidential pardons."

Pia clenched her fists and turned to Tania, who shrugged. She then turned to Jacob. He shook his head and pressed his hand down as if saying "later."

Watson crabbed to his feet and dusted himself off.

Jacob turned his gaze to the Army lieutenant. For a moment, the two had a telepathic conversation of some kind. If she didn't know better, it looked as if they were going through coded options like a pitcher and catcher. Jacob tilted his head a fraction of an inch. The lieutenant's eyes shifted from right to left, then settled on a young private. They repeated the odd dance a couple more times, all in the space of a second.

The officer shrugged apologetically. He turned to Watson. "Sir, my unit's moving out. You are free to remain here if you wish."

With that, the platoon double-timed their march to the C-130 and ran up the ramp.

Watson watched them for a second. He glanced over his shoulder to find the cold stares of Pia and her agents tracking him. He pointed at her and shouted, "You're dead, Sabel! It's only a matter of time."

He ran, grabbing the box as he went. The ramp was lifting and the plane rolling when he jumped on board. The bird rolled to the far end of the runway, where it almost disappeared in the mists. It wheeled around, throttled up, and came roaring back toward them. It lifted off, dipped a wing, then banked, tracking back to the mainland.

Pia looked at Tania. "Was he right? No satellite connection? Nothing uploaded to the cloud?"

"Nothing connected, and they crushed my phone just to make sure."

"How did he know we were here?"

Tania bit her thumbnail while staring at the ground. "Nothing tracks this piece of rock. He didn't follow Popov—that cagey old bastard never used a phone. Popov's soldiers relayed everything. There's no way they heard Popov say, 'Attu Island'. Yuri Belenov used a system Bianca couldn't trace. Gotta be a spy in Popov's group."

"CIA?"

"Or FSB. Or someone." Tania pursed her lips and nodded. "Given his timing, I'd say Hunter and Roche wanted you to kill Viktor Popov today. You tied up a loose end for them."

Pia turned to Jacob. "What was that thing you did with the lieutenant?"

"I asked him if he could arrange a weapons malfunction to end Watson's miserable life. He gave it some serious thought. But he had too many new guys fresh out of boot camp in the platoon. You can't jade them right off like that."

"You have a plan B then?"

Jacob looked left, then right, then spoke in a barely audible whisper. "Later."

CHAPTER 70

THE PILOT SAID WE WOULDN'T get into Sabel Satellite range to use our phones until we were near Hudson Bay. He went on about polar flight paths and other things that made my head hurt. I left the cockpit and tried sleeping on the divan in back. I didn't fit. Dhanpal slept just fine curled up on the facing couch. Miguel stretched out on two facing seats farther forward.

I was twisting and turning, trying to get comfy when I noticed Ms. Sabel's presence. Dhanpal woke up.

"Would you mind if I had a word with Jacob?" She gave him a nod toward the front.

Dhanpal grabbed his blanket and gave us the space.

She sat on the opposite sofa, crossed her legs and looked out the window, then at the floor. A troubled woman.

"Seeing recurring visions of Popov's shattered head?" I asked.

"No."

"Having regrets about the killing?"

"No."

I waited until her gaze met mine. I raised my brows, leaving it for her to speak next.

"What's the best way to kill David Watson?"

Whoa now. Mercury put his hands out as if pushing her away. *That's not a good ice-breaker for a Caesar, bro. She's going straight into conspiracy to commit and pre-meditated. You gotta talk her off the ledge. Killing Watson is your job. You can walk right up to him and pop him. Broad daylight.*

I said, *I'd get caught. He's a big deal in the government.*

Mercury said, *So? You do a few decades in the big house. No big deal. Your life sucks anyway. Vulcan will chill with you. He's got nothing going on these days.*

I shook my head. "A man like Watson needs to be put down worse than a rabid dog. I'll take care of it."

"He's mine." She drummed her fingers on the top of the sofa. "Killing Popov felt … good."

No, no, no. Mercury spun away and put his forehead against the mahogany wall. *You've got to talk some sense into her, homie. She's going whacko on me. She could go on a killing spree that would make Diocletian look like a puppy.*

I said, *Who?*

Mercury said, *Oh, just an old emperor I talked into killing all the Christians and confiscating their stuff. Got my ass hauled in front of the galactic god council for that one. And back in those days, the Christians weren't even rich. We didn't make enough to pay the Legion. Total waste of time.*

"You OK?" She tilted her head.

"Killing should never feel good."

"I didn't ask you to judge me." She gave me a long cold glare. "I asked you to advise me. Popov's dead. He left Roche in charge of our country. I'm going to take down Roche, one step at a time."

And killing Watson was her next step because he was the triggerman in her parent's murders and the traitor who told Strangelove how to snatch her. I blew out a long breath to ease my conscience. It didn't work.

"Ever hear of Sun Tzu?" I leaned forward, trying to keep my voice down. "A Chinese general in the sixth century BCE. He said, 'All warfare is based on deception; the supreme art of war is to subdue the enemy without fighting.'"

"'Let your plans be as dark and impenetrable as night, and when you move, fall like a thunderbolt.' Dad made me re-read *The Art of War* every year. I find it relevant in both soccer and business."

There was no talking her out of it. So, I gave her some hypothetical situations. I tried my best to make it sound impossible with all the surveillance cameras everywhere and the license plate readers and the response times for cops and the blood splatter nerds and the capacity of hospitals to save lives. She asked my theories about defeating those issues. I gave them to her reluctantly. The grilling went on for a long time. When she was satisfied, she thanked me and stood up and started back up the aisle.

"I forgot to tell you," she said over her shoulder. "I invited Sylvia to the Gardens to thank her for the help. She should be there when we land."

My heart attack commenced immediately, but Ms. Sabel never saw me dying because she'd already walked away.

Mercury laughed. *'So daring in love, and so dauntless in war; Have ye e'er heard of gallant like young Lochinvar?' That would be Sir Walter Scott, homie; old pal of mine from way back when white dudes' poetry was all the rage. Holy Luna, that was a long time ago. Your problem is: you ain't no kind of Lochinvar. You're scared shitless.*

I said, *Things ended badly last time we talked. Not the way I wanted it to go. I'll have to apologize.*

Mercury said, *See that? That's what I'm talking about, bro. That should be a warning sign right there. She should apologize to you. But that's how the Greeks are; it's all about them, all the time. Olympus this and Ares that. Hermes can suck my—*

I said, *Let it go.*

I gave up all hope of trying to sleep and sat there staring out the window, dreaming up ideas for putting my best-ever relationship (probably) back on track. Nothing came to mind since we had a fundamental disagreement on whether killing people was OK. She didn't think it was, but then, she'd never met some of the cretins I've run into. Plenty of people could be taken out, and no one would notice. Like the guy who cuts you off in traffic then flips you off. Or the mom who tells you her two-year-old is going to Harvard and has seven hundred pictures. Or the teenager who can't take your order because she's texting her friends.

Maybe those aren't the best death penalty examples.

Was all the angst worth it? I started to wonder why I even liked her. I knew nothing of her intellectual capacity or if she read books or could live with Mercury. I had no idea if she was healthy or drunk or tidy. I didn't know what kind of movies she liked.

But. She's pretty.

Good enough.

When we landed, the ground crew had my Ferrari warmed up and waiting. Tania jumped in the passenger's seat before I could say no. The others piled into one of Ms. Sabel's limos. I drove through the freezing air of dusk with the top down, the heater cranked up. We arrived at Sabel Gardens, where Tania had left her car.

I planned to run home for a quick nap before meeting Sylvia. But she was standing on the grand staircase when I circled around to drop Tania.

Tania opened the door and spoke to her. "You haven't figured out this guy's a loser yet?"

Sylvia cocked a hip. "Says the woman riding in his hot car."

"She's clever," Tania whispered over her shoulder at me. "This won't last long."

Sylvia slid right in when Tania stepped aside.

"I forgot to say something last time we parted. You saved my life. Thank you." She gave me a kiss, then pulled back. "But you kill people. I don't know what to do with that."

I cupped her face and kissed her again.

Her nose crinkled. "You need a bath."

We went straight to my place where she took a personal interest in the suds and the rinsing. Then we traded places. Before long the euphemism moved to the bedroom. My massage oil collection and candle selection made her giggle with anticipation. There are no substitutes for experienced hands in a situation of that kind. Unless one counts tongue tricks. Sylvia was satisfied twice before our dreamy romp came to a mutual conclusion.

It was the best afternoon of my entire life. The way she cuddled led me to believe she felt the same.

We stared at the ceiling.

"There's something magical about you," I said. "I've never felt such a magnetic attraction."

She purred. "Same."

Having never experienced a post-coital, single-word answer from a woman before, I sat up on an elbow and admired her cheekbones. "Call me crazy, but I feel like you're an ancient soul."

"I don't want to fight this time." She sat up and ran her fingertips along my jaw. "Let's enjoy the moment and talk about the future. Tell me your vision. What does Jacob Stearne's life look like in five years?"

"How about I tell you over a dozen oysters at the Old Angler's Inn?"

We dressed and drove out to the restaurant nestled in the trees on MacArthur Boulevard. Built out of a nineteenth-century stone farmhouse, the rooms were converted to dining and drinking areas decades ago. Each room was small and romantic even when it was crowded.

"Five years from now," I said after ordering wine, "Jacob Stearne is the luckiest guy in the world. He's married to a goddess, has two kids, and a modest home in Bethesda."

"A modest home—with a Ferrari parked out front?" she laughed.

"Yeah, well, that's going up for sale next week. I can't afford a flat tire much less the insurance." We sipped our wine. "What about you?"

"I would be married to a sensible man." She reached for my hand and held it. "One who believes in making love, not war."

Mercury appeared tableside with a serviette over his forearm and bowed to my ear. *That's what I'm talking about, bro. She's gotcha. Making you choose between love and war. Why not have both, like my boys did with the Sabine women?*

I said, *That's so not acceptable in modern moral terms. Say. Could you give me a little privacy? This is a complex negotiation.*

Mercury said, *You negotiate me out of the picture, and I'm calling Ukko. He be putting lightning bolts in your mouth and out your ass for eternity. Feel me?*

"I believe in making love and war." I smiled.

She didn't.

Not funny. Apparently.

"Well, someone has to keep the country safe." I shrugged. "I'm a militant pacifist—I'm willing to fight for peace."

"There's an oxymoron without any oxy."

A text came in just in time to save me from the daggers in her cold gaze. It was my insurance agent lamenting the fact that he couldn't sell me insurance because the car was already insured. It was registered to the company, paid in full, and I was listed as the primary operator. A grin grew across my face. Ms. Sabel was covering the expenses. I could keep the Ferrari as my company car. I was leading a charmed life. A beautiful woman and a cool car. This was, without a doubt, the best day of my life. Ever.

Then I returned to Sylvia's glare.

"Hey, you were that guy on TV, right?" A stranger stood next to our table pointing at me. "At the Sabel funeral, am I right?"

He was a veteran. I could tell by the way he carried himself. He had the confidence of a man carrying a sidearm and the knowledge of how and when to use it. And then there was the haircut. Dead giveaway. His smirking, almost angry attitude struck me as off-key.

"Yes, that was me." I gave him my soldier stare. "Not to be rude, friend, but we're having a private conversation here."

"Wow, she's gorgeous. Is she your girl?" He leered at her, leaning over and looking down her modest neckline.

I stood, put a hand on his chest and pushed him upright. "I take it you missed the manners sessions at boot camp."

He was a short, wiry guy. He grabbed my wrist and tried to wrench it off. My arm was immobile.

"We're watching you, Stearne." He pushed up to my face. "You and your little bitch."

He wrenched away and walked out of the room. I watched every step he took before sitting back down.

"I'm not a fan of toxic masculinity." Sylvia reached for my hand again. "He's an asshole, so what? I don't like men fighting for my honor—or whatever macho thing this is."

"I love honor more than I fear death."

"Ugh." Her nose crinkled. "That sounds so ... Roman."

"Julius Caesar." My eyes remained glued to the exit. If that guy came back, I intended to rearrange his nose.

"Romans were all about violence, oppression, and war."

Mercury stood behind her, pointing with an I-told-you-so face.

The guy stepped back into the room, holding his phone up. He snapped a couple pictures, his flash drawing everyone's attention.

"America's been running the world for two hundred years." I stood and started for the door. "The Romans ran it for a thousand." I got to the exit and called over my shoulder. "I'll be right back."

The guy wasn't in the next room or the bar. Then I heard the gasps of old ladies shocked about some impropriety or another. I circled back to the dining room to find Sylvia holding her napkin up in front of the guy's phone while he flashed pictures. He saw me and ran out the back of the room.

I chased him through the bar and out into the parking lot. He jumped in the passenger seat of a Toyota and spewed gravel out onto MacArthur Boulevard.

My Ferrari was the perfect weapon for the occasion. I jumped in, fired up the bi-turbo V8, and blew gravel until the tires found bedrock below and shot the car forward like a cannonball. The 488 Spider accelerated down the empty road with enough velocity to scare the hell out of me. In three seconds, I'd blown through sixty mph and saw the Toyota's taillights disappear around a bend in the lonely road.

I also saw Mercury flying horizontally next to me, the brass wings on his silver helmet flapping like a hummingbird's. *Dawg. You ever stop to think why some random guy would piss you off on purpose—then run like hell?*

I looked at him instead of the road. *Ambush?*

He said, *Or?*

We negotiated a sweeping turn. Ahead was the Toyota. I was closing extremely fast.

I slammed on the brakes, scrubbing speed as the ABS furiously chirped the tires. When it got below fifteen, I rolled out and let the car accelerate away.

I stood up, feeling my fresh scrapes and bruises.

I looked at Mercury. *They wanted me within range of their remote detonator.*

Mercury touched his nose.

The explosion blew the treetops backward several feet before they recovered to upright. The shock wave knocked me back on the pavement.

I called Ms. Sabel. No answer. I texted her. "You're in extreme danger."

CHAPTER 71

Yuri stood on the balcony overlooking the long, sweeping curve of beach that made Santos a popular destination for Brazilians. *Sheez Music* by Dumpstaphunk filled the apartment with New Orleans funk. Below him, people bathed in the afternoon sun and cars paraded up the beachfront boulevard. He took a deep breath and considered the wisdom of what he was about to do. Some might think him crazy, but he considered it an honorable course of action.

His front door buzzed.

He opened it to find Roman in the hallway, shocked and breathless. The bandages encircling his ribs bulged beneath his knit shirt.

"I'm not going to apologize." Yuri stepped back and waved Roman in.

Roman hesitated. Yuri shrugged, turned his back, and went to the living room. He pulled two glasses off the shelf, set them on the bar, and produced a bottle of Tovarich vodka and poured.

Roman came in like a wary cat, inching along the wall.

"Why didn't you tell me they approached you?" Yuri took one glass and held the other out to Roman.

"What do you want?" Roman asked.

"Your help."

They eyed each other for a silent minute. Roman took a step forward, then another until he reached the bar. He stared at the drink.

"Fine." Yuri set the glass down. "Don't drink. I'll talk. When Strangelove stabbed me, it was because I had betrayed him. This is how I know your fury, resentment, humiliation. I lived through it myself. However, there is a fundamental difference between Strangelove and me.

He did it to control me, to own me. What I did to you was in anger. It will remain a serious regret in my professional life. And even so, I know if the circumstance were repeated, I would do it again. I am a violent man."

Roman picked up the glass and tasted the vodka. He eased onto a bar stool. "Why are you telling me this?"

"If you accept my proposal, you should know not to keep things from me." Yuri drank. "It turned out OK, but you didn't know them. You trusted an outsider. That was stupid."

Roman regarded his former boss. He took another sip and didn't respond.

"The other members of SHaRC are excited about regrouping." Yuri waved around the room. "We've bought out the top half of this building for them. They're on their way."

Roman appeared to be thinking through which questions he should ask, or if he should ask any at all. His gaze took in the room until he spotted something on a bookshelf.

He pointed to a line of six antennae peeking above the books. "What's that?"

"An MG-40 electronics jammer." Yuri flicked open his switchblade and toyed with its weight. "4G, GSM, LTE, Bluetooth, WiFi—all signals blocked. My neighbors hate me right now."

Roman watched the blade for a moment, then met Yuri's gaze. They remained motionless and wordless. Yuri observed his lieutenant's pulse rising on his neck. Fine beads of sweat broke out on the man's forehead.

After a while, Roman blew out an exhausted breath. He pulled up his shirt and peeled off a layer of tape. From within the winds of the bandage, he pulled a Bluetooth microphone. He handed it to Yuri.

Yuri snapped the blade back in the stiletto. "Did you volunteer?"

"Not exactly." Roman slid the remaining vodka down his throat. "They wanted insurance."

"Put it back." Yuri rounded the bar, found the vodka, and poured another round. "Do you want to hear my offer?"

"Why offer me anything when you don't trust me?"

Yuri let out a laugh and handed Roman his drink.

"Over the last few months, I've learned one thing: trust no one." Yuri took a sip. "You are the best lieutenant I've ever had. If you don't take the job, I will settle for someone else. I won't trust him more than I don't trust you. He won't be as good, but I'll make it work. You owe me nothing."

"You're honest. I'll give you that." Roman picked up his glass. "You're offering me an opportunity with RULE?"

"Not exactly."

"They are dangerous people, Yuri." Roman's posture sank. "They found us twice. We cannot betray them."

Yuri motioned for Roman to follow him and crossed the room to the balcony. They stood side-by-side to admire the view.

"Rich men make everyone dance for them," Yuri said. "Soldiers, hackers, women, politicians—everyone dances when oligarchs snap their fingers. We have danced for them. You danced for them when you betrayed me on Saint Bart's. You danced for them in Liberia. I danced for them at a big dinner a few days ago." Yuri took another sip. "Yeschenko snapped his fingers and, very nicely, told me we would be his techno-slaves. To be fair, he promised we would be rich slaves, but we would not be Stateless Hactivists working for ourselves. We will dance for him."

"They gave us our families back."

"Yes," Yuri said through clenched teeth. "Some walking, others in urns."

Roman's gaze fell to his glass. Tears filled his eyes. Yuri waited for the moment of mourning to pass.

"We will make them pay for that treachery." Yuri let the hatred inside him seep into his hissed words. "We owe them nothing."

"They forced me—"

"Don't feel shame." Yuri grabbed him. "You did what was necessary. You are standing here because I know your weaknesses. I don't trust you. That is something I can deal with. To me, it is far more honest than the lies Yeschenko and Roche tell me."

"What is your plan?"

"For SHaRC to succeed, we will need to dance for them a little longer." Yuri leaned his forearms on the railing and let the breeze stroke his face. "We will lure them into a state of wonder at our accomplishments. All the while we will stockpile our malware on their devices. When we own their communications, we can move on them. Exactly as we did to Popov."

"Bold." Roman watched him as the waves rolled in and the beachgoers splashed near the shore. "There are many risks."

"They gave me a mercenary to do whatever needs to be done." Yuri paused for effect. "Brad."

"You're going to test him?"

Yuri nodded. "Sabel and Stearne are the immediate enemy of everyone combined: RULE, Roche, Hunter, us. No one will mind if we take them out."

"That's what Strangelove wanted."

"He was right. They are the only ones who can tie us to #HuntersFail. Roche will catch some terrorists in a few days, but the router logs in Sabel's possession could still upset that plan. Brad will rid us of Sabel."

"What if that doesn't work?"

"I also have a backup plan." Yuri grinned and took another sip.

"You plan to blame Roche?" Roman allowed himself a smile.

"If we need to, why not?" Yuri patted his friend's shoulder. "If not Roche, many members of RULE are not as sophisticated as they believe. We can pin it on anyone who pisses us off."

"What is our goal?"

"As it was in the beginning: to build a stateless world for virtuous hackers. To take all Yeschenko's money and Roche's money and make it our money. Why should we work for them when we can be oligarchs? You could buy Chelsea, I'll buy the LA Rams, Petr can buy the Yankees. We are not destined to be servants, Roman. We have the tools. We know how to control the minds of people from the USA to the People's Republic of China. Then we will build our own mercenary army. We will rule anywhere we wish." Yuri paused. "Are you in?"

Roman nodded then held up a finger. "They told me to record—"

"We will pick this up as if we are in the middle of the conversation they planned for you. The one they made you rehearse to test my loyalty.

We will dance for them, Roman." Yuri squeezed his lieutenant's shoulder. "Are you ready?"

Roman nodded.

Yuri unplugged the jammer.

CHAPTER 72

Pia knocked on Stefan's door and waited. She knew how calculated her appearance looked. He had told her on the phone that the kids were away on a play date for the afternoon. He had failed to invite her over. She didn't care.

A light snow drifted down from dark skies. She knocked again, folded her arms and checked the flowerbed strewn with straw for the winter. Her blood pressure had skyrocketed after Dad's death and hadn't come down since. She needed something tangible to make her feel real. She longed for the soothing warmth of love to quell the burning rage in her heart.

Brutal memories exploded in her mind. Her failed attempt to pull Kaspar from the flames. Shooting Popov without an ounce of remorse. Daydreaming about Watson's head exploding from three hollow-points fired at point-blank range. Why did the first image make her feel like crying when the second two made her feel like pumping her fists in the air? Rage and hate seared her insides. She felt herself breathing hard, angry, and tense. She needed the calmness Stefan had subsumed into his being.

Stefan opened the door. Water dripped from his hair, a towel covered his lower half. "Pia? I wasn't expecting—"

She pushed him back inside, kicked the door closed, and smashed her lips against his. In that instant, she wanted every emotion of love to burst forth at once. The safety of a trusted lover, the vulnerability of hot sex, the meaningful tenderness of a soft kiss, the cocoon of two lovers in temporary isolation, the suspension of all worldly problems for an afternoon of commingled spirits—even if it was fleeting. It would be worth the risk to her emotional state on the chance that he might love her as much as she needed to love him.

His towel fell to the floor, and she wanted to step back to apologize for her forwardness. Yet, nothing seemed more meaningless. She pressed into the kiss even harder, hoping to find salvation in his arms. Hoping to find the same kind of quiet he had found.

His arms encircled her. He pressed her against him. The pain in her soul melted. She felt the inner glow of love. Then, as if a veil had been lifted, she understood life's goal: peace. Couch potatoes sought peace through inaction. Champions sought peace through triumph. Alan Sabel sought peace in wealth. She sought peace through revenge. Was any of it worth as much as Stefan's embrace?

She pushed him to the edge of the bed, held up her hand to make him wait, and did her best impression of a stripper. Without his towel, she discovered her dance had the desired effect. When he couldn't take it anymore, he pulled her into his arms. She rode him for what felt like hours. He was a consummate gentleman and a knowledgeable lover. When neither could manage another round, they fell back exhausted, a slick sheen of sweat covering their jellied muscles. They stared at the ceiling.

Darkness dimmed the gray afternoon. Stefan reached for his watch on the nightstand and checked the time. He announced thirty minutes of quiet remained for them. Then the children would return.

She lay her head on his chest and drew lazy circles on his skin.

"What's on your mind?" he asked.

"Nothing."

"Don't lie." He ran his finger down the tip of her nose and over her lips. "Blurt it out."

"How did you do it?" She rolled on her back and stared up. "How did you find peace after you killed your father?"

"Have you killed someone?" He inhaled sharply and pressed a finger to her lips. "Don't answer that."

They lay still for a long time, each sorting through the next few words.

"I went to churches of all kinds," he said. "For days on end, I met with imams and rabbis and ministers and gurus. I took big checks with me and lavished money on their congregations in exchange for spiritual advice."

"Why not therapists?"

"I'd learned something from Alcoholics Anonymous: therapists will tell you why you're a drunk. AA will teach you how to stop drinking. I already knew why I was troubled. I turned to religion to find peace."

"Did you find it?"

"It's a work in progress." He sighed. "They all have similar advice. They asked me to shed everything I did for myself and start doing everything for someone else."

"That's when you gave away your fortune and adopted the kids?"

"No." He turned to face her, half of their faces buried in pillows. "Good advice never makes sense at first, it takes time to seep in. At least, that's how it's been for me. I was deep in lawsuits and criminal investigations and lawyers and … endless problems. Then one day, I stopped for coffee and just sat there staring out the window trying not to read a thousand emails from my attorneys. An older woman wearing a clerical collar smacked my table with a stick. At first, I thought it was a cane or a walking stick, but as we talked, I realized it was just a stick."

"Who was she?"

"I never found out. She sat down, quite uninvited, and told me we are most violent when we're afraid. Violence is the result of fear. She went on to explain that hate begets hate. That fighting with others, verbally, emotionally, legally or literally, gives hate room to flourish. The proper response to hate is not love, it's resistance. Turning the other cheek is not an act of submission or cowardice, it's an act of defiance. Then she left."

"How did that bring about Ethan and Emma?"

"She was right." Stefan rolled onto his back and stared up. "I was afraid. I lived in fear that the survivors of my father's evil enterprises would sue me. I feared the investigation might not clear me. I worried that I would never see you again. It made me violent with terror."

He smiled. "But, that's because it was all about me. What the spiritual leaders told me was true; the woman gave me the key to making it work. She empowered me to defy the things that made me afraid. Defying my attorneys, I paid the victims handsomely. I defied my estate planners and common sense and gave my fortune to charity. I threw myself on the mercy of the court. All my problems evaporated. I dedicated my life to doing something for two survivors who didn't have a lawyer to ask me for compensation: the orphans. From now on, everything I do is for them."

"A noble goal. You're a good parent." Pia heard words coming out of her mouth that she hadn't planned. "I want to be part of that. I want to help."

"That is a problem." Stefan sat up on an elbow and brushed a wisp of her hair back. "I must protect them from violence. You have not renounced it. I asked you to. Yet you have a loaded gun in your purse."

Pia rocked back. She felt as if she'd been punched. She thought through his ideas. They were vastly different from hers. Why did she find it so hard to put down her weapons? Did that make her a bad person? She had saved lives and governments. She had stopped terrorists and murderers. And yet, Stefan's life had turned from horrible to blissful. He lived with the inner peace she sought.

There had to be a way to compromise. She said, "I'm not sure I could—"

He asked, "If you walked into an apartment with a loaded gun in your purse and found a man seconds away from firing a missile at an elementary school, what would you do?"

"I would shoot him."

"Thus the Middle East has burned for centuries. The citizens kill the terrorists and the terrorists' friends rise up and kill the citizens' children, and the parents kill the new terrorists, and more terrorists kill more children. Who is brave enough to stop?"

"I make it stop." She pushed him. "What would you do?"

"I would stand in front of his missile. Defiance." He sounded angry. "Ten thousand years of recorded history and people like you have never prevailed. I'm asking you to renounce violence. Counter hate with defiance."

"That's what I do." Pia felt her head twisting in confused curiosity. "We defy the powerful people who prey on others."

He shook his head. "I'm talking about a higher level of defiance. That's what leads to inner peace. Be willing to die for the meek—not kill for them."

Someone pounded on the door—rapid, insistent and demanding beats.

They looked at each other for a second. Stefan kissed her and got up, put on a robe, and went to the door. Pia slipped on his shirt and followed. He pulled open the door.

Tania burst in, clenching body armor in both hands. She tackled Pia as a bullet tore through Stefan's door.

He slammed it closed. Another bullet ripped through the center. It pierced Tania's leg.

"Damn it." Tania rolled off Pia, clutching her wound. "Do NOT put your phone on total privacy mode, girlfriend! Saw snipers setting up. One out front, another in the back, and a third on the side street."

Stefan called 911.

Pia grabbed his phone and disconnected the call. "They'll kill the first responders."

She ran to the bedroom, grabbed her things, dressed in a flash, donned her armor, and came back.

Tania had made a bandage from Stefan's shirt. She stood and wobbled.

"What's the plan?" Pia asked.

Tania limped to the living room curtain and snuck a peek. "Attack at full speed and hope Miguel got on the other side of him."

A bullet shattered the window.

Pia checked her texts and saw Jacob's urgent warning.

Pia checked her magazines and felt Stefan staring at her. She hugged him with a pistol in each hand. "I can't renounce this. They follow me everywhere I go. I won't see you again until I end this thing." Tears filled her eyes. "It might be a few weeks, it might be the rest of my life, but I'm not going to endanger you or the kids again. I love you."

CHAPTER 73

I WAS SITTING AT THE bottom of the grand staircase in front of Sabel Gardens, whittling a stick for Anoshni to fetch on a beautiful, sunny day. Mercury sprawled out next to me, worshipping Sol Invictus (the sun god, faithless ones). Anoshni trotted back to me with the last stick I threw. He didn't quite get the concept of fetching. Which was why I was trimming the leaves and sharp edges off the new stick in my hand. He dropped to the ground just beyond my reach and proceeded to shred the old stick into toothpicks.

A limo pulled up. The driver got out, opened the rear door and stood by. A few seconds later, Sylvia emerged from the mansion. Sex over the last thirty-six hours had been frequent and heavenly. Unfortunately, the discussions about alternatives to violence between those sessions moved from bad to worse. Our last spoken words were not the words either of us wanted. Seeing her tore my heart in half. But we couldn't stay away from each other.

She stopped at the top of the stairs. The limo driver ran up and took her bag. She met me halfway down.

I opened my arms for a hug.

She hesitated, then closed her eyes and embraced me, squeezing tight. She said, "Thank you for saving my life."

There wasn't any reply to that. I kissed her cheek and ear. I wanted her to stay. I wanted her to quit her minor role in the French soap opera and move to Bethesda. But a warrior and a pacifist have issues to work out before they make lifetime commitments. I said, "When will you be back?"

"It's your turn to visit me." She pulled back to shine her pale-blues at me. "Maybe we could spend a weekend on Santorini."

Mercury squeezed into our cramped space. *You don't go anywhere near Greece. You hear me, dawg? She'll take you straight to Aeaea and that'll be the last anyone hears of you.*

I said, *Take me where?*

Mercury said, *Aeaea, Circe's island. Remember? Ulysses told Penelope the reason he couldn't get back to Ithaca for twenty years was because Circe drugged him and forced him to have sex with her.*

I said, *What's so bad about drugs and sex?*

Mercury smacked me and said, *Dude. Do not go to Greece with Sylvia—or we're done.*

"I'd love to watch you work." I kissed her lips. "Could I visit the set?"

"After I refused to give the producer a…" She huffed. "I'm pretty sure my character's going to get hit by a car."

"I don't care if it's dinner theater, I'd love to see you act."

The limo driver coughed politely. Sylvia reached in her purse and pulled out a book and handed it to me. *The Book of Forgiving* by Desmond Tutu, the wisdom of a man who healed his nation after generations of apartheid. "Read this before we meet again. Please."

I stepped away and grabbed my gift for her off the step. *The Forever War* by Dexter Filkins, a decade-old book about civilian and military service and sacrifice in Afghanistan and Iraq. "If you read this."

She gave me a long kiss, then broke it off and ran to the limo. She stopped before getting in. With tears in her eyes, she blew me a kiss. Then she got in, and the limo pulled away.

My sister once told me that all a woman wants is a man she can change from whoever he is into whoever she wants him to be. When I asked why women didn't look for men who didn't need to be changed, she said, "They all need to change." And walked away.

Would I change for Sylvia? Would I read the book? Would I make the trip to Monaco and Santorini? All that depended on how much I wanted a certain god hanging around.

Weighed in philosophical terms, the Mercury-experience has been interesting. Sure, he saved my life a bunch of times. Not to mention the lives of people around me. Then there's the Temple Ms. Sabel was planning to build in her backyard. She liked him even though she couldn't see or hear him. If he didn't exist—and I am a total whack-job like Dad says—my life was significantly better when I had faith in Mercury.

Minus the Sylvia part.

The decision came down to what's more important: a personal relationship with god, or babe-a-licious Sylvia?

Don't answer that until you hear me out, brutha. Mercury held up his hands. *The right answer will get you a free pass on your next murder rap—which is due in about three minutes. The wrong answer will bring down a pox that'll make you so ugly your own mother will say, 'pull the plug!'.*

I said, *Let me think on that for four minutes.*

Mercury said, *You suck.*

Behind me, the mansion's massive walnut doors slammed so hard I looked over my shoulder. Two men in suits looked pissed off but decided there was nothing they could say to a six-inch-thick hardwood door that would get them back inside.

Resigned to their humiliation, they dropped down the steps. I recognized them: DC detective Eddie Harris and Montgomery County Detective Czajkowski. They had once stopped by my crib after some anonymous person had invaded the Russian Embassy.

They recognized me.

"Ms. Sabel's attorneys are downright nasty people." Harris took a seat three feet away on the same marble tread.

CJ trotted down a couple steps and gave me his best evil eye. I would've quaked in my boots, but I'm not that good an actor.

Harris opened his mouth to speak, but CJ jumped him. "Harris is investigating a suicide."

Harris gave his local counterpart a long, cold stare.

"Just saying." CJ turned away.

"Suicide?" I looked at Harris. "What's the matter, can't figure out who done it?"

"I'd like to ask your professional opinion on a case." Harris opened his laptop. "You enlightened us once before."

I stopped trimming the stick and inspected the blade of my Fairbairn-Sykes dagger. "I'd love to help."

"You see, a top aide to President Roche committed suicide in DC last night. Had a long career with the FBI before joining Sabel Security. Man name of David Watson."

"You don't say."

"I do say." He regarded me, tilting his head to one side.

I went back to whittling my stick.

"You don't look bothered by it none," Harris said.

"Just so you're aware—" I tipped the knife at him to make a point "—that man tried to discredit me several times when he was with the FBI and tried to kill me after he joined Sabel. It doesn't bother me in the least if he finally succumbed to his shame. Besides, working for Roche would make anyone suicidal."

"Interesting." Harris's eyes narrowed. He drew a long, deep breath. "Consider your attitude duly noted. Just so *you're* aware: President-Elect Roche has demanded that the FBI investigate his death as a murder."

I twisted to look at him. "The FBI doesn't investigate murder."

"I didn't say Roche has a handle on the rule of law or even a passing understanding of basic civics, for that matter. I'm just explaining why the FBI handed this case to me."

"OK." I returned to my stick. "What do you want from me?"

"We have some surveillance video." He pointed to his laptop. "Watson had one of those kits from Costco with cameras all around his house. Seems there was an intruder at his place right around the time of death."

"Coffee?" I asked.

"I'd love me some." Harris grinned.

CJ shook his head. I texted Chef for some curbside service.

Harris started his video. Nighttime, suburban house. A large shadow crossed the driveway and slap-hammered the kitchen door. The stealthy figure opened it. Harris stopped it on the frame where the shadow was silhouetted against the light inside. The black-clad operative filled the doorframe. "Does this person look familiar to you?"

"Ninjas all look alike."

"Looks pretty tall, 'round six feet, wouldn't you say?"

"If you're implying that figure is me, I was on duty here at Sabel Gardens until ten this morning. Plenty of witnesses can verify me doing rounds."

Harris looked up at CJ. The man took a note to check my alibi. He looked back at me. "Roche says this here is Pia Sabel."

"Was he on drugs?" I asked. "Doesn't she get an ounce of credit for bringing in that sniper the other day?"

"Why not? She's a husky girl. Her profile from the National Team says she's six foot something. This person is definitely over six feet. How much does she weigh?"

"You think I'm dumb enough to guess a woman's weight?" I gave him the stink-eye. "Do you have any idea how much misinformation about that touchy subject is floating around western society, turning every girl in the country nearly apoplectic every time she steps on the scales?"

"Moving on." Harris rolled his hand. "Can you tell me if there is anything in this video that can prove it's not her?"

Mercury whispered and I spoke his words out loud. "Whatever happened to *ei incumbit probatio qui dicit, non qui negat?*"

Harris and CJ shared a glance with their noses crinkled up. "Say what?"

"*The burden of proof is on the one who declares, not on the one who denies,* according to Justinian the Great, the last Roman and founder of the legal concept, *innocent until proven guilty.*"

"Just answer the question."

I looked at the video still-frame. "Those are some shoulders. Ms. Sabel works out, but this person looks downright beastly."

CJ leaned over as Harris spun the laptop back for a look.

"And the last time I checked, women have hips. That person—"

"Yeah. I get it." Harris waved me off. "So, if you were going to disguise a woman, how would you do it?"

CJ leaned forward. "And let's skip the part about stuffing the balaclava with tissues to throw off facial-mapping software. We heard about that from an expert."

I flung my newly trimmed stick across the palace-sized turning circle in front of us and watched it sail into the manicured grass beyond. Anoshni watched it fall, then looked at me as if I were the most irresponsible stick-handler on the planet. He took off in a dead run to nab it.

"A woman might use shoulder pads." I concentrated and nodded as I thought. "Taped up to look smooth, they'd push a jury from 'reasonable doubt' over to the 'no-way-that's-a-woman' category. Later, she could disassemble the pads and toss the pieces into public trash cans from here to San Diego."

CJ and Harris shared another sour glance.

A maid came out of the main house bearing a silver tray with cups and saucers and pitchers and sugars fit for a royal visit. She began her careful descent.

"One thing I don't get, though." I paused to watch Anoshni bring back the stick. Instead of responding to my entreaties, he returned to his spot three steps down from me and commenced chewing. I sighed. "Motive. Why does the Liar-in-Chief think she'd want to hurt a former employee?"

Harris squinted at me for a long time. "Word is, Watson killed her dad. The first one."

The maid arrived and offered the coffee. Harris stood and bowed to her. He poured a cup and stirred in cream and sugar. She turned to CJ and offered the tray's lone glass of chocolate milk. Chef keeps a profile on every visitor's comfort-foods. CJ did a double-take and grinned like a kid. He grabbed the glass and chugged half.

I said, "Cock Roche is willing to testify to that?"

In unison, Harris, and CJ said, "No."

"No motive, no evidence—good luck with that case."

"We could offer you immunity for testimony." Harris sipped from his cup and hummed its goodness. He slipped a glance at the maid, who stood bearing the tray like a statue. "You believe in justice, don't you Stearne?"

"According to what you've just told me, justice was served when

Watson put a bullet in his brain." I looked at them. "Tell me he took the manly way out and ate his pistol. Cause if he took pills—that's just so wussy."

"You didn't answer my question. Where was she?"

"See for yourself." I pointed to one of several video cameras on the property.

"Where can I view those?"

Mercury waved his hands. *Whoa, dude. Never show the cops a video you haven't personally edited. Jupiter only knows what might be on there.*

"Get yourself a warrant, come back, I'll give you a personal screening."

Harris put his coffee cup on the tray and gave a polite bow to the maid. He looked at me and shook his head, then turned and took a step toward his car.

CJ pointed a finger at me. "You can't cover for her forever." Harris grabbed his associate by the arm and tried to turn him around. CJ kept talking, walking backward. "We're going to find where you tripped up, Stearne. We're going to find your Achilles heel, and we're going to tear you apart. You hear me?"

"Give it your best shot, boys." I smiled up into the sunshine. "I have god on my side."

CHAPTER 74

PIA WAITED IN THE SERVICE alley behind the Cincinnati Hilton. After ten minutes, a white-haired Secret Service agent stuck his head out the fire exit. He was an older guy with a youthful countenance. He waved her into a concrete stairwell.

"I'm Dan." He led the way upstairs at a strong pace. "Catherine will meet you on the landing. Kevin and Tony paused the video feeds but the shift changes soon. You need to be out of there in under five minutes."

"That's all I need," Pia said.

"I'm sick of his victory tours," Dan said. "So your visit is a welcome distraction. What's your business with the President-Elect?"

"I'm going to ask him to resign."

"Great idea. Do you have some leverage to encourage him?"

"Unfortunately, no." Pia didn't want to elaborate, but he waited for her, and she felt obliged. "Dad had some incriminating records, but the corroborating evidence was scooped up by the Feds and locked away. Starting today, getting rid of him is my top priority."

"How do you expect to do that?"

"You don't want to know." The truth was, Pia didn't know. But she owed it to her dad and her country. She would find a way.

"Fine." Dan stopped on a landing and regarded her a moment. "This is an incredibly risky visit. Good thing my former co-workers vouched for you." He resumed the climb. "There's an agent doing rounds who would blow the whistle if she saw you. Her name's Ellen—blonde, middle-aged, nice lady, but a big Roche fan and a stickler for the rules."

"Understood."

When they reached the forty-ninth floor, Dan was breathing as if they'd taken a stroll in the park. He checked with his partner over their comm link. "Catherine, how about pizza and beer after our shift?"

Pia heard his earbud squawk.

"Code." He turned to Pia. "We need a minute. Ellen is still on the floor."

A few seconds later, he opened the stairwell door and waved her through. An attractive, dark-haired woman waved to her from halfway down the hall.

The woman led her to the double door in front of a large suite. The agent whispered, "I'm Catherine, nice to meet you and all that. I'll give you a 30-second warning. If you aren't out of there in time…" Catherine gave her a once over. "Just get out of there when I say."

Catherine waved a keycard over the latch. It clacked open. Catherine stayed at the door, her gaze swiveling from the hall to the suite.

Pia went in.

When she turned the corner from the foyer into the sitting room, she found President Hunter sitting in President-Elect Roche's lap. Hunter's finger was in the middle of stroking the man's chin when they both turned to face Pia.

Hunter stumbled to her feet and smoothed her skirt. Roche stood with clenched fists.

"What the hell are you doing in here?" Roche roared. "Guard!"

Catherine ignored his call.

"Good to see you two are still … active." Pia approached the pair.

"Security!" Roche's face flared red.

Hunter backhanded his chest. "She owns them."

"Impossible. They're the best in the world. They'd never take a bribe." Roche looked past Pia's unmoving shoulders. "Security!"

Hunter smacked him again. "When Alan Sabel decided to protect his daughter from your men, he staffed Sabel Security entirely with retired Secret Service agents. They're incorruptible. But every single one of them knows, in the back of his mind, that if he gets sick of this job, he's welcome at Sabel."

"Done whining?" Pia put her foot on a chair.

"You owe me $100 million." Hunter scowled. "I released Sabel

Industries from the exclusive government contracts. You're going open-market now. You stand to make billions. Time to pay up. I have campaign debts I need to retire."

"Four years ago, you burned Dad." Pia frowned back. "Sucks, huh."

"What do you want?" Roche snarled at Pia.

"A truce. Leave Stefan Devoor and his children out of our disagreement."

Hunter's mouth fell open. "Chuck's people would never hurt—"

"I offered you a chance to get in on this." Roche picked up his cane. "You chose to play with fire. Whatever nonsense you're talking about, you can only blame yourself."

Pia pulled her phone and played a video. A man held in police custody identified himself as Brad from Roche Security. "He was shooting at Stefan's front door."

"Oh, my god, no." Hunter fell back into a chair. "That couldn't be. Chuck, tell me—"

"My people are contracted out." Roche glared up at Pia. "She probably hired my people and did this as a publicity stunt."

"Montgomery County will subpoena Roche Security records," Pia poked him in the chest. "Think up a better lie."

"What did you mean about a truce?" Hunter asked.

"You can come after me all you want, but things will get worse for you if you involve innocent children."

"You're just like Popov and Yeschenko, you know that?" Roche shouted as he swept a lamp off the side table. "You guys think I'm stupid and impotent. Well, news flash, I'm not. I'm the President of the United States."

"President-Elect," Hunter said.

"Who cares?" Roche's voice rattled the windows. He faced Pia and tipped up as tall as he could. "You came after me. So. Right back atcha, bitch."

Catherine poked her head around the corner from the foyer. "Sixty seconds, ma'am."

"Hey, wait a minute. You threatened me." Roche grabbed Pia's arm and turned her to face him. "You said things would get worse. What do you mean?"

"We have Strangelove's notes about Flight 1028."

"Big deal. We tracked down the Puerto Ricans who did it. On my Inauguration Day, they're going to get droned."

"We have the router logs, actual proof of who—"

"Forget it, Pia," Hunter said. "We can't escalate anything with the Russians without risking nuclear war. The public wants revenge. We'll give them some. They'll feel better."

Roche snarled, "Is that all you've got? Powder logs?"

"No." Pia pulled up her phone again and played the recording of Roche, Hunter, and Watson planning to throw the election. When it stopped, no one spoke for a few seconds.

"Oh, my god," Hunter said.

"It's nothing." Roche paced the room. "It's illegal. She can bring us down with that, but only by ruining her precious reputation. We'd drown her in the press: *Big Brother is alive and well and running Sabel Industries. No one is safe.* She'd never get another dollar of business after she gets out of jail. Go ahead, put it on YouTube. I'll call it a hoax."

"Take the truce," Hunter said.

"Yeah. Sure, why not? Truce on Devoor." Roche stuck out his bottom lip. "But I'm getting even with you for killing Watson. Tell that goon of yours, Jacob, to watch his back. Or maybe I'll send someone after that half-breed girl."

"Chuck!" Hunter screeched. "She could be recording this."

"I didn't kill David Watson." Pia displayed a photo on her phone. "I watched him die."

"He would never commit—" Roche stopped when he came close enough to the picture to see what it was. A smug-looking Watson held his undated pardon next to his face.

Roche turned away, and Hunter stepped in. She said, "That idiot. Why did he show you that?"

Catherine peeked around the corner. "Thirty seconds, ma'am."

"He got cocky on Attu Island," Pia said. "Told me everything. The night he died, I paid him a visit. I tried to trick him into repeating his confession. He bragged about the pardon, then figured out what I was recording him. He said he'd rather die than implicate you."

"Good man." Roche paced back. "That's loyalty."

Hunter covered her mouth as she inhaled in shock. "How did he die?"

"He pulled a pistol out of his desk and put it in his mouth." Pia stared hard at Hunter. "I tried to talk him down. I told him you two weren't worth it. But he knew."

"Knew what?" Hunter asked.

"If he wouldn't talk, I'd put him down."

"Oh my god" Hunter backed up a step. "Why?"

Pia stepped forward, towering over the President. "Someone paid him to kill Lloyd Aston."

"What did he tell you?" Roche shouldered Hunter aside. "Some lie about us being involved?"

"Pozdeeva detailed your meeting in the park. Watson confirmed it."

Hunter and Roche looked at each other, then back at Pia.

"Look, Pia, I'm sorry I ever got involved in that." Hunter's hands trembled as she reached out. "It's one of the biggest regrets—"

"Don't apologize to her," Roche shouted, slapping Hunter's hand. "We did what we had to do at the time. Popov would've skinned us if we turned him down. Besides, Aston was stupid." He faced Pia. "What do you want?"

"I want my democracy back."

"What the hell does that mean?"

Catherine stepped into the room. "Excuse me, ma'am. You need to go. Now."

"You resign." Pia looked at Catherine, who waved anxiously. She turned and crossed to the agent.

Roche followed her.

"You've made a powerful enemy." He stopped in the foyer. "Rest assured, the minute my hand touches the Bible on Inauguration Day, Feds will be swarming into Sabel Industries with search warrants for everything. We'll find the snuff films your bodycams recorded when you murdered Popov. We'll hang you and everyone who works with you."

Pia looked over her shoulder at him. She wanted to fire back that she had Pozdeeva's files and would run down every shell company that laundered money in his refineries. It was too early to play that card. Someday soon. She kept her mouth shut and followed agent Catherine.

"I worked hard to earn my reputation for being cruel and vindictive to losers. It keeps them from coming back." He raised his voice as she strode away. "Yeah. You can run now, girly. But you can't hide from me. Not anymore. I'm the President of the United States of America."

THANK YOU!

Thank you for choosing my book. I hope you enjoyed reading it as much as I enjoyed writing it. As an independent writer, I am dependent on word-of-mouth referrals and book reviews. If you liked this book, please tell everyone, and leave reviews all over the place. I will be eternally grateful.

When you do write a review, send me a link to it and I'll put you in the next drawing for an autographed book. I run at least three or four drawings a year.

If you can't get enough of Pia, Tania, Miguel and Jacob*, checkout the series at SeeleyJames.com/books. While you're there, join my newsletter to get discounts, drawings, fun, news, outtakes, and more about the Sabel Agents club on Facebook! Every week (or so, sometimes I'm lazy), I'll let you know about the book in progress, personal triumphs & tragedies, what I'm reading and other fun stuff. I even had one person write to me to say, "I don't like your books, but I love your newsletters." To which I replied, "Thanks, Mom." Yeah … whatcha gonna do?

I'd love to hear from you. Please write, message me on Facebook, let me know what you think.

*I like you already.

NOW THAT YOU'VE READ THIS BOOK, WHICH ONE SHOULD YOU READ NEXT?
HTTPS://SEELEYJAMES.COM/BOOKS

ACKNOWLEDGMENTS

My heartfelt thanks to the beta readers and supporters who made this book the best book possible. Alphabetically: Melissa "Iceterrors" Capo-Murray, Ken Newland, Gail Weiss, and Pam Safinuk.

- Extraordinary Editor and Idea man: Lance Charnes, author of the highly acclaimed *Doha 12, SOUTH,* and *THE COLLLECTION.* http://wombatgroup.com
- Medical Advisor and Character Diviner: Louis Kirby, famed neurologist and author of *Shadow of Eden.* http://louiskirby.com
- Amazing Editor: Mary Maddox, horror and dark fantasy novelist, and author of the Daemon World Series http://marymaddox.com

A special thanks to my wife whose support, despite being reluctant to say the least, has been above and beyond the call of duty. Last but not least, my children, Nicole, Amelia, and Christopher, ranging from age eighteen to forty-five, who have kept my imagination fresh and full of ideas.

ABOUT THE AUTHOR

His near-death experiences range from talking a jealous husband into putting the gun down to spinning out on an icy freeway in heavy traffic without touching anything. His resume ranges from washing dishes to global technology management. His personal life stretches from homeless at 17, adopting a 3-year-old at 19, getting married at 37, fathering his last child at 43, hiking the Grand Canyon Rim-to-Rim several times a year, and taking the occasional nap.

His writing career ranges from humble beginnings with short stories in The Battered Suitcase, to being awarded a Medallion from the Book Readers Appreciation Group. Seeley is best known for his Sabel Security series of thrillers featuring athlete and heiress Pia Sabel and her bodyguard, unhinged veteran Jacob Stearne. One of them kicks ass and the other talks to the wrong god.

His love of creativity began at an early age, growing up at Frank Lloyd Wright's School of Architecture in Arizona and Wisconsin. He carried his imagination first into a successful career in sales and marketing, and then to his real love: fiction.

For more books featuring Pia Sabel and Jacob Stearne, visit: SeeleyJames.com.

facebook.com/seeleyjamesauthor

instagram.com/seeleyjamesauth

bookbub.com/authors/seeley-james